EL SEÑOR PRESIDENTE

MIGUEL ANGEL ASTURIAS

EL SEÑOR PRESIDENTE

TRANSLATED FROM THE SPANISH BY
FRANCES PARTRIDGE

ATHENEUM

NEW YORK

1985

PART I

The 21st, 22nd and 23rd of April

CHAPTER I

In the Cathedral Porch

"BOOM, bloom, alum-bright, Lucifer of alunite!" The sound of the church bells summoning people to prayer lingered on, like a humming in the ears, an uneasy transition from brightness to gloom, from gloom to brightness. "Boom, bloom, alum-bright, Lucifer of alunite, over the sombre tomb! Bloom, alum-bright, over the tomb, Lucifer of alunite! Boom, boom, alum-bright . . . bloom . . . alum-bright . . . bloom, alum-bright . . . bloom, boom."

In the frozen shadow of the cathedral, the beggars were shuffling past the market eating-houses as they made their way through the ocean-wide streets to the Plaza de Armas, leaving the deserted city behind them.

Nightfall assembled them, as it did the stars. With nothing in common but their destitution, they mustered to sleep together in the Porch of Our Lord, cursing, insulting and jostling each other, picking quarrels with old enemies, or throwing earth and rubbish, even rolling on the ground and spitting and biting with rage. This confraternity of the dunghill had never known pillows or mutual trust. They lay down in all their clothes at a distance from one another, and slept like thieves, with their heads on the bags containing their worldly goods: left-over scraps of meat, worn-out shoes, candle-ends, handfuls of cooked rice wrapped in old newspapers, oranges and rotten bananas.

They could be seen sitting on the steps of the Porch with their faces to the wall, counting their money, biting the nickel coins to see if they were false, talking to themselves, inspecting their stores of food and ammunition (for they went out into the streets fully armed with stones and scapularies) and stuffing themselves secretly on crusts of dry bread. They had never been known to help each other; like all beggars they were miserly with their scraps, and would rather give them to the dogs than to their companions in misfortune.

Having satisfied their hunger and tied up their money with

7

seven knots in handkerchiefs fastened to their belts, they threw themselves on the ground and sank into sad, agitated dreams— nightmares in which they saw famished pigs, thin women, maimed dogs and carriage wheels passing before their eyes, or a funeral procession of phantom monks going into the cathedral preceded by a sliver of moon carried on a cross made of frozen shin-bones. Sometimes they would be woken from their deepest dreams by the cries of an idiot who had lost his way in the Plaza de Armas; or sometimes by the sobs of a blind woman dreaming that she was covered in flies and suspended from a hook like a piece of meat in a butcher's shop. Or sometimes by the tramp of a patrol, be- labouring a political prisoner as they dragged him along, while women followed wiping away the blood-stains with handkerchiefs soaked in tears. Sometimes by the snores of a scabby valetudi- narian, or the heavy breathing of a pregnant deaf-mute, weeping with fear of the child she felt in her womb. But the idiot's cry was the saddest of all. It rent the sky. It was a long-drawn-out inhuman wail.

On Sundays this strange fraternity used to be joined by a drunk man who called for his mother and wept like a child in his sleep. Hearing the word "mother" fall more like an oath than a prayer from the drunkard's lips, the idiot would sit up, search every corner of the Porch with his eyes and—having woken himself and his companions with his cries—burst into tears of fright, joining his sobs to those of the drunkard.

Dogs barked, shouts were heard, and the more irritable beggars got up and increased the hubbub by calling for silence. If they didn't shut their jaws the police would come. But the police wanted nothing to do with the beggars. None of them had enough money to pay a fine. "Long live France!" Flatfoot would shout, amidst the cries and antics of the idiot, who became the laughing- stock of the other beggars in the end, simply because this scoundrelly, foul-mouthed cripple liked to pretend to be drunk several nights every week. So Flatfoot would pretend to be drunk, while the Zany (as they called the idiot), who looked like a corpse when he was asleep, became more lively with every shriek, ignoring the huddled forms lying under rags on the ground, who jeered and cackled shrilly at his crazy behaviour. With his eyes far away from the hideous faces of his companions, he saw nothing, heard nothing and felt nothing, and fell asleep at last, worn out

8

with weeping. But it was the same every night—no sooner had he dropped off than Flatfoot's voice woke him again:

"Mother!"

The Zany opened his eyes with a start like someone who dreams he is falling into space; he shrank back with enormously dilated pupils as if mortally wounded and the tears began to flow once more; then sleep gradually overcame him, his body became flaccid, and anxious fears reverberated through his deranged mind. But no sooner was he thoroughly asleep than another voice would wake him:

"Mother!"

It was the voice of a degenerate mulatto known as the Widower, snivelling like an old woman, amidst bursts of laughter:

". . . mother of mercy, our hope and salvation, may God preserve you, listen to us poor down-and-outs and idiots . . ."

The idiot used to wake up laughing; it seemed that he too found his misery and hunger so amusing that he laughed till he cried, while the beggars snatched bu-bu-bursts of la-la-laughter from the air, from the air . . . la-la-laughter; a fat man with his moustaches dripping with stew lost his breath from laughing; and a one-eyed man laughed till he urinated and beat his head against the wall like a goat; while the blind men complained that they couldn't sleep with such a row going on, and the Mosquito, who was legless as well as blind, cried out that only sodomites could amuse themselves in such a fashion.

No one paid any attention to the blind men's protests and the Mosquito's remark was not even heard. Why should anyone listen to his jabber? "Oh yes, I spent my childhood in the artillery barracks, and the mules and officers kicked me into shape and made a man of me—a man who could work like a horse, which was useful when I had to pull a barrel-organ through the streets! Oh yes, and I lost my sight when I was on the booze, the devil knows how, and my right leg on another booze-up, the devil knows when, and the other in another booze-up, knocked down by a car the devil knows where!"

The beggars spread a rumour among the people of the town that the Zany went mad whenever anyone mentioned his mother. The poor wretch used to run through the streets, squares, courtyards and markets, trying to get away from people shouting "Mother!" at him from every side and at any hour of the day,

9

like a malediction from the sky. He tried to take refuge in houses, but was chased out again by dogs or servants. They drove him out of churches, shops and everywhere else, indifferent to his utter exhaustion and the plea for pity in his uncomprehending eyes.

The town that his exhaustion had made so large—so immensely large—seemed to shrink in the face of his despair. Nights of terror were followed by days of persecution, during which he was hounded by people who were not content to shout: "On Sunday you'll marry your Mother, my little Zany—your old woman!" but beat him and tore his clothes as well. Pursued by children, he would take refuge in the poorer quarters, but there his fate was even worse; there everyone lived on the verge of destitution, and insults were not enough—they threw stones, dead rats and empty tins at him as he ran away in terror.

One day he came to the Cathedral Porch from the suburbs just as the angelus was ringing, without his hat, with a wound in his forehead, and trailing the tail of a kite which had been fastened to him as a joke. Everything frightened him: the shadows of the walls, dogs trotting by, leaves falling from the trees, and the irregular rumbling of wheels. When he arrived at the Porch it was almost dark and the beggars were sitting with their faces to the wall counting their earnings. Flatfoot was quarrelling with the Mosquito, the deaf-mute was feeling her inexplicably swollen belly, and the blind woman was hanging from a hook in her dreams, covered in flies, like a piece of meat at the butcher's.

The idiot fell on the ground as if dead; he had not closed his eyes for nights, he had not been able to rest his feet for days. The beggars were silently scratching their fleabites but could not sleep; they listened for the footsteps of the police going to and fro in the dimly lit square and the click of the sentinels presenting arms, as they stood at attention like ghosts in their striped *ponchos* at the windows of the neighbouring barracks, keeping their nightly watch over the President of the Republic. No one knew where he was, for he occupied several houses in the outskirts of the town; nor how he slept—some said beside the telephone with a whip in his hand; nor when—his friends declared he never slept at all.

A figure advanced towards the Porch of Our Lord. The beggars curled themselves up like worms. The creak of military boots was answered by the sinister hoot of a bird from the dark, navigable, bottomless night.

Flatfoot opened his eyes (a menacing threat as of the end of the world weighed upon the air) and said to the owl:

"Hoo-hoo! Do your worst! I wish you neither good nor ill, but the devil take you all the same!"

The Mosquito groped for his face with his hands. The air was tense as though an earthquake were brewing. The Widower crossed himself as he sat among the blind men. Only the Zany slept like a log, snoring for once.

The new arrival stopped; his face lit up with a smile. Going up to the idiot on tiptoe he shouted jeeringly at him: "Mother!"

That was all. Torn from the ground by the cry, the Zany flung himself upon his tormentor, and, without giving him time to get at his weapons, thrust his fingers into his eyes, tore at his nose with his teeth and jabbed his private parts with his knees, till he fell to the ground motionless.

The beggars shut their eyes in horror, the owl flew by once more and the Zany fled away down the shadowy streets in a paroxysm of mad terror.

Some blind force had put an end to the life of Colonel José Parrales Sonriente, known as "the man with the little mule".

It was nearly dawn.

CHAPTER II

The Death of the Mosquito

THE sun was gilding the projecting terraces of the Second Police Station (a few people were passing along the street), the Protestant church (one or two doors stood open) and a brick building in process of construction.

It always seemed to be raining in the patio of the Police Station, and groups of bare-footed women were sitting on stone benches in the dark corridors waiting for the prisoners, with their breakfast baskets in the hammocks made by their skirts between their knees. Their children clustered round them, the babies glued to their pendulous breasts and the bigger ones threatening the loaves in the baskets with hungrily opened mouths. The women were telling each other their troubles in low voices, crying all the while, and mopping their tears with the ends of their shawls. A hollow-eyed old woman, shaking with malaria, wept copiously and silently as if to show that as a mother she suffered more acutely than the rest. The evils of life seemed without remedy here in this dismal place of waiting, with nothing to look at but two or three neglected shrubs, an empty fountain and these sallow-faced policemen cleaning their celluloid collars with saliva. They must put their trust in the power of the Almighty.

A ladino* policeman came by, dragging along the Mosquito. He had caught him at the corner by the Infants' School and was pulling him along by the hand, shaking him from side to side like a monkey. But the women did not notice anything comic in this; they were too busy spying on the movements of the gaolers as they carried in breakfasts and returned with news of the prisoners: "He says . . . not to worry about him, things are looking up already! He says . . . you're to buy him four *reals*-worth of mercury ointment as soon as the chemist opens! He says . . . not to count on what his cousin told you! He says . . . you're to get a lawyer for him; best look for a student, he won't rook you so

* Of mixed white and Indian blood.

much! He says . . . don't go on like that, they've got no women in there with them so you can't be jealous; they brought in one of *them* the other day and he soon found himself a boy-friend! He says . . . send him a few *reals*-worth of purge or he can't shit! He says . . . he's fed up with you for selling the cupboard!"

"Hey, you!" the Mosquito protested, indignant at the way this copper was knocking him about. "What d'you think you're doing? No pity, eh? Just because I'm poor? Poor but honest. Listen to me: I'm not your kid, nor your fancy-boy, for you to treat me like that! A fine idea to keep in with the Yankees by nabbing us and carting us to the workhouse! What a dirty trick! Like turkeys for the Christmas dinner! And it's not as if you even treated us right! Not you. When Mister Nosey-Parker got there we'd been there three days with nothing to eat, looking out of the windows dressed in blankets as if we were nuts . . ."

The captured beggars were taken straight to one of the narrow dark cells known as the "Three Marias". The Mosquito was dragged in like a crab. His voice was drowned at first by the noise of the keys in the locks and the curses of the gaolers, who stank of sweat-soaked clothes and stale tobacco, but afterwards it echoed loudly through the underground vault:

"Oh my God, what a copper! Holy Conception, what a bastard! Jesus Christ!"

His companions were whimpering like sick animals and snivelling with horror of the darkness (they felt they would never be able to free their eyes from it again), and with fear (so many other men had suffered hunger and thirst here till they died); they had a growing conviction that they would be boiled down and made into soap like dogs, or have their throats cut and be given to the police to eat. They seemed to see the faces of these cannibals, lit up like lanterns, advancing through the shadows, with cheeks like buttocks and moustaches like slobbered chocolate . . .

A student and a sacristan found themselves together in the same cell.

"I think I'm right in saying you were the first here. You and then me, isn't that so?"

The student talked for the sake of saying something, to get rid of the knot of anxiety which constricted his throat.

"Yes, I think so," replied the sacristan, trying to see the other's face in the darkness.

'Well, I was just going to ask what you're here for."

"For political reasons, so they say."

The student was trembling from head to foot as he enunciated with great difficulty: "Me too."

The beggars were hunting about for their inseparable bags of provisions, but everything had been taken away in the office of the Chief of Police, even what they had in their pockets, so that not even a match should be allowed in. Orders were strict.

"And what about your case?" went on the student.

"There's no case against me. I'm here by orders from above!"

The sacristan rubbed his back against the rough wall as he spoke, to scratch his lice.

"You were—?"

"Nothing," interrupted the sacristan violently. "I wasn't anything!"

At this moment the hinges of the door creaked as it opened to admit another beggar.

"Long live France!" cried Flatfoot as he came in.

"I'm in prison . . ." declared the sacristan.

"Long live France!"

". . . for doing something that was purely an accident. You see, instead of taking down an announcement about the Virgin of La O from the door of the church where I was sacristan, I went and removed a notice of the President's mother's anniversary."

"But how did he find out?" murmured the student, while the sacristan wiped away his tears with his fingers.

"I don't know. My own stupidity. Anyway, they arrested me and took me to the offices of the Chief of Police, who hit me once or twice and then gave orders for me to be put in this cell in solitary confinement—as a revolutionary, he said."

The beggars were crumpled up in the darkness, crying with fear, cold and hunger. They couldn't even see their own hands. Sometimes they relapsed into lethargy, and the heavy breathing of the pregnant deaf-mute could be heard circulating among them as if seeking a way out.

No one knew what time it was, perhaps midnight, when they were taken out of their dungeon. A squat little man with a wrinkled, saffron-coloured face, an unkempt moustache combed over his thick lips, a rather snub nose and hooded eyes, informed them that he was investigating a political crime. And he ended by asking them, first all together and then separately, whether they knew the perpetrator or perpetrators of the murder in the Cathedral Porch, committed the night before on the person of a Colonel in the army.

The room to which they had been taken was lit by a smoking lamp, whose feeble light seemed to be filtered through lenses full of water. What was happening? What wall was that? And that rack bristling more fiercely with weapons than the jaws of a tiger, and that policeman's belt full of cartridges?

The beggars' unexpected reply to his questions made the Judge Advocate General jump up from his chair.

"Tell me the truth!" he shouted, opening basilisk eyes behind his thick spectacles and banging his fist on the table he used as a desk.

One by one they repeated in the voices of souls in torment that the assassin had been the Zany, and described in detail the crime they had witnessed with their own eyes.

At a sign from the Judge Advocate the policemen who had been listening outside the door fell upon the beggars, beat them and pushed them into an empty room. From the almost invisible centre beam a long rope was hanging.

"It was the idiot!" screamed the first to be tortured, eager to escape by telling the truth. "It was the idiot, sir! It was the idiot! Before God, it was the idiot! The idiot! The idiot! The Zany! The Zany! It was him! Him! Him!"

"That's what they told you to say, but lies won't cut any ice with me. The truth or death, do you hear? Get that into your heads if it's not there already!"

The Judge Advocate's voice faded away like the roaring of blood in the ears of the unfortunate wretch, who was suspended by his thumbs with his feet some way off the ground. He went on shouting:

"It was the idiot! That's who it was! I swear to God it was the idiot! It was the idiot! It was the idiot! It was the idiot! . . . It was the idiot!"

"Lies!" declared the Judge Advocate, and then, during a pause: "Lies! You're a liar! I'll tell you who murdered Colonel José Parrales Sonriente, and we'll see if you dare deny it; I'll tell you myself. It was General Eusebio Canales and Abel Carvajal, the lawyer!"

A frozen silence followed these words; then there was a moan, and after a pause another moan and finally a "yes". When the rope was unfastened the Widower fell to the floor unconscious. Dripping with sweat and tears, the mulatto's cheeks looked like coal wetted by the rain. When they went on to interrogate his companions, who were trembling like dogs poisoned by the police and dying in the street, they all confirmed what the Judge Advocate General had said—all except the Mosquito. His face was contorted by a rictus of fear and disgust. They hung him up by the fingers because he went on insisting from the ground—seeming indeed half buried in the earth as all legless men do—that his companions were lying when they accused unknown persons of a crime for which the idiot alone was responsible.

"Responsible!" The Judge Advocate pounced on the word. "How dare you say an idiot is responsible? You see what lies you tell us—an irresponsible idiot responsible!"

"It's what he'll tell you himself—"

"He must be beaten," said a policeman with a woman's voice; and another struck him across the face with a lash.

"Tell the truth!" shouted the Judge Advocate as the whip lashed the old man's cheeks. "The truth, or you'll hang here all night!"

"Can't you see I'm blind?"

"Then stop saying it was the Zany."

"No, because that's the truth and I've got the spunk to say so!"

Two strokes from the lash covered his lips in blood.

"Listen, even if you are blind you can tell the truth like the rest."

"All right," agreed the Mosquito in a faint voice, and the Judge Advocate thought he had won. "All right, you clot, it was the Zany who did it . . ."

"You fool!"

The Judge Advocate's insult was lost to the ears of this half-man who would never hear anything again. When they loosed the rope, the Mosquito's dead body—or rather his torso, for he had lost both his legs—fell to the ground like a broken pendulum.

"The old liar, how could his evidence be any use when he was blind?" said the Judge Advocate General as he walked past the corpse.

And he hurried off to take the President the news of the first results of the inquiry, in a ramshackle cab drawn by two thin horses, and with its lamps shining like the eyes of death. The police flung the Mosquito's body into a garbage-cart on its way to the cemetery. The cocks were beginning to crow. Those of the beggars who had been set free went back to the streets. The deaf-mute was crying with fear of the child she felt moving in her womb.

CHAPTER III

The Flight of the Zany

THE Zany fled through the narrow twisting streets of the suburbs, but his frantic cries disturbed neither the calm of the sky nor the sleep of the inhabitants, who were as alike one another in their simulation of death as they would be different when they resumed the struggle for life at sunrise. Some lacked the bare necessities of life and were forced to work hard for their daily bread, others got more than enough from the privileged industries of idleness: as friends of the President; owners of house-property (forty or fifty houses); money-lenders at nine, nine and a half and ten per cent a month; officials holding seven or eight different public posts; exploiters of concessions, pensions, professional qualifications, gambling hells, cock-pits, Indians, brandy distilleries, brothels, bars and subsidised newspapers.

The blood-red juice of dawn was staining the edges of the funnel of mountains encircling the town, as it lay like a crust of scurf in the plain. The streets were tunnels of shadows, through which the earliest workmen were setting out like phantoms in the emptiness of a world that was created anew every morning; they were followed a few hours later by office workers, clerks and students; and at about eleven, when the sun was already high, by important gentlemen walking off their breakfasts and getting up an appetite for lunch, or going to see some influential friend, to get him to join in the purchase of the arrears of starving school-masters' salaries at half-price. The streets still lay deep in shadow when their silence was broken by the rustle of the starched skirts of some townswoman, working without respite—as swine-herd, milk-woman, street-hawker or offal-seller—to keep her family alive, or up early to do her chores; then, when the light paled to a rosy white like a begonia flower, there would be the pattering footsteps of some thin little typist, despised by the grand ladies who waited till the sun was already hot before they left their bedrooms, stretched their legs in the passages, told their dreams to the servants, criticised the passers-by, fondled the cat, read the newspaper or admired themselves in the looking-glass.

Half in the world of reality, half in a dream, the Zany ran on, pursued by dogs and by spears of fine rain. He ran aimlessly, with his mouth open and his tongue hanging out, slobbering and panting, and his arms in the air. Doors and doors and doors and windows and doors and windows flashed past him. Suddenly he would stop and put his hands over his face to defend himself from a telegraph pole, but when he realised it was harmless he burst out laughing and went on again, like a man escaping from a prison with walls made of mist, so that the more he ran the further they receded.

When he came to the suburbs, where the town gave way to the surrounding country, he sank on to a heap of rubbish, like someone who has reached his bed at last, and fell asleep. Above the dunghill was a spiders-web of dead trees, covered with turkey-buzzards; when they saw the Zany lying there motionless, the black birds of prey fixed him with their bluish eyes and settled on the ground beside him, hopping all round him—a hop this way, a hop that way—in a macabre dance. Ceaselessly looking about them, making ready for flight at the smallest movement of a leaf or the wind in the rubbish—a hop this way, a hop that way— they closed in upon him in a circle until he was within reach of their beaks. A savage croaking gave the signal for the attack. The Zany got to his feet as he woke, prepared to defend himself. One of the boldest birds had fastened its beak in his upper lip piercing it right through to the teeth like a dart, while the other carnivores disputed as to which should have his eyes and his heart. The bird which had hold of his lip struggled to tear off the morsel, caring nothing that its prey was alive, and would have succeeded had not the Zany taken a step backwards and rolled down a precipice of garbage, sending up clouds of dust and chunks of caked debris.

It was growing dark. Green sky. Green countryside. In the barracks the bugles were sounding six o'clock, echoing the anxiety of a tribe on the alert, or a besieged medieval town. In the prisons the agony of captives who were being slowly killed by the passage of the years began anew. The horizon withdrew its little heads into the streets of the town, a snail with a thousand heads. People were returning from audiences with the President, some in favour, some in disgrace. The lights from the windows of the gambling-dens stabbed the darkness.

The idiot was struggling with the ghost of the turkey-buzzard which he still seemed to feel attacking him, and also with the pain of a leg broken in his fall—an unbearable, black pain, which tore at his vitals.

All night long he whined like an injured dog, first softly then loudly, softly and loudly:

"Ee, ee, ee . . . Ee, ee, ee . . ."

As he sat beside a pool of water among the wild plants whose lovely flowers had been engendered by the filth of the town, the idiot's brain was brewing gigantic storms within its small compass.

"E-e-eee . . . E-e-eee. E-e-eee."

The steel finger-nails of fever were clawing at his forehead. Disassociation of ideas. A fluctuating world seen in a mirror. Fantastic disproportion. Hurricane of delirium. Vertiginous flight, horizontal, vertical, oblique, newly-born and dead in a spiral . . .

"Eee, ee, ee, ee, ee."

Curveofacurveinacurveofacurvecurveofacurveinacurveof Lot's wife. (Did she invent lotteries?) The mules pulling the tram were turning into Lot's wife and their immobility annoyed the tram conductors, who, not content with breaking their whips on their backs and throwing stones at them, invited the gentlemen passengers to use their weapons. The grandest of them carried daggers and made the mules go by stabbing them . . .

"Ee, ee, ee."

INRIdiot! INRIdiot!

"Ee, ee, ee."

The knife-grinder sharpens his teeth before he laughs! Smile-sharpeners! Knife-grinder's teeth!

"Mother!"

The drunkard's cry roused him.

"Mother!"

The moon was shining brilliantly between the spongy clouds. Its white light fell on the damp leaves giving them the gloss and texture of porcelain.

They're carrying off—!

They're carrying off—!

They're carrying off the saints from the church to bury them!

Oh what fun, oh they're going to bury them, they're going to bury them, oh, what fun!

The cemetery is gayer than the town and cleaner than the town! Oh what fun! They're going to bury them!

Ta-ra-ra! Ta-ra-ra-boom!

And on he went, through thick and thin, taking great leaps from one volcano to another, from star to star, from sky to sky, half awake, half asleep, amongst big mouths and little mouths, with teeth and without teeth, with lips and without lips, with double lips, with moustaches, with double tongues, with triple tongues, crying: "Mother! Mother! Mother!"

Toot-toot! He took the local train to get away from the town to the mountains as quickly as possible; the mountains would give him a leg-up to the volcanoes, beyond the wireless pylons, beyond the slaughter-house, beyond the artillery fort—a *vol-au-vent* stuffed with soldiers.

But the train returned to its point of departure like a toy on a string; and when it arrived—chuff-chuff, chuff-chuff—a snuffling vegetable-seller with hair like the withies her baskets were made of was waiting in the station, and cried out: "Some bread for the idiot, polly parrot? Water for the idiot! Water for the idiot!"

Pursued by the vegetable-seller who was threatening him with a gourd full of water, he ran towards the Cathedral Porch, but when he arrived—"Mother!" a cry, a jump, a man, night; a struggle, death, blood, flight, the idiot . . . "Water for the idiot, polly parrot! Water for the idiot!"

The pain in his leg awoke him. He felt there was a labyrinth inside his bones. His eyes grew sad in the daylight. Sleeping lianas covered in beautiful flowers invited him to sleep beneath their shade, close to a cool spring which moved its foaming tail as if a silver squirrel were hidden amongst its mosses and ferns.

No one. No one.

Once again the Zany took refuge in the night of his closed eyes and fought against pain, trying to find a position for his broken leg, holding his torn lip in place. But whenever he raised his burning lids, blood-red skies were passing above him. Between flashes of lightning the ghosts of caterpillars fled away as butterflies.

He turned his back on the alarum bell of delirium. Snow for

the dying! The ice-man is selling the viaticum! The priest is selling snow! Snow for the dying! Ting-a-ling! Snow for the dying! The viaticum is going by! The ice-man is passing! Take your hat off, you dribbling mute! Snow for the dying!

CHAPTER IV

Angel Face

COVERED in bits of paper, leather and rags, skeleton umbrellas, brims of straw hats, saucepans with holes in them, broken china, cardboard boxes, pulped books, pieces of glass, shoes curled up by the sun, collars, egg-shells, scraps of cotton and food—the Zany went on dreaming. Now he saw himself in a large patio surrounded by masks; soon he realised that they were the faces of people watching a cock-fight. The fight blazed up like paper in a flame. One of the combatants expired without pain before the spectators' eyes, which were glazed with pleasure to see the curved spurs drawn out smothered in blood. A smell of brandy. Tobacco-stained spittle. Entrails. Savage exhaustion. Somnolence. Weakness. Tropical noon. Someone was tiptoeing through his dream so as not to wake him . . .

It was the Zany's mother. The mistress of a cock-breeder who played the guitar with flinty fingernails, she had been the victim of his jealousy and his vices. The story of her troubles was endless: at the mercy of this worthless man and a martyr to the child born to her under the "direct" influence of a changing moon, so the midwives said, in her agony she had connected her baby's disproportionately large head—a round head with a double crown like the moon—with the bony faces of all the other patients in the hospital, and the expressions of fear and disgust, the hiccups, gloom and vomiting of the drunken cock-breeder.

The Zany became aware of the rustle of starched petticoats—wind and leaves—and ran after her with tears in his eyes.

He found relief in her motherly bosom. The entrails of the woman who had given birth to him absorbed the pain of his wounds like blotting-paper. What a deep and imperturbable refuge. What abundance of love! My pretty little lily! My fine big lily! How I love you! How I love you!

The cock-breeder was singing softly into the hollow of his ear:

23

Why not,
Why not,
Why not, my sugar-plum lollypop,
For I am a cock lollypop
And when I raise my foot lollypop
I drag my wing lollypop!

The Zany raised his head and without speaking said:
"I'm sorry, Mamma, I'm sorry!"
And the apparition stroked his face tenderly and replied:
"I'm sorry, my son, I'm sorry!"
From a long way off he heard his father's voice, emerging from a glass of brandy:

I was hooked
I was hooked
I was hooked by a white woman,
And when the yucca grows well
Only the leaves are torn up!

The Zany murmured:
"I'm sick to my soul, Mamma!"
And the apparition stroked his face tenderly and replied:
"I'm sick to my soul, my son!"
Happiness does not taste of flesh. Close beside them the shadow of a pine tree lay kissing the earth, as cool as a river. And in the pine tree a bird was singing, a bird that was also a little gold bell.
"I am the Rose-Apple of the Bird of Paradise, I am life, half my body is a lie, the other half is truth; I am a rose and I am an apple, I give to everyone one glass eye and one real eye; those who see with my glass eye see because they dream, those who see with my real eye see because they are looking! I am life, the Rose-Apple of the Bird of Paradise; I am the lie in every truth, and the truth in every fabrication!"
Suddenly the idiot left his mother's lap and ran to watch the circus go by: horses with long manes like weeping-willows ridden by women dressed in spangles; carriages decorated with flowers and paper streamers reeled along the paved streets as unsteadily as drunkards. A troupe of squalid street musicians, trumpeters,

fiddle-scrapers and drum-beaters. Floury-faced clowns were distributing bright-coloured programmes announcing a gala performance in honour of the President of the Republic, the Benefactor of his Country, Head of the Great Liberal Party and Protector of Studious Youth.

The idiot's gaze wandered round the high vaulted roof. The circus performers left him alone in a building standing above a bottomless abyss the colour of verdigris. The seats were hanging from the curtains like suspension bridges. The confessionals went up and 'down between the earth and sky like lifts carrying souls, operated by the Angel of the Golden Ball and the Devil with Eleven Thousand Horns. The Virgin of Carmel came out from her shrine through the wall of glass enclosing her, just as light passes through a window, and asked what he wanted and whom he was looking for. And he was delighted to stop and talk to her, to the owner of the house, the sweetest of the angels, the reason for the existence of the saints and the poor people's pastrycook. This great lady was less than three feet tall, but when she spoke she gave the impression of understanding everything like a full-grown person. The Zany explained by signs how much he enjoyed chewing wax; and half-smiling, half-serious, she told him to take one of the lighted tapers from the altar. Then, gathering up her too-long silver cloak, she led him by the hand to a basin full of coloured fish and gave him the rainbow to suck like barley-sugar. Perfect bliss! He felt happy from the tip of his tongue to the tip of his toes. It was something he had never had in his life : a piece of wax to chew like copal, peppermint-flavoured barley-sugar, a basin full of coloured fish, and a mother who sang as she massaged his injured leg: "Get well, get well, my little frog's bottom, seven little farts for you and your mamma!" All this was his as he slept on the garbage.

But happiness lasts no longer than a shower in the sunshine . . . Down the path of beaten earth the colour of milk leading to the rubbish-dump came a wood-cutter followed by his dog; he carried a faggot of sticks on his back, his coat folded over it and his machete in his arms like a baby. The gulley was not deep, but the falling dusk had plunged it in shadows and shrouded the rubbish piled up in its depths. The wood-cutter turned and looked back. He could have sworn he was being followed. Further on, he stopped again. He sensed the presence of some hidden person.

The dog howled, with its hair standing on end as if it saw the devil. An eddy of wind lifted some dirty bits of paper, stained as with women's blood or beetroot juice. The sky looked very far away, very blue, decorated like the vault of a very high tomb with sleepily circling turkey-buzzards. Suddenly the dog raced off to the place where the Zany was lying. The wood-cutter trembled with fear. He followed the dog cautiously, step by step, to see who the dead man was. He was in danger of cutting his feet on broken glass, bottle-ends and sardine-tins, and had to jump over foul-smelling excrement and nameless patches of darkness. The hollows were full of water, like harbours among the garbage.

Without putting down his load—his fear was a heavier burden —he caught hold of one of the supposed corpse's feet, and was astonished to find a living man, whose panting breath combined with his cries and the dog's barking to make a graph of his distress, like wind when it is laced with rain. The footsteps of someone walking through a little wood of pines and ancient guava-trees near-by agitated the wood-cutter even more. Suppose it was a policeman! Oh well, really, that would be the last straw!

"Quiet!" he said to the dog. And as it went on barking he gave it a kick. "Shut up, you brute, be quiet!"

Should he run for it? But flight would be a confession of guilt. Worse still, if it were a policeman. And turning to the injured man:

"Here quick, I'll help you get up! My God, they've half killed you! Quick, don't be scared, don't shout; I'm not hurting you! I was just coming along, and saw you lying there . . ."

"I saw you digging him out," interrupted a voice behind him, "and I turned back in case it was someone I knew; let's get him out of here."

The wood-cutter turned his head to reply, and nearly fainted with fear. He gave a gasp, and would have made off except that he was supporting a man who could barely stand. The man who had spoken was an angel: a complexion of golden marble, fair hair, a small mouth and an almost feminine appearance, in strong contrast with the manly expression of his black eyes. He was wearing grey. In the fading light he seemed to be dressed in a cloud. In his slender hands he held a thin cane and a broad-brimmed hat which looked like a dove.

"An angel!" The wood-cutter couldn't take his eyes from him. "An angel," he repeated, "an angel!"

"It's obvious from his clothes that he's very poor," said the newcomer. "What a sad thing it is to be poor!"

"That depends; everything in this world depends on something else. Look at me; I'm very poor; but I've got my work, my wife and my hut, and I don't think I'm to be pitied," stammered the wood-cutter like a man talking in his sleep, hoping to ingratiate himself with this angel, who might recompense his Christian resignation by changing him from a wood-cutter to a king, if he so wished. And for a second he saw himself dressed in gold, with a red cloak, a crown on his head and a sceptre set with jewels in his hand. The rubbish dump seemed far away . . .

"Strange!" remarked the new arrival, raising his voice above the Zany's groans.

"Why strange? After all, we poor men are more resigned than other people. And what can we do, anyway? It's true that with the schools and all that, anyone who learns to read gets ideas into his head. Even my wife gets sad sometimes and says she'd like to have wings on Sundays."

The injured man fainted two or three times as they descended the steeper part of the slope. The trees rose and sank before his moribund eyes like the fingers of Chinese dancers. The remarks of the men who were now almost carrying him zigzagged in his ears like drunk men on a slippery floor. There was a great black patch before his eyes. Sudden cold shivers blew through his body, setting ablaze the ashes of his burning fancies.

"So your wife wants wings on Sundays?" said the stranger. "Wings! And if she had them they'd be no use to her."

"That's right; she says she wants them to go out with, and when she's fed up with me she asks the wind for them."

The wood-cutter stopped to wipe the sweat from his forehead with his sleeve, and exclaimed:

"He's no light weight!"

The new arrival said:

"Her legs are quite good enough for that; even if she had wings she wouldn't go."

"Not she; nor yet out of good nature neither, but because women are birds who can't live without their cage, and because I carry home too few bits of wood to go breaking them on her

27

back"—he remembered at this point that he was talking to an angel and hastily gilded the pill—"for her own good, of course."

The stranger was silent.

"Who can have beaten up this poor chap?" went on the wood-cutter, changing the subject out of embarrassment at what he had just said.

"There are plenty . . ."

"It's true, some people'll do anything, but this chap looks as if—as if they'd had no mercy on him. A jab in the mouth with a knife and off with him to the rubbish dump!"

"He's probably got other wounds."

"Looks to me as if the one in his lip was done with a razor, and they chucked him away here so that the crime shouldn't be found out, eh?"

"But what a place!"

"Just what I was going to say."

The trees were covered with turkey-buzzards making ready to leave the gulley. The Zany's fear was stronger even than his pain, and kept him mute; he curled himself up like a hedgehog in a deathly silence.

The wind ran lightly over the plain, blowing from the town into the country, delicate, gentle, familiar . . .

The stranger looked at his watch, and after putting some money in the wounded man's pocket and bidding the wood-cutter a friendly goodbye, he walked quickly away.

The sky was cloudless and resplendent. The outermost houses of the town looked out at the countryside with their electric lights burning like matches in a darkened theatre. Sinuous groves of trees were beginning to appear out of the darkness near the first houses: mud huts smelling of straw, wooden cabins smelling of ladino, big houses with sordid front yards stinking like stables, and inns where it was usual to find fodder for sale, a servant girl with a lover in the barracks, and a group of muleteers sitting in the darkness.

When he reached the first houses the wood-cutter abandoned the injured man, after telling him how to get to the hospital. The Zany half-opened his eyes in search of help, or something to cure his hiccups; but it was on shut doors in a deserted street that his moribund gaze fastened itself like a sharp thorn. Far off bugles could be heard, testifying to the submission of a nomad race, and bells tremulously tolling thrice for the souls of dead Christians: Mer—cy! Mer—cy! Mer—cy!

He was terrified by a turkey-buzzard dragging itself through the shadows. The creature had a broken wing and its angry complaints sounded to him like a threat. Slowly he moved away, step by step, leaning against the walls, against the motionless trembling of the walls, giving moan after moan, not knowing where he was going, with the wind in his face, the wind which had bitten ice before it blew at night. He was shaken by hiccups . . .

The wood-cutter dropped his bundle of wood in the courtyard of his hut as usual. His dog had got home before him and received him effusively. He pushed it aside, and without taking off his hat opened his coat so that it hung on his shoulders like a bat's wings; then he went up to the fire in the corner of the room, where his wife was cooking pancakes, and told her what had happened.

"I met an angel on the rubbish dump."

The light from the flames flickered on the bamboo walls and the straw roof, like the wings of other angels.

From the hut there emerged a tremulous stream of white, vegetal smoke.

CHAPTER V

That Swine!

THE President's secretary was listening to Doctor Barreño.

"I must tell you, Mr Secretary, that I've been visiting the barracks daily for the last ten years, as military surgeon. And I tell you I've been the victim of an unspeakable outrage; I was arrested, and my arrest was due to—but I must tell you about it. This is what happened: a strange disease suddenly made its appearance in the Military Hospital; every day ten or twelve men died in the morning, ten or twelve in the afternoon, and ten or twelve more in the night. Well, the Chief of Military Hygiene commissioned me and some of my colleagues to enquire into the situation and find out what was the cause of the death of individuals who had been admitted to hospital the day before in good health, or nearly so. Well, after five autopsies I succeeded in proving that these unfortunate men had died of a perforation in the stomach, as big as a small coin, produced by some external agent that I didn't recognise, and which turned out to be the sodium sulphate they had been given as a purge—sodium bought from the soda-water factory, and therefore of poor quality. Well, my colleagues didn't share my opinion, and presumably for that reason were not arrested; in their view it was a new disease which needed further investigation. I tell you a hundred and forty soldiers died, and there are still two barrels of sulphate left. I tell you that in order to enrich himself by a few pesos, the Chief of Military Hygiene sacrificed a hundred and forty men, as well as those still to follow. I tell you . . ."

"Doctor Luis Barreño!" shouted one of the President's aides-de-camp from the door of the secretary's office:

"I'll tell you what he says to me, Mr Secretary."

The secretary took a few steps towards the door with Doctor Barreño. Humanitarian considerations apart, he was interested by the picaresque style of his story, built up step by step, monotonous and grey, in harmony with the grizzled head and dry beef-steak face of a man of science.

The President of the Republic received the doctor standing, his head held high, one arm hanging at his side in a natural position, the other behind his back, and without giving him time to greet him, he declaimed:

"Please get this straight, Don Luis: I am not going to stand the good name of my government being depreciated by gossiping medical quacks, even to the smallest degree. My enemies must be careful to remember this, because I'll have the head of the first man who forgets it. You may go! Get out! . . . and go and fetch that swine!"

Doctor Barreño went out backwards, hat in hand, his forehead wrinkled tragically and his face as pale as it would be the day he was buried.

"I'm done for, Mr Secretary, I'm done for! The only thing I heard him say was: 'You may go! Get out, and go and fetch that swine!' "

"I am that swine!"

So saying, a clerk got up from a table in a corner, and went into the President's room by the door Doctor Barreño had just shut behind him.

"I thought he was going to hit me! If you'd only seen—if you'd only seen!" gabbled the doctor, wiping away the sweat that was streaming down his face. "If only you'd seen! But I'm wasting your time, Mr Secretary, and you're very busy. I'm going now. And thank you very much."

"Goodbye, my dear Doctor. Don't mention it. Good luck."

The Secretary finished writing out the despatches which the President would sign in a few minutes' time. The town was soaking up the orangeade of dusk; it was clothed in pretty muslin clouds and a crown of stars like the angels in a prologue. The shining steeples let fall the Ave Maria like a life-belt into the streets.

Barreño went home, his world crumbling round him. How could he have parried such a treacherous blow? He shut the door, looking at the roofs from which murderous hands might descend and strangle him, and hid himself at the back of a wardrobe in his bedroom.

His coats were suspended in a solemn row like the corpses of hanged men preserved in naphthaline, and their funereal appearance reminded Barreño of the assassination of his father, many years ago, when walking alone at night. His family had

had to be content with a fruitless judicial inquiry; and after crime came melodrama in the form of an anonymous letter couched in more or less the following terms: "My brother-in-law and I were returning along the road from Vuelta Grande to La Canoa at about eleven o'clock at night when we heard a shot some way off; another, another, another—we counted five. We took refuge in a little copse near by. We heard horses coming towards us at full gallop. Riders and horses almost touched us as they went by, and after a while we went on our way again. Then all was silence, but soon our horses began to rear. While they were shying and whinnying we dismounted, pistol in hand, to see what was the matter, and there we found the dead body of a man lying on his face, and a little further on a wounded mule, which my brother-in-law put out of its pain. We immediately went back to Vuelta Grande to report our discovery. At Headquarters we found Colonel José Parrales Sonriente, 'the man with the little mule', and a group of his friends, sitting round a table covered with wine-glasses. We took him on one side and told him what we had seen. First the shots, then . . . He listened to us, shrugged his shoulders, turned his gaze to the guttering candle-flame and replied deliberately: 'Go straight home—I know what I'm talking about—and never mention this matter again!' "

"Luis! Luis!"
One of his overcoats slipped from its hanger like a bird of prey.
"Luis!"
With a quick movement Barreño stepped into his library and began turning the pages of a book. How frightened his wife would have been if she had found him in his hanging-cupboard!
"It's really past a joke! You'll kill yourself or go crazy with all this studying! I've told you so from the first! Can't you understand that it's tact rather than knowledge you need if you want to get on? What good does all this studying do you? What good does all this studying do you? None whatever! It won't even buy you a pair of socks! It's really too bad! It's too bad!"
Daylight, and his wife's voice restored him to calm.
"It's the last straw! Studying, studying . . . What for? So that when you're dead they'll say how learned you were, just as they always do about everyone. Pooh! Leave studying to quacks; you don't need it—that's the point of having a degree; you've got

knowledge and don't have to study. And don't look so cross! Clients are what you need, not a library. If you had a patient for each of these useless books, this house would be a healthier place. As for me, I'd like to see your clinic full up, hear the telephone ringing all the time, see you summoned to consultations—getting somewhere, in fact . . ."

"What do you mean by getting somewhere?"

"Well—be a success. And don't go and tell me that you must wear your eyes out reading for that. Other doctors get along with half of what you know. They're content to elbow their way to the front and make a name for themselves. The President's doctor here, the President's doctor there—that's what it means to get somewhere."

"We-e-ell." Barreño dwelt on the word as if to bridge a little gap in his memory. "Well, my dear, you'd better stop hoping; I suppose you'll fall over backwards when I tell you that I've just been to see the President. Yes, to see the President."

"Oh, my goodness! And what did he say to you? How did he receive you?"

"Badly. The only thing I heard him say was something about cutting my head off. I was afraid, and what was worse I couldn't find the way out of the room."

"He ticked you off? Well, you're not the first nor the last. He's pitched into plenty of others!" And after a long pause she added: "Timidity has always been your undoing."

"But, my dear girl, show me somebody who is brave when he meets a wild beast."

"No, my dear, that's not what I mean; I'm talking about surgery, since you can't manage to be the President's doctor. And for that the important thing is to lose your timidity. What a surgeon needs is courage, I tell you. Courage and determination in using his knife. A dressmaker who isn't ready to waste material will never succeed in cutting out a dress properly. And a dress is worth something, you know. On the other hand, a doctor can get his hand in by practising on the Indians in hospital. But don't worry about what's happened between you and the President. Come and have lunch. He must have been in a bad temper because of that horrible assassination in the Cathedral Porch."

"Be quiet, will you—or I'll do what I've never done before

and slap your face. It wasn't an assassination, and there's nothing horrible in the death of that odious brute who killed my father on a lonely road—an old, defenceless man!"

"Only according to an anonymous letter! What an extraordinary man you are! Who takes any notice of anonymous letters?"

"If I paid attention to anonymous letters . . ."

"It would be unworthy of you . . ."

"Will you let me speak? If I paid attention to anonymous letters you wouldn't be here with me in my house." Barreño searched feverishly in his pockets with a tense expression. "You wouldn't be here in my house. Hear, read that."

Pale-faced, with no colour but the chemical vermilion on her lips, she took the paper her husband handed her, and ran her eyes quickly over it:

"Doctor, pleese console your wife, now that 'the man with the little mule' has gone to a better plaice. The advice of friends who wish you well."

With an anguished laugh—a laugh which splintered and filled the test-tubes and retorts in Barreño's small laboratory, like a poison to be analysed—she returned the paper to her husband. A maid had just come to the door and announced:

"Lunch is served."

At the Palace, the President was signing papers with the assistance of the little old man who had entered the room as Doctor Barreño left, and whom he had referred to as "that swine".

"That swine" was a poorly dressed man with a pink skin like a young mouse, hair of inferior quality gold, and worried blue eyes lost behind bright yellow spectacles.

The President signed his name for the last time, and the little old man, trying to blot it in a hurry, upset the ink-pot over the signed sheet.

"SWINE!"

"Sir!"

"SWINE!"

A ring at the bell, another, another. Footsteps, and an officer appeared at the door.

"General, see that this man gets two hundred lashes, at once, at once!" roared the President, and immediately went into his own apartments. Luncheon was ready.

The eyes of "that swine" filled with tears. He said nothing because he was incapable of speech and because he knew it was useless to beg for forgiveness: the assassination of Parrales Sonriente had put the President in a furious temper. In the mists before his eyes he saw his wife and children begging for mercy for him: a hard-working woman and half a dozen thin children. With a claw-like hand he searched in his coat pocket for a handkerchief—if only he could relieve his feelings by crying!—he did not think, as anyone else would have done, that the punishment was unjust, but on the contrary that it was right he should be beaten to teach him to be less clumsy—if only he could relieve his feelings by crying!—and to be more efficient and not to spill ink over documents—if only he could relieve his feelings by crying!

His teeth projected between his tight lips like those of a comb, combining with his hollow cheeks and his anguished expression to give him the appearance of a man condemned to death. His shirt was glued to his back with sweat, and this caused him special dismay. He had never sweated like this before! If only he could relieve his feelings by crying! And the nausea of fear made him . . . him . . . him . . . shiver.

The President's aide-de-camp took hold of him by the arm; he was stupefied, sunk in a macabre torpor, his eyes staring, a terrible emptiness in his ears, his skin heavy as lead, his body doubled up, weak, growing ever weaker . . .

A few minutes later in the dining-room:

"May I come in, Mr President?"

"Come in, General."

"I've come to tell you that that swine was unable to stand the two hundred lashes, sir."

The President was at that moment helping himself to fried potatoes, and the maid-servant holding the dish began to tremble.

"Why are you trembling?" her master scolded her.

Then turning to the general who was standing at attention without blinking, his kepi in his hand: "Very good, you may go!"

Still holding the dish, the servant hurried after the aide-de-camp and asked him why the man had been unable to stand the two hundred lashes.

"Why? Because he died."

And, still holding the dish, she went back to the dining-room.

"Please, sir," she said to the President almost in tears, as he calmly ate his lunch, "the General says he couldn't stand it because he died!"

"Well, what of it? Bring the next course!"

CHAPTER VI

A General's Head

MIGUEL ANGEL FACE, the President's confidential adviser, came to see him after the dessert.

"Please forgive me, Mr President," he said as he appeared at the dining-room door. (He was as beautiful and wicked as Satan.) "Please forgive me if I'm late—but I had to go to the assistance of a wood-cutter who had found a wounded man on the rubbish-dump, and I couldn't get here sooner. It was no one you know, Mr President—a low sort of fellow!"

The President was dressed as usual in the deepest mourning: black shoes, black suit, black tie, and the black hat which he never took off; he concealed his toothless gums beneath a grizzled moustache combed over the corners of his mouth; he had thin pendulous cheeks and pinched eyelids.

"And did you take him to hospital?" he asked, allowing his frown to subside.

"Sir . . .?"

"What's this you're telling me? A man who prides himself on being the friend of the President of the Republic surely doesn't leave a poor wretch lying in the street, wounded by some unknown hand!"

A slight movement at the dining-room door made him turn his head.

"Come in, General."

"With your permission, Mr President."

"Are they ready, General?"

"Yes, Mr President."

"Go yourself, General; offer my condolences to his widow and present her with these three hundred pesos in the name of the President of the Republic, to help her with the funeral expenses."

The General, who was standing at attention, cap in hand, without blinking and almost without breathing, bent forward and took the money from the table, turned on his heel and was seen to

leave a few minutes later, in a motor-car with the coffin containing the body of "that swine".

Angel Face hastened to explain:

"I thought of going to the hospital with the injured man, but
then I said to myself: 'He'll be better looked after if I get an order
from the President.' And as I was coming here at your request,
and also to tell you again how horrified I am at the treacherous
assassination of our Parrales Sonriente—"

"I'll give orders . . ."

"That is only what one would expect from a man who they
say ought not to be governing this country."

The President started as if he had been stung.

"Who says so?"

"I do, Mr President—the first of many who believe that a man
like you ought to govern a country like France, or free Switzer-
land, or industrious Belgium or wonderful Denmark! But
France—France above all. You would be the ideal man to guide
the destinies of the great race to which Gambetta and Victor
Hugo belonged!"

An almost imperceptible smile appeared beneath the President's moustache, as he polished his spectacles on a white silk
handkerchief without taking his eyes from his friend's face. After a
short pause he embarked on a new subject of conversation.

"I asked you to come here, Miguel, because of an affair which
I want to have settled tonight. The competent authorities have
given orders for the arrest of that scoundrel General Eusebio
Canales, and it is to take place at his house first thing tomorrow.
For special reasons, although he was one of Parrales Sonriente's
assassins, it doesn't suit the Government for him to go to prison,
and it is essential that he takes to flight at once. Go and find
him, tell him what you know and advise him to escape tonight, as
though the idea were your own. You may have to help him do it,
because like every professional soldier he believes in honour and
would rather die than run away. If they catch him tomorrow he'll
be executed. He must know nothing of this conversation; this is
between you and me. And take care the police don't find out
you've been to see him; arrange matters so as not to arouse
suspicion and so that the ruffian escapes. You can go now."

The favourite left with his face half hidden in his black muffler.
(He was as beautiful and wicked as Satan.) The officers guarding

their master's dining-room instinctively gave him a military salute—or perhaps they had heard that he held a general's head in his hands. Seventy despondent people were yawning in the audience-chamber, waiting for the President to be at liberty. The streets surrounding the Palace and the President's House were carpeted with flowers. Groups of soldiers were decorating the front of the neighbouring barracks with lanterns, little flags and blue-and-white paper chains, under instructions from their commanding officer.

Angel Face took no notice of these festive preparations. He had to see the general and make plans for his flight. Everything seemed easy until the dogs began barking at him in the monstrous wood which separated the President from his enemies, a wood made up of trees with ears which responded to the slightest sound by whirling as if blown by a hurricane. Not the tiniest noise for miles around could escape the avidity of those millions of membranes. The dogs went on barking. A network of invisible threads, more invisible than telegraph wires, connected every leaf with the President, enabling him to keep watch on the most secret thoughts of the townspeople.

If only it were possible to make a pact with the devil, to sell one's soul to him on condition that the police were deceived and the general escaped! But the devil does not lend himself to charitable actions; although almost anything might be at stake in this strange undertaking. The general's head—and something else. He uttered the words as if he really held in his hands the general's head—and something else.

He arrived at General Canales' house in the district of La Merced. It was a large corner house, almost a hundred years old, whose eight balconies on the front and big carriage entrance on the back gave it something of the majestic appearance of an ancient coin. The favourite decided to listen outside the door and knock for admission if he heard anyone moving inside. But the presence of police patrolling the opposite pavement forced him to give up this plan. He walked quickly past, glancing at the windows to see if there were anyone to whom he could make a sign. He saw no one. It was impossible to stand about on the pavement without arousing suspicion. But on the corner opposite to the house was a disreputable little tavern, and the safest way to remain in the neighbourhood was to go in and have a drink.

A beer. He exchanged a few words with the woman who served him and then, with the glass of beer in his hand, turned his head to see who was sitting on a bench against the wall; he had glimpsed a man's silhouette out of the corner of his eye as he came in. His hat pulled down over his forehead almost to his eyes, a handkerchief round his neck, the collar of his coat turned up, wide trousers, high boots with the buttons unfastened, made of rubber, yellow leather and coffee-coloured cloth. The favourite raised his eyes absent-mindedly and looked at the bottles standing in rows on the shelves, the luminous S in the electric light bulb, an advertisement for Spanish wines (Bacchus astride a barrel amongst pot-bellied friars and naked women), and a portrait of the President, outrageously rejuvenated, with epaulettes like railway-lines on his shoulders, and a cherub crowning him with a laurel wreath. A portrait in the best of taste! Every now and then he turned and glanced at the general's house. It would be a serious matter if the man on the bench and the bar-keeper were more than friends and made any trouble. He unbuttoned his jacket and at the same time crossed one leg over the other, leaning his elbows on the bar as if he were in no hurry to leave. Suppose he ordered another beer? He ordered it and paid for it with a hundred peso note to gain time. Perhaps the innkeeper had no change. She opened the drawer of the till with a cross expression, rummaged among the grimy notes and shut it with a bang. She hadn't any change. Always the same story! She would have to go out and get some. She threw her apron over her bare arms and went out into the street, after a glance at the man on the bench, as if to warn him to keep an eye on her client: to take care he didn't steal anything. A useless precaution, because at that moment a young lady came out of the general's house as if she had dropped from the sky, and Angel Face was off like a shot.

"Señorita," he said, walking beside her, "would you tell the master of the house you've just left that I have something very urgent to say to him?"

"My papa?"

"You're General Canales' daughter?"

"Yes."

"Then, don't stop; no, no . . . Keep on walking; we must keep on walking. Here's my card. Please tell him that I shall expect

him at my house as soon as possible; that I'm going straight there now and will wait for him, that his life is in danger. Yes, yes, at my house as soon as possible."

The wind blew his hat off and he had to run after it. Twice or three times it escaped him. At last he caught it with the wild gesture of someone catching a fowl in a chicken-run.

He went back to the bar, on the pretext of picking up his change, but really to see what impression his sudden exit had made on the man on the bench, and found him struggling with the barkeeper; she had her back to the wall, while his eager mouth sought a kiss from hers.

"You miserable policeman, you! *Bascas** is the right name for you!" she cried when the man from the bench let go of her, alarmed by the sound of Angel Face's approaching steps.

It suited Angel Face's plans to intervene amicably; he took away the bottle the innkeeper was brandishing and looked indulgently at the man.

"Take it easy! Take it easy, Señora! Heavens, what a to-do! Here! Keep the change and make it up. You won't gain anything by kicking up a row, and the police might come along; besides if our friend here . . ."

"Lucio Vasquez, at your service."

"Lucio Vasquez? *Sucio Bascas,*† more likely! The police! It's always 'the police'. Let 'em try! Just let 'em try and come in here. I'm not afraid of anyone and I'm not an Indian neither, d'you hear? so that he can't frighten me with his Casa Nueva prison!"

"I'll put you in a brothel if I want to!" mumbled Vasquez, spitting out something he had swallowed the wrong way.

"Come on, man, make it up! That's enough!"

"All right, sir, I wasn't saying anything!"

Vasquez had a disagreeable voice; he spoke like a woman, in a small affected falsetto. Deeply enamoured of the barkeeper, he used to struggle with her day and night for one freely-given kiss—that was all he asked. But she refused on the grounds that giving him a kiss would mean giving him everything. Entreaties, threats, little presents, false or real tears, serenades, lies were all of no avail against the barkeeper's stubborn refusal, and she had never given in nor let herself be wheedled. "Anyone who tries to

* Vomit.
† Filthy vomit.

make love to me," she used to say, "knows that he's in for a free fight."

"If you've finished," went on Angel Face, speaking as if to himself and rubbing with his forefinger at a nickel coin nailed to the counter, "I'll tell you about the young lady opposite."

And he began to tell them that a friend of his had asked him to find out whether she had received a letter, when the barkeeper interrupted:

"Anyone can see that you're the one who's after her, you lucky bastard!"

The favourite had an inspiration . . . After her . . . say that her family was against it . . . pretend to kidnap her . . .

He went on rubbing his forefinger on the nickel coin fastened to the counter, but more vigorously now.

"That's true," said Angel Face, "but the trouble is her father doesn't want us to marry."

"Don't talk to me about that old man!" put in Vasquez. "The sour faces he makes at a chap, as if I could help being ordered to follow him everywhere!"

"That's the rich all over!" commented the barkeeper disagreeably.

"That's why I'm planning to run off with the girl. She's agreed. We were talking about it just this minute and we're going to do it tonight."

The barkeeper and Vasquez smiled.

"Let's have a drink," said Vasquez, "that's better." Then he turned and offered Angel Face a cigarette. "Smoke?"

"No thanks. Well—I don't want to be unfriendly."

The woman filled three glasses while they lit their cigarettes. A moment later, after the fiery liquid had burned its way down his throat, Angel Face said:

"Then I can count on you both? Whatever happens I shall need your help. Oh, but it must be today!"

"No good after eleven tonight; I'm on duty. But this one here . . ."

"*This one* indeed! I like your cheek! Watch out what you say!"

"La Masacuata here," said Vasquez, turning to look at the barkeeper, "she'll take my place—she's worth two men—unless you want me to send someone else; a friend of mine's meeting me in the Indian quarter tonight."

"Why must you always drag that milk-and-water Genaro Rodas into everything?" asked the woman.

"What's this about milk-and-water?" enquired Angel Face.

"It's because he looks half-dead. He's pasty-faced."

"What does that matter?"

"I don't see anything wrong with him . . ."

"Yes there is; I'm sorry to interrupt, sir. I didn't want to tell you, but Genaro Rodas' wife Fedina has been telling everyone that the general's daughter is going to be godmother to her child; so you see your pal Genaro isn't the chap for what this gentleman wants done."

"Poppycock!"

"Everything's poppycock to you!"

Angel Face thanked Vasquez for his amiability, but told him it would be better not to count on his milk-and-water friend, since (as the woman had said) he could not be considered neutral.

"It's a pity, Vasquez my friend, that you can't help me this time."

"I'm sorry too not to be in on it; if I'd known I'd have got leave of absence."

"If money would help fix matters . . ."

"No; that's not my game. It can't be done." And he put his hand to his ear.

"Well, it can't be helped. I'll be back before dawn, about a quarter to two or half past one, because in love affairs you must strike while the iron's hot."

He said goodbye and went to the door, lifting his wrist-watch to his ear to see if it was going—how portentous is the tiny tremor of that isochronous pulsation!—and then hurried away with his black muffler pulled up over his pale face. He was carrying the general's head in his hands—and something else.

CHAPTER VII

Archiepiscopal Absolution

GENARO RODAS stopped by the wall to light a cigarette. Just as the match scratched the side of the box, Lucio Vasquez appeared. A dog was vomiting against the grille of a shrine.

"Curse this wind!" growled Rodas when he saw his friend.

"Hullo there!" Vasquez greeted him, and they walked on together.

"How goes it, eh?"

"Where are you off to?"

"Where am I off to indeed! Are you trying to be funny? Didn't we fix to meet here then?"

"Oh, I thought you'd forgotten. I'll tell you about your affair, but come and have a drink. I could do with a drink, I don't know why. Come on, let's go by the Cathedral Porch and see what's doing."

"Nothing much, probably, but we'll go if you like: ever since they stopped the beggars sleeping there there's not a cat stirring."

"All the better, say I. We'll go through the close, shall we? What a devil of a wind!"

Ever since the assassination of Colonel Parrales Sonriente, the Cathedral Porch had been constantly occupied by the Secret Police. The toughest men were chosen to keep watch there. Vasquez and his friend traversed the Porch, climbed the steps at the corner of the Archbishop's Palace and went out by the Hundred Doors. The shadows of the columns lay on the ground occupying the places where the beggars had once slept. A ladder, and another and another, bore witness to the fact that a painter was going to rejuvenate the doors and windows of the building. And in fact, among the Municipality's plans for showing their unconditional support of the President of the Republic, the first on the list was that of painting and repairing the building which had been the scene of the odious assassination, at the expense of the Turks who kept a bazaar there redolent of burning rubbish.

44

"Let the Turks pay; they are in a way responsible for the death of Colonel Parrales Sonriente, because they live in the place where the deed was done," was the stern decision of the aldermen when the subject of money came up. And as a result of this vindictive arrangement, the Turks would have ended up poorer than the beggars who used to sleep on their doorsteps, had it not been for the help of influential friends who managed to pay for the painting, cleaning and improved lighting of the Cathedral, with receipts from the National Treasury bought at half their value.

But the presence of the Secret Police worried them. They asked each other in a whisper what could be the reason for such vigilance. Hadn't the receipts been converted into pails of whitewash? Hadn't paint-brushes as broad as the beards of the Prophets of Israel been bought at their expense? They prudently increased the number of bars, bolts and padlocks on the doors of their shops.

Vasquez and Rodas left the porch by the side nearest to the Hundred Doors. The silence swallowed up their heavy footsteps. Further on up the street, they slipped into a bar called The Lion's Awakening. Vasquez greeted the barman, ordered two glasses and a bottle of wine, and sat down beside Rodas at a small table behind a screen.

"Well, what news have you got for me?" asked Rodas.

"Cheers!" Vasquez raised his glass.

"Cheers!"

The barman who had come up to serve them, added mechanically: "Your healths, gentlemen!"

Both drained their glasses at a single gulp.

"Nothing doing." Vasquez spat out the words with his last mouthful of liquor diluted with frothy saliva; "the assistant director put up a bloke of his own, and when I spoke up for you they'd already given the job to the lousy fellow."

"You don't say?"

"But when the captain commands, the sailor has to do as he's told, you know. I let him see you were keen to join the Secret Police, that you had plenty of guts. Every trick I knew!"

"And what did he say?"

"What I've told you: that he already had a man of his own, and then he shut me up. I can tell you it's more difficult now than when I joined to get into the Secret Police. Everyone has spotted it as the career of the future."

Rodas shook off his friend's remarks with a shrug of the shoulders and an unintelligible comment. He had come there in hopes of getting work.

"Don't take it to heart! As soon as I hear of another vacancy you shall have it. I swear by God you shall have it; especially now that the place is becoming a regular ants' nest and there are sure to be more jobs going. Did I tell you . . .?" Vasquez looked about him nervously. "No—I'm not a blabber. Better not!"

"All right, don't tell me; what do I care?"

"It's a tricky business . . ."

"Look, old chap, don't tell me anything; do me a favour and shut up! You don't trust me, I see! You don't trust me!"

"I do, old chap, how touchy you are!"

"Look here, shut up, will you; I don't like this suspiciousness. You're just like a woman! Who's been asking you anything, that you go on like this?"

Vasquez stood up to see if anyone could hear, and spoke in a low tone, going close to Rodas, who listened to him sulkily, still offended by his reticence.

"I don't know if I told you that the beggars who were sleeping in the Porch on the night of the murder have already blabbed, and now there's not a single soul that doesn't know who did in the colonel." And raising his voice he asked: "Who do you think?" He lowered it to a pitch suitable to a State Secret. "Blowed if it wasn't General Eusebio Canales and Abel Carvajal, the lawyer."

"Are you telling me the truth?"

"The order for their arrest went out today. There, now you know the whole thing."

"So that's how it is," said Rodas in a more conciliatory tone; "so the famous colonel who could shoot a fly at a hundred yards and was such a devil of a fellow, wasn't finished off with a revolver or sword—he just had his neck twisted like a chicken! You can do anything in this world if you make up your mind to it! The murdering swine!"

Vasquez suggested another round of drinks and called out: "Two more short ones, Don Lucho!"

Don Lucho, the barman, displayed his black silk braces as he refilled their glasses.

"Knock it back!" said Vasquez; then he spat and added

between his teeth: "Hurry, or the bird will have flown! I hate to see a full glass, you know; or if you don't know you ought to. Cheers!"

Rodas had seemed preoccupied, but now he drained his glass hastily, and removing it from his lips exclaimed:

"The devils who sent the colonel into the next world won't be such fools as to come back to the Porch. Not bloody likely! It's not worth waiting for them; or is it for love of the Turks the Secret Police are there?"

"What the Secret Police are up to in the Cathedral Porch has nothing to do with the assassination. I promise you it hasn't. You'll never guess what we're doing there. We're waiting for a man with rabies!"

"Come off it!"

"You remember that scoundrel people used to shout 'Mother!' at in the streets? Tall fellow, bony, with twisted legs, who used to run about the streets like a loony. Remember? Yes, of course you do. Well, it's him we've been waiting for in the Porch these last three days, ever since he disappeared. We're going to pump him full of lead . . ." and Vasquez's hand went to his pistol.

"Don't be funny!"

"No, I'm not joking; it's true, I tell you, he's bitten a whole crowd of people and the dose the doctors have ordered is an ounce of lead injected into his skin. What do you say to that?"

"What d'you take me for? No man alive could make me believe it. I'm not such a fool as all that. The Police are waiting in the Porch for the men who wrung the Colonel's neck."

"God, no! What a stubborn mule you are! It's for the dumb chap, do you hear? The dumb fellow with rabies who has been biting everyone! Have I got to say it all over again?"

The Zany's moans filled the street, as he dragged himself along, sometimes on all fours, helping himself with the toes of one foot and scraping his stomach on the stones, and sometimes supported on the thigh of his good leg and one elbow, while pain tore at his side. At last the square came into view. The wind buffeting the trees in the park seemed to bring with it a sound of turkey-buzzards. The Zany was so terrified that he became almost unconscious for some time, his anguish manifested in the dryness of his swollen tongue, like a dead fish in the ashes, and the sweat-soaked scissors of his pants. Step by step he clambered up to the Porch of Our Lord, hauling himself along like a dying cat, and lay huddled in a shady corner with his mouth open, his eyes glazed and his ragged clothes stiff with blood and earth. The silence blended together the footsteps of late passers-by, the click of the sentinels' rifles and the sound of stray dogs padding along, noses to the ground, poking about for bones among the bits of paper and leaves the wind had blown to the foot of the porch.

Don Lucho refilled the large wine-glasses known as "two-storeys".

"Why the hell won't you believe me?" said Vasquez in a sharper voice than usual, between two expectorations. "Didn't I tell you that about nine this evening—or perhaps half-past nine—before I met you here, I was making up to La Masacuata, when into her bar comes a fellow and asks for a beer? She serves him one quick. The bloke asks for another and pays for it with a hundred peso note. She's got no change and goes out to get some. But I kept my eyes open, because as soon as I saw him come in I smelt a rat—and just as if I'd known it beforehand, a tart came out of the house opposite, and she'd hardly got her foot outside when this chap went after her. But that was all I saw, because just then La Masacuata came back, and then, you see, I had to get my hands on her again . . ."

"And the hundred pesos?"

"Wait and I'll tell you. We were hard at it, she and I, when this fellow comes back for the change; he finds us hugging each other, so he gets confidential and tells us he's crazy about General Canales' daughter and he's thinking of running off with her this very night if possible. General Canales' daughter was this tart who came out to meet him. You've no idea how he went on at me to help him; but what could I do with this business of the Porch on my hands?"

"What a story!"

Rodas accompanied this remark with a jet of saliva.

"And the funny thing is I've seen this chap often over by the President's House."

"Well I'm blowed, he must be one of the family!"

"Not him. That's not the way the land lies. What I'd like to know is: why such a hurry to kidnap the girl today? He knows something about the general's arrest and thinks he'll get away with her while the soldiers are nabbing her old man."

"You've hit it, and no mistake."

"One more little drink, and then we'll show 'em!"

Don Lucho filled the two friends' glasses, which were quickly emptied. They spat on to the gobbets of spittle and stubs of cheap cigarettes covering the floor.

"What's to pay, Don Lucho?"

"Sixteen, and four . . ."

"Each?" put in Rodas.

"No—the lot," the barman replied, while Vasquez counted out the notes and four nickel coins.

"So long, Don Lucho!"

"Be seeing you, Don Luchito!"

Their voices mingled with that of the barman, who came to the door with them.

"Oh Christ! it's damned cold!" exclaimed Rodas, thrusting his hands into his trouser pockets, as they went into the street.

Walking slowly, they reached the shops by the prison, at the corner nearest to the Porch of Our Lord, and there they stopped at Vasquez's suggestion; he was feeling happy and stretched out his arms as if to rid himself of a load of sluggishness.

"This is the lion awakening, all right, with his curly mane!" he said as he stretched himself. "And what a job it must be for a lion to be a lion! Cheer up a bit, d'you mind? because this is my lucky night; this is my lucky night, I tell you, this is my lucky night!"

And by dint of repeating these words in a piercing tone, increasing in shrillness each time, he seemed to transform the night into a black tambourine decorated with gold bells; to be shaking hands with invisible friends in the wind, and inviting the puppet-master of the Cathedral Porch and his marionettes to come and tickle his throat till he burst out laughing. He laughed and he laughed, and tried out a few dance steps with his hands in his waistcoat pockets, and then his laugh suddenly died and became a groan and his happiness turned to pain. He doubled up to protect his mouth against his stomach's revolt. He was suddenly silent. His laughter hardened in his mouth like the plaster dentists use for their models. He had caught sight of the Zany. His footsteps pattered through the silent porch and the old edifice multiplied them by two, by eight, by twelve. The idiot was whining, now softly now louder, like a wounded dog. A yell rent the darkness. The Zany had seen Vasquez approaching, pistol in hand, to drag him by his broken leg towards the flight of steps leading down to the Archbishop's Palace. Rodas watched the scene without moving, breathing heavily and damp with sweat. At the first shot the Zany rolled down the stone steps. Another shot finished the job. The Turks cowered and flinched between the two explosions. And no one saw anything.

But a saint was looking out from one of the windows of the Archbishop's Palace and helping the unfortunate man to die, and just as the body rolled down the steps, a hand wearing an amethyst ring gave him absolution and opened the door to the Kingdom of Heaven to him.

CHAPTER VIII

The Puppet-Master of the Porch

IMMEDIATELY after the pistol shots, the Zany's yells and the flight of Vasquez and his friend, the streets ran one after the other, all scantily clad in moonlight, and not knowing what had happened, while the trees in the square twisted their fingers together in despair because they could not announce the event either by means of the wind or the telephone wires. The streets arrived at the crossroads and asked one another where the crime had taken place, and then some hurried to the centre of the town and others to the outskirts, as if disorientated. No, it wasn't in Jew's Alley, which wound and zigzagged as though traced by a drunkard's hand. Nor in the Alley of Escuintilla, once famous because some younger sons of a noble family had revived the days of chivalry and musketeers by fleshing their swords in the bodies of some scoundrelly police there. Nor was it in King's Alley, frequented by gamblers, where it was said no one could pass without saluting the King. Nor in Saint Theresa's Alley, a steep hill descending through a dismal neighbourhood. Nor in Rabbit Alley, nor near the Fountain of Havana, nor the Five Streets, nor in the Martinique district.

It had been in the Plaza Central, where the water flows ceaselessly through the public urinals with a suggestion of tears, where the sentinels never stop presenting arms and the night turns and turns around the Cathedral under the icy vault of the sky.

The wind throbbed fitfully like the blood in temples wounded by shots, but could not blow away the leaves fixed like obsessions to the heads of the trees.

Suddenly a door opened into the Cathedral Porch and the puppet-master peered out like a mouse. With the curiosity of a fifty-year-old little girl, his wife pushed him into the street, so that he should see what was happening and describe it to her. What was up? What had been the meaning of those two reports, the second so soon after the first? The puppet-master did not care about showing himself at his door in his underwear to satisfy the whims of Doña Venjamon,* as his wife had been nicknamed (presumably because his name was Benjamin), and thought it indelicate of her to be so carried away by her desire to know if one of the Turks had been killed that she buried her fingers between his ribs like ten spurs to force him to poke his neck out as far as possible.

"But I can't see a thing, woman! What do you expect me to tell you? What's all the fuss about?"

"What d'you say? Was it over by the Turks?"

"I tell you I can't see a thing, and that all this fuss . . ."

"Don't mumble, for heaven's sake!"

When the puppet-master left his false teeth out, his mouth was drawn in and out as he talked, like a suction valve.

"Ah, now I see! Wait a moment! I see what it is!"

"But, Benjamin, I can't understand a thing you say!" she said, almost whimpering. "Don't you understand? I can't understand a thing you say!"

"I can see now! I can see now! There's a crowd collecting over there at the corner of the Archbishop's Palace."

"Come away from the door if you can't see anything—you're no good at all! I can't understand a word you say!"

Don Benjamin made way for his wife, who appeared at the door in a dishevelled state, with one of her breasts hanging out of her yellow cotton nightgown and the other entangled in the scapulary of the Virgin of Carmel.

"There—they're bringing a stretcher!" was Don Benjamin's final contribution.

"Oh, good, good! So it's over there, not by the Turks as I thought. Why didn't you say so, Benjamin? Well, of course, that's why the shots sounded so close."

"Look, don't you see them bringing the stretcher?" said the puppet-master. His voice seemed to come from the depths of the earth when he spoke from behind his wife.

"Be quiet! I don't know what you're talking about. You'd better go and put your teeth in—without them you might be talking English!"

"I said I saw them bringing the stretcher."

* Literally "Come ham".

52

"No, they're bringing it now!"

"No, my dear girl, it was there before!"

"I tell you they're bringing it now! I'm not blind, am I?"

"I don't know I'm sure, but I saw it with my own eyes . . .!"

"Saw what? The stretcher?"

Don Benjamin was hardly three feet tall and as slender and hairy as a bat; it was impossible for him to see what was interesting the groups of people and police over the shoulders of Doña Venjamon, a woman of colossal build, who required two seats in the tram (one for each buttock) and more than eight yards of material for a dress.

"But you're the only one who can see," Don Benjamin ventured to say in hopes of escaping from this state of total eclipse.

It was as if he had said: "Open sesame!" Doña Venjamon whirled round like a mountain and seized hold of him.

"Jesus Maria! I'll lift you up!" she cried. And she picked him up in her arms like a child and carried him to the door.

The puppet-master spat green, purple, orange and every other colour. While he was kicking his wife's chest and stomach, four drunken men were crossing the far side of the square carrying the Zany's body on a stretcher. Doña Venjamon crossed herself. The public urinals wept for the dead man, and the wind made a noise like the wings of turkey-buzzards in the pale dusty-coloured trees in the park.

" 'I'm giving you a nurse not a slave.' That's what the priest should have said on our wedding day—damn him!" growled the puppet-master as his feet touched solid ground again.

His better half let him talk—better half was hardly the word, for she would have made more than a whole grapefruit to his half tangerine. She let him talk, partly because she couldn't understand a word he said without his teeth and partly out of respect.

A quarter of an hour later, Doña Venjamon was snoring as if her respiratory organs were fighting for their life within this barrel of flesh, and he was still cursing the day he married with flashing eyes.

But this unusual event brought prosperity to his marionette theatre. The puppets took the tragedy as their theme, with tears oozing drop by drop from their cardboard eyes, thanks to a system of little tubes fed by a syringe and a basin of water. Hitherto the marionettes had only laughed, or if they wept it had been with smiling grimaces and without the eloquence given by the tears now trickling down their cheeks and falling in streams on to the stage which had been the scene of so many cheerful farces.

Don Benjamin thought that the painful element in the drama would make the children cry, and his surprise knew no bounds when he saw them laugh more heartily than before, with wide open mouths and happy expressions. The sight of tears made the children laugh. The sight of blows made the children laugh.

"Illogical! Illogical!" decided Don Benjamin.

"Logical! Relogical!" Doña Venjamon contradicted him.

"Illogical! Illogical! Illogical!"

"Relogical! Relogical! Relogical!"

"Don't let's quarrel!" Don Benjamin suggested.

"Don't let's quarrel!" she agreed.

"But it *is* logical . . ."

"Relogical, I tell you! Relogical, recontralogical!"

When Doña Venjamon argued with her husband she always added syllables to her words, like safety valves to prevent an explosion.

"Illolological!" shouted the puppet-master, nearly tearing out his hair in his frenzy.

"Relogical! Relogical! Recontralogical! Recontrarelogical!"

However, the little puppet went on for a long time using the device with the syringe, and making the marionettes cry to amuse the children.

CHAPTER IX

Glass Eye

THE smaller shops of the town used to shut at night-fall, after doing their accounts, taking in the newspaper and serving the last customers. Groups of boys would amuse themselves at street corners with the cockchafers blundering around the electric lamps. Each insect they caught was submitted to a series of tortures which were prolonged by the more vicious through lack of anyone sufficiently merciful to put his foot on the creatures and finish them off. At the windows, young couples could be seen, absorbed in the pangs of love; while patrols armed with bayonets or sticks ranged through the quiet streets in single file, keeping step with their leader. However, there were evenings when everything was different. The peaceful tormentors of cockchafers played organised games, waging battles whose duration depended on the supply of missiles, for the combatants refused to give in while there were stones left in the street. As for the lovers, the girl's mother would appear, put an end to the amorous display and send the young man running into the street, hat in hand, as if the devil were after him. And the patrol would fall on some passer-by for a change, search him to the skin and carry him off to prison, even if he was unarmed, as a suspicious character, vagrant, plotter or (as the leader of the patrol said): "Because I don't like his looks."

At this hour of the night, the poor quarters of the town made an impression of infinite solitude, grimy poverty and oriental decadence stamped with religious fatalism. The gutters carried the moon's reflection at ground level, and the water dripping from the drinking fountains measured out the endless hours of a race who believed themselves condemned to slavery and vice.

In one of these poorer quarters, Lucio Vasquez was saying goodbye to his friend.

"Goodbye, Genaro!" he said, his eyes enjoining secrecy. "I'm

55

off to see if it's not too late to lend a hand with kidnapping the general's daughter."

Genaro stood still for a moment with the undecided expression of someone hesitating to say a last word to a departing friend; then he went up to one of the houses—he lived in a shop—and tapped on the door.

"Who's there? Who is it?" said a voice from inside.

"It's me," replied Genaro, bending his head as if speaking to a very small person.

"Who's me?" said the woman who opened the door.

His wife, Fedina de Rodas, raised her candle to the height of his head to see his face; her hair was dishevelled and she was in her nightdress.

As Genaro went indoors, she lowered the candle, put back the bars of the door with a loud bang and went into the bedroom without a word. Then she set her light down in front of the clock, so that the reprobate should see at what time he had come home. He stopped to stroke the cat sleeping on the counter and tried to whistle a gay tune.

"Well, what's happened to make you so cheerful?" cried Fedina, rubbing her feet before she got into bed.

"Nothing!" Genaro replied hastily from the darkened shop, anxious lest his wife should detect the worry in his voice.

"You and that policeman with the woman's voice are thicker than ever these days."

"No!" interrupted Genaro, going into the back room where they slept, with his slouch hat pulled down over his eyes.

"Liar! You've just this minute left him! Oh, I know what I'm talking about; a man who talks in a little voice—neither cock nor hen—like that friend of yours, is never up to any good. You go about with him because you want to get into the Secret Police. A lot of lazy brutes! They ought to be ashamed of themselves!"

"What's this?" asked Genaro, to change the subject, taking a little dress out of a box.

Fedina took the frock from her husband like a flag of peace, and sitting on the bed began to tell him excitedly that it was a present from General Canales' daughter, who had been asked to be godmother to her first child. Rodas hid his face in the shadows surrounding his son's cradle, and without hearing what his wife was saying about the arrangements for the christening, he put up his hand irritably to ward off the light of the candle from his eyes; then he quickly snatched it away, shaking it to cleanse it of the red light which clung like blood to his fingers. The spectre of death arose from his child's crade as if it were a bier. The dead have to be rocked, like babies. The spectre was the colour of white of egg, with cloudy eyes; it had no hair, eyebrows or teeth, and it twisted itself spirally like the inner convolutions of the censers used in the funeral service. Genaro heard his wife's voice coming to him as if from a long way off. She was talking of her child, of the christening, of the general's daughter, of inviting her next-door neighbour, the fat man opposite and the one who lived on the corner, the pub-keeper, the butcher and the baker.

"Won't it be lovely?"

And then, sharply:

"What's the matter, Genaro?"

He started.

"Nothing's the matter."

His wife's voice had brought out a number of little black spots on the spectre of death, little spots which made it stand out against the dark corner of the room. It was a woman's skeleton, but no feminine attributes remained to it except the sunken breasts, limp and hairy like rats, hanging over the framework of the ribs.

"What's the matter, Genaro?"

"Nothing's the matter."

"That's what comes of your going out. You come home like a sleep-walker, with your tail between your legs. Why the devil can't you stay at home, you miserable man?"

His wife's voice dissolved the skeleton.

"No, nothing's the matter."

An eye was travelling over the fingers of his right hand like the circle of light from an electric bulb. From the little finger to the middle finger, thence to the ring finger, from ring finger to index, from index to thumb. An eye . . . A single eye. He could feel it throbbing. He tried to crush it by closing his hand hard, till his nails sank into his flesh. But it was impossible; when he opened his hand, there it was again on his fingers, no bigger than a bird's heart and more horrifying than Hell. Beads of hot sweat, like beef broth, broke out on his forehead. Who was looking at him with this eye, which rested on his fingers and jumped about like the ball of a roulette wheel to the rhythm of a funeral knell?

Fedina pulled him away from the cradle where her son was sleeping.

"What's the matter, Genaro?"

"Nothing."

And a little later he sighed several times and said:

"Nothing; there's an eye after me! I'm being pursued by an eye, an eye is chasing me! I can see my hands—no! that's impossible! They're my eyes, it's an eye . . ."

"Commend yourself to God," she advised him between her teeth, without comprehending this rigmarole.

"It's an eye—yes, a round, black eye with eyelashes, like a glass eye!"

"You're drunk, that's what's the matter with you!"

"How can I be, when I've had nothing to drink?"

"Nothing? Why, your breath reeks of it!"

Though he was standing in the middle of the bedroom alcove—the other half of the room was occupied by the shop—Rodas felt as if he were lost in a cellar full of bats and spiders, snakes and crabs, far from all possible help and comfort.

"You must have been up to something," went on Fedina, between yawns; "it's the eye of God watching you!"

Genaro took one leap on to the bed and got under the sheets fully dressed, shoes and all. The eye was there, dancing beside his wife's body, her fine young woman's body. Fedina put out the light, but that was worse; in the darkness the eye grew rapidly bigger and bigger, until it covered the walls, the floor, the ceiling, the roof, the houses, his whole life, his child . . .

"No!" he replied in answer to a remark from his wife, who had relit the candle when she heard his terrified cries and was wiping the cold sweat from his forehead with one of the baby's napkins. "No, it's not the eye of God, it's the eye of the Devil."

Fedina crossed herself. Genaro told her to put out the light again. The eye became a figure of eight as it moved from the light into darkness, then a thunderous noise came from it, it seemed as if it must break against something, and almost at once it did break against the footsteps echoing in the street.

"The Porch! The Porch!" cried Genaro. "Yes! Yes! Light! Matches! Light! For the love of God!"

She stretched her arm across him to reach the match-box.

There was a sound of distant wheels. Genaro had his fingers in his mouth and spoke as if he were choking: he didn't want to be left alone and called to his wife, who had thrown on a petticoat and gone to heat him up some coffee.

Hearing her husband's cries she came back to the bed in alarm.

"Is he ill—or what?" she said to herself, watching the flickering candle flame with her beautiful black eyes. She thought of the worms they had taken from the stomach of Henrietta—the girl from the inn by the theatre; of the fungus they found where brains should have been in an Indian in the hospital; of the dreadful creature called the Cadejo, which prevented one from sleeping. Like a hen which flaps its wings and calls to its chickens when she sees a sparrow-hawk, she got up and hung a medallion of St Blas round the little neck of her new-born child, reciting the words of the trisagion as she did so.

But the trisagion shook Genaro as though he were being beaten. He got out of bed with his eyes tight shut, found his wife beside the cradle and fell on his knees embracing her legs and telling her what he had seen.

"He rolled down the steps, yes, right to the bottom, bleeding from the first shot, and he never shut his eyes again. His legs apart, his eyes fixed in such a cold, glassy stare, I never saw anything like it! One of his eyes seemed to take in everything like a flash of lightning, and how it gazed at us! An eye with long eyelashes, which won't leave me, won't leave my fingers, here, oh my God, here!"

A wail from the baby silenced him. Fedina took the child from its cot, wrapped it in flannels and gave it her breast, without being able to get away from her husband, though she felt disgusted by him as he knelt there, grasping her legs and groaning.

"The worst thing of all is that Lucio—"

"Is the man with the woman's voice called Lucio?"

"Yes, Lucio Vasquez."

"The one they call 'Velvet'?"

"Yes."

"And why in heaven's name did he kill him?"

"He was ordered to; he had the rabies. But that's not the worst thing of all; the worst thing is that Lucio told me that a warrant for General Canales' arrest had been issued, and that a chap he knows means to kidnap his daughter tonight—"

"Señorita Camila? My child's godmother?"

"Yes."

On hearing this unbelievable news, Fedina wept with the facility and abundance with which women of the people weep over the troubles of others. Her tears fell on her child's little head as she lulled him—as warm as the water grandmothers take to church to add to the cold holy water in baptismal fonts. The baby fell asleep. The night passed, and they were still sitting as if under a spell when dawn drew a gold line under the door and the silence of the shop was broken by the baker's girl tapping on the door.

"Bread! Bread! Bread!"

CHAPTER X

The Princes of the Army

GENERAL EUSEBIO CANALES, alias Chamarrita, left Angel
Face's house with the bearing of a soldier at the head of his army,
but as soon as the door had shut behind him and he was alone in
the street, his military stride was transformed into the scuttling
run of an Indian going to market to sell a hen. He was aware of
eager pursuers close at his heels. He kept his hand pressed against
a hernia in his groin, for the pain from it sickened him. He was
gasping out disconnected words and broken exclamations of
despair, while his heart gave wild leaps, contracted and missed
several beats, by turns. With vacant eyes and his thoughts in
suspense, he pressed his hands against his ribs as if it were a broken
limb and he could force it to go on functioning. That was better.
He had just turned the corner which had seemed so far off a
minute ago. Now for the next one, but how far off it looked
through his exhaustion! He spat. His legs were almost giving
under him. A piece of orange peel. A cab slipped past at the end
of the street. He was the one who must slip away. But he could see
nothing except the cab, the houses and the lights. He walked
faster. There was nothing else to be done. Better. He had just
turned the corner which looked so far off a few minutes ago. And
now for the next, but how far off it looked through his exhaustion!
He clenched his teeth and tried to force his knees to make a further
effort. He was hardly making any headway now. His knees were
stiff and there was an ominous irritation at the base of his spine
and in his throat. His knees! He would have to drag himself back
to his house on all fours, helping himself along with his hands and
elbows and every instinct in him that was fighting for life. He
walked more slowly. Then came street corners, where there was no
shelter. What was more, they seemed to be multiplying in the
wakeful darkness, like glass screens. He was behaving ridiculously
in his own eyes and other people's, whether they saw him or not—
an apparent contradiction due to the fact that he was a person of

61

importance, always in the public eye even in the solitude of night time.

"Whatever happens," he muttered, "it's my duty to stay at home—all the more so if what that scoundrel Angel Face has just told me turns out to be true!"

And further on:

"Running away would be a confession of guilt!" The echo tapped out his footsteps behind him. "Running away would be a confession of guilt; it would—but I won't do it." The echo tapped out his footsteps behind him. "A confession of guilt! But I won't do it." The echo tapped out his footsteps behind him.

He put his hand to his chest as if to tear away a plaster of fear fastened there by what the favourite had told him. His medals were not there. "Running away would be a confession of guilt, but I won't do it." Angel Face's finger was pointing out the road to exile as the only possible way to safety. "You've got to save your skin, General! There's still time!" And everything that he was, everything that he stood for, and everything he loved with a child's tenderness: country, family, memories, traditions and his daughter Camila—all were revolving round that fatal forefinger, as if the disintegration of his ideas had brought the universe itself to chaos.

But after a few more steps, nothing remained of this vertiginous vision except tears of perplexity in his eyes.

" 'Generals are the Princes of the Army', I said in one of my speeches. What a fool! I've paid dearly for that little phrase! The President will never forgive me for those 'Princes of the Army', and as I was in his bad books, he's getting rid of me now by saddling me with the death of a colonel who always showed affectionate respect for my white hairs."

The ghost of an ironical smile appeared under his grey moustache. He was making room within himself for a new General Canales, a General Canales who walked at a snail's pace, dragging his feet like a penitent in a procession, silent, humble, sad, with the smell of burnt-out rockets clinging to his clothes. The real Chamarrita, the arrogant General Canales who had left Angel Face's house at the very height of his military career, with his powerful shoulders outlined against a background of all the glorious battles waged by Alexander, Julius Caesar, Napoleon and Bolivar, now suddenly found himself supplanted by a caricature of a general, by a General Canales without any gold embroidery, plumes or braid, without boots, without spurs. Beside this sombrely dressed, shaggy, deflated intruder, next to this pauper's burial, the other, authentic, true Chamarrita seemed (without any ostentation on his part) like a first-class funeral, complete with fringes, laurels, plumes and solemn salutations. The disgraced General Canales was advancing towards a defeat which would remain unknown to history, walking ahead of the real general, who remained behind like a puppet bathed in gold and blue light, his three-cornered hat pulled over his eyes, his sword broken, his hands dangling and the crosses and medals on his breast covered with rust.

Without slackening his pace, Canales removed his gaze from his likeness in full uniform; he felt himself morally defeated. He gloomily imagined himself as an exile, dressed in porter's trousers under a jacket that was too long or too short, too tight or too loose, but never the right size. He was walking among the ruins of his life, treading his gold braid underfoot.

"But I'm innocent!" And he repeated the words with the most heartfelt persuasiveness. "But I'm innocent! Why should I be afraid?"

"For that very reason!" his conscience answered, in Angel Face's own words. "For that very reason! It would be another story if you were guilty. Crime has the advantage of guaranteeing a citizen's adherence to the Government. Your country? You must escape, General; I know what I'm talking about. Neither country nor wealth can save you! The law? A fine lot of use! You must escape, General; death is lying in wait for you!"

"But I'm innocent!"

"Whether you're guilty or innocent is irrelevant, General; what matters is whether you're in favour or not with the President; it's worse to be an innocent man frowned on by the Government than a guilty one!"

He shut his ears against Angel Face's voice, and mumbled threats of vengeance; the beating of his own heart was suffocating him. Further on he began to think about his daughter. She must be waiting for him with her heart in her mouth. The clock on the tower of La Merced struck the hour. The sky was clear, studded with stars and without a cloud. When he came in sight of the corner of his house he saw lights in his windows, sending their anxious beams right into the middle of the street.

"I will leave Camila with my brother Juan until I can send for her. Angel Face offered to take her away tonight or early tomorrow morning."

He had no need of the latch-key he held in his hand, for the door opened at once.

"Papa darling!"

"Sh! Come—I'll explain everything! There's no time to lose. I'll explain. Tell my orderly to harness one of my mules—collect some money, a revolver. I'll send for my clothes later. I shan't want more than a suitcase with the barest necessities. I don't know what I'm saying, nor whether you understand! Tell them to saddle the bay mule, and you go and get my things together while I change and write a letter to my brother. You'll be staying with Juan for a few days."

Being suddenly confronted by a madman would have alarmed Camila less than to see her habitually calm father in this state of nervous agitation. His voice kept failing him. His colour came and went. She had never seen him like this. Driven by the urgency of his haste, and tormented by anxiety, unable to hear what he said nor to say anything but "Oh my God! Oh my God!", she ran to wake up the orderly and tell him to saddle the mule, a magnificent animal with eyes full of fire, and came back to pack the suitcase (towels, socks, bread—yes, with butter, but she forgot the salt); then she went to the kitchen to rouse her nurse, who was sitting on the wood basket nodding as usual in front of the dying fire beside the cat, which moved its ears at every unusual noise.

The general was writing a letter in great haste when the servant came into the room to shut and bar the windows.

Silence took possession of the house, but it was not the silken silence of sweet peaceful nights, whose nocturnal carbon-paper makes copies of happy dreams, lighter than the thoughts of flowers, less metallic than water. The silence which now took possession of the house and was broken by the general's coughing, his daughter's hurrying to and fro, the sobs of the servant, and a frightened opening and shutting of cupboards, chests and commodes, was a silence as tense, constrained and uneasy as an unfamiliar garment.

A small sly-faced man, with the body of a ballet-dancer, was writing silently without lifting his pen from the paper, as if he were spinning a spider's web.

"To His Excellency the Constitutional President of the Republic.

"Your Excellency,

"In accordance with instructions received, a careful watch has been kept on the movements of General Eusebio Canales. I now have the honour to inform the President that he has been seen in the house of one of your Excellency's friends, Señor Don Miguel Angel Face. I have been informed both by the cook in that house (who was spying on her master and the housemaid) and the housemaid (who was spying on her master and the cook), that Angel Face was shut in his room with General Canales for approximately three-quarters of an hour. They add that General Canales went away in a state of great agitation. In accordance with instructions, the watch on Canales' house has been redoubled, and orders have again been given that the slightest attempt at flight must result in his death.

"The housemaid—but this the cook does not know—has supplied further details. Her master gave her to understand—so she told me on the telephone—that Canales had come to offer him his daughter in exchange for his effective intervention on his behalf with the President.

"The cook—but this the housemaid does not know—was more explicit on this subject: she said that when the general left, her master seemed very pleased and gave her orders to go out as soon as the shops opened and buy preserves, liqueurs, biscuits and sweets, because a young lady of good family was coming to live with him.

"Such is the information I have the honour to impart to the President of the Republic . . ."

He wrote the date and his signature—a scrawled flourish like a dart—and, before taking his pen from the paper to scratch his nose with it, he added as an afterthought:

"Postscript to the message sent this morning: Doctor Luis Barreño—Three people visited his clinic this afternoon, two of whom appeared to be badly off; in the evening he went for a walk in the park with his wife. Abel Carvajal, the lawyer: This afternoon he visited the American Bank, the chemist's shop opposite the Capuchin monastery and the German Club; there he talked for a long while with Mr Romsth, who is being watched seperately by the police, and he returned home at half-past seven. He has not been seen to go out again, and the watch on his house has been redoubled, according to instructions received. Signed above. Date *ut supra. Vale.*"

CHAPTER XI

The Abduction

AFTER parting with Rodas, Lucio Vasquez went as fast as his unsteady legs would carry him to La Masacuata's bar, to see whether the time had come to lend a hand in the abduction of the girl. He hurried past the Fountain of La Merced, a region given over to terror and crime according to popular report and the lies of the women who threaded their needles of gossip with the dirty water trickling into their jugs.

"It would be a fine thing to take part in a kidnapping," said the Zany's executioner to himself without slackening his pace. "And as my business was so quickly over in the Cathedral Porch, thank God, I can treat myself to that pleasure. I've always been one for pilfering things or helping myself to a chicken, but Holy Mary! what must it be like to pinch a female?"

At last La Masacuata's bar came in sight, but he began to sweat when he saw the La Merced clock. It was nearly time unless his eyes deceived him. He greeted one or two policemen who were guarding Canales' house, and dived into the door of the bar like a rabbit into its burrow.

La Masacuata had gone to bed to await the appointed hour of two in the morning with her nerves on edge; she pressed her legs against each other, crushed her arms beneath her in uncomfortable positions and rolled her head about on the pillow sweating at every pore, but without succeeding in closing her eyes.

When Vasquez knocked she jumped out of bed and hurried to the door with a gasp of profound agitation.

"Who's there?"

"It's me, Vasquez. Open up!"

"I wasn't expecting you!"

"What time is it?" he asked as he came in.

"Quarter-past one," she replied immediately, without looking at the clock, but with the conviction born of having counted every minute, every five minutes, ten minutes, quarter-of-an-hour

67

and twenty minutes, while waiting for two o'clock to come round.

"Well, how is it the La Merced clock says a quarter to two?"

"You don't say so! It must be fast again."

"And, tell me this, has that chap come back yet?"

"No."

Vasquez took the barkeeper in his arms, fully expecting to be rewarded with a slap. But nothing of the sort; La Masacuata had become as gentle as a dove, and let herself be embraced and kissed on the mouth, so sealing a sweet and amorous pact that that night she would refuse him nothing. The only light in the room was burning in front of an image of the Virgin of Chiquinquira, beside a bunch of paper roses. Vasquez blew out the candle and tripped up La Masacuata. The Virgin's image vanished in the darkness as their two bodies rolled on the floor trussed together like a string of garlic.

Angel Face appeared from the direction of the theatre, walking fast and accompanied by a party of roughs.

"As soon as the girl is in my hands," he told them, "you can loot the house. You won't go away empty-handed, I promise you. But be careful, both now and later on, and don't blab, or I'd rather do without your help."

As they turned the corner they were stopped by a patrol. The favourite spoke to the commanding officer while the soldiers stood around.

"We're going to serenade a lady, Lieutenant."

"Will you kindly tell me where?" said the officer, tapping the ground with his sword.

"Here, in the Callejon de Jesus."

"And where are your guitars and marimbas?* A rum sort of serenade without any music!"

Angel Face discreetly slipped a hundred peso note into the officer's hand and his objections were at once overcome.

The end of the street was blocked by the bulk of the Church of La Merced—a church shaped like a tortoise with two eyes or windows in the dome. The favourite told his companions that they had better not arrive at La Masacuata's all together.

"Remember, we meet at the Two-Step Tavern," he said aloud

*A sort of xylophone especially popular in Guatemala and Mexico.

as they separated. "The Two-Step. Don't make any mistake—The Two-Step, next to the bedding-shop."

Their footsteps faded away in different directions. The plan of escape was as follows: when the La Merced clock struck two, one or two of Angel Face's men would go up on to the roof of General Canales' house, whereupon the general's daughter would open one of the windows at the front of the house and call for help at the top of her voice against burglars, so as to attract the police keeping watch on the house. Canales would profit from the general confusion to get away by the back door.

A fool, a madman or a child would never have concocted such an absurd plan. It was quite without rhyme or reason, and if the general and the favourite had adopted it in spite of its absurdity, it was because each of them secretly saw in it a second possibility. For Canales, the favourite's protection gave him a better chance of escape than any other—and for Angel Face success did not depend on his agreement with Canales but on the President, whom he had informed by telephone of the hour and the details of the plan as soon as the general had left his house.

April nights in the tropics are like the widows of the warm days of March—dark, cold, dishevelled and sad. From the corner between the tavern and Canales' house, Angel Face counted the shadowy dark-green figures of the police scattered here and there; then he walked slowly round the block, and afterwards stooped and slipped through the small covered doorway of the Two-Step Tavern; there was a gendarme in uniform at the door of each of the neighbouring houses, not to mention innumerable agents of the Secret Police, walking nervously up and down the pavement. He felt a foreboding of evil.

"I'm taking part in a crime," he said to himself; "they'll murder this man as he leaves his house." And the more he thought about this project the blacker it seemed; the idea of kidnapping the daughter of a man doomed to die seemed to him as horrible and repugnant as it would have been congenial and pleasant to help him to escape. It was not good nature which made such a naturally unfeeling man dislike the thought of ambushing a trusting and defenceless citizen in the very heart of the town, as he escaped from his house in the belief that he was being protected by a friend of the President. Nor the fact that this protection must in the end be revealed as an exquisitely cruel device to embitter

69

the victim's last appalling moments by making him realise that he had been played with, trapped and betrayed, as well as an ingenious method of giving the crime a legal aspect by explaining it as the final resort of the authorities to prevent the escape of a presumed criminal the day before his arrest. No. Very different were the sentiments which made Angel Face bite his lips with silent disapproval of this desperate and diabolical plan. He had believed in all good faith that as the general's protector he possessed certain rights over his daughter, but he now saw them sacrificed to his accustomed role of unreasoning tool, myrmidon and executioner. A strange wind was blowing across the plain of his silence, where a wild vegetation was growing, as thirsty as tearless eyelashes, as thirsty as prickly cactuses, as thirsty as trees unrefreshed by rain. What was the meaning of this desire? Why should trees be thirsty when it rains?

The idea flashed through his brain like lightning that he might turn back, ring Canales' door-bell and warn him. (He imagined his daughter smiling gratefully at him.) But he had already crossed the threshold of the little bar, and felt his courage revived by Vasquez's brave words and the presence of the other men.

"Just try me, that's all. I'm your man. Yes, you there, I'm ready to help you in anything, d'you hear? I'm not one to back out. I'm a cat with nine lives, a true son of the brave Moor!"

Vasquez was trying to pitch his feminine voice lower in order to give his pronouncements more virility.

"If you hadn't brought me good luck," he added in a low tone, "I wouldn't be talking as I am now. No, don't you believe it. But you've put me right with La Masacuata, and now she behaves as she should to me."

"I'm very glad to find you here and so full of courage; you're a man after my own heart!" exclaimed Angel Face, effusively shaking hands with the Zany's executioner. "You've given me back the spirits the police robbed me of, friend Vasquez; there's one of them at every door."

"Come and have a drop of Dutch courage!"

"Oh, it's not for myself I'm afraid—as far as that goes it's not the first time I've been in a tight place; I'm thinking of the girl. I wouldn't like it if they nabbed us coming out of her house, you understand?"

"But, look here, who's going to nab you? As soon as they find there's something to loot in the house there won't be a single copper left in the street. Not one, I'll stake my life on that. I promise you, when they see what there is to get their claws into, they'll all be busy carrying off what they can, not the least doubt of it . . ."

"Wouldn't it be a good thing if you went and talked to them, now that you're here, and as they know you're incapable of . . .?"

"Rubbish. No need to say anything to them. When they see the door wide open, they'll think: 'Come along, what's the harm?' Ah, but when they get wind of me! They all know what sort of a chap I am since the day Antonio Libelula and I broke into the house of that little priest, and he got the wind up so badly when he saw us drop into his room from the attic and put on the light, that he threw us the keys of the cupboard where his savings were, wrapped in a handkerchief to make no noise, and pretended to be asleep! Yes, that time I certainly got away with it! And now the boys are eager to go," finished Vasquez, pointing to the group of ill-favoured, silent, verminous men, who were drinking glass after glass of brandy, tossing the liquor to the back of their throats at one gulp and spitting disgustedly as soon as the glass left their lips. "Yes, I tell you, they're ready to go."

Angel Face raised his glass and invited Vasquez to drink to love. La Masacuata poured herself a glass of anisette. And they all three drank.

In the dim light—they had been chary of turning on the electric light, so that the only illumination in the room came from the candle in front of the Virgin of Chiquinquira—the disreputable figures of the men threw fantastic shadows, elongated like gazelles, against the yellowish walls, while the bottles on the shelves looked like coloured flames. They were all watching the clock. They spat on the floor with the sound of pistol shots. Some way from the rest, Angel Face was waiting with his back against the wall beside the Virgin's image. His large black eyes moved about the room, pursuing the idea which was persistently assailing him in these decisive moments: that he needed a wife and children. He smiled inwardly as he remembered the anecdote about the political prisoner under sentence of death, who was visited by the Judge Advocate General twelve hours before the execution, to offer him a favour, even his life, on behalf of the authorities, if he would change his testimony. "Very well, the favour I shall ask is to leave a son behind me," replied the prisoner point-blank. "Granted," said the Judge Advocate, and thinking himself smart he sent for a prostitute. The condemned man sent the woman away untouched, and when the Judge Advocate General returned he said to him: "There are quite enough sons of whores already!"

Another smile twitched the corner of his lips as he said to himself: "I've been governor of a school, editor of a newspaper, diplomat, deputy and mayor, and now here I am head of a band of toughs! Such is life in the tropics!"

A double chime issued from the tower of La Merced.

"Everyone outside!" cried Angel Face, and as he went out, revolver in hand, he said to La Masacuata: "I'll be back with my prize!"

"Let's get on with it!" commanded Vasquez, climbing like a lizard up to one of the windows of the general's house, followed by two of his gang. "And no blabbing, mind!"

The double chime from the church clock was also heard in the general's house.

"Ready, Camila?"

"Yes, Papa darling!"

Canales was wearing riding breeches and a blue military tunic stripped of its gold braid, above which his hair shone spotlessly white. Camila threw herself almost fainting into his arms, without a tear or a word. The meaning of happiness or despair can only be understood by those who have spelt it out in their minds beforehand, bitten a tear-soaked handkerchief, torn it to shreds with their teeth. For Camila all this was either a game or a nightmare; it couldn't, no, it simply couldn't be true; what was happening, happening to her, happening to her father, couldn't be true. General Canales took her in his arms and said goodbye.

"This is how I embraced your mother when I went to fight for my country in the last war. The poor darling got it into her head that I wouldn't return, but it was she who didn't wait for me."

Hearing steps on the roof, the old soldier thrust Camila aside and went across the patio with its beds and pots full of flowers to the back door. The scent of every azalea, every geranium and every rose-bush said goodbye to him. The water trickling into the jug said goodbye to him, so did the light streaming from the windows. Suddenly the house became dark, as if severed at a blow from its neighbours. Flight was unworthy of a soldier. The thought of returning to liberate his country at the head of a revolution, on the other hand . . .

According to the plan they had agreed upon, Camila went to the window to call for help.

"Burglars have broken in! Help! Burglars!"

Before her voice had faded into the immensity of the night the first gendarmes had arrived—those who had been watching the front of the house—blowing into the long hollow fingers of their whistles. There was a discordant sound of metal and wood and the street door yielded at once. Other police in plain clothes appeared at the cross-roads, ignorant of what was afoot, but for that very reason holding their well-sharpened knives ready, with their hats pulled down and their coat collars turned up. The wide open door swallowed them all—a turbulent river. Vasquez cut the electric wires as he went up to the roof; passages and rooms were all one solid shadow. Some of his companions struck matches to find their way to cupboards, dressers and chests. And without more ado they ransacked them from top to bottom after striking off padlocks, shooting at glass doors and reducing valuable wood to splinters. Others were at large in the drawing-room, upsetting chairs, tables and corner cupboards covered with photographs, like tragic playing-cards in the shadows, or striking the keys of a small grand piano; it had been left open and groaned like an animal in pain every time they strummed on it.

Far off was heard the laugh of forks, spoons and knives as they were thrown on the ground, and then a sudden cry cut short by a blow. The old nurse, La Chabelona, had hidden Camila in the dining-room between the wall and a sideboard. The favourite threw her to the ground. The old woman's hair had caught in the handle of the silver-cupboard and its contents were scattered on the floor. Vasquez silenced her with a blow with an iron bar. He struck at her blindly. He did not even see her hands.

PART II

The 24th, 25th, 26th and 27th of April

CHAPTER XII

Camila

SHE used to spend hours and hours in front of the looking-glass in her room. "If you make such faces the devil will come and look over your shoulder!" cried her old nurse. "He can't look more of a devil than me!" replied Camila. Her hair was a confusion of black flames, her dark-skinned face shone with coconut-butter cleansing-cream and her slanting green eyes were drowning in their deep sockets. "China" Canales, as her classmates had called her when she went out with her school cloak buttoned right up to the neck, looked more grown-up now, less ugly, capricious and challenging.

"I'm fifteen," she said to the looking-glass, "but I'm still just a little donkey trailing round everywhere with a swarm of uncles, aunts and cousins."

She tugged at her hair, cried out, made faces at herself. She hated always having to be among this crowd of relations; being the "little girl"; going everywhere with them: to the military review, to twelve o'clock Mass, to the Cerro del Carmen, for rides on the chestnut, for walks round the Teatro Colon or up and down the ravine of El Sauce.

Her uncles were moustachioed scarecrows with rings clinking on their fingers; her cousins untidy, fat, heavy as lead; her aunts repulsive. Or so they all seemed to her. She was exasperated when her cousins gave her paper cornets full of sweets with a little flap on top as if she were a child; when her uncles fondled her with hands smelling of cigar smoke, pinching her cheeks between finger and thumb and moving her face from side to side (Camila used to stiffen her neck instinctively); and when her aunts kissed her through their veils, leaving behind a feeling as if a spider's web were stuck to her skin with saliva.

On Sunday afternoons she would either go to sleep or sit bored to tears in the drawing-room looking at old photographs in the family album, or portraits hanging on the red-covered walls and ranged on the shelves of dark corner-cabinets, silver-topped tables and marble brackets, while her father looked out of the window at the empty street purring like a cat and replying to the greetings of passing neighbours and friends. Every so often someone would go by and take their hats off to him. That was General Canales. And the general would reply in a booming voice: "Good evening." "Au revoir!" "I'm delighted to see you." "Take care of yourself!"

There were photographs of her mother as a newly-married woman, with everything except her fingers and her face concealed by a fashionable dress reaching to the ankles, gloves nearly to the elbow, furs round her neck and a hat cascading ribbons and feathers under a sunshade wreathed in lace; there were photographs of her aunts, big-bosomed and stuffed like drawing-room furniture, with sculptured hair and little tiaras on their foreheads; and others of friends of past days, one in a manila shawl with combs and fans, another dressed as an Indian in sandals and embroidered tunic with a pitcher on her shoulder, others with beauty spots and jewels. They all induced in Camila a sense of crepuscular drowsiness, coupled with superstitious feelings about their inscriptions: "This portrait will follow you like my shadow." "This pale testimony of my affection will be with you always." "When these words are effaced my memory will fade." Some of the other photographs had only a few words written at the bottom between dried violets and bits of faded ribbon: "Remember 1898." "My adored one." "Until the grave and beyond." "Your incognita."

Her father's greetings were addressed to the friends who occasionally passed along the otherwise empty street, but his booming voice echoed through the drawing-room as if he were really replying to the inscriptions: "This portrait will follow you like my shadow." "I'm very glad. Good luck to you!" "This pale testimony of my affection will be with you always." "Good day, take care of yourself!" "When these words are effaced my memory will fade." "At your service! Remember me to your mother."

Sometimes a friend who had escaped from the album would stop outside the window to talk to the general. Camila would watch from behind the curtain. It was that man who had such a conquering air in his photograph, young, slim, with black eyelashes, loud check trousers, his overcoat buttoned up and a hat that was halfway between a topper and a bowler—the very latest thing at the end of the last century.

Camila smiled and thought to herself: "You'd better have stayed as you were in the photograph. You'd have looked old-fashioned and people would laugh at your museum outfit, all the same you wouldn't have been pot-bellied and bald with your cheeks blown out as though you were sucking bulls-eyes."

From the penumbra of the dusty smelling curtains, Camila's green eyes gazed through the window at the Sunday afternoon. There was no softening of the coldness in her frozen glassy eyes as they looked out of her house to see what was happening in the street. Her father, dressed in a gleaming linen shirt and no jacket and with his elbows resting on a satin cushion, was passing the time talking to someone who seemed to be an intimate friend, across the bars of the projecting balcony. He was a bilious-looking gentleman, with a hooked nose, a small moustache and a gold-handled walking stick. What a lucky chance! He had been strolling past the house when the general stopped him with: "What a pleasure to see you here in La Merced! How splendid!" And Camila found him in the album. It wasn't easy to recognise him; she had to look hard at the photo. The poor man had once had a well-shaped nose and a round amiable face. How true it was that time dealt harshly with people. Now his face was angular, with prominent cheekbones, thin eyebrows and a jutting jaw. As he talked to her father in his slow cavernous voice, he kept raising the handle of his stick to his nose as if to smell the gold.

Immensity in motion. Herself in motion. Everything in her that was by nature still was in motion. When she saw the sea for the first time, words expressing her astonishment bubbled to her lips, but when her uncles asked her what she thought of the spectacle she said with a stupidly important air: "I knew it already by heart from photographs!"

The wind was tugging at the wide-brimmed pink hat she held in her hands. It was like a hoop. Like a big round bird.

Her cousins looked at her in wide-eyed amazement, their mouths dropping open. The deafening sound of the waves swallowed up her aunts' remarks: "How beautiful! Almost incredible! What a lot of water! How angry it seems! And look—

79

over there—the sun is setting! We didn't leave anything in the train, did we, when we got out in such a hurry? Have you looked to see if everything's there? We must count the suitcases."

Her uncles, carrying suitcases full of thin clothes for the beach (the wrinkled clothes like dried raisins that summer visitors wear), bunches of coconuts which the ladies had bought at the stations on the way merely because they were cheap, and a collection of bundles and baskets, went off to the hotel in Indian file.

"Yes, I know what you mean," remarked the most precocious of her cousins. (A rush of blood to her skin tinged Camila's dark cheeks with faint carmine when she heard herself addressed). "I think it's because the sea looks the same as in the moving pictures, only bigger."

Camila had heard about the moving pictures which were being shown at the Hundred Doors, close to the cathedral, but she had no idea what they were like. However, after what her cousin had said, she could easily imagine them as she stared at the sea. Everything in motion. Nothing stable. Pictures mingling with other pictures, shifting, breaking in pieces to form a new image every second, in a state that was not solid, nor liquid, nor gaseous, but which was the state of life in the sea. A luminous state. Both in the sea and in the moving pictures.

With her toes curling inside her shoes, and her eyes darting everywhere, Camila went on contemplating the scene with insatiable delight. At first she felt that her pupils had to become empty to take in the immensity, but now that immensity filled them completely. The rising tide had reached her eyes.

Followed by her cousin, she went slowly down to the beach—walking on the sand was not easy. She wanted to get closer to the waves, but instead of offering her a polite hand, the Pacific Ocean aimed a liquid slap of transparent water at her and wet her feet. She was taken by surprise and only just retreated in time, leaving behind a hostage—her pink hat—dwindling to a mere point among the waves, and yelling out a spoiled child's threat to go and complain to her papa:

"Ah—*mar*!"*

Neither she nor her cousin noticed that she had uttered the words "to love" for the first time as she threatened the sea. The

* Ah *mar*! (Oh sea!) = *Amar* (to love).

80

tamarind colour of the sky above the setting sun made the deep green water look colder still.

Why did she kiss her own arms there on the beach, breathing in the smell of her sun-drenched, salty skin? Why did she do the same to the fruit she was forbidden to eat, touching it with her joined lips? "Acid is bad for little girls," her aunts had sermonized at the hotel, "so are wet feet and romping." Camila had not sniffed at her father and her nurse when she kissed them. She had held her breath when she kissed the foot of the Jesus of La Merced, which was so reminiscent of a broken root. And if one did not sniff at what one kissed, the kiss had no taste. Her salty flesh, as brown as the sand, and pine kernels and quinces all tempted her to kiss them with her nostrils flaring, eager and greedy. But after speculation came reality: she did not know whether she was sniffing or biting when, at the end of the summer, she was kissed on the mouth by the same cousin who had talked about moving pictures and could whistle an Argentine tango.

When they returned to the capital, Camila pestered her nurse to take her to the moving pictures. They were being shown at the corner of the Cathedral Porch, at the Hundred Doors. They went without her father's knowledge, biting their nails nervously and murmuring a prayer. After nearly turning away from the door when they saw how full the hall was, they took two seats close to a white curtain, on which a light as if from the sun was thrown from time to time. They were testing the apparatus, the lenses and the projector, which made a sputtering noise like the mantles of the street lamps.

Suddenly the room grew dark. Camila felt as if she were playing hide-and-seek. Everything on the screen was blurred. Figures moved about like grasshoppers. Shadowy people who seemed to be chewing as they talked, who walked in a series of jumps and whose arms moved as if they were dislocated. Camila was reminded so vividly of an occasion when she and a boy had hidden in a room with a skylight, that for a moment she forgot the moving pictures. A guttering candle had been standing in front of an almost transparent celluloid Christ in the darkest corner of the room. They hid under a bed. They had to lie flat on the ground and the bed creaked loudly and incessantly. It was an ancestral piece of furniture which could not be treated with disrespect. There was a shout of "Coming!" from the further patio. "Coming!" from the nearest patio. "Coming! Coming!" When she heard the footsteps of the "he" approaching, Camila wanted to laugh. Her companion in hiding looked at her sternly, warning her to be silent. She obeyed at first with a serious expression, but could hardly contain herself when the sickening smell coming from a half-open commode reached her nostrils, and she would have burst out laughing outright if her eyes had not begun to water from the fine dust under the bed, while at the same time something struck her on the head.

And exactly as she had left her hiding place long ago, so she now hurried away from the moving pictures with her eyes full of tears, among a crowd who were leaving their seats and hastening through the darkness to the exits. They did not stop till they reached the Portal del Comercio. And there Camila learnt that the audience had left so as to avoid excommunication: a woman in a tight-fitting dress had been shown on the screen dancing the Argentine tango with a long-haired, moustachioed man wearing a flowing artist's tie.

Vasquez went out into the street still holding the massive iron bar with which he had silenced La Chabelona; he gave a signal with his hand and Angel Face followed carrying the general's daughter in his arms. They disappeared inside the Two-Step Tavern just as the police were beginning to make off with their loot. Those who had not helped themselves to a saddle were carrying off on their backs a clock, a large mirror, a statue, a table, a crucifix, a tortoise, hens, ducks, doves or any other of God's creations. Men's clothes, women's shoes, Chinese knick-knacks, flowers, images of saints, basins, trivets, lamps, a chandelier, bottles of medicine, portraits, books, umbrellas for water from the sky and chamber-pots for human water.

The innkeeper was waiting in the Two-Step Tavern with a bar in her hand, ready to barricade the door behind them.

Camila had never dreamed of the existence of this hovel smelling of musty bedding, only a few yards from the house where she had lived so contentedly, spoiled by the old soldier (impossible to believe that he had been happy yesterday!), and looked after by her nurse (impossible to believe that she was now lying seriously injured). The flowers in the patio, untrodden yesterday were now laid flat; her cat had fled, her canary was dead—

crushed, cage and all. When the favourite removed the black scarf from her eyes, Camila had the impression that she was very far away from home. She passed her hand over her face two or three times, looking about her to see where she was. Her fingers stopped moving to stifle a cry of dismay when she realised her desperate plight. It was not a dream.

"Señorita"—the voice of the man who had broken the disastrous news to her that afternoon came floating towards her heavy numbed body, "at least you're in no danger here. What can we give you to quiet your fears?"

"Water and fire!" said the innkeeper as she hurriedly raked a few embers to the top of the earthenware pot which served her as an oven, while Lucio Vasquez seized the opportunity to attack a bottle of strong brandy, swallowing it without tasting it, as if he were drinking rat poison.

The innkeeper revived the fire by blowing at it, muttering all the time: "Burn up quickly! Burn up quickly!" Behind her, against the wall of the back room, now glowing red in the light from the embers, Vasquez's shadows slipped past on his way to the patio.

La Masacuata dropped a live ember into a bowl full of water, making it bubble and hiss like a terrified person, with the dead charcoal floating in it like the black kernel of some infernal fruit; then she removed it with the tongs. After a few sips Camila found her voice again.

"And my father?" was the first thing she said.

"Keep calm, don't worry, drink some more charcoal water; the general's all right," replied Angel Face.

"Are you sure?"

"I think so."

"But some misfortune—"

"Sh! Don't tempt fate!"

Camila turned and looked at Angel Face. The expression of a face is often more revealing than words. But her eyes lost themselves in the favourite's blank, dark pupils.

"You must sit down, my dear," remarked La Masacuata.

She was dragging the bench on which Vasquez had been sitting when the stranger who paid for his beer with a large note first came into the bar.

Had that afternoon been years ago, or only a few hours? The

favourite gazed first at the general's daughter, then at the candle flame alight in front of the Virgin of Chiquinquira. His pupils were darkened by the thought of putting out the light and having his will of the girl. One puff . . . and she would be his either willingly or by force. But his eyes moved from the Virgin's image to look at Camila; she had sunk on to the bench, and when he saw her pale face sprinkled with tears, her dishevelled hair and her body like an immature angel's, his expression changed and he took the cup from her hand with a fatherly air, saying: "Poor little girl!"

The innkeeper's discreet coughs to signify that she was going to leave them alone, and her foul language when she found Vasquez lying completely drunk in the tiny patio smelling of potted roses which lay behind the back room, brought a fresh outburst of tears from Camila.

"You've sozzled yourself pretty quick, you wretch," La Masacuata scolded him; "the only thing you know how to do is drive me crazy! It's true enough what they say; one can't close an eye without your swiping something! All very fine to say you love me! Oh yes—no doubt you do! Hardly turned my head and you've pinched the bottle! It doesn't cost you a thing, does it? Just because I trusted you! Get out of here, you thief, before I throw you out!"

The drunken man answered in a complaining tone; his head struck the ground as the woman began hauling him along by the legs. The door into the patio was blown to by the wind. Then silence.

"It's over now, it's all over," Angel Face was repeating into the ear of the weeping Camila. "Your father's not in danger, and you're quite safe in this hiding-place; I'm here to protect you. It's all over, don't cry; you'll only upset yourself more. Stop crying and look at me and I'll explain everything."

Camila's sobs gradually died away. Angel Face was stroking her hair, and he took her handkerchief from her hand to dry her eyes. Like whitewash mixed with pink paint the light of dawn coloured the horizon and shone between the objects in the room and under the doors. Human beings sensed each other's presence before they could see each other. Trees were driven demented by the first trilling of the birds and were unable to scratch themselves. Yawn after yawn from the fountains. And the sky flung aside the dark tresses of night, the tresses of death, and put on a golden wig.

"But you must keep calm—otherwise all will be lost. You'll endanger yourself, you'll endanger your father, you'll endanger me. I'll come back this evening and take you to your uncle's house. The chief thing is to gain time. We must be patient. One can't arrange everything all at once—some things are trickier than others."

"It's not myself I'm thinking of; I feel safer after what you've told me, and I'm grateful. I do understand that I must stay here. It's my father I'm worried about. I do so want to be sure that nothing's happened to my father."

"I promise to bring you news of him."

"Today?"

"Today."

Before he went out, Angel Face turned and gave her an affectionate little pat on the cheek.

"Feeling calmer?"

General Canales' daughter looked up at him with eyes that were again full of tears and answered:

"Bring me news . . ."

CHAPTER XIII

Arrests

GENARO RODAS' wife did not even wait for the bread to arrive before she hurried out of the house. God only knew whether the baskets of loaves would be delivered. She left her husband stretched on the bed fully clothed, limp as a rag, and her infant asleep in the basket which served for its cradle. Six o'clock in the morning.

The La Merced clock was striking just as she tapped on the door of Canales' house. "I hope they'll forgive me waking them so early," she thought, holding the knocker in her hand ready to let it fall again. "But are they coming to open the door or not? The General must know as soon as possible what Lucio Vasquez told my crazy husband in that bar called The Lion's Awakening."

She stopped knocking and waited for the door to open. "The beggars have laid the blame for the murder in the Cathedral Porch on him," she reflected. "They're going to come and arrest him this morning; worst of all they mean to kidnap the young lady. What an outrage! What an outrage!" she repeated inwardly as she went on knocking.

Her heart seemed to turn over again. "If they arrest the general—well, after all he's a man and he can go to prison. But if they kidnap the young lady! God help us! There'd be no getting over the disgrace. I'd bet anything there's one of those miserable ladinos at the bottom of all this—bringing his sly tricks to the city from the mountains."

She knocked again. The house, the street, the air echoed the sound like a drum. It drove her frantic that no one came. To pass the time she spelt out the name of the tavern on the corner: The Two-Step. There were only a few letters to decipher, but then she noticed two painted figures one on each side of the door: a man on one side, a woman on the other. From the woman's mouth came the legend: "Come and dance a little Two-Step!", and from behind the man, who was holding a bottle in his hand, came the reply: "No thanks! I prefer the bottle dance!"

Tired of knocking—either they weren't there or they were not going to open up—she pushed the door. It gave to her hand. Had it only been on the latch? Wrapping her fringed shawl round her shoulders, she entered the hall with a sense of deep foreboding, and went through into the passage hardly knowing what she was doing; the sight that met her eyes pierced her as a bird is pierced by a shot, leaving her drained of blood, short of breath, her eyes blank, her limbs paralysed: there were flower vases and quetzal plumes lying on the ground; screens, windows and mirrors broken; cupboards forced open; locks violated; papers, clothes, furniture and carpets all destroyed, all grown old in a single night, all converted into a worthless confusion of lifeless dirty rubbish, unfamiliar and soulless.

The old nurse, La Chabelona, was wandering about like a ghost in search of her young lady, with her head cracked open.

"Ha-ha-ha!" she laughed. "Tee-hee-hee! Where are you hiding, Camila my girl? I'm coming! Why don't you answer? Coming! Coming! COMING!"

She imagined she was playing at hide-and-seek with Camila, and looked for her over and over again in the same corners, among the flower pots, under beds, behind doors, turning everything upside-down like a whirlwind.

"Ha-ha-ha! Tee-hee-hee! Oh-ho-ho! Coming! Coming! Come out, Camila my girl, I can't find you! Come out, little Camila; I'm tired of looking for you! Ha-ha-ha! Come out! I'm coming! Tee-hee-hee! Oh-ho-ho!"

In the course of her search she happened to go up to the fountain and when she saw her own reflection in its still waters, she screamed like a wounded monkey, and with her laugh turning into a terrified chattering, her hair over her face and her hands over her hair she sank gradually to the ground to escape from this extraordinary vision. She whispered broken excuses as if to ask forgiveness from herself for being so ugly, so old, so small and so dishevelled. Suddenly she screamed again. Through the ragged cascade of her hair and between the bars of her fingers she had seen the sun leap upon her from the roof, and throw her shadow on to the floor of the patio. Frantic with rage, she stood up and attacked her own shadow and reflection, striking the water with her hands and the ground with her feet. She wanted to destroy them. Her shadow twisted and turned like an animal under the lash, but in spite of her furious kicking and stamping it was still there. Her reflection was shivered to pieces in the turbulence of the beaten water, but reappeared as soon as it was still again. She yelled like a wild beast with rage at her inability to destroy this sooty deposit sprinkled on the stones, which fled from her kicking feet as if it really felt the blows, or to batter to pieces this other luminous dust floating on the water, like a fish with a suggestion of her own image about it.

Her feet were beginning to bleed, her hands were dropping to her sides with fatigue, but her shadow and her reflection remained indestructible.

Convulsed with rage, she made a last desperate effort and threw herself head first against the fountain . . .

Two roses fell into the water . . .

The thorny branch of a rose tree had torn out her eyes . . .

After writhing on the ground like her own shadow, she lay at last still and apparently lifeless at the foot of an orange tree.

A military band was passing down the street. What vigorous martial music! What an eager vision of triumphal arches it summoned up! However, in spite of the trumpeters' efforts to blow hard and in time, the townspeople did not open their eyes impatiently that morning, like heroes tired of seeing the sword rust in the golden peace of cornfields, but rather to the pleasant prospect of a holiday, humbly resolving to pray that God should deliver them from evil thoughts, words or deeds directed against the President of the Republic.

After a brief spell of unconsciousness La Chabelona became aware of the band. She was in darkness. Her young lady must have crept up on tiptoe and covered her eyes from behind.

"Camila, my dear, I know it's you. Let me look at you!" she stammered, putting her hands to her face to take away the girl's hands which were hurting her horribly.

The wind blew the music away down the street in gusts. The music and the darkness with which blindness had bandaged her eyes as if in a child's game, brought back the memory of the school where she had learnt her letters, down in the Old Town. Then with a leap through the years she saw herself grown-up, sitting in the shade of two mango trees, and then, gradually, little by little, another leap and she was in an ox-cart, rumbling along a flat road smelling of hay. The creaking of the wheels was like a double crown of thorns drawing blood from the silence of the beardless carter who made a woman of her : chewing as they went, the patient oxen dragged along the nuptial couch. Rapture of the sky above the springy fields . . . But her memories suddenly dissolved, and she saw a crowd of men pouring into the general's house with the force of a torrent, panting like black animals; heard their fiendish cries, blows, blasphemies, coarse laughter, and the piano screaming as if they were wrenching its teeth out by main force. Her young lady vanished like a perfume, and she felt a violent blow in the middle of her forehead accompanied by a strange cry and all-pervading darkness.

Genaro Rodas' wife, Niña Fedina, found the old servant lying in the patio with her cheeks bathed in blood, her hair dishevelled, her clothes torn to pieces, fighting to keep off the flies which invisible hands were throwing at her face—and fled in terror through the house like someone who has seen a ghost.

"Poor thing ! Poor thing !" she kept muttering to herself.

Beneath one of the windows she found the letter the general had written to his brother Juan. He asked him to look after Camila. But Niña Fedina did not read it all, partly because she was distracted by La Chabelona's cries—they seemed to come from the broken mirrors, the splintered window-panes, the damaged chairs, the forced cupboards and the fallen pictures—and partly because of her urgent need to escape from the house. She wiped the sweat from her face with a handkerchief folded in four, nervously crushed in a hand ornamented with cheap rings, slipped the letter into her bodice and hurried out into the street.

Too late. A rough-looking officer stopped her at the door. The house was surrounded by soldiers. From the patio came the tortured cries of the nurse.

Lucio Vasquez, who had been egged on by La Masacuata and Camila to watch from the door of the Two-Step Tavern, held his breath when he saw them arrest the wife of his friend Genaro Rodas, to whom he had revealed the plan for the general's arrest in his cups last night at the Lion's Awakening.

A soldier came up to the tavern. "They're looking for the general's daughter !" thought the innkeeper with her heart in her boots. The same thought made Vasquez's hair stand on end. But the soldier had come to tell them to close the bar. They shut the doors and stood watching what went on in the street through the cracks.

In the darkness Vasquez rallied a little and began fondling La Masacuata on the pretext of being afraid, but she stopped him out of force of habit. She would have boxed his ears for two pins.

"Don't be so stuck-up!"

"So that's what you think? Well you're wrong! And I'd like to know why I should let you mess me about. Didn't I tell you last night that that fool of a woman said the general's daughter . . ."

"Look out! They'll hear you!" interrupted Vasquez. They were stooping to look out into the street through the cracks in the door as they talked.

"Don't be a fool, I'm talking quietly enough! If I hadn't told you that woman was going to get the general's daughter to be godmother to her brat, you'd have brought Genaro into it and then the fat would have been in the fire."

"I dare say," answered the other, hawking to get rid of some immovable substance stuck between his gullet and the back of his nose.

"Don't be so disgusting, you uneducated brute!"

"Very dainty all of a sudden!"

"Sh!"

At that moment the Judge Advocate General was seen getting out of a ramshackle cab.

"It's the Judge Advocate," said Vasquez.

"What's he come for?" asked La Masacuata.

"To arrest the general."

"And he's dressed himself up like a peacock for that? I ask you! Just look at him! Why don't you pinch one of those feathers he's got on his head?"

"No thanks. What a one for questions you are. He's dressed like that because he's on his way to see the President."

"Lucky fellow! If they didn't arrest the general last night I'm a whore!"

"Why don't you shut up?"

When the Judge Advocate General got out of his carriage, orders were given in a low tone and a captain went into the house at the head of a squad of soldiers, carrying his naked sword in one hand and a revolver in the other, like the officers in the colour prints of the Russo-Japanese war.

And a few minutes later—they were centuries to Vasquez, who was watching everything that happened with his heart in his mouth—the officer returned looking pale and extremely agitated, to tell the Judge Advocate what had happened.

"What's that?" shouted the Judge Advocate. "What's that?" The words came bursting out between explosions of air.

"What? What? What? You say he's escaped?" he roared, with the veins on his forehead swelling up like black question marks. "And that—that—that—the house has been looted?"

Without a moment's hesitation he disappeared through the front door, followed by the officer; after a rapid survey he was back in the street, his fat hand angrily grasping the hilt of his sword, and so pale that his lips were indistinguishable from his blanched moustache.

"How did he get away? That's what I want to know!" he exclaimed as he came out of the house. "What was the telephone invented for? To see that orders were carried out! To arrest the enemies of the Government! The old fox! I'll hang him if I catch him! I wouldn't care to be in his shoes!"

The Judge Advocate General's gaze suddenly fell on Niña Fedina. An officer and a sergeant were dragging her by main force towards him as he stood there shouting.

"The bitch!" he cried, and without taking his eyes off her he added: "We'll make her talk! Lieutenant, take ten men and convey her as quickly as possible where she belongs! And solitary confinement, you understand?"

A petrified cry filled the air, a sharp, lacerating, inhuman cry.

"Oh my God, what are they doing to that poor crucified Christ?" groaned Vasquez. La Chabelona's increasingly piercing shrieks made his blood run cold.

"Christ?" the bartender corrected him sarcastically. "Can't you hear it's a woman? I suppose you think all men whistle like female blackbirds!"

"Shut your trap . . ."

The Judge Advocate gave orders for the neighbouring houses to be searched. Parties of soldiers dispersed in all directions under corporals or sergeants. They ransacked patios, bedrooms, private offices, attics, fountains. They went on to the roofs and rummaged among linen cupboards, beds, carpets, sideboards, casks, dressers and chests. If anyone was slow to open his door they felled him with their rifle butts. Dogs barked frenziedly beside their white-faced masters. The sound of barking spouted from each house as from a watering-can.

"Suppose they come here?" said Vasquez, who was almost speechless with terror. "We've got ourselves into a fine mess! If we'd got something out of it it might be different, but for less than nothing . . ."

La Masacuata hurried off to warn Camila.

"If you want to know what I think," said Vasquez, following her, "she ought to cover her face and get away from here." And he backed to the door again without waiting for an answer.

"Wait! Wait!" he said with his eye to the crack. "The Judge Advocate has countermanded the order; they've stopped searching. We're saved!"

The barkeeper took two steps to the door to see with her own eyes what Lucio had announced so jubilantly.

"Just look at your crucified Christ!" whispered the woman.

"Who is she?"

"The nurse—can't you see?" and she withdrew her body out of range of Vasquez's lustful hand: "Will you be quiet! Be quiet! Be quiet, blast you!"

"Poor thing, look at the way they're dragging her along!"

"She looks as if a tram had run over her!"

"Why do people squint when they're dying?"

"Ugh! I don't want to see!"

The unfortunate nurse, La Chabelona, had been dragged out of the general's house by a squad of men led by a captain with a drawn sword. It was impossible for the Judge Advocate to interrogate her. Twenty-four hours earlier this relic of a human being, who was now breathing her last, had been the mainstay of a house in which the only political activity had been the canary's schemes to get bird seed, the concentric circles spreading beneath the jet of the fountain, the general's interminable games of patience and Camila's whims.

The Judge Advocate jumped into his carriage, followed by an officer. They were held up at the first corner. Four ragged, filthy men had arrived with a stretcher to take La Chabelona's corpse to the dissecting room. The soldiers filed off to their barracks and

La Masacuata opened up her bar. Sitting on his usual seat, Vasquez made little attempt to disguise the agitation caused in him by the arrest of Genaro Rodas' wife; his head was as hot as a brick kiln; he was full of wind from the alcohol he had drunk, and waves of intoxication kept returning to him, along with fears about the general's escape.

Meanwhile Niña Fedina was hustled away to prison by her guard, who pushed her off the pavement every few minutes into the middle of the street. She let herself be manhandled in silence, but suddenly lost patience as they went along and struck one of them full in the face. A blow with a rifle butt was the unexpected reply, while another soldier hit her from behind so violently that she staggered, her teeth rattled in her head and she saw stars.

"So that's what your weapons are for, is it, you cowardly blackguards? You ought to be ashamed of yourselves!" intervened a woman returning from market with a basket full of vegetables and fruit.

"You shut up!" shouted one of the soldiers.

"None of your cheek, you bully!"

"Now then, Señora, get along will you? Hurry on wherever you were going. Or have you got nothing to do?" shouted a sergeant.

"What about you, you fat swine!"

"Be quiet!" interrupted an officer, "or we'll bash your face in for you!"

"Bash my face in indeed! That's enough of that, you dirty Indians with your sleeves out at elbows and no seats to your trousers! Better have a look at yourselves and keep your traps shut, you lousy lot—insulting people just for the fun of it!"

And the unknown defender of Genaro Rodas' wife was left behind among the startled passers-by, while the captive herself went on her way to prison, a tragic figure, her drawn face covered in sweat, and with the fringe of her bombazine shawl sweeping the ground.

The Judge Advocate General's carriage arrived at the house of Abel Carvajal the lawyer just as he was leaving for the palace in his top hat and morning coat. The Judge Advocate leapt from the step on to the pavement, setting the carriage rocking behind him. Carvajal had shut the door and was meticulously pulling on one of his gloves when his colleague arrested him. Dressed in his ceremonial clothes, he was escorted by a picket of soldiers along the middle of the street to the Second Police Station, the outside of which was decorated with flags and paper chains. They took him straight to the cell where the student and the sacristan were imprisoned.

CHAPTER XIV

Let the Whole World Sing!

THE streets were gradually being revealed to view in the fugitive light of dawn; around them lay roofs and fields redolent of the freshness of April. The milk mules could be seen arriving at a gallop with the lids of their cans jangling, urged along by grunts and blows from their muleteers. The morning light shone on the cows drawn up outside the porticos of the richer houses or at the street corners in the poorer quarters, while their patrons—some on the way to convalescence others to extinction—with their eyes still sunk and glazed with sleep, waited on their chosen cow and came up in turn to receive their milk, skilfully tilting the jug so as to get more liquid than froth. The bread delivery women went by with their heads sunk on their chests, backs bowed, straining legs and bare feet, threading their way with short, unsteady steps under the weight of their huge baskets. Baskets were piled on baskets in pagodas, leaving in the air an aroma of pastry covered in sugar and toasted sesame seeds. And the alarum clocks announced the beginning of a national holiday, setting in motion phantoms of metal and air, a symphony of smells and an explosion of colours; while between darkness and dawn there sounded from the churches the timid yet daring bell announcing early Mass—timid and daring, because if on ordinary holidays its chime suggested chocolate cake and canonical biscuits, on a national holiday it savoured of forbidden fruit.

A national holiday . . .

Up from the streets along with the smell of the good earth, rose the jubilation of the inhabitants as they emptied basins of water out of their windows to settle the dust raised by the troops carrying the flag to the Palace (it smelt like a new handkerchief), or by the carriages of important people dressed in full regalia, doctors in frock coats, generals in brilliant uniforms smelling of moth-balls—the former in shining toppers, the latter in three-cornered hats with plumes; or by the trotting horses of lesser officials, the value of whose services was measured by the sum the State would one day pay for their funerals.

Señor! Señor! Heaven and earth are full of your glory! Pleased at the response his efforts for their welfare met with from the people, the President allowed himself to be seen, a long way off, among a group of his intimate friends.

Señor! Señor! Heaven and earth are full of your glory! The women felt the divine power of their Beloved Deity. The more important priests paid him homage. The lawyers imagined they were attending one of Alfonso el Sabio's tournaments. The diplomats, excellencies from Tiflis perhaps, put on grand airs as if they were at the court of the Sun King at Versailles. Native and foreign journalists congratulated themselves on being in the presence of a second Pericles. Señor! Señor! Heaven and earth are full of your glory! The poets felt they were in Athens, so they announced to the world at large. A sculptor of saintly figures imagined he was Phidias, smiled, rubbed his hands and turned his eyes to heaven when he heard the cheering in the streets in honour of their eminent ruler. Señor! Señor! Heaven and earth are full of your glory! A composer of funeral marches, a devotee of Bacchus and also of religion, craned his tomato-coloured face from a window to see what was happening in the street.

But if the artists believed they were in Athens, the Jewish bankers imagined they were in Carthage as they passed through the rooms of the statesman who had given them his confidence and entrusted the nation's savings to their bottomless coffers at an interest of zero and nothing per cent—by which transaction they had managed to get rich and replace the gold and silver currency with the foreskins of the circumcised. Señor! Señor! Heaven and earth are full of your glory!

Angel Face made his way among the guests. (He was as beautiful and as wicked as Satan.)

"The people want you to come out on to the balcony, Mr President."

"The people?"

The leader put a germ of interrogation into these two words. There was silence all round him. Weighed down by a deep sadness which he angrily suppressed as soon as he became aware of it, he got up from his chair and went out on to the balcony.

He appeared before the crowd surrounded by a group of his

intimates. Some women had come to congratulate him on the happy anniversary of his escape from death, and one of them, who had been given the task of making a speech, began as soon as she saw the President:

"Son of the people . . .!"

The leader swallowed a bitter mouthful of saliva, perhaps remembering his student years, when he lived in poverty with his mother in a town paved with bad intentions; but the favourite interposed in a sycophantic undertone:

"So was Jesus a son of the people."

"Son of the pe-eople!" repeated the speechifier, "of the people, I say. On this radiantly beautiful day the sun is shining in the sky, shedding its light on your eyes and on your life, and exemplifying by the blessed succession of day and night in the dome of heaven, the blackness of that unforgivable night when criminal hands—instead of sowing the seed as you, Señor, had taught them—laid a bomb at your feet, which in spite of every European scientific device left you scatheless."

A burst of organised applause drowned the voice of the "Talking Cow", as the female orator was unkindly nicknamed, and a succession of acclamations fanned the air around the hero of the day and his suite.

"Long live the President!"

"Long live the President of the Republic!"

"Long live the Constitutional President of the Republic!"

"Let our applause go on echoing throughout the world for ever: Long live the Constitutional President of the Republic, Benefactor of his Country, Head of the great Liberal Party, and Liberal-hearted Protector of Studious Youth!"

The "Talking Cow" went on:

"There would have been a hundred stains on our flag had the plans of these wicked sons of our Fatherland succeeded, supported as they were in their criminal attempt by the President's enemies. They never paused to reflect that God's hand was protecting your precious life, with the support of all those who recognise that you are worthy to be First Citizen of the Nation and who therefore surrounded you at that terrible moment, and who surround you now and will continue to do so as long as it is necessary!

"Yes, gentlemen—ladies and gentlemen; today we realise more fully than ever that if those dreadful plans had been successful on that day of tragic memory for our nation—now marching at the head of civilised peoples—our Fatherland would have been bereft of its father and protector, and at the mercy of those who sharpen their daggers in darkness to plunge them into the breast of Democracy, as that great statesman Juan Montalvo said!

"Thanks to your escape, our flag still flutters above us unstained. And that is why we are here today, gentlemen, to honour the illustrious protector of the poorer classes, who watches over us with a father's love and has brought our nation, as I have already said, into the vanguard of that progress to which Fulton gave the first impulse with his discovery of steam, and which Juan Santa Maria defended from piracy by setting fire to the fatal powder in Lempira. Long live our Fatherland! Long live the Constitutional President of the Republic, Head of the Liberal Party, Benefactor of the Nation, Protector of defenceless women and children, and of education!"

The "Talking Cow's" vivats were lost in a conflagration of cheering which was extinguished by a sea of clapping.

The President said a few words in reply, with his right hand grasping the marble balcony; he turned slightly sideways so as not to expose his breast and moved his head from left to right to embrace the crowd, his brows drawn together, his eyes watchful. Men and women alike wiped away a few tears.

"Won't you come indoors again, Mr President?" put in Angel Face, hearing him sniff, "as you find the crowd so affecting . . ."

As the President returned from the balcony followed by one or two friends, the Judge Advocate hurried forward to inform him of General Canales' flight and also in order to be the first to congratulate him on his speech; but like everyone else who approached with this intention he stopped dead, suddenly inhibited by a strange feeling of fear, as of some supernatural agency, and rather than remain with his hand outstretched, he offered it to Angel Face.

The favourite turned his back, and it was with his hand still in mid-air that the Judge Advocate General heard the first of a series of explosions, following each other rapidly like a discharge of artillery. Already screams could be heard; already people were jumping, running, kicking over chairs, and women were fainting; already there was the tramp of soldiers, as they scattered among the crowd like grains of rice, their hands on the stiff fastenings of their cartridge-pouches, their rifles loaded, accompanied by machine-guns, red mirrors, officers, guns . . .

A colonel disappeared upstairs, revolver in hand. Another ran down a spiral staircase, revolver in hand. It was nothing. A captain went past a window, revolver in hand. Another stood at a door, revolver in hand. It was nothing. It was nothing! But the air felt cold. The news spread through the agitated crowd. It was nothing. Gradually the guests formed into groups; some had made water in their terror, others had lost their gloves; those whose colour returned to them had not regained the power of speech, and those who had recovered the power of speech had lost their colour. The one question nobody could answer was where and when the President had disappeared.

On the floor at the foot of a little staircase lay the leading drummer of the military band. He had rolled down from the first floor, drum and all, and thus provoked the panic!

CHAPTER XV

Uncles and Aunts

THE favourite left the Palace between the Lord Chief Justice—
a little old man in a top hat and frock coat looking like a child's
drawing of a rat—and a member of parliament, as cadaverous
as some ancient statue of a saint. They were arguing in the most
mouth-watering way as to whether the Grand Hotel or an inn
near by would most effectively drive away the fright they had
all been given by that ridiculous drummer, whom they consigned
without a twinge of remorse to prison, Hell, or worse. When the
member of parliament put the case for the Grand Hotel he seemed
to be laying down obligatory rules as to the most aristocratic
setting in which to lift the elbow, an activity which had favourable
repercussions on the exchequer. When the judge spoke it was with
the emphasis of someone pronouncing sentence: "intrinsic
excellence is always to be found where there is lack of outer
display, and that is the reason, my friend, why I prefer the humble
inn, where one is at ease and among friends, to the luxurious hotel
where all is not gold that glitters."

Angel Face left them still arguing at the corner of the Palace—
it was better to wash one's hands of a dispute between two such
authorities—and set off for the El Incienso quarter, in search of
Juan Canales' house. It was of urgent importance that this
gentleman should fetch or send for his niece from the Two-Step
Tavern. "What does it matter whether he goes himself or sends
for her?" he said to himself, "so long as she ceases to be my
responsibility, so long as she ceases to exist for me any more than
she did yesterday, when she was nothing to me." Two or three
passers-by made way for him respectfully, stepping off the pavement into the road. He thanked them without noticing who
they were.

Don Juan, the general's brother, lived at El Incienso in a house
close to "The Coin", as the Mint was called, a building, it must be
said, of patibulary gloom. The peeling walls were reinforced with

flaking beams of wood, and through the iron bars of the windows one could glimpse rooms like the cages of wild beasts. Here the devil's millions were kept safe.

When the favourite knocked a dog answered. It was clear from the frenzied way this Cerberus barked that he was tied up.

Hat in hand, Angel Face entered the door—he was as beautiful and as wicked as Satan; he was pleased to be in the house where the general's daughter was to be taken, but distracted by the dog's barking, and repeated invitations to "Come in" from a florid-complexioned, smiling, pot-bellied man who was none other than Don Juan Canales.

"Do come in, I beg you; come in! This way, if you'll be so kind! And to what do I owe the pleasure of this visit?" Don Juan said all this like an automaton, in a tone of voice which was far from expressing the agitation he felt in the presence of this exquisite satellite of the Presidents.

Angel Face glanced round the room. With what a chorus of barking that bad-tempered dog greeted visitors to the house! He noticed a collection of portraits of the Canales brothers, and that the general's had been removed. A looking-glass at the other end of the room reflected the place where the picture had hung and a section of the room papered in yellow—the colour of a telegram.

While Don Juan went on exhausting his stock-in-trade of formally polite remarks, Angel Face reflected that the dog was still the guardian of the house as in primitive times. The defender of the tribe. Even the President himself owned a kennel of foreign dogs.

The master of the house could be seen in the mirror gesticulating distractedly. Don Juan Canales, having used up every phrase in his repertory, felt like a swimmer who has plunged into deep water.

"Here, in my house," he was saying, "we (my wife and your humble servant) have felt genuine indignation at my brother Eusebio's behaviour! What a story it is! Crime is always a detestable thing, and more so in this case, when the victim was in every way estimable, a man who was a credit to our Army, and above all—I ask you!—a friend of the President!"

Angel Face maintained the terrible silence of someone watching a man drown because he has no means of saving him—a silence only comparable to that of visitors who are too timid either to confirm or contradict what is said.

Finding that his words fell on deaf ears, Don Juan lost his nerve completely and began to beat the air with his hands and search for solid ground with his feet. His brain was in a ferment. He believed himself implicated in the murder in the Cathedral Porch and all its far-reaching political ramifications. The fact that he was innocent made no difference. How complicated it all was. How complicated! "It's a lottery, my friend, it's a lottery! It's a lottery, my friend, a lottery!" This phrase, describing the typical state of affairs in the country, used to be shouted by Old Fulgencio, a good old man who sold lottery tickets in the street, and was a devout Catholic with a sharp eye for business. Instead of Angel Face, Canales saw the skeleton silhouette of Old Fulgencio, whose bony limbs, jaws and fingers all seemed to be jerking on wires. Old Fulgencio used to grip his black leather portfolio under his angular arm, smooth out the wrinkles in his face, slap at the pendulous seat of his trousers, stretch out his neck and say in a voice which emerged simultaneously from his nose and his toothless mouth: "The lottery is the only law on this earth, my friend! The lottery can send you to prison, have you shot, make you a deputy, a diplomat, President of the Republic, a general or a minister! What's the good of work, when all this can be got by the lottery? It's a lottery, my friend—so come on and buy a lottery ticket!" And the whole of that knotted skeleton, that twisted vine-stem, was shaken by laughter, which spouted from his mouth like a list of winning lottery numbers.

Angel Face gazed at Canales in silence, asking himself quite a different question: how could this cowardly and repellent man have anything to do with Camila?

"It's being said—anyway my wife was told so—that they want to implicate me in the murder of Colonel Parrales Sonriente!" went on Canales, pulling a handkerchief out of his pocket with great difficulty and mopping the large drops of sweat that rolled down his forehead.

"I know nothing about that," the other man said shortly.

"It would be unjust! As I told you just now, my wife and I have disapproved of Eusebio's behaviour from the very first. Besides, I don't know if you're aware of it, but my brother and I have seen very little of each other lately. Almost nothing. In fact nothing. We used to meet like strangers: good morning, good morning; good evening, good evening; that was all. Goodbye, goodbye, but that was all."

Don Juan's voice was full of uncertainty. His wife, who had been following the interview from behind a screen, thought it was time to come to her husband's help.

"Introduce me, Juan," she exclaimed as she came in, with a nod and a polite smile to Angel Face.

"Oh yes, of course!" answered her distraught husband, as he and the favourite got up from their chairs. "Let me introduce my wife!"

"Judith de Canales."

Angel Face heard the name of Don Juan's wife, but he had no recollection of mentioning his own.

This visit was prolonging itself unnecessarily, because of the inexplicable influence which had begun to trouble his heart and disturb his entire life, and any remarks which had nothing to do with Camila failed to penetrate his ears.

"But why don't these people talk about their niece?" he wondered. "If they talked of her I should be all attention; if they talked of her I should tell them they needn't worry, that Don Juan couldn't be mixed up in any murder; if only they'd talk of her! But what a fool I am! It's she and they, not I; I'm out of it, out of it, miles away, nothing to do with her . . ."

Doña Judith sat down on the sofa and wiped her nose with a little lace handkerchief to keep herself in countenance.

"You were saying? I'm afraid I interrupted you. I'm so sorry . . ."

"Of . . . !"

"If . . . !"

"Have . . . !"

All three of them started speaking at once, and after several polite "do go on"s, Don Juan was left in possession of the floor, he didn't quite know why. ("Idiot!" his wife's eyes shouted at him.)

"I was just telling our friend here that you and I were outraged when we were told, in the most confidential way, that my brother Eusebio had been one of Colonel Parrales Sonriente's assassins."

"Oh, yes, yes, indeed!" agreed Doña Judith, thrusting forward her prominent breasts. "Juan and I said that my brother-in-law the general should never have degraded his uniform with such a barbarous action; and the worst of it is, the very last straw, that now they tell us people are trying to implicate my husband!"

"I've also been explaining to Don Miguel that my brother and I had drifted apart a long time ago, that we were enemies . . . yes, deadly enemies; he couldn't bear the sight of me, nor I of him!"

"Not quite so bad as that, but family matters always lead to anger and quarrelling," added Doña Judith, allowing a sigh to float away on the air.

"I know," put in Angel Face; "but Don Juan mustn't forget that there's always an indestructible bond between brothers . . ."

"What do you mean, Don Miguel? That I was his accomplice?"

"Excuse me!"

"You mustn't believe that," put in Doña Judith hurriedly, with lowered eyes. "All bonds are destroyed when money matters come up; it's sad that it should be so, but one sees it happen every day. Money is no respecter of blood ties!"

"Excuse me! I said just now that there is an indestructible bond between brothers, because in spite of the deep differences of opinion between Don Juan and the general, when the general saw that he was ruined and must leave the country, he told me . . ."

"If he tried to mix me up in his crime, he's a villain! Oh, what a slander!"

"But he did nothing of the sort!"

"Juan, Juan, do let our visitor speak!"

"He told me that he counted on you both to see that his daughter should not be left destitute, and he asked me to come and talk to you about having her here in this house . . ."

This time it was Angel Face who felt that his words were falling on deaf ears. He seemed to be talking to people who didn't understand Spanish. His words rebounded as from a mirror, unheeded either by the portly clean-shaven Don Juan or by Doña Judith, encased in her breasts as if in a wheelbarrow.

"And it's for you to consider what can best be done for the girl."

"Yes, of course!" As soon as Don Juan realised that Angel Face had not come to arrest him, he recovered his normal presence of mind. "I don't really know what to say to you; the truth is you've quite taken me by surprise! Of course it's out of the question to have her here. One can't play with fire, you know! I'm sure the poor girl would have been happy here, but my wife and I can't risk losing our friends; they would hold it against us if we opened the doors of our respectable home to the daughter of one of the President's enemies. Besides, it's common knowledge that my fine brother offered—how shall I say?—well, he offered his daughter to an intimate friend of the Chief of State, so that . . ."

"Simply to avoid being put in prison!" interrupted Doña Judith, letting her prominent bosom subside in yet another sigh. "But, as Juan says, he offered his daughter to a friend of the President's, who was to offer her in his turn to the President himself, who (it's natural and logical to suppose) rejected the disgraceful suggestion. And then, the Prince of the Army (as they nicknamed the general after his famous speech) saw that there was no way out for him, and decided to escape and leave his daughter to us. That was it! What can one expect from a man who has infected his relations with suspicion like the plague, and dishonoured the family name! Don't imagine we haven't suffered as a result of this affair. It's quite turned our hair white, as God and the Virgin are my witness!"

A flash of anger shot through the black depths of Angel Face's eyes.

"Then there's nothing more to be said . . ."

"We're sorry you should have had the bother of coming to see us. If you had sent a message . . ."

"And if it hadn't been utterly impossible for us," added Doña Judith, "we should have accepted with pleasure for your sake."

Angel Face went out without another word or glance in their direction.

The dog barked frenziedly, dragging its chain across the ground from side to side as far as it would go.

"I shall go and see your brothers," were his final words at the front door.

"You'll be wasting your time," Don Juan hastened to say. "I have the reputation of being a conservative as I live in this district, yet I won't take her into my house; but they are liberals . . . Oh well, they'll just think you're mad, or simply joking . . ."

He was standing on the door-step as he said these words; he

shut the door slowly, rubbed his fat hands together, hesitated for a moment, then walked away. He felt an irresistible desire to caress someone, but not his wife; and he went to get the dog which was still barking.

"Leave the dog if you're going out," shouted his wife from the patio, where she was pruning her rose trees now that the sun was off them.

"Yes, I'm going out now."

"Well, hurry, because I'm going to church for my Hour of Prayer, and I'd rather not be out in the streets after six."

CHAPTER XVI

In the Casa Nueva

Towards eight o'clock in the morning (how fortunate people were in the days of the clepsydra, when there were no grass-hopper clocks reckoning the time by leaps and bounds!) Niña Fedina was shut into a tomb-like cell the shape of a guitar, after the usual formalities and an exhaustive examination of everything she had on. They searched her from head to foot, her finger-nails, her arm-pits, everywhere—a most offensive process—and they became even more thorough after they found a letter written by General Canales in her bodice, the letter she had picked up from the floor of his house.

Tired with standing, and having no room to take even two steps, she sat down—after all it was better to sit. But after a little she got up again. The cold from the floor had penetrated her buttocks, her shins, her hands, her ears—human flesh is very susceptible to cold—and she remained standing for a while, then sat down again, stood up, sat down, and stood up by turns . . .

She could hear the prisoners who had been let out of their cells for an airing in the yard, singing songs as fresh as raw vegetables, in spite of the misery in their hearts. At times they hummed these airs sleepily; then their cruel monotony, the sense of doomed oppression they conveyed, would suddenly be broken by cries of desperation. The singers blasphemed, they hurled insults, they swore . . .

From the very first, Niña Fedina was frightened by a discordant voice which repeated over and over again like someone intoning a psalm:

> From the Casa Nueva
> to the houses of ill-fame,
> O pretty little sky,
> is only a step,
> and now that we are alone,
> O pretty little sky,
> Give me a kiss.

Ay, ay, ay, ay!
give me a kiss,
for from here to
the houses of ill-fame,
O pretty little sky,
is only a step.

The two first lines did not go with the rest of the song; however, this trifling circumstance seemed to emphasise the close relationship of the houses of ill-fame and the Casa Nueva. The break in the rhythm, though a sacrifice to realism, underlined the tormenting truth which filled Niña Fedina with fear of being afraid, making her tremble before she had experienced to the full that obscure and horrifying terror she was to feel later, when the voice on the worn gramophone record, pregnant with a more than criminal secrecy, had penetrated to her very bones. It was unfair that she had only this bitter song to feed upon. If she had been flayed alive she would not have suffered more torment than she did in her dungeon, listening to something which to the other prisoners, who forgot that a prostitute's bed is colder than prison, was the fulfilment of all their hopes of freedom and warmth.

She found some comfort in thinking of her child. She thought of him as if she still carried him in her womb. Mothers never reach a state of feeling completely empty of their children. The first thing she would do when she got out of prison was get him baptized. Everything had been arranged. The dress and bonnet Señorita Camila had given him were very pretty. And she planned to celebrate the occasion with tamal and chocolate for breakfast, Valencian rice and stew for midday, cinnamon water, almond syrup, ices and wafers in the evening. She had ordered the little invitation cards for her friends from the printer with the glass eye. And she wanted to hire two carriages from Shumann's, drawn by those big horses like locomotives, with tinkling silver-plated harness and drivers in tall hats and frock coats. Then she tried to drive these thoughts from her brain, so as to avoid sharing the fate of the man who said to himself on the eve of his wedding: "This time tomorrow you'll be mine, my little sweetheart!" and who had the misfortune to be knocked on the head by a brick in the street on his way to the church next day.

And she began thinking of her child again, with such happy absorption that without realising it she found herself gazing at a network of obscene drawings traced on the wall, which were a fresh source of agitation to her. Crosses, texts, men's names, dates, cabalistic figures, were jumbled up among sexual organs of all sizes. There was the word of God beside a phallus, the number thirteen on top of an enormous testicle, devils with their bodies twisted like candelabra, little flowers with fingers instead of petals, caricatures of judges and magistrates, small boats, anchors, suns, cradles, bottles, interlaced hands, eyes, hearts pierced by daggers, suns with policemen's moustaches, moons with faces like old maids, three or five-pointed stars, watches, sirens, guitars with wings, arrows . . .

Panic-stricken, she tried to escape from this world of madness and perversion, only to bump into the obscenities covering the other walls. She closed her eyes, mute with terror; she was like a woman beginning to slide down a slippery slope, with chasms opening around her instead of windows, and the sky displaying its stars as a wolf displays its teeth.

On the ground a party of ants were carrying off a dead cockroach. Still under the influence of the obscene drawings, Niña Fedina thought she was looking at female genitals being dragged by their own hair towards the beds of vice.

> From the Casa Nueva
> to the houses of ill-fame,
> O pretty little sky . . .

And the song again began rubbing at her living flesh gently with little splinters of glass, as if to wear away her feminine modesty.

In the town the celebrations in honour of the President of the Republic were still going on. In the evenings a cinema screen was erected like a gallows in the Plaza Central, and blurred fragments of films were exhibited to the crowd, who watched as enthusiastically as if they were witnessing an auto-da-fé. The flood-lit public buildings stood out against the dark sky. A stream of passers-by rolled themselves like a turban around the sharp-pointed railings of the circular public garden. The flower of society used to gather there and stroll round the gardens in the evenings, while the populace watched the cinema in religious silence under the stars. Packed together like sardines, old men and old women, bachelors and married couples were already yawning with undisguised boredom and watching the passers-by from their chairs and benches in the square, with a compliment for every girl and a greeting for their friends. From time to time, rich and poor alike looked up at the sky: a coloured rocket exploded and let fall its threads of rainbow silks.

The first night in a prison cell is a terrible thing. The prisoner feels that he is cut off from life in a nightmare world, there in the darkness. The walls vanish, the ceiling fades, the ground is lost to view, but this brings no feeling of freedom—rather of death.

Niña Fedina began a hurried prayer: "Oh most merciful Virgin Mary, it is said that you never abandon anyone who has sought your aid, implored your help and claimed your protection! So it is with confidence I turn to you, oh Virgin of Virgins, and throw myself at your feet, weeping for my sins. Do not reject my·prayers, oh Virgin Mary, but listen with a favourable and receptive ear. Amen." The darkness was choking her. She could not pray any more. She slipped to the floor, stretching out her arms—they seemed very long, very long—to embrace the cold floor, all the cold floors of all the prisoners who were being persecuted in the name of justice, the dying and the homeless . . .

She repeated the litany:

Ora pro nobis
Ora pro nobis
Ora pro nobis
Ora pro nobis
Ora pro nobis
Ora pro nobis
Ora pro nobis
Ora pro nobis

She sat up slowly. She was hungry. Who would suckle her child? She went to the door on all fours and beat on it in vain.

Ora pro nobis
Ora pro nobis
Ora pro nobis

In the distance she heard a clock strike twelve.

Ora pro nobis
Ora pro nobis

In the outside world where her child was . . .

Ora pro nobis

She had counted twelve strokes—rallying her forces, she made an effort to imagine she was free, and succeeded. She pictured herself at home among her belongings and friends, saying to Juanita: "Goodbye, it was lovely to see you!", going out and clapping her hands to call Gabrielita, seeing to the stove, bowing to Don Timoteo. She seemed to see her shop as if it were alive, some part of herself and others . . .

Outside the celebrations went on, with the cinema screen standing like a scaffold and people walking round the garden like slaves round a water-wheel.

The door of the cell opened when she was least expecting it. The noise of the lock unfastening made her start back as if from the brink of a precipice. Two men had come to find her in the darkness; they pushed her in silence along a narrow corridor swept by the night breeze and through two darkened rooms into another where lights were burning. When she came in, the Judge Advocate General was talking to his clerk in a low voice.

"That's the gentleman who plays the harmonium at the Virgin of Carmel!" thought Niña Fedina. "It seemed to me I recognised him when I was arrested; I've seen him in church. He can't be a bad man!"

The Judge Advocate gave her a long look, then he asked her some general questions: her name, age, state, profession, address. Rodas' wife answered in a firm voice, adding a question of her own when the clerk had written down a final answer—a question which went unheard because just then the telephone rang and a harsh woman's voice was clearly heard in the silence of the adjoining room, saying: "Yes! How's it going? I'm so glad! I sent to Canducha to enquire this morning. The dress? The dress is all right, yes, it's well cut. What? No, no, it isn't stained . . . I said it wasn't stained . . . Yes, without fail. Yes, yes . . . yes, come without fail. Goodbye. Sleep well. Goodbye."

Meanwhile the Judge Advocate was answering Niña Fedina's question in a familiar, cruelly mocking and ironical tone:

"Don't worry; that's what we're here for, to tell people like you, who don't know, why they've been arrested."

Then in a different voice, with his toad-like eyes bulging from their sockets, he added slowly:

"But first you must tell me what you were doing in General Eusebio Canales' house this morning."

"I'd gone—I'd gone to see the general on business."

"What was the business, may I ask?"

"Only a little matter, Señor! An errand I'd undertaken! To—look here, I'll tell you everything: I went to tell him that he was going to be arrested for the murder of that colonel (I forget his name) who was assassinated in the Cathedral Porch."

"And you've got the nerve to ask me why you're in prison? Does that seem a little thing, a little thing, you slut? Does that seem a little thing, a little thing?"

Each time he said "little" the Judge Advocate's rage increased.

"Wait a moment, Señor, let me explain! Wait a moment, Señor, it's not what you think! Wait! Listen! For heaven's sake! When I got to the general's house the general wasn't there; I didn't see him, I didn't see anyone, they had all gone, the house was empty, except for the servant who was running around!"

"And that seems a little thing? A little thing? And what time did you get there?"

"The clock of La Merced was just striking six in the morning, Señor!"

"You've got a good memory! And how did you know that the general was going to be arrested?"

"Me?"

"Yes, you!"

"I heard it from my husband."

"And what's your husband's name?"

"Genaro Rodas."

"Who did he hear it from? How did he know? Who told him?"

"A friend of his, Señor, called Lucio Vasquez, a member of the Secret Police. He told my husband and my husband . . ."

"And you told the general!" interrupted the Judge Advocate.

Niña Fedina shook her head as much as to say: "It's not true! NO!"

"And which way did the general go?"

"But, good heavens, how can I say when I never saw the general? Don't you understand, I never saw him, I never saw him! Why should I lie about it? Especially as this gentleman's writing everything I say down."

She pointed to the clerk, who stared back at her with his pale freckled face, like white blotting-paper which has blotted a great many dots.

"It's nothing to do with you what he's writing. Answer my question! Which way did the general go?"

There was a long silence. Then the Judge Advocate's voice rapped out, more sternly: "Which way did the general go?"

"I don't know! How can I possibly tell? I don't know, I never saw him—I never spoke to him!"

"You're making a mistake in denying it, because the authorities know everything—including the fact that you talked to the general."

"You make me laugh!"

"Listen to me; it's no laughing matter. The authorities know everything—everything, everything!" At each "everything" he made the table shake. "If you didn't see the general how did you come by this letter? I suppose it jumped into your bodice of its own account?"

"That's the letter I found lying in his house; I swiped it off the ground when I went out. But it's no good saying anything, since you don't believe me any more than if I was a liar!"

"*Swiped* it! She can't even talk properly!" grumbled the clerk.

"Look here, stop telling stories, Señora, and confess the truth, because all you'll get with your lies is a punishment that'll make you remember me for the rest of your life!"

"But I've told you the truth, and if you won't believe me I can't beat it into you with a stick as if you were my son!"

"You're going to pay for this, you just mark my words! And another thing: what had you to do with the general anyway? What were you, what are you, to him? His sister or what? What did you get out of him?"

"Me? Out of the general? Nothing. I only saw him twice, but you see it just happened that his daughter had promised to be godmother to my son."

"That's not a reason!"

The clerk put in from behind:

"All stupid lying!"

"And if I was upset, and lost my head, and ran off where you know I went, that was because Lucio told my husband that a man was going to carry off the general's daughter."

"Stop lying! You'd much better make a clean breast of it and tell me where the general is hiding; because I know you know, and that you're the only person who does know, and that you're going to tell us here and now—to tell us—to tell me. Stop crying and talk! I'm listening!"

And in a softer voice, almost in the tone of a confessor, he added:

"If you tell me where the general is—look here, listen to me: I know you know and are going to tell me—if you tell me where the general is hiding I'll let you off; I'll have you set free and you can go straight home to your house in peace. Think of that. Just think of that!"

"Oh dear, Señor, I'd tell you if I knew! But I don't know, unfortunately I don't know. Holy Mother of God, what shall I do?"

"Why do you deny it? Can't you see that you're ruining your own chances?"

In the intervals between the Judge Advocate's remarks, the clerk went on sucking his teeth.

"Well, if it's no use treating you kindly, if you're such scum as all that . . ." (the Judge Advocate said these words more quickly and with the increasing fury of a volcano about to erupt) ". . . then we'll make you talk by other means. You realise you've committed a grave crime against the security of the State, and that the law holds you responsible for the flight of a seditious traitor, rebel, assassin and enemy of the President? And that's saying quite a lot, quite a lot, quite a lot!"

Señora Rodas did not know what to do. This diabolical man's words concealed an urgent and terrible threat, perhaps even of death. Her teeth chattered, her fingers and legs trembled. When the hands tremble it seems as if they had no bones and were being shaken like gloves. When the teeth chatter and one cannot speak, one seems to be telegraphing one's anxiety. And when the legs tremble it seems as if one were standing in a carriage dragged along by two runaway horses, like a soul carried off by the devil.

"Señor!" she implored.

"I'm not joking! Come on, quickly now! Where is the general?"

A door opened some way off and a baby's crying was heard. Passionate, despairing crying.

"Do it for your child!"

Even before the Judge Advocate had spoken, Niña Fedina had thrown back her head and was looking in every direction to see where the crying came from.

"He's been crying for the last two hours, and it's no use your trying to find him. He's crying from hunger and he'll die of hunger if you don't tell me where the general is."

She rushed to the door, but was stopped by three men, three sinister-looking brutes who had very little trouble in overcoming her poor female strength. Her hair came down in the course of the futile struggle, her blouse came out of her skirt and her petticoats fell to the ground. Little she cared. Almost naked, she crawled back to the Judge Advocate General and begged him on her knees to let her suckle her baby.

"Anything you please, but first tell me where the general is!"

"I implore you by the Virgin of Carmel, Señor," she entreated, embracing his shoe. "Yes by the Virgin of Carmel, let me feed my little boy. Listen, he hardly has the strength to cry any more; listen, he's dying! Afterwards you can kill me if you want to!"

"No Virgin of Carmel will do you any good here! If you don't tell me where the general is hiding, here we stay, and your son too till he cries himself to death!"

Like a madwoman she threw herself on her knees in front of the men guarding the door. Then she struggled with them. Then she came back and knelt to the Judge Advocate again, trying to kiss his shoes.

"Señor, for my child's sake!"

"Well, for your child's sake, where is the general? It's useless to kneel and play the actress like this, because if you don't answer my question you have no hope at all of suckling your baby!"

As he said this, the Adjutant General stood up. The clerk was still sucking his teeth and holding his pen ready to write down the statement which would not come from the lips of the unfortunate mother.

"Where is the general?"

Just as water weeps in the gutters on winter nights, the baby went on crying, blubbering and whimpering.

"Where is the general?"

Niña Fedina was as silent as a wounded animal, biting her lips and not knowing what to do.

"Where is the general?"

Five, ten, fifteen minutes passed in this way. At last the Judge Advocate wiped his mouth on a black-edged handkerchief and added a threat to his questions:

"Well if you won't answer we'll make you crush some quicklime and see if that reminds you which way the general went!"

"I'll do whatever you like; only first let me—let me feed my little boy. Don't be so unjust, Señor, the poor little thing has done nothing! You can punish me as much as you like!"

One of the men guarding the door pushed her roughly to the ground; another gave her a kick which laid her flat. Her tears and indignation blurred the bricks in the wall, the objects in the room. She could take in nothing but her child's cries.

At one o'clock in the morning she began pounding quicklime to stop them hitting her about. Her little boy was still crying . . .

From time to time the Judge Advocate repeated:

"Where is the general? Where is the general?"

One o'clock.

Two.

And at last three. Her little boy was crying.

Three o'clock; it seemed like five.

Would four o'clock never come? And her child went on crying.

And four o'clock. Her child was still crying.

"Where is the general? Where is the general?"

With her hands covered all over in innumerable deep cracks, which opened wider with every movement she made, with the tips of her fingers raw, wounds between them, and bleeding nails, Niña Fedina groaned with pain as she lifted and rolled the stone on the quicklime. When she stopped, to beg pity for her child rather than for her own sufferings, they beat her.

"Where is the general? Where is the general?"

She wasn't listening to the Adjutant General's voice. Her baby's wailings, growing feebler every moment, filled her ears.

At twenty to five they left her lying unconscious on the ground.

A viscous stream was coming from her lips, and milk whiter than the lime itself was flowing from her breasts, which were lacerated with almost invisible fistulas. Now and again a few furtive tears escaped from her inflamed eyes.

Later on, when the first light of dawn was appearing, they took her back to her cell. There she watched over her frozen, dying baby, lying as limp as a rag doll in his mother's lap. The child revived a little and seized avidly upon her breast, but when he took the nipple in his mouth and tasted the sharpness of the lime, he dropped it and began crying again, and nothing would induce him to return to it.

She shouted and beat on the door with the baby in her arms. He was growing cold. He was growing cold. They couldn't possibly let an innocent creature die like this; and she began banging on the door and shouting again.

"Oh my son is dying! Oh my son is dying! Oh my life, my little one, my life! For God's sake come! Open up, for God's sake, open the door! My son is dying! Holy Virgin! Blessed Saint Anthony! Jesus of Saint Catherine!"

Outside the celebrations went on. The second day was just like the first, with the cinema screen like a scaffold, and people walking round the garden like slaves round a water-wheel.

CHAPTER XVII

Love's Stratagems

"WILL he come or not?"

"He'll turn up any minute, you'll see."

"He's already late, but if only he comes it doesn't matter, does it?"

"You can count on it, as sure as it's night now; I'll eat my boots if he doesn't come. Don't you worry."

"And you think he'll bring me news of Papa? He suggested it himself . . ."

"Of course. All the more reason."

"Oh, I hope to God it's not bad news! I don't know what I'm doing. I feel I'm going mad. I want him to come quickly to relieve my fears, yet I don't want him to come at all if he brings bad news."

From the corner of her little improvised kitchen, La Masacuata was listening to Camila, who lay on the bed, talking in a tremulous voice. A lighted candle had been stuck to the floor in front of the Virgin of Chiquinquira.

"With you in such a fix I'm sure he'll come, and with news which'll please you, you'll see. How can I tell, d'you say? . . . Because that's my line and there's nothing I don't know about affairs of the heart. One swallow may not make a summer but men are all the same . . . like bees round a honey-pot . . ."

The sound of the bellows interrupted the barkeeper's remarks. Camila watched her absent-mindedly as she blew up the fire.

"Love is like an iced drink, my dear. If you drink it as soon as it's made there's plenty of good syrup, but it runs out everywhere, and you must drink it up quick or it'll spill over; and then afterwards—afterwards there's nothing left but a lump of ice with no colour and no taste."

Footsteps were heard in the street. Camila's heart beat so violently that she had to press her two hands over it. They passed the door and went quickly away.

"I thought it was him."

"He won't be long now . . ."

"It must be because he went to my uncle's house before coming here; very likely he'll bring my Uncle Juan with him."

"Pst! The cat! The cat's drinking your milk; scare it away!"

Camila turned to look at the animal; it had been frightened by the barwoman's shout and was licking its milky whiskers beside her forgotten cup on a chair.

"What's the cat's name?"

"Benjie."

"I had one called Dewdrop. It was a female."

Again footsteps were heard, and perhaps . . .

Yes, it was Angel Face.

While La Masacuata unbarred the door, Camila tried to smooth her hair back a little with her hands. Her heart was pounding in her breast. At the end of this eternal, interminable day, as it had sometimes seemed, she felt numb, weak, lifeless and haggard, like a sick person who hears whispered preparations for her operation.

"Good news, Señorita, it's all right!" said Angel Face from the door, removing the troubled expression from his face.

She was waiting for him beside the bed, standing with one hand on the head-board, her eyes full of tears and her expression cold. The favourite took her hands.

"First the news about your father; that's the most important thing to you." After saying this he looked at La Masacuata, and changed his mind without altering his tone of voice. "But your father doesn't know that you're hiding here . . ."

"And where is he?"

"You must keep calm!"

"If only I knew nothing had happened to him, I could bear anything!"

"Sit down," interrupted the barkeeper to Angel Face, pointing to the bench.

"Thanks."

"And as you've got plenty to talk about, if there's nothing you want perhaps you'll let me go off for a little while. I want to go and see what's happened to Lucio. He went out this morning and hasn't been back since."

The favourite was on the point of asking the woman not to leave

119

him alone with Camila. But she had already disappeared into the dark little patio to change her skirt, and Camila was saying:

"God will reward you for everything, Señora! Poor thing, she's so kind. And everything she says is amusing. She says you are very good, very rich and charming, and that's she's known you a long time."

"Yes she's a good sort. However we couldn't talk openly in front of her and it's better she should go. The only thing that's known about your father is that he's on the run, and until he's crossed the frontier we can have no definite news. But tell me, did you say anything about your father to this woman?"

"No, because I thought she knew all about it."

"Well it's better not to breathe a word to her."

"And my uncle and aunt—what did they say?"

"I've not been able to go and see them because of trying to get news of your father; but I've told them I'll visit them tomorrow."

"I'm sorry to be such a nuisance, but I'm sure you understand I should feel happier there with them; especially with my Uncle Juan; he's my godfather and has always been like a second father to me."

"Did you see each other often?"

"Almost every day. Almost—yes. Yes, because if we didn't go to his house he came to ours, either with his wife or alone. He was the brother my father loved the best. He always said to me: 'When I go I shall leave you with Juan; you must go to his house and obey him as if he was your father.' And last Sunday we all dined together."

"Anyway, you must realise that I only hid you here to prevent your being bothered by the police, and because it's nearer."

The tired flame of the untrimmed candle fluttered like the gaze of a short-sighted person. Angel Face felt himself enfeebled and diminished in stature in its light. Camila looked paler, more alone, and more seductive than ever in her little lemon-yellow frock.

"What are you thinking about?"

His voice was intimate and relaxed.

"About what my poor father must be suffering, on the run through unknown dark places—I'm not explaining myself properly—hungry, tired, thirsty and with no one to help him.

May the Virgin go with him! I've kept her candle burning all day."

"You mustn't think of that sort of thing, don't go to meet misfortune; things will happen as it's written they will. You never guessed you would get to know me, nor I that I could be of use to your father!" He took one of her hands in his and she allowed him to stroke it as they both gazed at the Virgin's picture.

The favourite was thinking:

> In the keyhole of heaven
> You would fit neatly, for the locksmith
> Printed your outline in snow
> On a star, when you were born!

These lines were running through his head at the moment, just as if they embodied the rhythm now uniting their two hearts.

"You tell me that my father is going a long way away. When shall we know more?"

"I really haven't an idea, but it must be a matter of days."

"Many days?"

"No."

"Perhaps my Uncle Juan has had news of him."

"Very likely."

"You seem embarrassed when I talk about my uncle and aunt."

"What on earth can you mean? Not in the least. Quite the reverse. I realise if it wasn't for them my own responsibility would be greater. Where should I take you if not to them?"

Angel Face's tone of voice changed when he talked of her uncle, and could stop drawing imaginary pictures of the general's flight while all the time expecting to see him return handcuffed and under escort, or as cold as marble on a bloodstained hurdle.

Suddenly the door opened. It was La Masacuata in a state of great agitation. The bars of the door clattered to the floor. A gust of air nearly blew the candle out.

"You must excuse me for interrupting you and coming in so suddenly. They've arrested Lucio! I'd just heard the news from a friend when this paper arrived. He's in prison. It's that Genaro Rodas' doing! What a man! I've been worrying my head off the whole blessed evening! Every few moments my heart was going pom-pom, pom-pom, pom-pom. That fellow went and told them it was you and Lucio who carried off the young lady from her house."

The favourite could do nothing to prevent the catastrophe. A handful of words had been enough to cause the explosion. He and Camila and their unlucky love affair had been sent sky-high in a second, in less than a second. When Angel Face began taking stock of the situation, Camila was lying face downwards on the bed, weeping inconsolably; the innkeeper was still describing the abduction in detail, without the smallest idea that she was precipitating a whole little world into the abyss; and as for him, he felt as if he were being buried alive with his eyes open.

After crying for some time, Camila got up like a sleep-walker and asked the barkeeper for a wrap so that she could go out.

"And if you're really a gentleman," she said, turning to Angel Face, when the woman had handed her a shawl, "please take me to my Uncle Juan's house."

The favourite wanted to say what could not be said: words inexpressible by the lips, but which dance in the eyes of those whose dearest hopes have been frustrated by fate.

"Where's my hat?" he asked, his voice hoarse with anxious swallowing.

And before leaving he turned, hat in hand, for a last look at the inn room which had just seen the shipwreck of his dreams.

"But I'm afraid," he objected as he was just going out, "I'm afraid it may be too late."

"If we were going to a strange house it would be, but we're going to my house; any of my uncles' houses are home to me."

Angel Face held her back gently by the arm, and, as if wrenching the words from himself by force, told her the brutal truth:

"You mustn't think of your Uncle Juan's house any more; he doesn't want to hear anything about you, or the general, he disowns him as a brother. He told me so today."

"But you said just now that you hadn't seen them, that you'd only made an appointment to go! What am I to think? You forget what you told me a moment ago and say dreadful things about my uncle, so as to keep me a prisoner here in this inn and prevent my escaping! You say my uncle and aunt didn't want to hear anything about us, that they wouldn't take me into their house? Well, you must be mad. Come there with me and I'll prove the contrary to you!"

"I'm not mad. You must believe me. I'd give my life to prevent exposing you to humiliation, and if I lied it was because—I don't know. I think I lied out of tenderness to you, to spare you the pain you're feeling now as long as I could. I meant to go back tomorrow and renew my entreaties, pull some other string, beg them not to abandon you in the street; but that's impossible now that you're going away. That's impossible now."

The brightly lit streets seemed lonelier than ever. The innkeeper followed them outside holding the candle that had been burning in front of the Virgin, to light their first steps. The wind blew it out; the little flame seemed to cross itself as it died.

CHAPTER XVIII

Knocking

RAT-TAT-TAT! Rat-tat-tat!

The sound of knocking ran through the house like an exploding squib, waking the dog, which instantly began to bark in the direction of the street. The noise had burnt into its dreams. Camila turned to look at Angel Face—she felt safe here in the doorway of her Uncle Juan's house—and said to him proudly:

"He's barking because he doesn't recognise me! Ruby! Ruby!" she cried to the dog, but it went on barking. "Ruby! Ruby! It's me! Don't you know me, Ruby? Run and get them to come and open the door."

And turning to Angel Face again:

"We must just wait a moment!"

"Yes, yes, don't worry about me. We'll wait."

He spoke disconnectedly, like someone who has lost everything and is indifferent to everything.

"Perhaps they haven't heard; we must knock louder."

And she raised and let fall the knocker a good many times; it was a brass knocker in the shape of a hand.

"The servants must be asleep; they've had plenty of time to come to the door! My father used to sleep badly and he was quite right when he said, after a bad night, 'Oh, if I could only sleep like a servant!' "

Ruby gave the only sign of life in the whole house. His barking came sometimes from the hall, sometimes from the patio. He rushed tirelessly to and fro as the blows from the knocker fell like stones into the silence, tightening Camila's throat with anxiety.

"It's very odd!" she remarked, without leaving the door. "They really must be asleep. I'll knock harder still and see if that'll bring them."

Rat-tat-tat-tat! Rat-tat-tat-tat!

"Now they'll come. They can't have heard before."

"The neighbours are going to be the first to come!" said Angel

Face, for although they could see nothing in the mist, they heard the sound of doors opening.

"There can't be anything wrong, can there?"

"Oh no! Knock, knock, don't worry!"

"Let's wait a moment and see if they're coming now."

And Camila began to count in her head to pass the time: one, two, three, four, five, six, seven, eight, nine, ten, eleven, twelve, thirteen, fourteen, fifteen, sixteen, seventeen, eighteen, nineteen, twenty, twenty-one, twenty-two, twenty-three, twenty-three, twenty-three . . . twe-nty-four . . . twe-nty-five . . ."

"They're not coming!"

"Twenty-six, twenty-seven, twenty-eight, twenty-nine, thir-ty, thirty-one, thirty-two, thirty-three, thirty-four, thirty-five," she was terrified of reaching fifty, "thirty-six . . . thirty-seven . . . thirty-seven, thirty-eight."

Suddenly, without knowing why, she realised that what Angel Face had told her about her Uncle Juan was true, and seized with anguish and alarm she knocked again and again. Rat-tat-tat! She wouldn't let go of the knocker. Rat-tat-tat-tat! It's impossible! Rat-tat-tattattattattattattattattat.

She got the same reply as before: the dog's ceaseless barking. What could she have done, unknown to herself, to prevent them opening the door to her? She knocked again. She put fresh hope into every blow of the knocker. What would become of her if they left her in the street? The mere thought made her strength fail her. She knocked and knocked. She knocked furiously, as if she were hammering away at an enemy's head. Her feet felt heavy, her mouth had a bitter taste, her tongue was rough as a dish-cloth and her teeth tingled with fear.

There was the creak of an opening window and she thought she heard voices. Her whole body came to life. They were coming at last, thank God! She was glad to be leaving this man whose black eyes sparkled with diabolical fire like a cat's—this individual who repelled her in spite of his angelic beauty. During this brief instant, the world of the house and the world of the street, separated from one another by the door, brushed against one another like two extinct stars.

A house makes it possible to eat one's bread in privacy—and bread eaten in privacy is sweet, it teaches one wisdom—a house enjoys the safety of permanence and of being socially approved.

it is like a family portrait with the father wearing his best tie, the mother displaying her finest jewels and the children's hair brushed with real eau de Cologne. The street, on the other hand, is an unstable, dangerous, adventurous world, false as a looking-glass—the public laundry of all the dirty linen in the neighbourhood.

How often she had played in that doorway as a child! How many times too, while her father and Uncle Juan talked business just before they parted, she had amused herself staring up at the eaves of the neighbouring houses, silhouetted like scaly backbones against the blue sky.

"Didn't you hear them come to that window? Surely you did? But they don't open the door. Or—can we have mistaken the house? That would be funny!"

And letting go the knocker she stepped down from the pavement to look at the front of the house. She had made no mistake. It was indeed her Uncle Juan's house. "Juan Canales, Engineer," said a metal plate on the door. She screwed up her face like a child's and burst into tears. Her tears ran down like galloping horses, bringing with them from the innermost recesses of her brain the sombre thought that Angel Face had spoken the truth as they left the Two-Step Tavern. She didn't want to believe it even though it was true.

The streets were swathed in mist, a mist which smelt of verdure and stuccoed the houses in pale greenish cream.

"Please come with me to see my other uncles. We'll go and see my Uncle Luis first, shall we?"

"Wherever you say."

"Then come along." The tears were falling from her eyes like rain. "They don't want to let me in here."

They set off. At every step she turned her head—she couldn't give up hope that they would open the door at the last moment. Angel Face walked in gloomy silence. He would go and see Don Juan Canales again; such outrageous behaviour could not be left unavenged. The dog's barks were still heard, growing more distant with every step. Soon this last comfort vanished. Even the dog was now inaudible. Opposite the Mint they met a drunken postman, throwing his letters into the street as he went along like a sleepwalker. He could hardly stand. Every now and then he raised his arms in the air and burst into a cackle like a farmyard fowl, as he struggled to disentangle the buttons of his uniform from the streams of his saliva. Camila and Angel Face, moved by an identical impulse, began to pick up the letters and put them in his bag, at the same time advising him not to throw them away again.

"Tha-ank you; tha-ank you ve-ry much!" he enunciated carefully, leaning against the wall of the Mint. Then, when the letters were all back in his bag and they had left him, he moved on again, singing:

> To get up to heaven
> You must have
> a tall ladder and
> also a little one!

And half-singing, half-talking, he began on another tune:

> Ascend, ascend
> Oh Virgin to heaven,
> ascend, ascend,
> you will ascend to your kingdom.

"When Saint John gives the signal, I, Gup-Gup-Gumercindo Solares, will stop being a postman, will stop being a postman, will stop being a postman . . ."

And then, singing again:

> When I die
> Who will bury me?
> Only the Sisters
> Of Charity!

"Oh, you're no good, you're no good, you're no good!"

He staggered away into the mist. He was a little man with a big head. His uniform was too big for him, and his cap too small.

Meanwhile Don Juan Canales had been doing his utmost to get in touch with his brother José Antonio. The telephone exchange wouldn't answer and he began to be sick of the noise of the handle as he wound it. At last a sepulchral voice answered.

127

He asked for Don José Antonio Canales' house, and contrary to his expectations at once heard the voice of his eldest brother come over the line.

"Yes, yes, it's Juan speaking . . . I thought you didn't recognise me . . . Well, look here . . . the girl and that fellow, yes, of course, of course . . . certainly . . . yes, yes . . . what d'you say? No! We didn't let them in! The very idea! And no doubt they went straight to you from here . . . What? What's that? Just as I thought. We were trembling in our shoes by the time they left. The same with you? And it's not good for your wife to be alarmed; my wife wanted to go to the door, but I wouldn't let her. Naturally! Naturally! That's obvious! Yes, and have all the neighbourhood up in arms! Yes, indeed. And even worse here. They must have been furious. And I suppose they went to Luis after you? No? Oh well, they will . . ."

Beginning as a faint pallor, rapidly brightening to a subdued lemon colour, then to orange, and then to the red of a newly-lit fire mixed with the dull gold of the first flames, the dawn surprised them in the street as they came away from knocking in vain on Don José Antonio's front door.

At every step Camila kept repeating:

"I'll manage somehow!"

Her teeth were chattering with cold. Her large tearful eyes gazed at the dawn with unconscious bitterness. She walked uncertainly like someone pursued by fate and unaware of what she was doing.

The birds were greeting the dawn in the public parks and in the little patio gardens. A celestial concert of musical trills arose into the heavenly blue morning sky, while the roses unfolded and the chiming bells wishing God good morning alternated with the soft thuds of meat being chopped up in the butchers' shops; the rising notes of the cocks, as they beat time with their wings, with the muted report of bread falling into the bakers' trays; and the voices and footsteps of all-night revellers with the noise of a door opening, as some little old woman set off to Communion or a servant hurried out to get bread for a traveller with a train to catch.

Day was dawning . . .

The turkey-buzzards were quarrelling and pecking one another over the corpse of a cat. The dogs were running panting after the bitches, with burning eyes and tongues hanging out. A mongrel limped by with its tail between its legs, turning to cast a sad, frightened look behind it, with teeth bared. The dogs left Niagara-like patterns along all the walls and doors.

Day was dawning . . .

The parties of Indians who swept the central streets of the town at nights were returning home, one after another, like phantoms dressed in serge, laughing and talking in a language which sounded like a cicada's song in the morning silence. They carried their brooms under their arms like umbrellas. Teeth as white as almond paste in copper faces. Bare feet. Rags. Sometimes one of them would stop at the edge of the pavement and blow his nose by squeezing it between thumb and forefinger and leaning forward. They all took their hats off as they passed a church door.

Day was dawning . . .

Inaccessible monkey-puzzle trees, like green spiders-webs thrown out to catch the disappearing stars. Crowds going to Communion. Whistle of railway engines from afar.

La Masacuata was delighted to see them come back together. She hadn't been able to sleep a wink all night for worrying, and she was on the point of setting off for the prison with Lucio Vasquez's breakfast.

Angel Face said goodbye to Camila, who was weeping over the unbelievable misfortune that had befallen her.

"I'll see you soon," he said without knowing why; there was nothing more for him to do here.

And as he went out he felt his eyes fill with tears for the first time since his mother's death.

CHAPTER XIX

Accounts and Chocolate

THE Judge Advocate General finished drinking his chocolate with rice, tipping the cup up twice so as to drain it to the dregs; then he wiped his greyish moustache on the sleeve of his shirt, and moving closer to the lamp, peered into the bowl to see if it was really empty.

It was impossible to say, when he had taken off his collar, whether this Bachelor of Law was a man or a woman as he sat there amongst his official papers and his grimy law books, silent and ugly, short-sighted and greedy, like a tree made of official stamped paper—a tree whose roots drew their nourishment from all social classes down to the most humble and poverty-stricken.

When he looked up from the chocolate bowl which he had been exploring with his fingers to see if there was any left, he saw the servant come in at the only door of his study—a spectral figure dragging her feet slowly one after the other, one after the other, as if her shoes were too large for her.

"You don't mean to say you've drunk your chocolate already?"

"Yes, and God bless you for it, it was delicious! I always love feeling the last of it slip down my gullet."

"Where did you put the cup?" asked the servant, hunting about amongst the books which cast a shadow on the table.

"Over there! Can't you see it?"

"And while I remember it, just look at those drawers full of official stamped paper! Tomorrow if you like I'll go out and see if I can sell it."

"Well be careful not to let anyone know. People are so malicious."

"I wasn't born yesterday! There must be more than four hundred sheets at twenty-five centavos there, and two hundred at fifty. I was counting them while my iron was heating up only this afternoon."

A loud knock on the street door made her break off.

"What a way to knock! The fools!" grumbled the Judge Advocate.

"Yes they always knock like that. Who can it be this time? I often hear them right over in the kitchen."

She was on her way to see who was at the door as she said these last words. The poor creature looked like an umbrella, with her small head and long faded skirts.

"I'm not at home!" shouted the Judge Advocate General. "Wait a moment. Better go to the window . . ."

After a few moments the old woman returned, still with dragging feet, and handed him a letter.

"They're waiting for an answer."

The Judge Advocate tore open the envelope crossly, glanced at the little card inside it, and said in a milder tone:

"Say I've received the note!"

She went off, with dragging feet, to give the message to the boy who had brought it, afterwards shutting and fastening the window.

It was some time before she returned; she was seeing that the doors were locked. She had not yet taken away the dirty chocolate cup.

Meanwhile, her master was lolling in an armchair, carefully re-reading the little card he had just received, down to the last full-stop and comma. It was from a colleague who was making him a proposition.

"Concepcion Gold-Tooth," wrote the lawyer Vidalitas, "a friend of the President's and proprietress of a well-known brothel, came to see me this morning at my office to tell me that she had seen a pretty young woman in the Casa Nueva prison who would do for her establishment. She offers 10,000 pesos for her. As I know the prisoner is held on your orders, I'm writing to ask if it would be inconvenient for you to accept this small sum and hand over the woman to my client."

"If there's nothing more you want, I'll go to bed."

"No, nothing, goodnight."

"Goodnight. May the souls in Purgatory rest in peace!"

As the servant went away with dragging feet, the Judge Advocate was running over the sum he would get from the proposed transaction, figure by figure—one, nought, nought, nought—ten thousand pesos!

The old woman reappeared:

"I forgot to tell you that the priest sent to say he'll be saying Mass earlier than usual tomorrow."

"Ah yes! Tomorrow's Saturday. Call me when the bells start ringing, will you? Because I got no sleep last night and I may not wake."

"Very well, I'll wake you."

So saying she went slowly away with dragging feet. But she was soon back again. She had forgotten to carry away the dirty cup to the sink. She was already undressed when she remembered. "How lucky I remembered," she muttered to herself. "Just supposing I hadn't!" She struggled into her shoes. "Just supposing I hadn't." And she ended up with: "Well, thank God I did!" muffled by a sigh. If she hadn't been incapable of leaving a piece of crockery unwashed she would have been in bed by now.

The Judge Advocate was unaware of the old woman's final entry and exit; he was too deeply absorbed in reading his latest masterpiece: the indictment concerning General Eusebio Canales' escape. There were four accused: Fedina de Rodas, Genaro Rodas, Lucio Vasquez, and—he passed his tongue over his lips, for he had a score to settle with the last of the four—Miguel Angel Face.

The abduction of the general's daughter was like the black cloud expelled by a cuttlefish when attacked—merely a ruse to deceive the watchful authorities, he reflected. Fedina Rodas' statement proved this conclusively. The house was empty when she arrived there in search of the general at six in the morning. Her statement had made an impression of truth on him from the first, and if he put on the screw a little it was just to make quite certain: what she said convicted Angel Face irrefutably. The house was already empty by six o'clock, and since it appeared from the information given by the police that the general arrived home exactly at midnight, it followed that the wanted man must have escaped at two in the morning while the other was making a pretence of carrying off his daughter.

What a disillusionment for the President when he discovered that his most trusted confidant had arranged and supervised the flight of one of his bitterest enemies! What would he do when he learned that the intimate friend of Colonel Parrales Sonriente was concerned in the flight of one of his assassins?

Although he knew them by memory, he read and re-read all the articles relating to accomplices in the military statute-book, and his basilisk eyes shone with pleasure to find in every other line of this legal volume the following little phrase: "pain of death" or else its variant "capital punishment".

"Ah, Don Miguelin Miguelito, at last I have you in my power and for just as long as I want! When you insulted me yesterday at the Palace I never thought we should meet again so soon! And there will be endless turns of the screw of my vengeance I promise you!"

With his thoughts inflamed by the idea of revenge, and his heart a ball of cold steel, he went up the steps of the Palace at eleven o'clock next morning. He was carrying his indictment and a warrant for the arrest of Angel Face.

"Look here, Mr Judge Advocate," said the President after the facts had been set before him, "I must ask you to drop this case and listen to me: neither the Señora de Rodas nor Miguel is guilty; you must set the woman free and countermand the arrest. It is you who are the guilty ones, you fools! Government servants indeed! You are servants in no sense of the word! What use are you? None whatever! At the first sign of an attempt at flight the police should have riddled General Canales with bullets. Those were their orders! But the police can't see an open house without their fingers itching to loot it! It's your contention that Angel Face played a part in Canales' escape? He was not planning his escape but his death. But the police are such a lot of officious fools . . . you can go. And as to the other two accused men, Vasquez and Rodas, they can take what's coming to them. They're a pair of ruffians, especially Vasquez who knows more about the affair than he has any right to. You can go."

CHAPTER XX

Wolves of the Same Pack

ALL Genaro Rodas' tears had not been enough to wash away his recollection of the expression in the dying Zany's eyes, and he now stood before the Judge Advocate General with hanging head, his last spark of courage destroyed by his family misfortunes and the despondency into which loss of liberty casts even the most hardened. The Judge Advocate gave orders for his handcuffs to be removed, and told him to come closer in the tone of voice used to servants.

"My boy," he said, after a silence so long that it amounted to an accusation, "I know everything, and I'm only questioning you because I want to hear from your own lips how this beggar died in the Cathedral Porch."

"What happened . . ." began Genaro precipitately, and then stopped, as if afraid of what he was about to say.

"Yes, what happened . . .?"

"Oh, Señor, for the love of God don't do anything to me! Oh no, Señor, I'll tell you the truth but don't do anything to me, for mercy's sake, Señor!"

"Don't be afraid, my boy. The law may treat hardened criminals severely, but not a good chap like you. Stop worrying and tell me the truth."

"Oh I'm so afraid you'll do something to me!"

He writhed in a supplicating manner as he spoke, as if to defend himself from some threat floating in the air around him.

"No, no, come along now!"

"What happened? It was that night—you know the one—the night I'd arranged to meet Lucio Vasquez by the Cathedral and I went up through the native quarter. You see, Señor, I wanted a job and this Lucio had told me he could get me one in the Secret Police. We met, as I say, and it was 'How goes it?' and this and that; then this fellow asked me to have a drink in the bar a little way beyond the Plaza de Armas, called The Lion's Awakening.

But one drink turned into two, three, four, five drinks, and to make a long story short . . ."

"Yes, yes," agreed the Judge Advocate, turning to look at the freckled clerk who was taking down the accused man's statement.

"Well then, you see, it turned out he hadn't managed to get me the job in the Secret Police. Then I said it didn't matter. Then— oh yes, I remember, he paid for the drinks. And then the two of us went out again to the Cathedral Porch, where Lucio had to go on duty, so he told me, and keep an eye open for a dumb chap with rabies, who had to be shot. So I said to him: 'I'm off!' When I got to the Porch, I was a bit behind him. He crossed the road slowly, but when he reached the entrance to the Porch he came running out again. I ran after him, thinking someone was chasing us. Vasquez caught hold of something which was up against the wall—it was this dumb chap, who began yelling as if the wall had fallen on top of him when he felt himself caught. Then Vasquez pulled out his revolver and never said a word but let him have it, and then again. Oh no, Señor, I wasn't the guilty one; don't do anything to me, I didn't kill him! Just from looking for a job, Señor—you see what happened? I'd better have stayed a carpenter. Whatever got into me to want to be a policeman?"

Once again the Judge Advocate's cold gaze seemed to meet Rodas full in the eye. Without changing his expression, the Judge Advocate silently pressed a bell. Footsteps were heard and several gaolers preceded by a chief warder appeared at the door.

"Warder, see that this man gets two hundred lashes, will you?"

The Judge Advocate's voice did not change in the very smallest degree as he gave the order; it was as if a bank manager had given instructions for two hundred pesos to be paid to one of his clients.

Rodas did not understand. He raised his head and looked at the barefooted myrmidons who were waiting for him. And he understood still less when he saw their calm impassive faces devoid of any trace of surprise. The clerk turned his freckled countenance and expressionless eyes towards him. The warder said something to the Judge Advocate. The Judge Advocate said something to the warder. Rodas was deaf. Rodas understood nothing. But he felt as if he was going to shit in his trousers when the warder shouted to him to go into the next room, a long hall with a vaulted roof, and gave him a brutal shove as he came within reach.

When the other prisoner, Lucio Vasquez, came into the room, the Judge Advocate was still fulminating against Rodas.

"It's no use treating that sort well! What they need is the stick and then some more of the stick!"

Although Vasquez felt he was among his own sort, he didn't trust them an inch, especially when he heard this remark. It was too serious a matter to have had a hand in General Canales' flight, even against his will—and what a fool he had been!

"Your name?"

"Lucio Vasquez."

"You were born where?"

"Here."

"In prison?"

"No, of course not: in the capital."

"Married? Single?"

"Single all my life!"

"Answer the questions properly! Profession or occupation?"

"Employed in Government service."

"You were arrested?"

"Yes."

"For what offence?"

"Murder when on patrol."

"Age?"

"I have no age."

"What d'you mean you have no age?"

"I don't know how old I am; but put me down as thirty-five, if I must have an age!"

"What do you know about the murder of the Zany?"

The Judge Advocate General hurled this question at the prisoner point-blank, staring him full in the eye, but contrary to his expectations his words produced no effect on Vasquez's assurance, and he answered quite naturally and almost with satisfaction:

"What I know about the murder of the Zany is that I killed him myself"; and with his hand on his breast he repeated so that there should be no mistake: "I did!"

"Do you take this for some sort of a joke?" roared the Judge Advocate. "Or can you be so ignorant that you don't realise it may cost you your life?"

"Perhaps."

"What d'you mean 'perhaps'?"

For a moment the lawyer didn't know what attitude to take. He was disconcerted by Vasquez's placidity, his high guitar-like voice, his sharp eyes. To gain time he turned to the clerk.

"Write . . ."

And in a tremulous voice he added:

"Write down that Lucio Vasquez states that he murdered the Zany, with Genaro Rodas as accomplice."

"I've written that already," muttered the clerk between his teeth.

"It's clear to me," put in Lucio calmly, and in a slightly bantering tone which made the lawyer bite his lips, "that the Judge Advocate doesn't know much about this affair. What does that statement amount to? Anyone could see that I wouldn't have dirtied my hands for a slobbering idiot like that . . ."

"Show respect for the tribunal, or you'll suffer for it!"

"What I was saying was altogether to the point. I'm saying that I wouldn't have been so daft as to kill that fellow just for the pleasure of killing him, and that I did it because I was obeying the President's explicit orders . . ."

"Silence, you liar! Ah, our task would be easy if . . ."

He left the sentence unfinished, because at this moment the gaolers came in dragging Rodas, with dangling arms, and legs trailing along the floor like a rag doll or Saint Veronica's veil.

"How many did you give him?" the Judge Advocate asked the warder, who was smiling at the clerk, with his whip-lash rolled round his neck like a monkey's tail.

"Two hundred!"

"Well—"

The clerk came to the Judge Advocate's rescue:

"I should give him another two hundred," he muttered, running the words together so that the others shouldn't hear.

The Judge Advocate took his advice:

"Yes, Chief, see that he gets another two hundred while I attend to this fellow."

"What a nerve! That's just what one would expect from someone with a face like an old bicycle seat!" thought Vasquez.

The gaolers retraced their steps dragging their wretched burden and followed by the chief warder. They threw him down on a mattress in the corner where punishment was administered. Four of them held his hands and feet, while the others beat him. The warder kept the count. Rodas shran̄. before the first strokes, but he was at the end of his tether now and could not struggle and howl with pain as he had done when they began beating him a few minutes ago. Beneath the blows of the wet, flexible, greenish-yellow quince twigs the clotted blood oozed out of the wounds left by the first session, which had already begun to dry up. Strangled cries as of an animal dying without being clearly conscious of its pain were his final protest. He buried his face in the mattress, his expression contorted, his hair in confusion. His piercing cries were mingled with the panting of the gaolers, whom the warder punished with his whip for not hitting hard enough.

"Our task would be easy, Lucio Vasquez, if we allowed every citizen who committed a crime to go free if he simply asserted it had been done on the President's orders! What proof have you? The President isn't a madman, to give such an order. Where is the paper showing that he instructed you to treat this poor wretch in such a wicked and cowardly manner?"

Vasquez turned pale and put his trembling hands in his trouser pockets while he searched for an answer.

"When you're before a tribunal you must support your statements with documents, you know; otherwise where should we be? Where is the order you received?"

"Well, you see, I haven't got the order. I gave it back. The President must know that."

"How did that happen? And why did you give it back?"

"Because it said at the bottom that it must be given back after the order was carried out! I wasn't to keep it, you see? I think— you understand—"

"Not a word, not one word more! Trying to humbug me with your big talk about the President! I'm not a schoolboy to believe that kind of foolishness, you blackguard! A person's statement is no proof, except in cases specified in the Legal Code, when a police statement can function as full proof. But I'm not going to give you a lecture on Criminal Law. And that's enough— enough; I've said quite enough . . ."

"Well, if you don't want to believe me, go and ask him; perhaps you'll believe what he tells you. Perhaps I wasn't with you when the beggars accused—"

"Silence! Or I'll have you beaten till you shut up! I can just see myself going to ask the President! I tell you, Vasquez, that you know a great deal more about the matter than you have any right to, and your head is in danger!"

Lucio bent his head as if guillotined by the Judge Advocate General's words. The wind was roaring angrily against the windows.

CHAPTER XXI

Vicious Circle

ANGEL FACE tore off his collar and tie in a fury. Nothing could be stupider, he thought, than the little explanations people invented for the behaviour of others. The behaviour of others . . . of others! Sometimes their criticism would amount to no more than an acrimonious muttering. Anything in one's favour was suppressed, the rest exaggerated. What a lot of filth! It was as painful as a brush on a sore place. And a veiled reproach, disguised as ordinary friendly or even charitable comment, could wound one more deeply still, like a brush with extra fine hairs. Even the servants! To hell with all tittle-tattlers!

A tug, and all the buttons flew off his shirt. He had ripped it down the front. It was as if he had torn open his breast. His servants had been telling him in great detail what people were saying about his love affair. Men who are reluctant to marry for fear of sharing their house with a woman who repeats what everyone says about them except the good things, like a schoolgirl on prize day, end by hearing it all from the lips of their servants, as Angel Face had done.

He drew the curtains of his room before finally taking off his shirt. He badly needed sleep or (at least) that his room should appear to exclude the coming day—a day, as he told himself bitterly, which could not fail to be as bad as the last.

"Sleep!" he repeated as he sat on the edge of his bed, unbuttoning his trousers, with no shoes or socks on and his shirt open. "Oh, but what an idiot! I've not taken off my jacket!"

Walking on his heels with his toes curled up so as to keep the soles of his feet away from the cold concrete floor, he succeeded in hanging his coat on the back of a chair, and then returned to his bed by means of a series of rapid, chilly little hops on one foot like a heron. Then bang! down he came, defeated by this brute of a floor. The legs of his trousers revolved in the air like the hands of an enormous clock. The floor seemed to be made of ice rather than concrete. How horrible! Ice with salt on it. Ice made of tears. He jumped into bed as if from an iceberg on to a lifeboat. He wanted to escape from everything that had happened, and as he fell on the bed he imagined that it was an island, a white island surrounded by semi-darkness, and by motionless pulverised events. He was going to forget, to sleep, to cease to exist. He was tired of arguments that could be assembled and taken to pieces like the parts of a machine. To the devil with the tortuosities of common sense! Better far unreasoning sleep, that gentle stupor, at first blue in colour, then green and afterwards black, which distils itself from the eyes throughout the organism and annihilates the personality. Oh, desire! The desired object is at once possessed and not possessed. It is like a gold nightingale, caged by our ten joined fingers. Integral, restorative sleep, free from intrusions, entering through the mirrors of the eyes and leaving by the windows of the nose—that was what he longed for, sleep as relaxed as that of the old days. Soon he became aware that sleep was high above him, above the roof of his house, in the clear light of day—that unforgettable day. He turned on his face. No use. On his left side, to quiet the beating of his heart. On his right side. It was all the same. A hundred hours separated him from the perfect sleep of the days when he went to bed free from sentimental preoccupations. His instinct accused him of suffering these torments because he had not taken Camila by force.

The dark side of life looms so close at times that suicide seems the only means of escaping it. "I shall cease to exist!" he thought. And trembled inwardly. He touched one foot with the other. He was troubled by the absence of nails on the cross from which he was hanging. "There's something about drunkards walking that reminds one of hanged men," he thought, "and hanged men remind one of drunkards when they kick their legs or swing in the wind." His instinct accused him. A drunkard's sex. A hanged man's sex. And you, Angel Face, are no better! . . .

"An animal makes no mistake in its sexual reckonings," he thought. "We piss children into the graveyard. The trumpets of Judgement Day—very well, it won't be a trumpet. Golden scissors will cut through the continuous stream of children. We men are like pigs' tripes stuffed with mincemeat by a demon butcher to make sausages. And when I mastered my own nature so as to save Camila from my desire, I left a part of myself unstuffed; that's why I feel empty, uneasy, angry, ill, caught in a trap. Woman is the mincemeat into which man stuffs himself like a pig's tripes for his own gratification. What vulgarity!"

The sheets clung to him like skirts. Skirts unendurably soaked with sweat.

The Tree of Dreadful Night must feel pain in its leaves. "Oh my poor head!" The liquid sound of the carillon. Bruges, the city of the dead. Corkscrews of silk round his neck. "Never..." But there's a phonograph somewhere in the neighbourhood. I've never heard it. I didn't know it existed. First news of it. They've got a dog in the house at the back. There must be two. But here they have a phonograph. Only one. "Between the phonograph's trumpet here, and the dogs in the house at the back listening to their master's voice, is my house, my head, myself. To be close and to be far away is to be neighbours. That's the worst of being someone's neighbour. But as for them they've got work to do. They play the phonograph, and speak ill of everyone. I can imagine what they say about me. What a couple of dried-up aniseeds! They can say what they like about me, what do I care? but about her—! If I can prove that they've said as much as a single word against her I'll make them members of the Young Liberals. I've often threatened to do it but today I think I will. That'll embitter their lives! But perhaps I won't; they're not worth it. I can hear them saying everywhere: 'He kidnapped the poor girl after midnight, he took her to an inn belonging to a procuress and violated her; the secret police guarded the door so that no one should come in!' They'll imagine the scene with me undressing her, tearing her clothes, and Camila like a bird caught in a trap with trembling flesh and feathers. 'And he took her by force,' they'll say, 'without caressing her, and with his eyes shut as if he were committing a crime or swallowing a purge.' If they only knew that it wasn't like that at all, and that here I am half repenting of my chivalrous behaviour! If they realised that everything they say is false. It's the girl they'd really like to be imagining. Imagining her with me, with me and with themselves. Themselves undressing her, themselves doing what they think I did. The young Liberals are too good for such a pair of angels. I must think of something worse. The ideal punishment, since they are both bachelors—yes they really are old bachelors—would be to saddle them with two of those women who hang round the President. That would do fine! But one of them is pregnant. That doesn't matter. Better still. When the President arranges a marriage it doesn't do to look at the bride's belly. So let them marry out of fear, let them marry . . ."

He curled himself up in bed with his arms between his legs, and buried his head in his pillows, seeking for some respite from the agonising lightning-flashes of his ideas. There were physical shocks in store for him in the cold corners of the bed, giving him temporary relief from the reckless flight of his thoughts. In the end he pursued these welcome if painful sensations even further by stretching his legs outside the sheet till they touched the brass bar at the foot of the bed. Then he gradually opened his eyes. As he did so he seemed to be breaking a fine seam between his lashes. He was suspended from his eyes; they were fixed to the ceiling like cupping-glasses; he was weightless as the shadows, his bones flaccid, his ribs reduced to cartilage and his head to putty. A cotton-wool hand was going through the motions of knocking in the semi-darkness. A sleep-walker's cotton-wool hand . . . The houses are made of knockers. The towns are forests of trees made of knockers . . .

Leaves of sound fell to the ground as she knocked. The tree-trunk of the door stood intact after the leaves of intact sound had fallen. There was nothing for her to do but knock . . . there was nothing for them to do but open the door . . . But they didn't open. She might have knocked down the door. Blow after blow, she might have knocked down the door; blow after blow, and then nothing; she might have knocked down the house . . .

"Who is it? What?"

"They have just brought the notification of a death."

"Yes, but don't take it to him, because he must be asleep. Put it here on his desk."

" 'Señor Joaquin Ceron died last night, fortified by the last Sacraments. His wife, children and other relatives have the sad duty of informing you of this fact, and beg you to commend his soul to God and attend the obsequies at the General Cemetery today at 4 p.m. The mourners will meet at the door of the cemetery. House of the deceased: Callejon del Carrocero.' "

He had involuntarily listened to one of his servants reading aloud the announcement of Don Joaquin Ceron's death.

He disengaged one of his arms from the sheets and folded it

under his head. Don Juan Canales was marching through his brain dressed in feathers. He had snatched up four hearts made of wood and four Sacred Hearts, and was playing on them like castanets. And in his occiput he could feel Doña Judith, with her cyclopean breasts imprisoned in her creaking corsets made of metal thread and sand, and her hair dressed in the Pompeian style with a magnificent comb in it which made her look like a dragon. He was seized with cramp in the arm which was pillowing his head, and he stretched it cautiously, like a garment with a scorpion on it . . .

Cautiously . . .

A lift full of ants was ascending towards his shoulder. A lift full of magnetic ants was descending towards his elbow. The cramp went through the tube of his forearm and vanished among the shadows. His hand was a jet of water—a jet of double fingers. He felt ten thousand finger-nails gush to the floor.

"Poor little girl, knocking and knocking and then nothing . . . they are brutes, obstinate mules; if they open the door I'll spit in their faces. As sure as three and two make five . . . and five ten . . . and nine, nineteen, I'll spit in their faces. At first she knocked cheerfully, but in the end she seemed to be hitting the ground with a pick. She wasn't knocking, she was digging her own grave. What a desolate awakening! I'll go and see her tomorrow if I can. On the pretext of bringing her some news of her father. Oh, if only I could get news of him today. I could— although she may not believe what I say . . ."

"I do believe what you say! I'm convinced, I'm absolutely convinced that my uncles have disowned my father and told you that they never want to set eyes on me in their houses again." So Camila was thinking as she lay in bed with a pain in her side in La Masacuata's house, while in the tavern itself, separated from the bedroom by a partition made of old planks, sailcloth and bundles, the customers were discussing the events of the day between glasses: the general's flight, the abduction of his daughter, the favourite's activities. The barkeeper pretended not to hear anything they said but did not miss a word of it.

A sudden violent wave of faintness carried Camila far away from this pestilent crew. A sensation of falling vertically and in silence. After hesitating whether to cry out—which would be rash—or not cry out, and perhaps lose consciousness completely, she decided to cry out. Then a feeling of cold, as from the feathers of dead birds, enveloped her. La Masacuata ran to her at once—what had happened?—and as soon as she saw her lying there as green as bottle-glass, with her arms as stiff as broomsticks, her jaws clenched and her eyes closed, she hurriedly took a mouthful of brandy from the nearest bottle and sprayed her face with it. She was so worried that she didn't hear her customers leave. She implored the Virgin of Chichinquira and all the saints not to let the girl die here in her house.

"When we parted this morning, what I said made her cry. What else could she do? When something that seems impossible comes true, one cries either from joy or sorrow . . ."

So thought Angel Face as he lay in bed, half asleep, half awake, aware of an angelic bluish conflagration, and gradually floating, asleep now, with the drift of his own thoughts, disembodied, without shape, like a warm current of air moved by his own breath . . .

As his body sank into nothingness, Camila alone remained—tall, sweet and cruel as a cross in a graveyard.

The god of Sleep, who sails the dark seas of reality, took Miguel on board one of his many boats. Invisible hands dragged him away from the gaping jaws of events—the hungry waves quarrelling fiercely over morsels of their victims.

"Who is it?" asked Sleep.

"Miguel Angel Face," replied his invisible henchmen. Their impalpable hands emerged from the blackness like white shadows.

"Take him to the boat of . . ." Sleep hesitated. ". . . of lovers who have given up hope of loving and resigned themselves to being loved."

And Sleep's men were obediently conveying him to this boat, moving across the blanket of unreality which covers life's daily happenings with a fine dust, when a sudden noise wrenched him from their grasp like a clutching hand . . .

The bed . . .

The servants . . .

No; the note, no. A child!

Angel Face rubbed his eyes and raised his head in terror. Two yards from his bed stood a child, so short of breath that he couldn't speak. At last he said:

"The innkeeper . . . sent me . . . to tell you . . . to go there . . . because . . . the young lady . . . is very ill."

If he had heard these words from the President himself the favourite could not have dressed himself so quickly. He rushed out into the street wearing the first hat he could seize from the rack, with his shoes unlaced and his tie untidily knotted.

"Who is it?" asked Sleep. His men had just fished up a fading rose from the dirty waters of life.

"Camila Canales," they replied.

"Very well, put her in the boat for unhappy lovers, if there's room . . ."

"What do you think, doctor?" Angel Face's voice had softened to a paternal tone. Camila was very seriously ill.

"I think the fever is likely to increase. She is developing pneumonia . . ."

CHAPTER XXII

The Living Tomb

HER son had ceased to exist. With the automaton-like movements of those who are losing their sanity in the chaos of their collapsing lives, Niña Fedina lifted the corpse to her fevered face. It weighed no more than a dried husk. She kissed it. She stroked it. Suddenly she went down on her knees—a pale yellow gleam was filtering in under the door—and bent down close to the crack through which this bright streak of dawn light was coming at ground level, to get a better view of all that was left of her little one.

With his little face puckered like the surface of a scar, two black circles round his eyes and clay-coloured lips, he looked more like a swaddled foetus than a child of several months old. She took him hastily away from the light, pressing him against her swollen breasts. She reproached God in an inarticulate language made up of words and tears mixed; at moments her heart stopped beating and she would stammer out her grief in lament upon lament, like the hiccup of a dying person. "My son . . . son . . . son !"

The tears rolled down her expressionless face. She wept until she almost lost consciousness, forgetting her husband who had been threatened with death by starvation in prison if she didn't confess; ignoring her own physical pain, her ulcerated hands and breasts, her burning eyes, her bruised back; setting aside all worries about her neglected business; completely stunned and stupefied. And when her tears dried up and she could weep no more, she felt that she had become her son's tomb, that he was again enclosed in her womb, that his last endless sleep was hers. For an instant a sharp joy cut into the eternity of her suffering. The idea of being her son's tomb was like soothing balm to her heart. She felt the joy of Eastern women who are buried with their lovers. And a greater joy still, for she was not being buried with her son ; she was his living tomb, his last cradle, the maternal lap, and they would wait together, closely united, until they were summoned to their God. Without drying her tears she tidied her hair as if she were getting ready for a party, and crouched in a corner of the cellar with the corpse pressed against her breasts and between her arms and legs.

Tombs do not embrace the dead, therefore she must not kiss him; but they press heavily, heavily upon them, as she was doing. They are stiff corselets of strength and tenderness, forcing the dead to suffer the irritation of worms and the heat of decomposition in silence and without moving. The wavering gleam from the crack under the door would only grow brighter every thousand years. The shadows, pursued by the rising light, clambered slowly up the walls like scorpions. They were walls of bones . . . bones tattoed with obscene drawings. Niña Fedina shut her eyes—tombs are dark inside—and did not utter a word nor a moan—tombs are silent.

It was the middle of the afternoon. A smell of cypresses washed by water from the sky. Swallows. A half moon. The streets were still bathed in sunlight and full of boisterous children. The schools were emptying a river of new lives into the town. Some were playing tag as they came out, zigzagging to and fro like flies. Others made a ring round two of their schoolmates who were attacking each other like fighting-cocks. Bloody noses, snivelling, tears. Some ran along knocking on doors. Others raided the confectioners' shops for treacle toffees, coconut cakes, almond tarts, and meringues, or fell like pirates on baskets of fruits, leaving them like empty dismantled boats. Behind came those who were busy swopping stamps or trying to cut a dash by smoking.

A cab stopped in front of the Casa Nueva and set down three young women and a very stout old one. There was no mistaking what they were from their appearance. The young women were dressed in bright-coloured cotton stuffs, red stockings, yellow shoes with exaggeratedly high heels, skirts above the knee exposing knickers with long, dirty lace flounces, and blouses opening to the navel. Their hair was done in the Louis XV style as it was called, consisting of a large quantity of greasy curls tied on either side with a green or yellow ribbon; and the colour of their cheeks was reminiscent of the red electric lamps over the doors of brothels. The old woman, who was dressed in black with a purple shawl, descended unsteadily from the carriage, clutching at the door with a fat hand thickly covered in diamonds.

"The cab is to wait, isn't it, Niña Chonita?" asked the youngest of the three Graces, raising her shrill voice so that even the stones in the deserted street could hear her.

"Yes, of course, it can wait here," answered the old woman.

And all four went into the Casa Nueva, where the concierge received them warmly.

Some other people were waiting in that inhospitable hall.

"Tell me, Chinta, is the secretary in?" the old woman asked the concierge.

"Yes, Doña Chon, he's just arrived."

"Then tell him, for heaven's sake, that if he'll see me I've brought him a little written order, which is very important to me."

The old woman remained silent while the concierge was away. For persons over a certain age the building still retained the atmosphere of a convent, for before becoming a prison for delinquents it had been a prison of love. Nothing but women. The sweet voices of the Teresian nuns floated down from its great walls like a flight of doves. There were no lilies to be seen, but the light was white, caressing and cheerful, and fasting and sackcloth had been replaced by the thorns of all the tortures that had flourished under the spiders-webs and the sign of the cross.

When the concierge returned, Doña Chon went in to explain her business to the secretary. She had already spoken to the Prison Governor. The Judge Advocate General had given orders that in exchange for ten thousand pesos—but that he did not mention—they should hand over to her the prisoner Fedina de Rodas, who from that moment would become an inmate of The Sweet Enchantment, as Doña Chon Gold-Tooth's brothel was called.

Two knocks echoed like thunder through the cell where the unhappy woman still sat crouched with her child, motionless, her eyes closed, almost without breathing. With a great effort she pretended not to hear. Then the bolts groaned. A prolonged squealing of disused hinges sounded in the silence like a lament. They opened the door and seized her roughly. She shut her eyes tightly so as not to see the light—tombs are dark inside. And so they dragged her away like a blind woman, with her little treasured corpse pressed to her breast. She had been bought like an animal for the basest of trades.

"She's acting dumb!"

"She's shutting her eyes so as not to see us!"

"She's ashamed, that's what it is!"

"Perhaps she doesn't want them to wake her baby!"

Such were the comments of Chon Gold-Tooth and the three Graces during the journey. The cab rumbled along the unsurfaced road, making an infernal noise. The driver, a Spaniard of Quixotic appearance, heaped insults on his horses; they were destined for the bull-ring, for he was a picador. Sitting beside him, Niña Fedina made the short journey from the Casa Nueva to the houses of ill-fame (as in the song) in total ignorance of her surroundings, without moving her eyelids or her lips, but clutching her child to her with all her strength.

While Doña Chon paid off the cab the others helped Fedina to get down and pushed her with friendly hands inside The Sweet Enchantment.

One or two clients, nearly all soldiers, were spending the night in the saloon of the brothel.

"What time is it, you there, eh?" Doña Chon called to the barman as she came in.

One of the soldiers answered:

"Twenty past six, Doña Chompipa."

"So you're here, you old troublemaker, are you? I didn't notice you!"

"And it's twenty five past by this clock," put in the barman.

They were all interested in the new girl. They all wanted to spend the night with her. Fedina still obstinately maintained a tomblike silence, with her child's body clasped in her arms; she kept her eyes shut, she felt cold and heavy as stone.

"Go along," Gold-Tooth said to the three Graces, "take her to the kitchen and get Manuela to give her a bite to eat, and make her tidy herself up a bit."

An artillery captain with pale blue eyes went up to the new girl to feel her legs. But one of the three Graces defended her. Then another soldier put his arms around her as if she had been a palm-tree trunk, rolling his eyes and showing his splendid Indian's teeth, like a dog with a bitch in heat. And afterwards he kissed her, rubbing her icy cheek, salt with dried tears, with his brandy-flavoured lips.

These were good times for both barracks and brothel! The warmth of the whores was a compensation for the cold of the shooting-range.

"Now then, you old trouble-maker, you womaniser, be quiet, will you?" interrupted Doña Chon, putting an end to this indecent behaviour. "Ah well, we'll have to tie you up!"

Fedina didn't defend herself from this lustful manhandling, but contented herself with pressing together her eyelids and lips to protect her tomblike blindness and silence from assault, while she clutched her dead child to her and rocked him in her arms as if he were asleep.

They led her to a little patio, where the afternoon was gradually drowning in a fountain. There was the sound of women moaning, weak voices, whispering of invalids, schoolgirls, prisoners or nuns, affected laughter, harsh little cries and the tread of stockinged feet. Someone threw a pack of cards out of the door of a room, and it fell in a fan on the floor. No one knew who had done it. A woman with dishevelled hair put her head out through a hatch, stared at the cards as if they represented Fate itself, and wiped a tear from her pale cheek.

A red lantern hung over the street door of The Sweet Enchantment. It looked like the inflamed eye of an animal. Men and stones took on a sinister hue. The mystery of the developing-room. Men came to bathe themselves in this red light like victims of smallpox hoping to cure their scars. They exposed their faces to the light shamefacedly, as if they were drinking blood, and afterwards returned to the street lights, to the white light of the municipal lamps and the clear light of their homes, with the uneasy feeling that they had fogged a photograph.

Fedina still took in nothing that was happening around her, but was possessed with the idea that she had no existence except for her child. She kept her eyes and lips more tightly shut than ever, and the little corpse still clutched to her over-full breasts. Her companions did everything they could think of to shake her out of this state on the way to the kitchen.

Manuela Calvario, the cook, had for many years reigned over the region between the coal-bin and the rubbish heap at The Sweet Enchantment; she looked like God the Father without a beard and wearing starched skirts. The flabby jowls of this respectable and gigantic cook were filled with an airy substance which found vent in words as soon as she caught sight of Fedina.

"Another shameless hussy! Well, where did this one come from? And what's that she's holding so tightly?"

The three Graces, not daring to speak though they didn't know why, made the cook understand by signs, such as putting one hand above another to represent bars, that she had come from the prison.

"Dirty bitch!" was the woman's next remark. And after the others had gone she added: "I ought to give you poison instead of food! Here's your snack! Here . . . take that . . . and that!"

And she dealt her several blows on the back with the spit.

Fedina sat down on the ground holding her little corpse, without answering or opening her eyes. She had carried him so long in the same position that she no longer felt his weight. Manuela walked up and down, gesticulating and crossing herself.

In the course of her comings and goings she noticed a bad smell in the kitchen. She returned from the sink carrying a dish. Without more ado she began kicking Fedina and shouting:

"You've got something rotten there and it stinks. Take it away from here! Get rid of it! I won't have it here!"

Her noisy shouts brought Doña Chon to the kitchen, and between them, by main force as if they were breaking the branches of a tree, they succeeded in opening the wretched woman's arms; but when she realised that they were taking away her child she opened her eyes, let out a yell and fell senseless.

"It's the child that stinks! It's dead! How horrible!" exclaimed Doña Manuela. Gold-Tooth was speechless, and while the prostitutes poured into the kitchen she ran to the telephone to inform the authorities. Everyone wanted to see and kiss the child; they covered it in kisses and snatched it from each other's hands and lips. The little wrinkled face of the corpse was masked by the saliva of vice, and it was now beginning to give out a bad smell. There was loud weeping and talk of arrangements for a wake. Major Farfan went to get the authorisation of the police. The largest of the private bedrooms was cleared; they burned incense to remove the smell of stale semen from the hangings; Manuela burned tar in the kitchen, and the child was laid on a black enamel tray, among flowers and linen, where it lay curled up, dry and yellow, like a sarsaparilla seed . . .

It was as if each of them had lost a son that night. Four wax candles were burning. A smell of maize-cakes and brandy, of ailing flesh, of cigarette-ends and wine. A half-drunk woman, with one of her breasts bare, was chewing rather than smoking a cigar, and kept repeating, amid floods of tears:

> Sleep, my little boy,
> My pumpkin-head,
> for if not, the wolf
> will kill you dead!
>
> Sleep, my life,
> for I must go
> to wash your linen
> and sit down to sew!

CHAPTER XXIII

The President's Mail-Bag

(1) The widow Alexandra Bran, domiciled in this town, proprietress of the bedding shop called La Ballena Franca, states that as her business adjoins the Two-Step Tavern she has been in a position to observe several persons who frequent the aforesaid tavern, especially at night, on the Christian pretext of visiting a sick woman. She is bringing these circumstances to the notice of the President because, from the conversations she has heard through the wall, it seems to her that General Eusebio Canales may be hiding in the Tavern, and that the persons who go there are conspiring against the safety of the State and the President's invaluable life.

(2) Soledad Belmares, resident in this town, states: that she now has nothing to eat because she has come to the end of her resources, and since she is a stranger and unknown here no one will lend her money, that in these circumstances she begs the President to set her son Manuel Belmares H. and her brother-in-law Federico Horneros P. at liberty; the Minister of her country can certify that they are not involved in politics, but only came here to earn their living by honest work, their sole offence having been that they accepted a recommendation from General Eusebio Canales to assist them to get work at the railway station.

(3) Colonel Prudencio Perfecto Paz states: that his recent journey to the frontier was undertaken with the object of seeing what was the condition of the land, roads and foot-paths, in order to decide what places should be occupied. He gives a detailed description of a plan of campaign which could be developed at favourable strategic points in case of a revolutionary rising; he confirms the report that men are being enlisted at the frontiers for that purpose and that Juan Leon Parada and others are so engaged, and that they possess by way of arms: hand grenades, machine-guns,

small-bore rifles, dynamite and everything else necessary for mine-laying; and that the revolutionaries have from 25 to 30 armed men who could attack the forces of the Supreme Government at any moment. He has not been able to confirm the report that Canales is their leader, but if that should be the case, they will certainly invade our territory unless diplomatic steps are taken to intern the revolutionaries. He is ready to carry through the invasion announced for the beginning of next month, but he lacks arms for his brigade of riflemen, having nothing else but what is in ammunition dump Cal. 43; and with the exception of a few sick, who are requiring proper treatment, the troops are in good shape and are receiving instruction from six to eight every morning; a head of cattle is provided for their provisions each week, and the signatory has already asked for sacks of sand from the port to build block-houses.

(4) Juan Antonia Mares thanks the President for the interest he was so kind as to show him, in getting his doctors to look after him. He is now ready again for service and begs permission to come to the capital to attend to various matters arising from his special knowledge of the political activities of Abel Carvajal, the lawyer.

(5) Luis Raveles M. states that in view of his illness and lack of means to regain his health he wishes to return to the United States, where he begs for some employment in one of the Consulates of the Republic, not at New Orleans, nor under the same conditions as before, but as a sincere friend of the President's. At the end of last January he was so extremely fortunate as to have his name on the audience list, but when he was in the anteroom and about to enter he noticed a certain air of suspicion on the part of the General Staff, who altered the position of his name on the list, and when his turn arrived an officer took him into a separate room, searched him as if he was an anarchist and told him he was doing so because of information that he had been paid by Abel Carvajal, the lawyer, to assassinate the President. On his return he found his audience had been cancelled, and though he has since done everything possible to speak to the President, in order to tell him certain things which could not be entrusted to paper, he has met with no success.

(6) Nicomedes Aceituno writes stating that on his way back to the capital after one of his frequent journeys on business, he noticed that the poster fastened to the reservoir, on which the President's name appears, had been almost completely destroyed; six letters having been torn away and others damaged.

(7) Lucio Vasquez, detained in the Central Prison by order of the Judge Advocate General, begs for an audience.

(8) Catarino Regisio states: that he is manager of the property "La Tierra" belonging to General Eusebio Canales, and that one day last August the gentleman in question was visited by four friends, to whom he declared (being drunk at the time) that if the revolution should take place he had two battalions at his disposal: one was under the orders of one of themselves, Major Farfan, and the other of a Lieutenant-Colonel whose name was not mentioned. Since the rumours of revolution continue, the signatory is writing to inform the President of this, as he has been unable to do so in person in spite of several requests for an audience.

(9) General Megadeo Rayon forwards a letter received by him from the priest, Antonio Blas Custodio, who states therein that Father Urquijo has been slandering him (on account of his replacing the Father in the parish of San Lucas by order of the Archbishop), and stirring up the Catholic population with his lies, assisted by Doña Arcadia de Ayuso. Since the presence of Father Urquijo, a friend of Abel Carvajal the lawyer, might have serious consequences, the signatory is communicating the facts to the President.

(10) Alfredo Toledano, of this town, states that as he suffers from insomnia and never goes to sleep till late, he surprised one of the President's friends, Miguel Angel Face, knocking violently on the door of the house of Don Juan Canales, brother of the general of the same name who is always criticising the government. He is informing the President in case it may be of interest.

(11) Nicomedes Aceituno, commercial traveller, states that the man who defaced the President's name on the reservoir was

Guillermo Lizazo, the accountant, in a state of intoxication.

(12) Casimiro Rebeco Luna states: that he will shortly have completed two and a half years' detention in the Second Police Station; that as he is poor and has no relatives to intercede on his behalf he begs the President to be so good as to order him to be set at liberty; that the offence of which he is accused is that of having removed the announcement of the President's mother's anniversary from the door of the church where he is sacristan, on the instigation of enemies of the Government; that it is not certain that he did so, and that if he did, it was because he mistook it for another notice, since he cannot read.

(13) Doctor Luis Barreño begs the President's permission to travel abroad for the purpose of study, accompanied by his wife.

(14) Adelaida Peñal, inmate of the brothel called The Sweet Enchantment in this town, wishes to inform the President that Major Modesto Farfan told her when drunk that General Eusebio Canales was the only general worth his salt he had known in the army, and that his disgrace was due to the President's fear of able leaders, but that the revolution would be triumphant in spite of all.

(15) Monica Perdomino, patient in the General Hospital, in bed No. 14 in San Rafael ward, states that her bed being next to that of the patient Fedina Rodas, she has heard the aforesaid patient talking about General Canales in her delirium; that as she was not fully in her right mind she did not understand what the woman said, but that it might be advisable for someone to keep watch and take notes. The signatory sends the President this information out of her humble admiration for his Government.

(16) Tomas Javeli announces his marriage to Señorita Arquelina Suarez, and desires to dedicate it to the President of the Republic.

April 28th.

CHAPTER XXIV

The Whore-House

"Be quiet, will you? Be quiet! What a way to go on! Ever since God's dawn we've had nothing but chatter and jabber; anyone would think you were senseless animals!" cried Gold-Tooth.

Dressed in a black blouse and purple skirt, Her Excellency was digesting her dinner in a leather chair behind the bar counter.

A little while later she said to a copper-skinned servant with smooth, shining hair:

"Pancha, go and tell the women to come here; this'll never do—the clients will be arriving any moment and they ought to be here ready and waiting! God only knows one has to keep on hurrying these girls all the time!"

Two girls came running in on stockinged feet.

"Not so much noise, Consuelo! Oh what pretty little dears! Jesus Maria, just look what games they get up to! And look here, Adelaida—Adelaida, I'm talking to you!—if the Major comes it would be a good idea to take his sword away as security for what he owes us. What does he owe the house, you great ape?"

"Exactly nine hundred, plus the thirty-six I lent him last night," replied the barman.

"A sword isn't worth as much as that; no, not even if it's made of gold; still it's better than a poke in the eye! Adelaida! Am I talking to the wall or to you?"

"I heard you, Doña Chon, I heard," said Adelaida Peñal between bursts of laughter, and went on frolicking with her companion, whom she had hold of by the hair.

The assortment of women provided by The Sweet Enchantment were sitting about on the old divans in silence. Tall, short, fat, thin, old, young, adolescent, meek, farouche; blondes, redheads, brunettes, with small eyes or large eyes, white-skinned, dark-skinned, and mulattas. Though they were all different they seemed alike; they smelt alike—they smelt of men, all of them smelt of men, the acrid smell of stale shellfish. Inside their cheap little cotton chemises their breasts swung to and fro as if they were almost liquid. As they sat lolling with thighs apart, they displayed legs as thin as drain-pipes, bright-coloured garters, and knickers that were either red trimmed with white lace, or pale salmon-pink trimmed with black.

Waiting for the clients made them irritable. They waited like emigrants with animal expressions in their eyes, sitting in huddled groups in front of the mirrors. To avoid getting too fidgety, some slept, some smoked, some ate peppermints, and others counted the spots of fly-dirt on the blue and white paper-chains decorating the ceiling; enemies were quarrelling, friends slowly and immodestly caressing each other.

Nearly all of them had nicknames. A girl with large eyes would be called Codfish; if she was short Little Codfish, and if she was getting on in years and buxom, Big Codfish. A girl with a turn-up nose was Snubby; a brunette, Blackie; a mulatta, Darkie; a girl with slanting eyes, China; a blonde, Sugar; a stammerer, Stutter.

Besides these general appellations there was the Convalescent, the Sow, Big Feet, Honey-tongue, the Monkey, the Tape-worm, the Dove, the Bombshell, No-guts, Deaf-ears.

During the early hours of the night, a few men would come in to amuse themselves for a little by amorous talk, and by kissing and pestering any of the girls who were free. They all had plenty of assurance. Doña Chon would have liked to box their ears for them, for they had committed the crime in her eyes of being poor, but she put up with them in her house instead of sending them packing for the sake of the "queens". Poor queens! They got involved with these men, who exploited them as ponces and cheated them as lovers, out of their craving for affection and to have someone of their own.

Some inexperienced boys would also turn up during the early part of the night. They used to come in trembling all over, hardly able to speak, moving awkwardly like dazzled butterflies, and did not recover until they were out in the street again. Fair game. Docile and up to no tricks. Fifteen years old. "Good night." "Don't forget me." Instead of the guilt and bravado with which they had entered, they left the brothel with a bad taste in their mouths, and that pleasant fatigue that comes from much laughing and repeated tumbles with a woman.

159

Ah, how good it was to be outside that stinking house! They munched the air as if it was new-mown hay and gazed at the stars as though they reflected their own strength.

Afterwards the serious clients began to arrive in relays. A respectable businessman, ardent and pot-bellied, with an astronomical amount of flesh surrounding his thoracic cavity. A shop assistant, who embraced the girls as if measuring cloth by the yard, in contrast to the doctor, who looked as if he were auscultating them. A journalist who always left something behind in pawn, even if it was only his hat. A lawyer who suggested both a cat and a geranium with his air of vulgar and uneasy domesticity. A countryman with milk-white teeth. A round-shouldered civil servant, unattractive to women. A portly tradesman. A workman smelling of sheepskin. A rich man who was always slyly touching his pocket-book or his watch or his rings. A chemist, more taciturn than the hairdresser but less polite than the dentist.

By midnight the room was in a ferment. Men and women were using their mouths to inflame each other's passions. Kisses—lascivious contacts of flesh and saliva—alternated with bites, confidences with blows, smiles with bursts of coarse laughter, and the popping of champagne corks with the popping of bullets, when some blustering individual was present who wanted to cut a dash.

"This is the life!" said an old man with his elbows on a table, his eyes roving here and there, his feet moving restlessly and a network of veins standing out from his burning forehead.

And with mounting excitement he enquired of one of his companions in debauchery:

"Can I go with that woman over there?"

"Why yes, old man, that's what they're here for."

"And that one next her? I like her even better!"

"Well, you can have her too."

A dark girl with provocatively bare feet was crossing the room.

"And that one walking over there?"

"Which? The very dark mulatta?"

"What's she called?"

"Adelaida; they call her the Sow. But I shouldn't pick her because she's with Major Farfan. I think he keeps her."

"Look how the Sow's making up to him," remarked the old man in a low voice.

The girl was using all her most serpentine arts to make the Major lose his head—she gazed at him from close range with the bewitching love-philtres of her eyes, made more beautiful than ever by belladonna; she exhausted him by pressing kisses on him with her fleshy lips and tongue as if sticking on stamps, and leaned against him with all the weight of her warm breasts and protruding stomach.

"Take off this beastly thing," whispered the Sow into Farfan's ear. And without waiting for an answer—it was too late for that—she unfastened the sword from his belt and handed it to the barman.

A railway-train of cries went by at full speed, passed through the tunnels of every ear in the room, and speeded on its way . . .

Couples were dancing, in time and out of time to the music, with the movements of two-headed animals. A man with his face daubed to look like a woman was playing the piano. Both his mouth and the piano had a few ivories missing. "Because I'm a flirt, a dreadful flirt, and terribly refined!" he replied to people who asked him why he painted his face, adding ingratiatingly: "My friends call me Pepe and the boys call me Violeta. I wear a low-cut vest (although I don't play tennis) to show off my dove's breasts; a monocle for smartness and a frock-coat out of absent-mindedness. I use powder (oh how spiteful people are!) and rouge to hide the smallpox scars I have on my face—there they are and there they'll stay. The beastly disease scattered them all over me like confetti. Oh well—what does it matter! It's just my little way!"

A railway-train of cries went by at full speed. Crushed between the wheels and the pistons, a drunk woman lay writhing limply, her face the colour of bran. She was pressing her hands against her groins, while the tears washed away the paint from her cheeks and lips.

"Oh my ovaaAAries! Oh my ovAAAries! Oh my ovaa-AAAAAAries! My ovaries! Oh . . . my ovaries! Oh!"

Everyone but those too drunk to move joined the group that had collected to see what was happening. In the general confusion the married men tried to find out if someone had attacked her, thinking to make their escape before the police arrived; while the rest took a less serious view of the matter and ran to and fro for the pleasure of being jostled by the crowd.

More and more kept joining the group round the woman, who lay twisting and shivering, with rolling eyes and protruding tongue. At the height of the crisis her false teeth became loose. There was frenzied excitement among the spectators. A loud laugh went up when her teeth slipped suddenly to the concrete floor.

Doña Chon brought this disgraceful scene to an end. She had been somewhere behind the scenes and came running to the rescue like a fat hen, cackling after her chicks; she took the unfortunate shrieking girl by one arm and swept the floor with her as far as the kitchen, where with Manuela's help she shut her in the coal-shed, after the cook had dealt her several blows with the spit.

The old man who had become enamoured of the Sow took advantage of the confusion to snatch her from the Major, who was too drunk to see anything.

"What a filthy bitch, eh, Major Farfan?" exclaimed Gold-Tooth when she returned from the kitchen. "Her ovaries didn't hurt her enough to stop her gorging herself and sleeping all day; it's just as if, when the battle began, a soldier got a pain in his . . . !"

A burst of loud drunken laughter drowned her voice. They laughed as if they were spitting out toffee. Meanwhile Doña Chon turned to the barman and said:

"I wanted to have the big girl I fetched from the Casa Nueva yesterday, instead of that obstinate brute; what a pity she was taken bad!"

"Ah yes, she was a fine girl!"

"I told the lawyer he must fix it that the Judge Advocate pays back my money. The son of a whore isn't going to hold on to my ten thousand pesos. Not he—the fool!"

"You're quite right! As for that lawyer, I happen to know he's a bad lot!"

"Dirty swindlers all of them!"

"And lecherous into the bargain, you know!"

"Anything you like, but I promise you one thing: he won't catch me twice! If he thinks he can sit there on his fat arse . . . !"

She left the sentence unfinished and went to the window to see who was knocking.

"Holy Jesus Maria and all the angels! Talk of the devil and here he comes!" she said aloud to the man who was standing at the door, bathed in the purplish light from the lantern, with his scarf pulled up to his eyes; and without answering his "Good evenings", she went off to tell the concierge to open the door at once.

"Come along quick and open the door, Pancha! Hurry! Open up quick, it's Don Miguelito!"

Doña Chon had recognised him from pure intuition and also from his satanic eyes.

"Well! What a miracle!"

Angel Face glanced round the room as he greeted her, and was reassured by the sight of a recumbent form which must be that of Major Farfan; a long stream of saliva was coming from his open mouth.

"A great miracle, because it isn't often the likes of you visit us poor folk!"

"No, Doña Chon, true enough!"

"You've come in the nick! I was just calling on the Saints to help me because of some trouble I'm in, and they've sent you to me!"

"Well, I'm always at your service, you know."

"Thank you. I'll tell you about my trouble but first you must have a drink."

"Don't bother . . ."

"It's no bother! Just a little something, a little of what you like, whatever you have a fancy for! To show there's no ill-feeling! How would a whisky be? But I'll have it served in my room. Come this way."

Gold-Tooth's private apartments were completely separate from the rest of the house and seemed to be a world apart. Tables, chests of drawers and sideboards were crowded with engravings, sculptures and religious images and relics. A Holy Family caught the eye by its great size and the skill with which it was executed. The Infant Christ was as tall as a lily; the only thing he lacked was speech. A brilliantly painted Saint Joseph, with the Virgin in a star-spangled dress, were on either side. The Virgin was decked in jewels, and Saint Joseph was holding a cup ornamented with two stones, each worth a fortune. Under a large glass case was a dark-skinned dying Christ, covered in blood, and in a wide glass case framed in shells a Virgin was ascending to heaven—an imitation in sculpture of Murillo's picture. The most valuable

163

thing about it was the serpent made of emeralds coiled at her feet. Between the sacred images were portraits of Doña Chon (the diminutive of Concepcion, which was her real name) at the age of twenty, when she had a President of the Republic at her feet offering to take her to "Paris, France", as well as two magistrates of the Supreme Court and three butchers who fought each other with knives for her sake at a fair. And over in a corner, out of sight of the visitors, was a portrait of the survivor, a hairy individual who had in the end become her husband.

"Sit down here on the sofa, Don Miguelito, you'll be better off here."

"You do yourself well, Doña Chon."

"I do my best . . ."

"It's like a church!"

"Now you mustn't tease me! Don't make fun of my saints!"

"And what can I do for you?"

"Drink up your whisky first."

"Very well. Cheers!"

"Cheers, Don Miguelito! And please forgive me for not joining you, but I'm a little upset in my stomach. Put your glass here—put it on this little table. Here give it to me."

"Thank you."

"Well as I was saying, Don Miguelito, I'm in great trouble and I'd be glad of your advice—the sort only people like you can give. One of the women I've got here suddenly became no good to me, so I set about looking for another; then a friend of mine told me there was a prisoner in the Casa Nueva, shut up by order of the Judge Advocate, a fine girl and just what I wanted. Well, I know what's what, so I went straight to my lawyer, Don Juan Vidalitas, who has got hold of women for me before, and made him write a proper letter to the Judge Advocate General— offering ten thousand pesos for her."

"Ten thousand pesos?"

"That's right. I didn't have to say it twice. He answered on the spot that that would be all right, and as soon as he got the cash (which I counted out myself in 500 peso notes on his desk) he gave me a written order to the Casa Nueva to hand over the woman to me. They told me she was there for political reasons. It seems they nabbed her in General Canales' house . . ."

"What did you say?"

Angel Face had been following Gold-Tooth's story inattentively with his ears pricked towards the door to make sure that Major Farfan did not leave (he had been looking for him for many hours) but when he heard Canales' name it was as if a network of fine wires had suddenly spread before him. This unhappy woman must be the servant Chabela, about whom Camila had talked in her feverish delirium.

"Excuse my interrupting . . . where is this woman?"

"You shall hear, but let me go on with my story. I took the Judge Advocate's order and went myself with three of my girls to fetch her from the Casa Nueva. I wasn't going to be given a pig in a poke. We went in a cab to be more comfortable. So there we are arriving; I hand in the order, they examine it and read it carefully, they fetch the girl, they hand her over, and, to make a long story short, we bring her back here where they're all waiting for her and they all like her. Nothing wrong so far, eh, Don Miguelito?"

"And where have you put her?"

Angel Face would have liked to take her away that same night. The minutes seemed like years whilst this horrible old woman was telling her story.

"You're all the same, you young nobs, no holding you! But just let me tell you. After we'd left the Casa Nueva, I noticed that this woman refused to open her eyes or say one word. You might as well have talked to the wall! I thought she was up to some game or other. And what's more I noticed that she was hugging a bundle about the size of a baby in her arms."

The image of Camila in the favourite's mind lengthened out until it split in half like a figure of eight, with the rapidity of a soap-bubble that is burst by a shot.

"A baby?"

"That's right. My cook, Manuela Calvario Cristales, found out that what the wretched woman was rocking in her arms was a little dead baby, already beginning to stink. She called me, I ran to the kitchen, and between the two of us we took it away by main force; but we'd hardly got her arms apart—Manuela almost broke them to do it—and taken the brat away from her, when she opened her eyes as wide as the dead on Judgement Day, and let out a yell that must have been heard as far away as the market, and fell flat on the floor."

165

"Dead?"

"We thought so for a moment. They came and fetched her away, wrapped in a sheet, to San Juan de Dios. I didn't want to look. It quite upset me. They say the tears came running from her shut eyes like the water which is no use to any of us."

Doña Chon paused for breath, then she muttered:

"The girls who were visiting the hospital this morning asked after her and it seems she's very bad. Now here's what worries me. As you can imagine I won't dream of letting the Judge Advocate keep my ten thousand pesos, and I'm trying to think how I can get him to pay them back, because why in heaven's name should he keep what's mine? Why in heaven's name? I'd a thousand times rather make a present of them to the poor-house!"

"Your lawyer must get them back for you, and as for this poor woman . . ."

"Exactly! And he's been twice today—sorry to interrupt—my lawyer Vidalitas went twice to see him; once to his house and once to his office, and each time he said the same thing—that he wasn't going to give me back a thing. You see what a dirty swindler that man is! He says if a cow dies after it's been bought it's not the seller's but the buyer's loss. Talking about people as if they were animals! That's what he said. Oh really, I'd like to . . . !"

Angel Face was silent. Who was this woman who had been sold? Who was the dead child?

Doña Chon displayed her gold teeth as she said menacingly:

"Ah, but what I'm going to do is give him such a basting as he never had before, even from his mother. If they put me in prison it'll be for something. It's hard enough to earn one's living, God knows, without people robbing one like this! Damn the old ruffian! Already this morning I told them to throw earth from the graveyard on to his doorstep. We'll see if that brings him bad luck . . ."

"And did they bury the child?"

"We held a wake for it here in this house; the girls are very sentimental. There were maize cakes . . ."

"A regular party?"

"That's right!"

"And the police? What are they doing?"

"We paid them to give us a death certificate. Next day we buried the brat on the island in a beautiful coffin lined with white satin."

"And aren't you afraid that there may be relatives who'll claim the body, or at least want to be notified?"

"That would be the last straw! But who's going to claim it? The father, Rodas, is in prison, and the mother's in hospital as you know."

Angel Face smiled inwardly; an enormous weight had been lifted from his mind. This was no relation of Camila's.

"Do advise me, Don Miguelito—you're so clever—how can I prevent that old miser hanging on to my money? It was ten thousand pesos—remember? Not a flea-bite exactly!"

"My advice is to go and see the President and complain to him. Ask for an audience, and tell him the story. He'll put it right. He has it in his power."

"That's what I thought, and I'll do it too. Tomorrow I'll send him an urgent telegram asking for an audience. Luckily we're old friends. When he was only a Minister he had a passion for me. It's a long time ago now. I was young and pretty then; slim as a reed, just like that photograph over there. I remember we lived at El Cielito with my mother—may she rest in peace! And a parrot gave her a peck in the eye and blinded her—did you ever hear of such bad luck! I must admit I roasted that parrot—I would gladly have roasted two of them—and gave it to my dog and the stupid brute ate it and got rabies. The most cheerful thing that I remember about those days is that all the funerals used to go past the house. Corpses were always going by. It was because of that that we broke for good with the President. He was afraid of funerals; what did I care? They weren't my fault. He was just like a child; his head full of stories. He believed every little thing anyone told him, whether it was bad or good. At first I was very struck on him and I used to keep kissing him when that endless procession of corpses went by in different coloured coffins. Afterwards I got fed up with that and dropped it. What he liked best was for someone to lick his ear, though it sometimes tasted like death. I can see him now, sitting there where you're sitting, with his white silk handkerchief tightly knotted round his neck, his wide hat, his spats with pink tabs and his blue suit."

"And afterwards—I suppose he must have been President already when he was a witness at your wedding?"

"Not a bit of it. My late husband—may he rest in peace—didn't care for such things. 'Only dogs need witnesses and people staring at them when they get married,' he used to say, 'and then off they go with a string of other dogs behind them, all slobbering with their tongues hanging out . . .' "

CHAPTER XXV

Death's Halting-Place

THE priest arrived at a cassock-splitting speed. "Some people would be willing to hurry for much less than this," he reflected. "What can be more precious in the whole world than a human soul?" And some people would get up from the dinner-table with a rumbling belly for much less. Bel-ly! I bel-ieve in the three separate persons of the Trinity, and one true God. The belly-rumbling is not there, but here with me, me, me, in my own stomach, stomach, stomach . . . From your belly, Jesus . . . there is the table already laid, with a white cloth, clean china, and a dried-up old servant.

When the priest came in, followed by some female neighbours addicted to witnessing death agonies, Angel Face tore himself from the head of Camila's bed, his footsteps sounding like the tearing-up of roots. The barkeeper brought a chair for the priest, and then they all withdrew.

"I, a miserable sinner, confess to God," they were saying.

"*In Nomine Patris et Filii et* . . my daughter, how long is it since your last confession?"

"Two months."

"Have you made your act of contrition?"

"Yes, Father . . ."

"Tell me your sins."

"Father, I confess to having lied—"

"Over a serious matter?"

"No, and I disobeyed my father, and . . ."

(*Tick-tock, tick-tock, tick-tock*)

". . . and Father, I confess to . . ."

(*Tick-tock*)

". . . failing to go to Mass."

The sick girl and her confessor seemed to be talking in a crypt. The Devil, the Guardian Angel and Death were present at the confession. Death emptied his vacant stare into Camila's eyes;

the Devil sat at the head of the bed spitting out spiders, and the Angel wept in a corner, with long-drawn-out sobs.

"Father, I confess to not saying my prayers night and morning, and . . ."

(*Tick-tock, tick-tock*)

". . . to quarrelling with my girl-friends!"

"Over some matter affecting your reputation?"

"No . . ."

"My daughter, you have committed very grave offences against God."

"Father, I confess to riding astride like a man."

"Were there other people present, and did it create a scandal?"

"No, there were only a few Indians."

"So you felt you could do anything a man could do? That also is a grave sin, for Our Lord God created a woman to be a woman, and she should not try to be otherwise and imitate a man; that would be following the example of the Devil, who wanted to be equal with God."

In the other part of the room, in front of the bar-counter, covered like an altar with bottles of every colour, Angel Face, La Masacuata and the neighbours were waiting, not uttering a word but exchanging glances full of fear and hope, and breathing out a symphony of sighs, heavy with the oppressive idea of death. The half-shut door gave a glimpse of the brightly lit street, the porch of the Church of La Merced, some houses and a few passers-by. It enraged Angel Face to see these people coming and going, indifferent to the fact that Camila was dying—large grains of sand in a sieve of sun; shadows possessed of common sense; walking factories of excrement . . .

The confessor's voice dragged little chains of words through the silence. The sick girl coughed. The air tore at the drums of her lungs.

"Father, I confess to all those venial and mortal sins that I have committed but forgotten."

The Latin words of the absolution, the hurried disappearance of the Devil, and the Angel's return like a light to spread his warm white wings over Camila, put an end to the favourite's anger against the passers-by, his childish hatred tinged with tenderness, and gave him the idea—grace comes by devious paths—of saving a man who was in grave danger of death. Perhaps

God would grant him Camila's life in exchange, although this seemed impossible according to medical science.

The priest went noiselessly away; he stopped in the doorway to light a maize-leaf cigarette and gather up his cassock, for according to the law he had to keep it hidden under his cloak while he was in the street. He seemed harmless and gentle, a burnt-out ash of a man. The news went around that he had been summoned to confess a dying woman. The neighbours left the house behind him, and Angel Face went off to carry out his plan.

The Callejon de Jesus, the White Horse, and the Cavalry Barracks. Here he inquired of the corporal on guard for Major Farfan. He was told to wait a moment and the soldier went inside calling out:

"Major Farfan! Major Farfan!"

His voice died away in the huge courtyard, and the only response was a tremulous echo from the eaves of distant houses: "Jor fan fan! Jor fan fan!"

The favourite stood waiting a few steps from the door, taking no part in what was happening around him. Dogs and turkey-buzzards were quarrelling over the dead body of a cat in the middle of the road, directly opposite a window from which an officer was amusedly watching the ferocious battle and twirling the ends of his moustaches. Two ladies were drinking fruit-juice in a little shop swarming with flies. From the front door of the next house emerged five little boys in sailor suits, followed by a gentleman as pale as a turnip and a pregnant lady (papa and mamma). A butcher pushed his way between the boys, lighting a cigarette; his clothes were covered in bloodstains, his sleeves were rolled up, and he carried his sharp butcher's cleaver close to his heart. Soldiers came in and out, and a serpentine trail of the wet prints of bare feet wound over the tiles of the entrance hall to be lost in the courtyard. The barrack keys jingled against the sentinel's rifle as he stood at attention beside the officer on guard, who was sitting on an iron chair in the middle of a ring of gobbets of spittle.

Walking softly like a little deer, a white-haired woman, whose skin was burnt copper-colour by the sun and wrinkled with age, went up to the officer and respectfully covering her head with her cotton shawl said imploringly:

"Excuse me, Señor, but I beg you for mercy's sake to let me talk to my son. The Virgin will reward you."

Before replying the officer expelled a jet of saliva smelling of tobacco and dental decay.

"What is your son's name, Señora?"

"Ismael, Señor."

"Ismael what?"

"Ismael Mijo, Señor."

The officer spat again.

"But what's his surname?"

"It's Mijo, Señor."

"Look, here, you'd better come back another day, we're busy."

The old woman withdrew without lowering her shawl, slowly, counting out her steps as if measuring her misfortune; she paused briefly at the edge of the pavement and then turned back again and approached the officer who was still sitting on his chair.

"Excuse me, Señor, but I can't stay here any longer; I come from very far away, more than twenty leagues, and so if I don't see him today I don't know when I can come back. Please won't you send for him?"

"I've told you already, we're busy. Go away and don't bother me!"

Angel Face had witnessed this scene and, impelled by the desire to do good so that God should reward him by saving Camila, he said to the officer in a low voice:

"Send for the boy, Lieutenant, and here's something for cigarettes."

The soldier took the money without glancing at the stranger and gave orders for Ismael Mijo to be sent for. The little old woman stood gazing at her benefactor as if he were an angel.

Major Farfan was not in the barracks. A secretary appeared at one of the balconies with his pen behind his ear, and told the favourite that at this hour of the night he could usually be found at The Sweet Enchantment, because the noble son of Mars divided his time between duty and love. However, it wouldn't do any harm to go to his house. Angel Face took a cab. Farfan rented furnished rooms in a remote suburb; through the cracks made by the damp in the unpainted door Angel Face could see into the darkened interior. He knocked twice, three times. There was no one there. He left at once, and went to see how Camila was, before going on to The Sweet Enchantment. The cab made a surprisingly loud noise on the paved road after leaving the unsurfaced lanes—horses' hooves, and wheels, wheels and horses' hooves.

When Gold-Tooth had finished her story of her love affair with the President, Angel Face went back to the saloon. It was vital not to lose sight of Major Farfan, and also to find out rather more about the woman who had been arrested in General Canales' house and sold by that swine the Judge Advocate General for ten thousand pesos.

Dancing was in full swing. Couples were revolving to the strains of a waltz, accompanied in a quavering voice by Farfan, who was as drunk as a lord:

> Why do the whores
> all love me so?
> Because I sing them
> the "Flor del Café"

All of a sudden he sat up, and realising that the Sow was no longer with him, he stopped singing and exclaimed between hiccups:

"So the Sow's gone away, has she, you bastards? She's busy, is she, you bastards? . . . well I'm off . . . I tell you I'm off, I t-ell you I'm off . . . I'm off . . . well, why don't I go? . . . I'm off, I do believe . . ."

He got up with difficulty, supporting himself on the table, to which he had been anchored, and on chairs and walls, and staggered towards the door. The servant ran to open it.

"I t-ell you I'm o-off! The whore will come back, won't she, Ña Chon? But I'm off! There's nothing left for us regular soldiers to do but drink ourselves to death, and afterwards they can distil us instead of cremating us! Hurrah for pork stew and the working man!"

Angel Face caught up with him at once. He was walking along the tight-rope of the road like an acrobat; now he would stop with his right foot in the air, now with the left, now again with the right, now with both . . . On the point of falling, he saved himself and remarked: "That's the way, as the mule said to the bridle."

173

The open windows of another brothel shed their light into the street. A long-haired pianist was playing Beethoven's Moonlight Sonata. There was no one to listen to him in the empty room, except the chairs arranged like guests around a small grand piano, no larger than Jonah's whale. The favourite stood still, pierced by the music. He propped the Major against the wall—poor tractable puppet that he was—and went closer so as to subject the fragments of his broken heart to the notes: he was returning to life among the dead—a dead man with burning eyes, suspended far above the earth—while the eyes of the street lamps were extinguished one by one, and the night dew dripped from the roofs like nails for crucifying drunkards or fastening down coffin lids. Each little hammer inside the magnetic box of the piano joined together the fine sand of musical sounds, and, after holding them together for a while, let them go again in the fingers of arpeggios, doubled to knock on the permanently shut door of love; always the same fingers; always the same hand. The moon was drifting through a paved sky towards the sleeping fields, leaving dark groves behind her, full of terror for the birds, and for those who find the world as supernaturally vast when love is born as it is small and empty when love dies.

Farfan awoke to find himself lying on the bar counter of a small tavern, and being shaken by a stranger as a tree is shaken to bring down the ripe fruit.

"Don't you recognise me, Major?"

"Yes—no—for the moment—in a moment—"

"You remember?"

"Ah—oOOh!" yawned Farfan, getting off the counter where he had been lying, as damp with sweat as a pack-mule.

"Miguel Angel Face, at your service."

The Major saluted.

"Excuse me; I didn't recognise you, you see. But yes, of course it's you one sees about always with the President."

"Good! Don't be surprised at my waking you up like this, Major—so suddenly—"

"Don't worry about that."

"But you have to get back to barracks, and it's important I talk to you privately; it happens that the proprietress of this—café, shall we say?—is out. I hunted for you everywhere, like a needle in a haystack, yesterday afternoon—in the barracks, at your rooms. You must promise not to repeat to a single soul what I'm now going to tell you."

"Word of honour."

The favourite shook the Major's hand warmly, and with his eyes on the door said in a low voice:

"I'm in a position to know that orders have been issued to do away with you. Instructions have been sent to the Military Hospital that when next you're confined to bed after a drinking-bout you shall be given a fatal dose of sedative. The harlot you've been going with at The Sweet Enchantment has informed the President of your revolutionary outbursts."

Farfan had been rooted to the spot by the favourite's words. He raised his clenched fists:

"Oh the bitch!"

And after going through the motions of hitting her, he bowed his head as if crushed.

"My God, what am I to do?"

"For the moment don't get drunk; that's the way to stave off the immediate danger, and don't—"

"Yes, that's what I was thinking; but I may not be able to do it; it'll be difficult. What were you going to say?"

"I was also going to say that you shouldn't eat in barracks."

"I don't know how to thank you."

"With silence—"

"Naturally, but that's not enough. However, some chance will turn up, and from now on here's a man you can count on—who owes you his life."

"I'll give you another piece of good advice as a friend. Try and find a way of getting on the right side of the President."

"Yes, that's the thing, isn't it?"

"It'll cost you nothing."

Both were silently adding to these words: "To commit a crime for example," the most effective means of gaining the leader's good will; or "to commit a public outrage on defenceless people"; or "to demonstrate the superiority of force to public opinion", or "to get rich at the expense of the nation"; or . . .

A murderous crime would be best; the annihilation of one of his fellows was the clearest proof of a citizen's complete adherence to the President. Two months in prison for appearance's sake, and immediately afterwards a public position of trust, such as was only given to those with a law suit pending, so that they could be conveniently sent back to prison if they didn't behave well.

"It'll cost you nothing."

"You're extremely kind."

"No, Major, don't thank me; my decision to save you is my offering to God for the health of someone who is very, very seriously ill. Your life for hers."

"Your beloved perhaps?"

The most beautiful word in the Song of Songs floated for a moment, like some charming embroidery, among trees full of cherubs and orange blossom.

After the Major had left, Angel Face pinched himself to find out if it were really he—the man who had driven so many to their deaths—who was now pushing a man towards life, and the inviolable blue of the morning.

CHAPTER XXVI

Whirlwind

DISMISSING the portly figure of the Major from his mind, Angel Face shut the door and went on tiptoe into the darkened back room. He felt as if he were dreaming. The difference between reality and dreams is purely artificial. Asleep, awake, which was he? In the half-darkness he seemed to feel the earth moving beneath him. The clock and the flies kept Camila company as she lay close to death. The clock let drop the little rice grains of its pulsations to mark out the path of return when she had ceased to exist. The flies ran over the walls, cleaning the cold of death off their little wings. Others buzzed about tirelessly and swiftly. He stepped quietly up to the bed. The sick girl was still delirious . . .

The ingenuity of dreams . . . pools of camphorated oil . . . the slow dialogue of the stars . . . the invisible, salty, naked contact of empty space . . . the double hinge of the hands . . . the uselessness of hands within hands . . . scented soap . . . the garden in the reading-book . . . in the tiger's den . . . in the great beyond of parakeets . . . in God's cage . . .

In God's cage, midnight Mass for a cock—a cock with a drop of moonlight on its comb . . . it pecks at the host . . . it is lit and extinguished, lit and extinguished, lit and extinguished. The Mass is sung . . . it isn't a cock; it's a flash of celluloid lightning in the neck of a large bottle surrounded by little soldiers . . . lightning from the White Rose pastry-shop, made by Saint Rose . . . Beer-froth of the cock for the chicken . . . for the chicken . . .

> Lay her now upon her bier
> Matatero, tero, la!
> For she is not happy here
> Matatero, tero, la!

No one is blowing his nose; it is the sound of a drum; a drum tracing down-strokes in the school of the wind . . . Stop! it's not a drum; it's a door echoing to a blow from a knocker shaped like a brass hand! The knocks penetrate into every corner of the intestinal silence of the house, like augers. Rat-tat-tat . . . The drum of the house. Every house has its door-drum to summon the people who are its life, and when it is shut it is as if they lived death . . . Rat-tat of the house . . . door . . . rat-tat of the house . . . the water in the fountain is all eyes when it hears the sound of the door-drum, and people say crossly to the servants: "Oh they're knocking!" and the walls send back an echo which repeats over and over again: "Oh they're knocking, go and open the door-r-r-r!" "Oh they're knocking, go and open the door-r-r-r!" and the ashes stir restlessly but can do nothing (while the cat sits like a watchful sentinel) except send a gentle shiver through the bars of the grate; and the roses take fright, innocent victims of the intransigence of their thorns; and the mirrors speak with the living voices of rapt mediums through the spirits of the dead furniture: "Oh they're knocking, come and open!"

The whole house, trembling as if in an earthquake, wants to go and see who is knocking, knocking, knocking at the drum-door: casseroles dance about, flower-pots move softly, wash-basins go rataplan! rataplan!, plates give a china cough, cups and cutlery scatter like silver laughter, empty bottles follow the bottle decorated with candle-grease tears which is used and not used for a candlestick in the back room; prayer-books, Easter palm-branches try to defend the house against the storm of knocking, scissors, shells, portraits, old locks of hair, cruets, cardboard boxes, matches, nails . . .

Only her uncles pretend to be asleep among these wakeful inanimate objects, in the islands of their double beds, under the protective covering of quilts smelling of gastric juices. In vain does the door-drum take bites out of the spacious silence. "They're still knocking!" murmurs the wife of one of her uncles, the most double-faced of her aunts. "Yes, but it would be risky to open the door," her husband answers in the darkness. "What time is it? Oh, my dear, I was so fast asleep! . . . They're still knocking!" "Yes, but it would be risky to open the door!" "What will the neighbours think?" "Yes, but it would be risky to open the door! If we only had ourselves to consider of course we'd open the door, but just think what people would say about us! . . . They're still knocking!" "Yes, but it would be risky to open the door!" "It's outrageous, did you ever hear of anything like it? So inconsiderate, so rude!" "Yes, but it would be risky to open the door!"

Her uncle's harsh voice grew softer, and came now from the throats of the servants. Chattering phantoms smelling of veal have arrived in their master's bedroom: "Sir! Madam! Listen how they're knocking! . . ." and they go back to their pallet beds, their fleas and their dreams, repeating over and over again: "Oh dear! but it would be risky to open the door! Oh dear! . . . but it would be risky to open the door!"

Rat-tat-tat on the drum of the house . . . darkness of the street . . . the dogs cover the sky with the tiles of their barking, making a roof for the stars, for black reptiles and clay washer-women who plunge their arms deep in foam of silver lightning . . .

"Papa . . . papa darling . . . papa!"

She called out to her father in her delirium, to her old nurse lying dead in the hospital, to her uncles, who would not let her into their houses even when she was dying.

Angel Face laid his hand on her forehead. "Every recovery is a miracle!" he thought as he caressed her. "If only I could drive away the disease with the warmth of my hand!" He was suffering the inarticulate grief of those who watch a young creature die, a tremulous tenderness which sent anguish creeping under his skin and through his flesh. What could he do? His mind began mechanically introducing prayers among his thoughts: "If only I could get beneath her eyelids and remove the tears of pity and loneliness from her eyes—from those pupils coloured like the wings of hope. May God preserve you! We exiles pray to you, oh Lord!"

"It's a crime to go on living every day . . . when one loves. Grant us today, oh Lord!"

When he thought of his own house it was as if it were a stranger's. His home was here—with Camila; it was not his house, but Camila was here. And supposing Camila were not here? A vague, wandering pain pierced his body. Supposing Camila were not here?

A lorry went by, shaking the house. There was a clinking of bottles on the shelves in the bar; a knocker rattled, the neighbouring houses shook. Angel Face was so startled that he felt he must have been falling asleep where he stood. Better sit down. There was a chair beside the medicine table. A moment later it was supporting his body. The tiny sound of the clock, the smell of camphor, the light from the candles offered up to the all-powerful Jesus of La Merced and Jesus of la Candelaria, the table, the towels, the medicines, Saint Francis' rope belt (lent by a neighbour to keep the devil at bay), were all gently disintegrating to a slow rhythm, a descending scale of somnolence, a momentary dissolution, a pleasurable discomfort full of more holes than a sponge, invisible, semi-liquid, hidden, traversed by the shadows of disconnected dreams:

Who is playing the guitar? . . . Little bones are breaking in the dark cellar, whence rises the song of the agricultural engineer . . . It is bitterly cold among the leaves . . . From all the pores of the earth rises an interminable, demoniac laugh, like a four-cornered wing . . . Are they laughing, are they spitting, what are they doing? It isn't night, but he is separated from Camila by darkness, the darkness of the skulls laughing in the confusion of the mortuary . . . The laughter comes from teeth that are blackened and horrible, but when it reaches the air it mingles with water vapour and rises up to form clouds. Fences made out of human intestines divide up the earth. Perspectives made by human eyes divide up the sky . . . A horse's ribs serve as a violin for the raging hurricane. He sees Camila's funeral passing by. Her eyes are swimming in foam from the bridles of the river of black carriages . . . the Dead Sea must have eyes!

Her green eyes! . . . why are the drivers waving their white gloves in the darkness? . . . Behind the funeral procession an ossuary full of children's thighbones is singing; "Moon, moon, take your prune and throw the stone in the lagoon!" Each tender little bone is singing this song: "Moon, moon, take your prune and throw the stone in the lagoon!" Hip-bones with eyes like buttonholes: "Moon, moon, take your prune and throw the stone in the lagoon!" . . . Why does daily life have to go on? . . . Why does the tram go on running? . . . Why doesn't everyone die? . . . After Camila's funeral nothing can be the same, everything is superfluous, artificial, does not exist . . . It would be better if he could laugh . . . The tower leans over with laughing . . . they search her pockets for souvenirs . . . The dust left by Camila's days . . . Trivial rubbish . . . A thread . . . Camila should be here now . . . A thread . . . A dirty card . . . Oh the cheek of that diplomat who brings in wine and tinned goods without paying the duty and then sells them in a shop kept by a Tyrolese! . . . Letthewholeworldsing . . . Shipwreck . . . Lifebelts, like white crowns . . . Letthewholeworldsing . . . Camila, motionless in his arms . . . Meeting . . . The bell-ringer's hand . . . They are turning the corners of the street . . . Pale with emotion . . . Livid, silent, disembodied . . . Why don't they offer her an arm? . . . She is letting herself down with the spiders-web of her sense of touch, and leaning on the arm she needs; she only holds on to the sleeve . . . In the telegraph wires . . . he has wasted time looking at the telegraph wires, and out of a big house in the Callejon del Judio come five men made of opaque glass, who bar his way, each with a trickle of blood coming from his temple . . . He fights desperately to get to the place where Camila is waiting for him, smelling of postage-stamp gum . . . Far off he sees Mount Carmel . . .

In his dream Angel Face tries to fight his way out. He is blind . . . He is weeping . . . He tries to bite through the thin thread of darkness which separates him from the human anthill which is being installed under straw awnings on the little mound, to sell toys, fruit and toffee . . . He puts out his claws . . . his hair bristles . . . He succeeds in crossing a little bridge and runs to find Camila, but the five men made of opaque glass bar his way again. "They're dividing her into little bits for Corpus Christi!" He shouts at them: "Let me pass! before they destroy her completely. She can't defend herself because she's dead!" "Don't you see?" "Look! Look! Every shadow has a fruit and a little piece of Camila is threaded into every fruit!" "How can one believe one's eyes? I saw her buried and I was sure it wasn't her, she's here at the feast of Corpus Christi, at this cemetery, smelling of quinces, mangoes, pears and peaches; and they have made little white doves out of her body, dozens, hundreds of little white cotton doves fastened to coloured ribbons embroidered with legends such as 'Remember Me', 'Eternal Love', 'I am thinking of You', 'Love me for Ever', 'Do not Forget Me'." His voice is drowned in the strident sound of toy trumpets, and drums made out of the guts of the bad years and stale bread; in the crowd of people (fathers climbing with dragging footsteps, children running after each other); in the clanging of bells in the steeples, in the heat of the sun, in the warmth of blind candles at noon, in the glittering monstrance . . . The five opaque men are joining together into a single man, a shape made of sleeping smoke . . . From a distance they no longer look solid . . . they are drinking soda-water . . . A flag of soda-water held in hands waving like cries . . . Skaters . . . Camila is gliding among invisible skaters, across a public mirror which reflects good and bad impartially. The cosmetic quality of her perfumed voice cloys as she tries to defend herself by saying: "No, no, not here!" "But why not here?" "Because I'm dead." "And what of that?" "It's just that . . ." "What, tell me, what?" Between the two of them there passed a current of cold air from the vast sky and a column of men in red trousers. Camila walks off behind them. On the impulse of the moment he walks off behind her . . . At the last rat-tat of the drum, the column suddenly comes to a halt . . . The President is approaching . . . a gilded figure . . . Tantarara! . . . The crowd retreats, trembling . . . The men in red trousers are having a game with their heads . . . Bravo! Bravo! Done it again! Have another go, well done! The men in red trousers do not obey orders. They obey the voice of the public and go on playing with their heads . . . Three times . . . One! off with his head . . . Two! throw it up high to be combed among the stars . . . Three! Catch it in your hands and put it back . . . Bravo! Bravo! Again! Have another go! That's it! Have another go! . . . It makes the flesh creep . . . gradually the voices die away . . . the drum is heard . . . Everyone sees something they don't want to see. The men in red trousers take off their heads and throw them in the air, but do not catch them when they fall. The skulls smash on the ground in front of the two rows of motionless figures with their arms tied behind their backs.

Angel Face was woken by two loud knocks on the door. What a horrible nightmare! Thank heaven reality was quite different. Returning from a nightmare produces the same feeling of well-being as returning from a funeral. He ran to see who was knocking. Was it news of the general or an urgent summons from the President?

"Good morning."

"Good morning," replied the favourite to an individual taller than himself, with a rather pink face, who bent his head and peered at him through his thick spectacles.

"Excuse me. Perhaps you can tell me if the lady who cooks for the musicians lives here. She is a lady dressed in black . . ."

Angel Face shut the door in his face. The short-sighted man was still peering about looking for him. Seeing that he wasn't there he asked at the next house.

"Goodbye, Niña Tomasita. Good luck!"

"I'm going to the little market place."

The two voices had spoken at once. La Masacuata was already at the door when Angel Face went to open it.

"How did it go?" he asked La Masacuata, who had just returned from the prison.

"Same as usual."

"What did they say?"

"Nothing."

"Did you see Vasquez?"

"Did I see him? Not likely. They took in his breakfast basket and brought it back again, and that was that!"

"Then he's not in the prison?"

"You could have knocked me down with a feather when they brought out the basket untouched, but a gentleman there told me he'd been sent out to work."

"The governor?"

"No. I gave the brute a piece of my mind. He tried to mess me about."

"How do you think Camila is?"

"It's taking its course. Yes, poor girl, it's taking its course!"

"She's very very bad, isn't she?"

"She's lucky. What could be better than to go before ever you know what life is about! You're the one I'm sorry for. You ought to go and pray to Jesus of La Merced. Who knows, he might perform a miracle for you. This morning before I went to the prison I left a candle there and I said to him: 'Look here, my little negro, here I am coming to you, because you're not our papa for nothing, and you must listen to me: you can save that girl's life; I asked the Virgin to save her before I got up and now I'm bothering you for the same reason; I'll leave you this candle and I'm going away trusting in your power, but I'll be back again soon to remind you of my prayer!' "

Half asleep, Angel Face remembered his dream. Among the men in red trousers, the Judge Advocate General—with the face of an owl—was fencing with an unknown man, kissing him, licking him, eating him, excreting him, eating him again . . .

183

CHAPTER XXVII

The Road to Exile

GENERAL CANALES' mount stumbled on in the dim light of dusk, drunk with fatigue under the dead weight of the rider clinging to the pommel. The birds flew over the woods, and the clouds passed over the mountains, climbing here, descending there, descending here, climbing there, just as (before sleep and exhaustion had overcome him) the rider himself had climbed and descended—over pathless hills, through wide and stony rivers whose rushing waters refreshed his mule, across slopes laced with mud down which stones slid to shatter themselves over precipices, through inextricable thickets full of angry brambles, and along goat-tracks evocative of witches and highwaymen.

The night's tongue was hanging out. A league of marshy land. Then a shadowy form appeared, lifted the rider from his mount, led him to a deserted hut and went silently away. But he returned at once. He must have gone outside among the cicadas singing: cricricri, cricricri, cricricri! He stayed in the cabin for a short while and then vanished like smoke. Now he was back again. He came in and out, in and out. It was as if he went away to report his find and returned to make sure he was still there. The starlit landscape seemed to follow his lizard-like comings and goings, like a faithful dog wagging a tail of sounds (cricricri, cricricri, cricricri) in the silence of the night.

In the end he returned to the hut for good. The wind was leaping through the branches of the trees. Day was dawning in the night-school where the frogs had been learning to read the stars. An atmosphere of happy digestion. The five senses of light. Objects began to take shape to the eyes of the man squatting by the door, a timid good man who was silenced by the impressiveness of dawn and the innocent breathing of the sleeping horseman. Last night he had been a mere shape, today he was a man; it was he who had taken the rider from his horse. When it grew light he made a fire, placing the rough-hewn smoky hearthstones crosswise, scraping the old ashes with a piece of candlewood, and putting together dry twigs and green wood. Green wood does not burn quietly; it talks like a parrot, sweats, contracts, laughs and cries. The horseman awoke frozen with terror at what he saw, and not yet fully himself; he took one jump to the door, pistol in hand, determined to sell his life dearly. Undisturbed by the barrel of the weapon pointing at him, the other man silently pointed to the coffee-pot simmering beside the fire. But the rider paid no attention. He advanced slowly towards the door—the hut was sure to be surrounded by soldiers—and saw before him nothing but a wide plain bathed in rosy mist. Distance. Like a blue lather. Trees. Clouds. A titillation of bird-trills. His mule was dozing under a fig-tree. He stood listening unwinkingly to test the evidence of his eyes, and heard nothing at all except the harmonious concert of the birds and the slow gliding of a stream, whose copious waters left an almost imperceptible ssss on the youthful air, like castor sugar falling into a bowl of hot coffee.

"You're not from the Government?" murmured the man who had unhorsed him, carefully stowing away forty or fifty corn-cobs behind him.

The horseman raised his eyes and looked at his companion. He shook his head from side to side without moving his mouth from his mug of coffee.

"Tatita!"* murmured the other with a sly expression, letting his eyes wander round the room like those of a lost dog.

"I'm on the run . . ."

The man stopped hiding his corn-cobs and went to pour out more coffee for his visitor. Canales could not speak of his misfortunes.

"Same as me, Señor! I'm running away because of the corn-cobs I took. But I'm not a thief; it was my land until they took it away from me; and my mules too . . ."

General Canales was interested in what the Indian was saying, and wanted to hear his explanation of how one could steal without being a thief.

"I'll tell you, Tatita, how it is I steal although I'm not a thief by trade; before this I was the owner of a little bit of land close by, and eight mules. I had my house, my wife and children, and I was as honest as you are . . ."

* Little father. Term of respect used by the Indians to the Whites.

"Yes, and then?"

"Three years ago the Political Commissioner came here and told me to take a load of pinewood on my mules' backs for the President's fête-day. I took them, Señor, what else could I do? When he arrived and saw my mules, he put me in prison in a cell by myself, and he and the mayor, a ladino, divided my animals between them, and when I asked for the money they owed me for my work, the Commissioner told me I was a brute and if I didn't hold my jaw at once he'd put me in irons. 'Very well, Señor Commissioner,' I said to him, 'do what you like to me, but the mules belong to me.' I couldn't say anything more, Tatita, because he hit me such a whack on the head with his belt that it was nearly the death of me . . ."

A bitter smile came and went under the grey moustache of the old soldier in disgrace. The Indian went on in the same tone without raising his voice:

"When I left hospital they came and told me they had put my children in prison but they'd set them free if I gave them ten thousand pesos. As my children were young and tender, I hurried off to the Governor and asked him to keep them in prison and not send them to the barracks, and I would mortgage my land and raise the three thousand pesos. I went to the capital and the lawyer there arranged with a foreign gentleman to sign a paper saying they would give me three thousand pesos on a mortgage. That's what they read out to me, but it wasn't what they wrote. Soon afterwards they sent a man from the law-courts to tell me I was to leave my land because it wasn't mine any longer, because I'd sold it to the foreigner for three thousand pesos. I swore to God that this wasn't true, but they believed the lawyer and not me, and I had to leave my land, and in spite of their taking the three thousand pesos from me my sons went to the barracks: one died guarding the frontier; the other was so badly wounded he'd have been better dead, and their mamma, my wife, died of malaria. And that's why I came to steal, although I'm not a thief, Tata, even if they beat me to death or throw me in jail."

"And that's what we soldiers are defending!"

"What did you say, Tata?"

A storm of feelings was raging in old Canales' breast, such feelings as are always aroused in the heart of a good man when confronted with injustice. He suffered on behalf of his country, as though its very blood was corrupt. He suffered in his skin, in the marrow of his bones and the roots of his hair, under his nails, between his teeth. Which was the truth? Had he never thought with his head hitherto, but always with his kepi? It is a more despicable and therefore a sadder thing to be a soldier simply in order to keep a gang of ruffians, exploiters and self-important betrayers of their country in power, than it is to die of hunger in exile. By what right are soldiers forced to be loyal to régimes which are themselves disloyal to ideas, to the world and to their nation?

The Indian was gazing at the general as if he were some strange fetish, but without understanding the few words which he had uttered.

"You must go, Tatita, before the mounted police get here!"

Canales asked the Indian to go with him into the neighbouring state, and the Indian agreed; for he was like a rootless tree without his land. And the pay was good.

They left the cabin without putting out the fire. They cut their way through the forest with their machetes. The tracks of a jaguar wound away ahead of them. Darkness. Light, Darkness. Light. Patchwork of leaves. They saw the hut shining behind them like a meteor. Noon. Motionless clouds. Motionless trees. Dejection. Blinding whiteness. Stones and more stones. Insects. Skeletons, bare of flesh and warm like newly ironed underclothes. Decomposition. Flustered birds, circling overhead. Water and thirst. The tropics. Timeless change, and always, always the same heat.

The general was wearing a handkerchief to keep the sun off the nape of his neck. The Indian walked beside him, keeping pace with the mule.

"I think if we walk all night we may reach the frontier tomorrow morning, and it wouldn't be a bad idea to risk taking to the main road, because I have to stop at the house of some friends at Las Aldeas."

"The main road, Tata! What are you thinking of? You'll run into the mounted police!"

"Come along! Follow me! Nothing venture, nothing have, and these friends of mine may be very useful to us!"

"Oh no, Tata!"

And the Indian gave a sudden start and said:

"Don't you hear? Don't you hear, Tata?"

A troop of horses could be heard approaching, but soon afterwards the wind dropped. The sound seemed to be left behind, as if they were going away.

"Quiet!"

"It's the mounted police, Tata, I know what I'm talking about, and now we'll have to take this path, even though it's a longer way round to Las Aldeas!"

The general plunged down a side track after the Indian. He had to dismount and lead the mule. As the gully swallowed them up they had the feeling of being inside a snail-shell, sheltered from the danger threatening them. It grew suddenly dark. The shadows were gathering in the depths of the sleeping ravine. Trees and birds seemed like mysterious portents in the gentle, continuously fluctuating breeze. A cloud of reddish dust between them and the stars was all they saw of the mounted police as they galloped past the place they had just left.

They had been travelling all night.

"When we get to the top of the hill we'll see Las Aldeas, Tata."

The Indian went on ahead with the mule to announce their arrival to Canales' friends, three unmarried sisters who divided their lives between hymns and quinsy, novenas and ear-ache, pains in the face and pains in back and side. They breakfasted on the news. They nearly fainted. They received the general in their bedroom. The drawing-room did not inspire them with confidence.

In country villages visitors enter a house unannounced and go right into the kitchen calling out: "Ave Maria! Ave Maria!"

The soldier told them the story of his misfortunes in a slow, dispassionate tone, shedding a few tears when he mentioned his daughter.

His friends wept with grief; so great was their grief that for the moment they forgot their own sorrow, the death of their mother, for whom they were wearing deepest mourning.

"But we'll arrange for your escape—the crossing of the frontier at any rate. I'll go and ask the neighbours. This is the moment to remember which of them are smugglers. And I know nearly all the possible crossing-places are guarded by the authorities."

It was the eldest sister speaking and she looked questioningly at the others.

"Yes, we'll take care of your escape as my sister says, General; and as I don't think some provisions would come amiss I'll go and get them ready," said the second sister, whose toothache had yielded to the shock of Canales' arrival. The youngest added:

"Since you're going to spend the day with us I'll stay and talk to you and cheer you up a bit."

The general looked gratefully at the three sisters—the service they were doing him was beyond price—and begged them in a low voice to forgive him for being such a nuisance.

"Not another word, General!"

"No, General, you mustn't talk like that!"

"I realise how good and kind you are, my dears, but I know I'm compromising you by being in your house."

"But we're you're friends after all—you can imagine that since Mamma died . . ."

"And tell me, what did your dear Mamma die of?"

"My sister will tell you, we'll go and get things ready."

So said the eldest. Then she sighed. She was carrying her stays rolled up in her shawl and she went off to put them on in the kitchen, where the second sister was preparing some provisions for the general, surrounded by pigs and poultry.

"It wasn't possible to take her to the capital and they didn't understand her illness here; you know how it is, General. She got worse and worse. Poor darling! She died weeping because she was leaving us alone in the world. It couldn't be helped. But just imagine, we hadn't anything to pay the doctor, who sent in a bill for fifteen visits amounting to something like the entire value of this house—all that our father left us. Excuse me a moment, I must go and see what your servant wants."

When the younger sister went out, Canales fell asleep. Eyes closed. Feather-light body.

"What do you want, boy?"

"For the love of heaven tell me where I can go and relieve myself . . ."

"Over there—in the pigsty!"

The peace of the countryside wove itself into the sleeping soldier's dreams. The gratefulness of the cornfields, the tenderness of the pastures with their simple little flowers. The morning was soon over, what with the terror of some partridges spattered with shot by sportsmen, the black terror of a burial spattered with holy water by the priest, and the troublesome behaviour of an active young bullock. Several important events took place in the dove-cote in the spinsters' patio: the death of a seducer, a courtship and thirty marriages in the sunshine. Nothing at all, as you might say!

Nothing at all, as you might say! said the pigeons, looking out of the little windows of their houses. Nothing at all, as you might say!

At twelve o'clock they woke the general for lunch. Rice with herbs. Beef broth. Stew. Chicken. Beans. Bananas. Coffee.

"Ave Maria!"

The voice of the Political Commissioner broke in upon their lunch. The spinsters turned pale and did not know what to do. The general slipped behind a door.

"Don't be alarmed, my dears; I'm not the Devil with Eleven Thousand Horns! Good gracious, how frightened you are, and after I've been so kind to you too!"

The poor things had quite lost the power of speech.

"And aren't you going to ask me to come in and sit down— even if it's on the floor?"

The youngest brought up a chair for the most important official in the village.

"Thanks very much. But who was having lunch with you? I see there's a fourth place laid."

All three stared at the general's plate.

"It was—you know—" stammed the elder, twisting her fingers in her misery.

The second sister came to the rescue:

"It's rather difficult to explain, but although Mamma is dead, we always lay a place for her, so as not to feel too lonely."

"Why, it looks as if you're turning into spiritualists."

"Won't you have something, Commissioner?"

"That's kind of you but I've already eaten. My wife has just given me lunch, and I couldn't take my siesta because I received a telegram from the Minister of the Interior instructing me to take proceedings against you if you don't pay the doctor."

"But, Commissioner, that's not fair, you know it isn't . . ."

"That may be so, but needs must when the devil drives."

"Of course," exclaimed the three sisters, with tears in their eyes.

"I'm very sorry to have to come and upset you like this, but that's how it is, as you know already; nine thousand pesos, the house or . . ."

The doctor's odious stubbornness was plainly expressed in the way the Commissioner turned on his heel, and presented them with his back—a back which looked like a tree-trunk.

The general heard them weeping. They locked and barred the street-door, in terror lest the Commissioner should return. Their tears splashed on to the plate of chicken.

"How cruel life is, General! You're lucky to be leaving this country for ever."

"What did he threaten you with?" asked Canales, addressing the eldest of the three who said to her sisters without drying her tears:

"One of you tell him."

"With taking Mamma out of her grave," stammered the youngest.

Canales stared at all three sisters, and stopped eating.

"What do you say?"

"Exactly that, General; with taking Mamma out of her grave."

"But that's iniquitous!"

"Tell him."

"All right. But you must understand, General, that our village doctor is a scoundrel of the deepest dye; we were told so before, but one can only learn from experience. What were we to do? It's difficult to believe people can be so wicked."

"A few radishes, General?"

The second sister handed the dish, and while Canales helped himself to radishes the youngest went on with her story:

"We fell into his trap. This is his game: when one of his patients falls seriously ill, and the last thing the relatives are thinking about is a funeral, he has a burial vault built. Then, when the moment comes—this was what happened to us—rather than let Mamma lie in the bare earth we accepted one of the recesses in his vault without realising what we were letting ourselves in for."

"And he knew we were unprotected women," remarked the eldest sister between sobs.

"I can tell you, General, the day he sent in the bill we were all three thunderstruck: nine thousand pesos for fifteen visits; nine thousand pesos or this house, because it appears he wants to get married, or . . ."

"Or if we didn't pay—he told my sister—oh it's too abominable—'you can take your rubbish out of my vault!' "

Canales struck the table with his fist.

"Dirty little quack!"

He thumped on the table again, making the plates, cutlery and glasses rattle, and opening and shutting his fingers as if he wanted to strangle this particular scoundrel and also destroy the whole social system which produced one shameful abuse after another.

"Have simple people been promised a Kingdom of Heaven on earth—what sanctimonious rubbish!—merely so that they should put up with such rogues?" he reflected. "No! We've had quite enough of this Reign of Camels! I swear I will work for total revolution; everything must be turned upside down! The people must rise against these parasites, exploiters of official positions and idlers who would be better off cultivating the soil. Everyone must take his share in destruction! destruction! destruction! Not a single puppet among them shall keep his head."

His departure was fixed for ten o'clock that night, according to an arrangement with a smuggler who was a friend of the family. The general wrote several letters, including an urgent one to his daughter. The Indian was going to pass himself off as a carrier and return by the main road. There were no good-byes. The horses moved off with their hooves wrapped in rags, whilst the sisters stood against the wall in a dark alley, weeping bitterly. When he reached the wider road the general felt a hand seize the bridle of his horse. He heard dragging footsteps.

"What a fright they gave me," whispered the smuggler. "I almost stopped breathing! But don't worry—they're only some men going with the doctor to serenade his sweetheart."

A candlewood torch was burning at the end of the street, sending out tongues of flame to join and separate the shapes of the houses and trees, and of five or six men standing together under a window.

"Which of them is the doctor?" asked the general, with his pistol in his hand.

The smuggler reined in his horse, raised his arm and pointed to a man holding a guitar. A shot tore through the air, and a man fell to the ground, as a banana falls from the bunch.

"Jesus Maria! Look what you've done! We must get away, quick—or they'll get us! Come on, spur your horse!"

"It's what . . . everyone must . . . do to . . . free the . . . people!" The words were jerked out of Canales between the strides of his galloping horse.

The noise of the horses' hooves woke the dogs, the dogs woke the hens, the hens woke the cocks, the cocks woke the villagers, who came reluctantly back to life, yawning, stretching and afraid.

The party of serenaders lifted up the doctor's dead body. People came out with lanterns from the surrounding houses. The lady who had been the object of the serenade could not weep, but stood stunned with shock and half undressed, holding a Chinese lantern in her white hand, her gaze lost in the murderous darkness.

"We're alongside the river now, General, but it needs a brave man to get across where we mean to cross, I don't mind telling you. Oh life, if only you lasted for ever!"

"Who's afraid?" answered Canales, who was riding behind on a black horse.

"Bravo! A man feels as strong as a lion when someone's after him! Hold on to me, tight, tight, or you'll lose the way!"

Everything was indistinct around them, the air was warm but with icy currents in it. They could hear the river rushing through the reeds.

They dismounted and plunged into a gully. The smuggler tethered the horses in a place he knew of, where he could collect them on his return. Between the shadows, patches of river reflected the starlit sky and a strange floating vegetation of mottled green trees with eyes the colour of talc, and white teeth. The water gurgled past the sleepy, greasy banks, smelling of frogs.

The smuggler and the general leapt from islet to islet in silence, each with his pistol in his hand. Their shadows followed them like alligators; the alligators followed them like shadows. Clouds of insects stung them, there was a winged poison in the air. There was the smell of the sea, of the sea caught in the net of the forest, with all its fish, its stars, corals and madrepores, its profundities and currents. The moss dangled overhead like the slimy tentacles of moribund octopuses. Even the wild beasts dared not go where they were going. Canales kept turning his head in every direction, lost in this ominous, inaccessible region, as destructive by nature

193

as its fauna. An alligator which had obviously tasted human flesh attacked the smuggler, but he had time to jump out of the way. It was not so with the general, who turned round to defend himself and stopped dead to find another alligator waiting for him with open jaws. It was a crucial moment. A deathly shiver ran down his spine. His hair stood on end. He was speechless with horror. He clenched his fists. There were three successive shots and the echo repeated them, before he took advantage of the wounded beast's flight to leap to safety. The smuggler fired again. Recovering from his terror the general ran forward and shook him by the hand, burning his fingers on his pistol barrel.

The sun was rising when they parted at the frontier. Over the emerald fields, over the mountains with their dense clump of trees like musical boxes for the birds, and over the forest, alligator-shaped clouds floated by, carrying treasures of light on their backs.

PART THREE

Weeks, Months, Years . . .

CHAPTER XXVIII

Conversation in the Darkness

The first voice:

"What day is it?"

The second voice:

"Why yes, what day can it be?"

The third voice:

"Wait a moment. I was arrested on a Friday. Friday, Saturday, Sunday, Monday . . . Monday. But how long have I been here? So what day is it?"

The first voice:

"I feel as if we were very far away, don't you? very far away."

Third voice:

"Don't talk like that!"

The first two voices:

"We mustn't . . ."

". . . talk like that!"

The third voice:

"But don't stop talking. I'm terrified of the silence; I'm afraid. I keep imagining a hand stretching out through the darkness, to seize me by the neck and strangle me."

The second voice:

"Talk for God's sake! Tell us what's happening in the town; you were the last to see it. What people are doing; how every thing's going . . . Sometimes I imagine the whole city buried in shadows as we are, shut in between very high walls, and the streets deep in the dead mud of winter. I don't know if it's the same with you, but at the end of the winter I couldn't bear to think that the mud was drying up. When I talk about the town it gives me a damnable craving to eat; I long for some Californian apples . . ."

The first voice:

"Or oranges perhaps! As for me I'd rather have a cup of hot tea."

The second voice:

"And to think that everything must be going on as usual in the town, as if nothing had happened, as if we weren't buried alive here! The trams must all be running. What time is it, for that matter?"

The first voice:

"It must be about . . ."

The second voice.

"I haven't the faintest idea."

The first voice:

"It must be about . . ."

The third voice:

"Talk! Go on talking. For heaven's sake don't stop talking! I'm terrified of the silence; I'm afraid, I keep imagining a hand stretching out through the darkness, to seize me by the neck and strangle me!"

And he added in a voice of anguish:

"I didn't want to tell you, but I'm afraid we may be flogged . . ."

The first voice:

"Don't talk about it. It must be terrible to be beaten!"

The second voice:

"Even the grandchildren of men who have been flogged feel the shame of it!"

The first voice:

"You're talking wickedly! Much better keep quiet!"

The second voice:

"Everything's wicked to a sacristan."

The first voice:

"Nothing of the sort! What stories have they been stuffing you with?"

The second voice:

"I tell you that everything that other people do is wicked to a sacristan!"

The third voice:

"Talk! Go on talking! Don't stop, for the sake of whatever you love most in the world! The silence terrifies me; I'm afraid. I keep imagining a hand stretching out through the darkness to seize me by the neck and strangle me!"

The student and the sacristan were still imprisoned in the jail where the beggars had spent one night, but they now had the lawyer Carvajal for company.

"My arrest happened in a very terrible way," said Carvajal. "The servant who went out to buy bread in the morning came back with the news that the house was surrounded by soldiers. She told my wife and my wife told me, but I thought nothing of it, and imagined that they were after some brandy-smuggler or other. I finished shaving, had my bath and my breakfast and dressed myself to go and congratulate the President—up to the nines in fact! 'Hallo, my friend, what a surprise,' I said to the Judge Advocate General when I found him on my doorstep in full uniform. 'I've come for you,' he replied, 'and be quick because I'm late already!' I went with him a little way and when he asked me if I had no idea why the soldiers were surrounding the house, I said no I hadn't. 'Well then I'll tell you, you little rat,' he said. 'They've come to arrest you.' I looked at his face and saw he wasn't joking. Just then an officer took hold of me by the arm, and they escorted me away, dressed as I was in my morning coat and top hat, and threw my carcass into this jail."

And after a pause he added:

"Now you two talk! I'm terrified of the darkness. I'm afraid!"

"Oh dear! Oh dear! What's happening?" exclaimed the student. "The sacristan's head is as cold as a millstone!"

"What d'you mean?"

"I've been touching him, and he can't feel anything any more and . . ."

"It wasn't me, take care what you say!"

"Who was it then? You, Carvajal?"

"No."

"Then . . . is there a dead man among us?"

"No, it's not a dead man. It's me . . ."

"But who are you?" put in the student. "You seem very cold!"

An extremely weak voice replied:

"I'm one of you."

The first three voices:

"Ohhh!"

The sacristan told Carvajal the story of his own misfortunes.

"I left the sacristy"—and he pictured himself coming out of the tidy sacristy with its smell of extinguished censers, old woodwork, gold ornaments and locks of dead people's hair. "I crossed the church"—and he saw himself traversing the church, overawed by the proximity of the Blessed Sacrament, the immobility of the candles and the mobility of the flies—"and I went to take down the notice of the Virgin of La O's novena, because one of the brothers had told me to, now that it was over. But the trouble was that as I can't read, I removed a paper announcing the anniversary of the President's mother instead by mistake. It was by the President's orders that the Blessed Sacrament had been exposed. I couldn't have done anything worse. They arrested me and put me in this prison as a revolutionary!"

The student was the only one who kept silent about the reason for his arrest. Talking about his diseased lungs caused him less pain that speaking ill of his country. He dwelt on his physical infirmities in order to forget that he had seen the light during a shipwreck, that he had seen the light among corpses, that he had opened his eyes in a school with no windows, where they had extinguished the small light of faith in him as soon as he arrived, without putting anything in its place except darkness, chaos, confusion and the astronomical melancholy of a eunuch. And in a low voice he began reciting this poem to lost generations:

> We anchor in the ports of nothingness,
> With no lights on the masts of our arms;
> We are wet with tears, brine-soaked
> As sailors returned from the sea.
>
> Your mouth is my delight—kiss me!
> and your hand in my hand lay yesterday.
> Ah! how useless does life flow again
> through the cold river-bed of the heart!
>
> The knapsack torn and the honey spilt,
> the bees flew away through space
> like meteors. Not yet,
> The rose of the winds had lost its petals;
> the heart bounded over the graves.
>
> Ah, ri-ri-ri, rumbling, rumbling cart!
> Through the moonless night go the horses
> Filled with roses to the hooves,

As if returning from the stars
And not from the cemetery.

Ah ri-ri-ri, rumbling, rumbling cart,
funicular of tears, ri-ri-ri,
between feathered brows, ri-ri-ri.

Riddle of dawn in the stars
illusion of bends in the road,
and how far from the world and how early!

Waves of tears strive in the ocean
to reach the strand of the eyelids.

"Talk, go on talking!" said Carvajal after a long silence. "Go
on talking!"

"Let's talk about liberty!" murmured the student.

"What an idea!" interrupted the sacristan. "Fancy talking
about liberty in prison!"

"And don't you suppose sick people talk about health in
hospital?"

The fourth voice murmured faintly: "There's no hope of
freedom for us, my friends; we must put up with this as long as
God wills. The men of this town who desired their country's good
are far away now: some of them begging outside houses in a
foreign land, others rotting in a common grave. A day will come
when no one dares walk the streets of this town. Already the trees
don't bear fruit as they used to. Maize is less nourishing than it
was. Sleep is less restful; water is less refreshing. The air is
becoming impossible to breathe. Plagues follow epidemics,
epidemics follow plagues, and soon an earthquake will put an end
to us all. My eyes tell me that our race is doomed! When it
thunders, it is a voice from heaven crying: 'You are evil and
corrupt, you are accomplices in wickedness!' Hundreds of men
have had their brains blown out against our prison walls by
murderous bullets. Our marble palaces are wet with innocent
blood. Where can one turn one's eyes in search of freedom?"

The sacristan:

"To God, who is omnipotent!"

The student:

"What's the use, if He doesn't answer?"

The sacristan:

"Because it is His Blessed Will."

The student:

"What a pity!"

The third voice:

"Talk! Go on talking, for heaven's sake! Don't stop! I'm terrified of the silence; I'm afraid. I keep imagining a hand stretching out through the darkness to seize us by the neck and strangle us!"

"Better to pray."

The sacristan's voice spread Christian resignation throughout the prison cell. Carvajal, who had passed as a liberal and a priest-hater among his neighbours, murmured:

"Let us pray . . ."

But the student broke in:

"What's the good of praying! We ought not to pray! We ought to try and break this door down and go to meet the revolution!"

Two arms belonging to someone he could not see embraced him warmly, and he felt against his cheek the bristles of a small beard wet with tears:

"You can die in peace, ex-master of the Infant School of San José. There's hope yet in a country where youth can talk like that!"

The third voice:

"Talk, go on talking, go on talking!"

CHAPTER XXIX

Council of War

THE indictment charging Canales and Carvajal with sedition, rebellion and treason, with all possible aggravating circumstances, ran to so many pages that it was impossible to read it right through at a sitting. Fourteen witnesses stated unanimously on oath that on the night of April 21st they had been in the Cathedral Porch, in which they habitually spent the night owing to their extreme poverty; and that they saw General Eusebio Canales and Abel Carvajal, the lawyer, fall upon a soldier who had been identified as Colonel José Parrales Sonriente and strangle him, in spite of the resistance he put up; he fought hand to hand like a lion, but was unable to use his weapons to defend himself against superior strength. They stated also that as soon as the murder had been committed, Carvajal addressed the following or similar words to Canales: "Now that we have killed 'the man with the little mule' the military leaders will have to hand over their weapons and recognise you, General, as the Supreme Head of the Army. It will soon be dawn; let's hurry off with the news to those who are collected in my house, so that they may proceed with the arrest and execution of the President of the Republic, and the organisation of a new government."

Carvajal was astounded. Every page of the indictment had a surprise in store for him. It would have been laughable except that the accusation was much too serious. And he went on reading. He was reading by the light of a window giving on to a shut-in patio, in the little unfurnished room reserved for those condemned to death. The Council of War which was to try the case was meeting that night, and they had left him alone with the indictment to prepare his defence. But they had left it till the last moment. He was trembling all over. He read without understanding or pausing, tormented by the fact that the darkness was devouring the manuscript, which seemed to be dissolving gradually into damp ashes in his hands. He did not succeed in reading much of it. The sun was setting. Its light was growing dim and his eyes were clouded with anguish at its loss. A last line, two words, the stroke of a pen, a date, a page . . . He tried in vain to read the number of the page; darkness was flooding over the paper like a black ink stain, yet he still hung impatiently over the dossier as if, instead of his having to read it, it was to be tied round his neck like a stone before he was hurled into the abyss. The rattling of the non-political prisoners' chains could be heard all along the invisible courtyards, and from further off still came the muted sounds of the traffic in the city streets.

"Oh God! My poor frozen body needs warmth and my eyes need light more desperately than do those of all the inhabitants of the hemisphere the sun is now shining on put together. If they knew of my sufferings they would be more merciful than you, oh God, and give me back the sun so that I could finish reading . . ."

Again and again he counted the pages he had not read, by touch alone. Ninety-one. Again and again he passed his finger-tips over the surface of the rough-grained sheets, trying to read as the blind do in his desperation.

Last night, in the small hours, they had moved him in a locked van with a great display of force from the Second Police Station to the Central Prison; however, so great was his pleasure at seeing and hearing and feeling the street around him that for a moment he thought they were taking him to his own house: the words died on his lips in bitter tears and longing.

The myrmidons of the law found him with the indictment in his arms and the sweet taste of the wet streets in his mouth; they snatched the documents from him and pushed him without a word into the room where the Council of War was sitting.

"But, Mr President," Carvajal plucked up courage to say to the general who was presiding over the council, "how can I defend myself when you don't even give me time to read the indictment?"

"That is nothing to do with us," answered the president; "the intervals between sessions are short, time is passing, and this matter is urgent. We have been summoned here to pronounce sentence."

What followed was like a dream to Carvajal, half ritual, half farce. He was the principal actor and faced them all from his position on the see-saw of death, in the middle of a hostile void.

But he did not feel afraid; he felt nothing; his anxieties lay dormant under his numbed skin. He made an impression of great courage. The table round which the tribunal sat was covered by a flag, as prescribed by the regulations. Military uniforms. Reading of the documents. Of numerous documents. Taking of oaths. The military statute-book lay like a stone on the table, on top of the flag. The beggars were sitting in the witnesses' seats. Flatfoot sat stiffly erect, with his cheerful toothless drunkard's face, his hair neatly brushed, not missing a word of what was read out, nor an expression on the President's face. Salvador the Tiger followed the proceedings with the dignity of a gorilla, picking his flattened nose or the few teeth scattered in his huge mouth, stretching from ear to ear. The tall, bony, sinister-looking Widower twisted his face into a corpselike rictus to smile at the members of the tribunal. Plump, wrinkled, dwarfish Lulo gave way to sudden outbursts of laughter or anger, amiability or hatred, and then shut his eyes and stopped his ears to show that he wanted to hear and see nothing that was going on. Don Juan, a small, moody-looking figure, was dressed in his inevitable frock-coat and other shabby garments exhaling a bourgeois and family atmosphere (a broad tie stained with tomato-juice, down-at-heel patent leather shoes, false cuffs, a removable dickey) and was given an air of gentlemanly elegance by his straw hat and stone deafness. Don Juan, who could not hear a thing, was counting the soldiers posted all round the walls of the room at intervals of two yards. Close to him was Ricardo the Musician, with his head and part of his face swathed in a coloured bandanna, a scarlet nose and his bristly beard greasy with food. Ricardo the Musician was talking to himself, with his eyes fixed on the swollen belly of the deaf-mute, who was dribbling over the seat and scratching the lice in her left armpit. After the deaf-mute came Pereque, a negro with only one ear the shape of a small chamber-pot. After Pereque, Little Miona, who was exceedingly thin, blind in one eye, moustachioed and stank of old mattresses.

After reading the indictment, the Prosecutor, a soldier with his hair *en brosse* and his small head emerging from a military tunic with a collar twice too big for it, got to his feet to ask for a sentence of death. Carvajal turned and looked at the members of the tribunal, searching for signs of wisdom and judgement. The first one his eyes encountered was as drunk as it was possible to be.

His brown hands were outlined against the flag; they were like the hands of a peasant acting in a play about a trial at a village fête. Next to him was a dark-skinned officer, also drunk. And the President, who was giving the most finished performance of them all as an alcoholic, seemed on the point of passing out.

He could not say anything in his defence. He tried to utter a few words, but at once received the painful impression that no one was listening—and in fact no one was listening. His words crumbled in his mouth like damp bread.

The sentence had been drawn up and written out in advance; there was something portentous about it, in contrast to the simplicity of those who were putting it into effect and would sign it (puppets made of gold and dried beef, bathed from head to foot in the diarrhetic light of the oil lamp) or in contrast to the beggars with their toads' eyes and their snakelike shadows lying like black moons on the orange floor—or to the little soldiers sucking their chin-straps, or to the furniture, as silent as if it stood in a house where a crime had been committed.

"I appeal against the sentence!"

Carvajal's voice was in his boots.

"Let's keep to the point," grumbled the President, "there's no question of an appeal or peal, or any other such rubbish here!"

A glass of water as large as the immensity he was holding in his hands helped him to swallow what he was trying to expel from his body: the idea of suffering, of the mechanism of death, of the impact of bullets on bones, blood on the living skin, glazed eyes, warm linen, the earth. Terrified, he gave back the glass and kept his hand outstretched until he could summon up the courage to withdraw it. He refused the cigarette he was offered. He fingered his neck with trembling hands, while his unfocused gaze, unrelated to the pale cement of his face, wandered round the whitewashed walls of the room.

More dead than alive, he was pushed along a draughty passage; there was a sharp taste in his mouth, his legs were giving under him, and he had a tear in each eye.

"Here, have a drink," said a lieutenant with eyes like a heron's.

He raised the bottle to his mouth—it seemed enormous—and drank.

"Lieutenant," said a voice from the shadows, "you will join

the batteries tomorrow. We have orders that no indulgences of any description are to be granted to political offenders."

A few steps further on they entombed him in an underground dungeon three yards long by two and a half wide, in which twelve prisoners condemned to death were already standing packed together like sardines, motionless for lack of space, satisfying their physical needs where they stood and trampling on their own excrement. Carvajal was Number 13. When the soldiers left them, the painful breathing of the mass of doomed men filled the silence of the cell, already disturbed by the distant cries of a walled-up prisoner.

Two or three times Carvajal caught himself mechanically counting the cries of this poor wretch, who had been condemned to die of thirst: Seventy-two! Seventy-three! Seventy-four!

The stench of the trampled excrement and the lack of fresh air made him feel faint, and carried him away from this group of human beings to wander along the brink of infernal precipices of despair, counting the prisoner's cries.

Lucio Vasquez was pacing to and fro in a neighbouring cell, completely yellow with jaundice, with his nails and eyeballs the colour of the underside of an ilex leaf. The only thing that sustained him in his misery was the idea that he would one day have his revenge on Genaro Rodas, whom he believed to be responsible for his troubles. He was kept alive by this remote hope, as black and sweet as molasses. He would wait there in the shadows for all eternity if only he could avenge himself. Such pitch-black night inhabited his ignoble breast, that nothing but the image of the knife cutting into Rodas' entrail and leaving a wound like an open mouth could let any light in upon his malevolent thoughts. With his hands cramped by the cold, Vasquez spent hour after hour motionless as a worm made of yellow mud, savouring his revenge. Kill him! Kill him! And as if his enemy were already at hand, he would stretch out in the darkness, feel the ice-cold handle of his knife, and hurl himself on Rodas in his imagination, like a ghost going through its accustomed movements.

He was jolted back to reality by the cries of the walled-up prisoner:

"*Per Dio, per favori* . . . water! Water! Water! Water! Tineti, water, water! *Per Dio, per favori* waaater, waaater . . . water!"

The walled-up man threw himself against the door of his cell, which had been completely obliterated on the outside by a layer of bricks cemented to the floor, cemented to the walls.

"Water, Tineti! Water, Tineti! Water, *per Dio*, water, *per favori*, Tineti!"

Devoid of tears, devoid of saliva, devoid of anything that was wet or cool, with his throat a burning thorn-bush, revolving in a world of lights and patches of darkness, he hammered out his incessant cry:

"Water, Tineti! Water, Tineti! Water, Tineti!"

A Chinaman with his face scarred with smallpox looked after the prisoners. Every few centuries he would come by like a last breath of life. Did this strange semi-divine being really exist, or was he a fiction of all their imaginations? The trampled excrement and the cries of the walled-up prisoners were making their heads swim and it was possible, yes possible, that this benevolent angel was only a fantastic vision.

"Water, Tineti! Water, Tineti! *Per Dio, per favori*, water, water, water, water!"

Soldiers came in and went out again, tramping across the tiled floor in their leather sandals, and among them there were some who used to roar with laughter and shout back at the walled-up prisoner:

"Tyrolese, Tyrolese! What did you do to the green parrot who talks like a man?"

"Water, *per Dio*, water, Signori, water *per favori*!"

Vasquez was brooding over his revenge, and the cries of the Italian left the air as dry and thirsty as a husk of sugar cane. The sound of a shot made him catch his breath. The executions had begun. It must be three in the morning.

CHAPTER XXX

Marriage in Extremis

"THERE's someone dangerously ill in our neighbourhood!"

A spinster came out of the door of every house.

"Someone dangerously ill in our neighbourhood!"

A woman called Petronila, with a face like a conscript's and the manner of a diplomat, who (for lack of other attractions) would at least have preferred to be called Berta, came out of the House of the Two Hundred. Next came a friend of the Two Hundred called Silvia, with a face like a chick-pea and clothes of Merovingian cut.

Then Silvia's friend Engracia, with her stays—or rather her armour—eating into her flesh, and her tight shoes into her corns, and a watch-chain hanging round her neck like a halter. Then Engracia's cousin, with a heart-shaped head like a viper's; she was harsh-voiced, dumpy and masculine-looking, hardly bigger than one of Engracia's legs, and had a habit of forecasting disasters out of the almanac and prophesying the coming of comets, anti-Christ, or an age when men would climb up trees to escape from the ardent pursuit of women, and women would go up and fetch them down again.

Someone seriously ill in our neighbourhood! What a godsend! They were not aware of entertaining such a thought, yet it was almost explicit in the way their soft voices tried to conceal their gratification over an event which might give many of them work for their scissors, and leave plenty of material over for all of them to cut a dress-length for themselves.

La Masacuata was waiting for them.

"My sisters are ready," declared Petronila from the Two Hundred, without saying what they were ready for.

"If you're short of linen of course you can count on me," remarked Silvia.

And Engracia, little Engracia, who smelt of beef broth when she didn't smell of hair-lotion, added, only half-enunciating the words because her stays were suffocating her:

"I thought of her and said a prayer for the souls of the dying after I had finished my Hour of Prayer."

They were gathered in the room behind the shop, speaking in undertones and trying not to disturb the silence which hung round the invalid's bed like some pharmaceutical product, nor to worry the gentleman who sat with her night and day. A real gentleman, yes indeed. They went up to the bed on tiptoe, more from desire to get a look at his face than at Camila lying there, a ghostly figure with her long eyelashes, her thin thin neck, her hair in confusion; and, scenting a mystery of some sort—isn't there always a mystery where there is love?—they refused to rest till they had extracted the key to it from the barkeeper. He was her sweetheart! Her sweetheart! Her sweetheart! Her sweetheart! Of course that was it. He was her sweetheart! They all repeated the golden word—all except Silvia, who went discreetly away as soon as she found out that Camila was General Canales' daughter, and did not return. Better not get mixed up with enemies of the Government. He may very well be her sweetheart, she said to herself, and on the President's side as well, but I'm my brother's sister, and my brother is a deputy, and I might compromise him. "We must trust in God!"

"We must trust in God," she repeated, out in the street by now.

Angel Face was hardly aware of the old maids, although they were anxious to complete their errand of mercy to the sick girl by consoling her lover. He thanked them without hearing what they said—mere words—with his whole soul involved in Camila's involuntary but agonising moans, nor did he respond to their demonstrations of emotion when they shook his hand. Crushed by his own misery, he felt his body growing cold. He had the impression that it was raining, that his limbs were numb, that he was entangled with invisible phantoms in a space larger than life, a space in which air, light, shadows and objects were isolated and alone.

The doctor broke in on the vicious circle of his thoughts.

"Then, doctor . . .?"

"Only a miracle can save her!"

"You'll come back, won't you?"

The barkeeper never sat down for a moment; yet nothing seemed to exhaust her. She was laundress to the neighbourhood, and used to put the linen to soak very early in the morning before taking Vasquez's breakfast to the prison; she had had no news of him lately. When she got back she would soap, rub and hang out the washing, and while it dried she would hurry home to do her housework and other chores, see to the invalid, light candles in front of the saints, try and make Angel Face take a little food, wait for the doctor, go to the chemist, put up with the "she-priests" as she called the spinsters, and quarrel with the pro-prietress of the mattress-shop. "Mattresses for lazy pigs!" she shouted from her doorway, pretending to whisk away the flies with a rag. "Mattresses for lazy pigs!"

"Nothing but a miracle can save her!"

Angel Face repeated the doctor's words. A miracle, the arbitrary persistence of what is perishable, the triumph of a fragment of humanity over the sterile Absolute. He felt a craving to cry out to God to perform the miracle; yet all the while the world was revolving out of reach—useless, hostile, uncertain and purposeless.

They were all expecting the crisis from one moment to the next. The howling of a dog, a loud knock on a door, the chiming of the La Merced clock would make the neighbours cross them-selves and exclaim between sighs: "She's at peace at last! Yes, her hour has struck! Poor young man! But it had to be! It was God's Will! We shall all come to it!"

Petronila was reporting on the state of affairs to a friend of hers: one of those men who go on looking like little boys even when they are old; he taught English and other more unusual subjects and was familiarly known as the Teacher. She wanted to know whether it was possible to save Camila's life by super-natural means, and the Teacher ought to know, because as well as giving English lessons he devoted his spare time to the study of theosophy, spiritualism, magic, astrology, hypnotism, and the occult sciences, and was even the inventor of a method which he called: "A repository of witchcraft useful for finding hidden treasure in haunted houses". The Teacher had never been able to account for his addiction to the unknown. As a young man he had been attracted to the Church, but a married woman more experienced and domineering than himself intervened when he was going to sing the Epistles, and he hung up his cassock and other priestly garments and was left looking rather foolish and lonely. He left the theological college for a commercial school, and would have successfully finished his training had he not been obliged to fly from his professor of accountancy who fell madly in love with him. Mechanics, in the strenuous shape of the iron-works, now opened its grimy arms to him, and he was taken on by a work-shop near his house to blow the bellows, but as he was neither used to hard work nor sufficiently strong for it, he soon gave up the job. Why should he work, when he was the only nephew of a very rich lady who had intended him for the priest-hood, a purpose which she had still not abandoned? "Go back to the Church," she used to say, "instead of yawning your head off here; go back to the Church. Can't you see that you're sick of the world, and that you're a bit crazy anyway and as weak as water; that you've tried everything and nothing satisfies you—soldier, musician, bullfighter! Or if you don't want to be a priest why don't you take up teaching—give English lessons for instance? If you're not one of the Lord's chosen, why don't you choose children? English is easier than Latin and more useful, and if you give English lessons your pupils will suppose you're speaking English although they can't understand—and if they don't understand, all the better."

Petronila lowered her voice, as she always did when she was wearing her heart on her sleeve.

"A lover who adores her, who worships her, Teacher; although he kidnapped her, he has treated her with respect and hopes the Church will bless their lifelong union. One doesn't see that sort of thing every day . . ."

"Less often than ever nowadays, my child," put in the tallest member of the Two Hundred, a woman who seemed to have climbed a few rungs of the ladder of her own body, as she came into the room carrying a bunch of roses.

"And this lover of hers has overwhelmed her with kindness, Teacher, and certainly won't survive her—oh dear!"

"Did you say, Petronila," said the Teacher slowly, "that the medical faculty declare they can't do a thing to snatch her out of the hands of the Fates?"

"Yes indeed; they've given her up three times."

"And did you say, Nila, that nothing but a miracle could save her?"

"Just think of it! My heart bleeds for that poor young man . . ."

"Well I've got the key; we'll bring about that miracle. The

only thing that can fight death is love, because they are equally strong, as the Song of Songs tells us. And if, as you say, this girl's sweetheart adores her—loves her deeply, I mean, with all his heart and soul and intends to marry her, we can save her life by means of the sacrament of marriage. According to my theory of grafting, that is what should be done in this case."

Petronila very nearly fainted into the Teacher's arms. She aroused the whole household, went back to her friends' house, and sent La Masacuata to speak to the priest, and that same day Camila and Angel Face were married on the very threshold of the next world. The favourite grasped a long, delicate hand, as cold as an ivory paper-knife, in his own feverish right hand, while the priest read the Latin words of the sacrament. The members of the Two Hundred were present—Engracia and the Teacher dressed in black. When the ceremony was over the Teacher exclaimed:

"Make thee another self, for love of me!"

CHAPTER XXXI

Sentinels Made of Ice

In the entrance to the prison two rows of gleaming bayonets could be seen; the soldiers on guard were sitting opposite one another like travellers in a dark railway-carriage. Suddenly one of the passing vehicles stopped at the door. The driver leant back to get more purchase on the reins, rocking from side to side like a dirty rag doll and spitting out an oath. He had nearly lost his balance! Punished by the brakes, the wheels screeched their way along the smooth high walls of the sinister building, and a pot-bellied man whose legs could hardly reach the ground slowly alighted. Feeling his cab relieved of the weight of the Judge Advocate General, the driver gripped his unlit cigarette between his dry lips—what a relief to be left alone with the horses!—loosened the reins and drove off to wait opposite, beside a garden as stony as a traitor's heart, just at the moment that a woman threw herself on her knees at the Judge Advocate's feet, begging him loudly to listen to her.

"Get up, Señora; I can't listen to you like that! No, no, get up please; I haven't the honour of your acquaintance . . ."

"I'm the wife of Carvajal the lawyer . . ."

"Get up . . ."

But she burst out again:

"I've been looking for you all day and night, Señor, at all hours, everywhere; in your house, in your mother's house, in your office, but without success. You are the only person who knows what has become of my husband; only you know, only you can tell me. Where is he? What has happened to him? Tell me if he is alive, Señor? Tell me that he is alive, Señor?"

"As it happens, Señora, the Council of War which is to hear my colleague's case has received an urgent summons for tonight."

"Aaaaah!"

The intensity of her relief kept her trembling lips apart. Alive! There was hope in the news. Alive! And as he was innocent—free . . .

But the Judge Advocate's cold expression did not change as he added:

"The political situation of our country does not permit of the Government showing any pity whatsoever to its enemies, Señora. That is all I can say to you. Go and see the President and beg for your husband's life, or he may be sentenced to death and shot within twenty-four hours, by the law of the land . . ."

"La . . . la . . . la . . ."

"The law comes before individuals, Señora, and unless the President reprieves him . . ."

"La-La-La . . ."

She could not speak. She stood there white as the handkerchief she was tearing to pieces with her teeth, otherwise motionless, abstracted, twisting her fingers together.

The Judge Advocate General disappeared between the two rows of bayonets. After a moment of animation, while carriages full of smart ladies and gentlemen came by on their way home from the most fashionable promenade in the town, the street was left exhausted and alone. A tiny tram came sparking and whistling out of a side road, and went off heeling over on its rails.

"La-La-La . . ."

She could not speak. A pair of ice-cold pincers had her by the neck in a tenacious grip, and her body was gradually slipping downwards from her shoulders to the ground. She was nothing but an empty dress, with a head, hands and feet. The sound of a cab approaching along the street resounded in her ears. She stopped it. The horses seemed to swell like tears as they arched their necks, drew back on their haunches and came to a halt. She told the driver to take her to the President's country house as fast as possible, but she was in such a hurry—such a desperate hurry—that although the horses set off at full speed she never stopped insisting that the driver must make them go faster . . . Surely they ought to be there by now? . . . Faster . . . she must save her husband . . . Faster, faster, faster . . . she snatched the whip from the driver . . . she must save her husband . . . the horses increased their speed under her cruel lashing . . . The whip scorched their flanks . . . save her husband . . . They ought to be there by now . . . But the carriage wouldn't move . . . she could feel that it wasn't moving, the wheels were revolving round the sleeping axles without advancing at all; they were standing still in the same place . . . yet she must save her husband . . . yes, yes, yes, yes, yes . . . her hair had come down—save him—her blouse came unfastened—save him. But the carriage wouldn't move . . . she could feel that it wasn't moving, only the front wheels were turning, she could feel the back wheels lagging behind so that the carriage was lengthening out like the bellows of a camera, and she could see the horses getting smaller and smaller in the distance . . . The driver had taken his whip away from her . . . they couldn't go on like this . . . yes, yes, yes, yes they could . . . No, they couldn't . . . yes . . . no, yes . . . no . . . But why not? . . . Why not? . . . yes . . . no . . . yes . . . no . . . She tore off her rings, her brooch, her ear-rings, her bracelet, put them in her jacket pocket and threw them to the driver, begging him not to stop. She must save her husband. But still they hadn't got there . . . She must get there, get there, get there, but still they hadn't arrived . . . She must get there, beg for her husband's life and save him . . . but still they hadn't arrived. Stones, ruts, dust, dried mud, grass, but still they hadn't arrived . . . They were stuck fast like telegraph wires, or rather they were going backwards like the telegraph wires, like the plantations of trees, like the fallow fields, like the clouds gilded by the setting sun, the lonely crossroads and the motionless oxen.

At last they turned aside towards the President's house, along a narrow ribbon of road disappearing between stream-beds and trees. Her heart was beating suffocatingly. The road wound its way between the little houses of a clean deserted village. Here they began to meet vehicles returning from the President's estate—landaus, sulkies, buggies—in which sat people whose faces and clothes all seemed alike. The noise of the wheels and of the horses' hoofs advanced along the paved road; but they still hadn't arrived; they still hadn't arrived . . . Amongst those returning in the carriages—bureaucrats out of a job, and corpulent, smartly dressed officers—they met others on foot: farm-owners who had been urgently summoned by the President months and months ago; countrymen in boots like leather bags; school-mistresses, stopping every few minutes to get their breath, their eyes blinded with dust, their shoes falling to bits, their skirts turned up to their knees; and parties of Indian policemen who understood little of what was going on around them. She must save him . . . yes, yes, but would they ever get there? The first thing was to get there, to get there before the audience was over, to get there, to beg for his life, to save him, but would they ever get there? There was not much further to go, only just beyond the village. They should be there by now, but there was no end to the village. This was the road along which the figures of Jesus and the Virgin of Sorrows had been carried on Maundy Thursday. The hounds had howled at the melancholy music of the trumpets as the procession passed in front of the balcony where the President stood under a canopy of purple stuff and bougain-villeas. Jesus passed in front of Caesar, bowed under the weight of the wooden cross, but it was to Caesar that men and women turned their admiring gaze. Suffering was not enough, it was not enough to weep for hours on end, it was not enough for fami-lies and towns to be aged by despair; the culminating outrage must take place—the image of Christ in his agony must pass before the President with his eyes shadowed by an infamous golden canopy, between two rows of grotesque puppets and to the rattle of pagan music.

The carriage stopped at the gate of the magnificent house. Carvajal's wife hurried up an avenue of pollarded trees. An officer came out and barred the way.

"Señora, Señora . . ."

"I've come to see the President . . ."

"The President cannot see anyone, Señora; you must go away . . ."

"Yes, yes, yes, he can. He will see me. I am Carvajal's wife." And she pushed forward, escaping from the soldiers who hurried after her, protesting loudly, and came to a little house with its lights shining dimly through the shadows of dusk. "They are going to shoot my husband, General!"

Walking up and down the passage of this doll's-house, with his hands behind his back, was a tall, swarthy man, tattooed all over with gold braid. She went up to him bravely:

"They are going to shoot my husband, General!"

The officer who had followed her from the door kept repeating that it was impossible for her to see the President.

In spite of his natural good manners the general answered bluntly:

"The President can see no one, Señora. You must go away . . ."

"Oh General! Oh General! What will become of me without

217

my husband? What will become of me without my husband? No, no, General! He will see me! Let me 'pass, let me pass! Tell him I'm here! They are going to shoot my husband!"

The beating of her heart was audible through her dress. They would not let her go down on her knees. Her ear-drums were buzzing in the silence with which they greeted her requests.

Dead leaves crackled in the dusk, as if afraid of the wind blowing them along the ground. She sank on to a bench. The soldiers were made of black ice. Her sobs rose to her lips with a sound like the rustle of starched flounces, almost with the sound of knives. The saliva was bubbling from the corners of her mouth with each moan. She sank on to a bench and watered it with her tears as though it had been a whetstone. They had hustled her away from the place where the President probably was to be found. The sound of a passing patrol made her shiver with cold. They smelt of garlic sausage, molasses and peeled pinewood. The seat vanished into the darkness like a plank into the sea. She moved from place to place so as not to be shipwrecked on her seat in the darkness, so as to stay alive. Twice, thrice, many times she was stopped by the sentinels posted among the trees. In harsh voices they refused to let her pass, and threatened her with the butts or barrels of their rifles when she insisted. Frustrated on the right, she ran to the left. She stumbled over stones and hurt herself on thorny bushes. Her way was barred by more sentinels made of ice. She entreated, she fought, she stretched out her hand like a beggar, and when none of them would listen to her she started running in the opposite direction.

The trees swept her shadowy figure towards the cab, but no sooner had she put her foot on the step than she turned and rushed back like a lunatic to try one last entreaty. The driver woke up suddenly, nearly throwing away the trinkets lying warm in his pocket as he pulled his hand out to take the reins. The time passed very slowly for him; he was impatient to make an impression on La Minga. Ear-rings, rings, bracelet . . . they should stand him in good stead! He scratched one foot with the other, pulled his hat over his eyes and spat. What had been going on here in the darkness? Carvajal's wife returned to the cab like a sleepwalker. She took her seat in the cab and told the driver to wait a little, perhaps they would open the door . . . Half an hour . . . an hour . . .

The cab made no noise; or was it that she could not hear very well, or was it still motionless? The road dipped sharply down a very steep hill into a ravine. Afterwards it rocketed up again towards the town. The first dark walls. The first white house. An advertisement for Onofroff in the hollow of a wall.

Everything seemed to be welded together with her grief . . . the air . . . everything. A solar system in every tear . . . Centipedes of dew were falling from the roofs on to the narrow pavements . . . Her blood was hardly circulating in her veins . . . How are you? . . . I'm ill, very ill indeed . . . And how will you be tomorrow? . . . Just the same, and the day after as well . . . She was answering her own questions . . . and the day after tomorrow too . . .

The weight of the dead makes the earth turn by night, and by day it is the weight of the living . . . When there are more dead than living there will be eternal night, night without end, for the living will not be heavy enough to bring the dawn . . .

The cab stopped, the road went on further, but not for her, for she was at the door of the prison where almost certainly . . . she walked slowly along, step by step, leaning against the wall. She was not wearing mourning. She had acquired a bat's sense of touch in the darkness . . . Fear, cold, disgust, she overcame them all in order to press herself against the wall which would echo the sound of the shots . . . After all, while she stood there how could they possibly shoot her husband, just like that, with a fusillade, with bullets, with weapons? How could men like him, people like him, with eyes, with a mouth, with hands, with hair on their heads, with nails on their fingers, with teeth in their mouths, with a tongue, with a throat . . . It was impossible that they should shoot men thus, men with the same coloured skin, with the same tone of voice, with the same way of seeing, hearing, going to bed, getting up, loving, washing their faces, eating, laughing, walking, with the same beliefs and the same doubts . . .

CHAPTER XXXII

The President

URGENTLY summoned to the Presidential house, Angel Face brooded anxiously over Camila's state, with a new resilience in his worried gaze, a new humanity mirrored in his eyes. He turned and twisted among his doubts, like a snake in its own coils: should he go or not; the President or Camila, Camila or the President?

He could still feel the barkeeper pushing him gently on the shoulder, and hear the thread of entreaty running through her voice. He would have a chance to put in a word for Vasquez. "You go, I'll stay here and look after her." Once in the street he drew a deep breath. He was on his way to the President's house in a cab. Clatter of horses' hoofs on the stones, liquid flow of the wheels. "The Red Pad-lock" . . . "The Bee-Hive" . . . "The Vol-can-o" . . . He carefully spelt out the names of the shops he passed; they were more visible at night than by day. "The Rail-way" . . . "The Hen and Chickens" . . . Sometimes his eye fell on a Chinese name: "Lon Ley Lon and Co" . . . "Quan See Chan" . . . "Fu Quan Yen" . . . "Chon Chan Lou" . . . "Sey Yon Sey" . . . He went on thinking about General Canales. They must have sent for him to tell him the latest news . . . Impossible! . . . Why impossible? . . . They had caught him and killed him . . . or else they hadn't killed him but brought him back a prisoner. A cloud of dust blew up suddenly. The wind played at bull-fights with the cab. Anything was possible! When they reached the country the cab travelled more smoothly, like a solid body that had suddenly become liquid. Angel Face gripped his knees with his hands and sighed. The noise of the cab was lost among the thousand sounds of the slowly moving, advancing, numismatic night. He thought he heard the wings of a bird. They passed a few scattered houses. Some half-dead dogs barked at them . . .

The Under-secretary for War was waiting for him at the door of his office, and after barely as much time as it took to shake hands and lay his cigar on the edge of a bowl he led him straight to the President's apartments.

"General," said Angel Face, taking the Under-secretary by the arm, "you don't happen to know what the boss wants me for?"

"No, Don Miguelito, I am 'not aware' of the reason."

He knew now what it was. A short laugh, repeated two or three times, confirmed the truth of what the Under-secretary's evasive reply had led him to suppose. When he reached the door he saw a forest of bottles standing on a round table beside a plate of cold meat with avocado and pimento salad. The picture was completed by several chairs lying on the floor. The windows with their panes of opaque white glass each surmounted by a red crest fought to keep out the light coming from the lamps in the gardens. The officers and soldiers on guard were fully armed, there was an officer at the door and a soldier in the tree outside. The President advanced from the far end of the room; the ground seemed to advance under his feet and the house over his head.

"Mr President," the favourite began, but was interrupted before he could go on:

"Ni-ni-mierva!"

"Are you referring to the goddess, Mr President?"

His Excellency went up to the table with a springy gait, and ignoring the favourite's eulogy of Minerva, he exclaimed:

"Do you know, Miguel, that the man who discovered alcohol was looking for an elixir to produce long life?"

"No, Mr President, I didn't know that," the favourite hastened to reply.

"That's odd."

"It would be odd, certainly, for a man of such wide knowledge as you, Mr President, who have every right to consider himself as one of the foremost statesmen of modern times, but not for me."

His Excellency dropped his lids over his eyes, to shut out the chaotic vision of his surroundings that his alcoholic state was presenting him with at the moment.

"H'm, yes, I do know a lot!"

So saying he let his hand drop among the black forest of whisky bottles, and poured out a glass for Angel Face.

"Drink, Miguel." He choked on the words. Something had caught in his throat; he struck himself on the chest to get rid of it, while the muscles of his thin neck tightened and the veins in his forehead swelled. The favourite made him swallow some soda-water and after a few belches he regained the power of speech.

"Ha ha! Ha ha!" He burst out laughing and pointed at Angel Face. "Ha ha! Ha ha! At the point of death . . ." Explosion after explosion of laughter. "At the point of death. Ha ha! Ha ha!"

The favourite turned pale. The glass of whisky, from which he had just drunk the President's health, trembled in his hand.

"The Pres—"

"—IDENT knows everything," interrupted His Excellency. "Ha ha! Ha ha! At the point of death. And on the advice of a half-wit—all spiritualists are that! Ha ha! Ha ha! Ha ha!"

Angel Face stopped his mouth with his tumbler and drank his whisky so as to stifle his own indignant outburst; he had just seen red, he had just been on the point of hurling himself at his master and ramming his miserable laughter down his throat. It was the flame from his alcohol-saturated blood. If a train had gone over his body it would have caused him less pain. He felt sick with disgust, yet he still went on behaving like a well-trained, intelligent dog, content with its portion of filth and full of the instinct of self-preservation. He smiled to conceal his animosity, but there was death in his velvety eyes; he was like a poisoned man who feels his face beginning to swell.

His Excellency was pursuing a fly.

"Do you know the fly game, Miguel?"

"No, Mr President."

"Oh, it's true youUUU . . . at the point of death! Ha ha! Ha ha! Tee hee, tee hee! Ho ho! Ho ho! Hoo hoo! Hoo hoo!"

And still roaring with laughter he went on pursuing the fly as it flew from place to place, with his shirt-tails coming out of his belt, his fly-buttons undone, his shoes untied, dribbling at the mouth and with his eyes exuding a bright yellow rheum.

"Miguel," he said, stopping from shortage of breath without having caught his prey. "The fly game is the most amusing and the easiest game to learn in the world; the only thing you need is patience. We used to play the fly game for *reals* in my village when I was a boy."

When he mentioned his native village he frowned, and a

222

shadow darkened his face; he turned to look at a map of the Republic which was hanging behind him, and directed a blow at the name of his village.

He had a vision of the streets where he had walked as a poor boy, an unjustly poor boy, where he had walked as a young man, obliged to earn his living while the well-born ladinos spent their time going from one spree to the next. He saw himself as an insignificant figure, isolated in his local rut, sitting under the lamp by which he used to study at night, while his mother slept in a camp bed and the wind buffeted the deserted streets with gusts impregnated with the smell of mutton. And he saw himself later on in his third-rate lawyer's office, amongst prostitutes, gamblers, offal-sellers, horse-thieves, despised by his colleagues who had important law-suits on their hands.

He swallowed a great many drinks, one after another. His puffy eyes were shining in his green face and his nails with their black edges outlined his small hands.

"Ungrateful beasts!"

The favourite supported him by the arm. The President's eyes seemed to be seeing corpses as they travelled about the disorderly room, and he said again:

"Ungrateful beasts!" Then he added under his breath: "I loved and shall always love Parrales Sonriente; I was going to have made him a general, because he trampled on my countrymen and humiliated them, and if it hadn't been for my mother he would have finished them off altogether and avenged me for all the grudges I bear against them, things I alone know about. Ungrateful beasts! And it's intolerable that they should have assassinated him, now that people are plotting against my life on all sides, my friends are deserting me, my enemies increasing and—no, no! Not a stone shall be left standing in the Cathedral Porch."

Words slithered from his lips like vehicles on a slippery road. He leant on the favourite's shoulder, with his other hand pressed to his stomach, his head spinning, his eyes discoloured, his breath ice-cold, and soon threw up a jet of orange-coloured fluid. The Under-secretary came running in with an enamel basin with the arms of the Republic on the bottom—and when the deluge was over—most of it went over the favourite—the two of them half-carried, half-dragged him on to a bed.

He was crying and repeating over and over again:

"Ungrateful brutes! Ungrateful brutes!"

"I congratulate you, Don Miguelito, I congratulate you," murmured the Under-secretary as they went out. "The President gave orders that the announcement of your marriage should be published in all the papers, with his own name at the head of the sponsors."

They went into the passage. The Under-secretary raised his voice:

"And that in spite of the fact that he wasn't best pleased with you at first. 'No friend of Parrales Sonriente should have done what Miguel did,' he said to me. 'He should have at least asked my permission before marrying the daughter of one of my enemies.' There are some people who would like to do you an injury, Don Miguelito; yes, they would like to do you an injury. Of course I tried to make him understand that love is an obstinate, over-confident, unscrupulous, deceitful emotion."

"Thank you very much, General."

"Well then, come and look at this!" went on the Under-secretary in a jovial tone, and giving Miguel a series of friendly little pushes towards his office, laughing all the time, he went on: "Come and look at the newspaper! We got the lady's photograph from her Uncle Juan. Splendid, my dear fellow! Splendid!"

The favourite dug his nails into the low rag of a newspaper. Beside the portrait of the Chief Witness, was that of Don Juan Canales, the engineer, and his brother Don José Antonio.

"Wedding in the fashionable world. Last night a marriage was celebrated between the beautiful Señorita Camila Canales and Señor Don Miguel Angel Face. Both parties . . ." From here his eyes moved on to the list of witnesses. ". . . the witnesses to the wedding were His Excellency the Constitutional President of the Republic, in whose house the ceremony was performed, and the Ministers of State, Generals . . ." he skipped the list of their names ". . . and the esteemed uncles of the bride, Don Juan Canales the engineer and Don José Antonio of the same name. A portrait of Señorita Canales will be found in the social columns of today's issue of *El Nacional*," the paragraph concluded, "and we have pleasure in congratulating the contracting parties and wishing them every happiness in their new home."

Angel Face did not know where to look. "The Battle of Verdun still continues. The Germans are expected to launch a desperate offensive tonight."

His eyes left the page of telegrams and he re-read the paragraph under Camila's portrait. The only person he loved had already been drawn into this grotesque farce in which they were all taking part.

The Under-secretary took the paper from him.

"You can hardly believe your eyes, eh, you lucky man!"

Angel Face smiled.

"But you need a change of clothes, my friend. Take my carriage."

"Thank you very much, General."

"Look—it's out there. Tell the driver to take you home as fast as possible and then come back for me. Good night and my congratulations . . . Oh and by the way, do take the paper for your wife to see, and congratulate her from your humble servant . . . !"

"I'm very grateful for everything. Good night."

The carriage moved off with the favourite inside, as soundlessly as a black shadow pulled by two horses made of smoke. The song of the crickets formed a roof over the solitude of the mignonette-scented fields, the warm solitude of the fields of early maize, the dew-soaked pastures and the garden hedges thick with jasmine.

"Yes, if he goes on making fun of me I'll strangle him," he thought, hiding his face in the seat behind him, lest the driver should read in his eyes what they were picturing: a lump of frozen meat with the presidential scarf across the chest, the flat face stiff and still, the hands covered by cuffs so that only the fingers were visible, the patent-leather shoes covered in blood.

His bellicose mood did not adapt itself easily to the jolting of the carriage. He would have liked to sit quite still, as motionless as a murderer reconstructing his crime in prison—in an apparent and external immobility which was the necessary compensation for the tempest raging in his thoughts. His blood tingled in his veins. He thrust his face out into the cool night, while he wiped himself clean of the President's vomit with a handkerchief damp with sweat and tears. He was cursing and weeping with rage. "Oh if only I could clean away the laughter that he vomited over my soul!"

A carriage with an officer in it overtook and brushed past them.

The sky was blinking over its eternal game of chess. The horses were galloping wildly towards the town in a cloud of dust. "Check to the Queen!" said Angel Face to himself, looking at the dust cloud in which the officer was hurrying off to fetch one of the President's concubines. He seemed like a Messenger of the gods.

In the central railway station goods were being unloaded with a shattering noise, amongst the snorts of the steaming locomotives. The street was dominated by the figure of a negro leaning on the green balcony of an upper window. Some drunks were reeling by and a stupid-looking man was pulling along a barrel-organ like a gun after a military defeat.

CHAPTER XXXIII

Dotting the I's

CARVAJAL's widow wandered from house to house, but was received coldly in them all; few of them dared show the grief they felt over her husband's death for fear of being taken for enemies of the Government, and in some cases the servants came to the window and shouted disagreeably:

"Who is it you want to see? Oh they're not at home."

The ice she had collected from these visits melted as soon as she got home. She returned to shed floods of tears in front of her husband's portrait, with no other companion but her little son, a deaf servant who kept on telling the child at the top of her voice: "A father's love is the best thing in the world!", and a parrot which repeated again and again: "A royal parrot from Portugal, dressed in green and without a *real*! Shake hands, Polly! Good morning, lawyer! Polly, shake hands! The turkey-buzzards are in the laundry. It smells of burnt rags. Blessed be the Holy Sacraments on the altar, the Queen of all the angels, and the Virgin conceived without sin! Ay! Ay!"

She had gone out to ask for signatures to a petition begging the President to let her have her husband's body, but she had not dared mention the subject in any of the houses she visited; they had received her so ungraciously, so reluctantly, with little coughs and ominous silences. And now she had brought the paper home under her black shawl and it still had no other signature but her own.

They had turned their heads aside, pretending not to see her; they had received her at the door without the usual: "Do come in"; she began to feel as if she had some invisible infectious disease, something worse than poverty, worse than cholera, worse than yellow fever, yet she was flooded with "anonymous letters", as the deaf servant described the notes she found pushed under the little door between the kitchen and a dark unfrequented alley. Left there under cover of darkness and written in a trembling

227

hand, they spoke of her as a saint, martyr and innocent victim, elevated her unfortunate husband to the skies and described the crimes of Colonel Parrales Sonriente in horrifying detail.

Early next morning there were two anonymous letters under the door. The servant brought them wrapped in her apron, because her hands were wet. The first said:

"Señora, this is not the most suitable means of conveying to you and your afflicted family the deep respect I feel for the character of your husband, our esteemed fellow citizen Don Abel Carvajal, but please allow me to make use of it out of caution, since there are certain truths which cannot be trusted to paper. Some day I will tell you my real name. My father was one of the victims of the man for whom all the torments of Hell are waiting— Colonel Parrales Sonriente—that hired assassin whose deeds will some day figure in history, if there is anyone prepared to dip his pen in snake-poison to write it. My father was murdered by this cowardly man on a lonely road many years ago. Nothing was proved, naturally enough, and the crime would have remained a mystery except for a perfect stranger who wrote anonymously to my family describing the horrible murder in detail. I do not know whether that exemplary man, your husband, a hero who already has a monument erected to him in the hearts of his fellow-townsmen, was in fact the avenger of Parrales Sonriente's victims, for there are many different stories circulating about this; but in any case I believe it to be my duty to express my sympathy, and to assure you, Señora, that we all weep with you for the loss of a man who delivered his country from one of the numerous bandits in gold braid who have used North American gold to subject it to a reign of blood and squalor.

I kiss your hands,

Cruz de Calatrava."

Drained and empty, paralysed by a deep-seated inertia which kept her lying on her bed for hours on end like a corpse, or sometimes more motionless even than a corpse, she reduced her activities to the sphere of her bed-table (which was covered with objects in immediate use so as to avoid getting up) or to attacks of hysteria if anyone opened the door, used a broom or made a noise anywhere near her. The darkness, the silence, the dirt gave tangible shape to her desolation, to her desire to be alone with her grief, with that part of her which had died with her husband and was slowly gaining the mastery of her body and soul.

"Most respected and esteemed Señora"—she began reading the other anonymous letter aloud—"I heard from some friends that you had your ear to the prison wall the night your husband was shot. Even if you heard and counted nine detonations, you will not know which among them snatched the lawyer Carvajal, God rest his soul, from among the living.

"After much hesitation for fear of causing you pain, I have decided to write under an assumed name—it is not safe to trust to paper these days—and communicate everything I know about the matter, for I witnessed the execution. A thin, dark-skinned man with almost white hair falling over his broad forehead was walking in front of your husband. I have not been able to find out his name. In spite of the suffering shown by his tears, there was great human kindness in his deep-sunk eyes, and one could read in them that their owner was a noble and generous man. The lawyer stumbled after him without raising his eyes from the ground—perhaps he couldn't even see it—his forehead damp with sweat and one hand on his breast as if to keep his heart from bursting. When he came out into the courtyard and found himself surrounded by soldiers, he rubbed his eyes with the back of his hand as if he couldn't believe what he saw. He was wearing a faded suit too small for him, the sleeves of the coat only reaching to his elbows and the trousers to his knees—old, crumpled, dirty, tattered clothes, such as all condemned prisoners wear, having given their own to the friends they leave behind entombed in underground prison cells, or to the warders in exchange for some special indulgence. His threadbare shirt was kept together by one little bone button. He wore no tie and no shoes. The presence of his companions in misfortune, half naked like himself, revived his courage. When they had finished reading the death sentence, he raised his head, looked sadly at the row of bayonets and said something inaudible. The old man next to him also tried to speak, but the officers silenced him by threatening him with their swords. Their hands were trembling from drink, and the swords looked like the blue flames of burning alcohol in the pale dawn light. Meanwhile a voice clashed with its own echo rebounding from the walls as it pronounced the words: 'For the Nation!' One, two, three, four, five, six, seven, eight, nine rounds of firing followed. Without knowing what I was doing I was counting them on my fingers, and so I got the strange impression that I had one finger too many. The victims shut their eyes and twisted their bodies as if to grope their way out of range of death. A veil of smoke hung between us and this handful of men, who tried in vain to catch hold of each other as they fell, rather than roll into the void alone. The final shots rang out like a burst of damp rockets, exploding late and badly. Your husband was fortunate enough to be killed by the first round of firing. Above, in the blue, inaccessible sky, we heard the almost imperceptible sound of bells, birds, rivers. I was told that the Judge Advocate had undertaken to bury the bod—"

She turned the page anxiously. "Bod—" But the rest of the word was not there, nor on any of the other pages; the letter had broken off suddenly, and the rest was missing. She re-read the letter, but in vain; she searched inside her envelope, unmade the bed, looked inside the pillows, on the floor and the table, turned everything upside down in her eagerness to know where her husband was buried.

In the patio the parrot was chattering:

"Royal parrot from Portugal, dressed in green, and without a *real*! Ah, here comes the lawyer! Hurrah, royal parrot! The liar told me! I don't cry, but I don't forget!"

The Judge Advocate General's servant left Carvajal's widow standing on the doorstep while she attended to two women talking at the tops of their voices in the entrance hall.

"Listen, just listen to me," one of them was saying; "you just go and tell him I'm not waiting for him any longer. I'm not an Indian, damn him, to be left freezing my arse on this stone seat! It reminds me of his pretty face! Tell him I've come to see if he's at last going to give me back the ten thousand pesos he swindled me out of for a woman from the Casa Nueva, who was no use to me, because the day I brought her home with me she fell down in a fit. And look here! tell him it's the last time I shall bother him; what I'm going to do now is go and complain to the President."

"Don't work yourself up so, Doña Chon, take that miserable old expression off your face," said the other woman.

"Señorita," the servant was beginning, but the Señorita interrupted:

"Shut up, will you?"

"Tell him what I said, and don't let him say I didn't give him fair warning: tell him Doña Chon and one of the girls came to see him, that they waited for him, and when they saw he wasn't coming, they went away saying he'd soon see what stuff they were made of . . ."

Absorbed in her own thoughts, Carvajal's widow did not take in what was happening. In her black clothes, with nothing showing but her face, she looked like a corpse in a coffin with a window in it. The servant tapped her on the shoulder—the old woman's fingers felt as though they were covered in spiders-webs—and told her to come in. They entered the house. The widow could not speak distinctly, but muttered like someone tired out by reading aloud for a long time.

"Yes, Señora, leave your letter with me. When he comes in—and he can't be long now, he ought to be here already—I'll give it to him, and tell him what you want."

"For the love of God . . ."

An individual wearing a coffee-coloured cotton suit, followed by a soldier with his Remington rifle over his shoulder, a knife in his belt and a well-filled cartridge-belt round his hips, came in just as Carvajal's widow was leaving.

"Excuse me," he said to the servant, "is the Judge Advocate in?"

"No, he's not."

"And where can I wait for him?"

"Sit down there, and the soldier too."

The prisoner and his guard sat down in silence on the stone bench ungraciously indicated by the servant.

The patio was full of the scent of verbena and begonias. A cat was walking on the roof. A mocking-bird was trying to fly inside its wicker cage. From far off came the sound of the water sleepily running into the fountain, as if dazed with falling.

The Judge Advocate locked the door with a rattle of keys, put them in his pocket and went up to the prisoner and the soldier. Both stood up.

"Genaro Rodas?" he enquired, sniffing. Whenever he came in from the street his house seemed to smell of cat-shit.

"Yes, Señor, at your service."

"Does your guard understand Spanish?"

"Not very well," replied Rodas, and turning to the soldier he added: "What d'you say? Do you understand Castillian?"

"Half understand."

"Very well," put in the Advocate General. "You'd better stay here. I'll talk to him. Stay here till he comes back. He's going to talk to me."

Rodas stopped at the door of the study. The Judge Advocate told him to go in, and laid the weapons he was carrying on a table covered with books and papers—a revolver, a knife, a knuckle-duster and a truncheon.

"I expect you've been notified of the sentence."

"Yes, Señor, I have."

"Six years and eight months, if I remember right."

"But, Señor, I wasn't Lucio Vasquez's accomplice; whatever he did he did without my help; by the time I got there the Zany was already rolling down the steps of the Porch covered in blood and as good as dead. What could I do? It was an order. It was an order, so he said."

"Well, God has already judged him . . ."

Rodas turned to look at the Judge Advocate General, as if unable to credit what the sinister expression of his face confirmed, and remained silent.

"And he wasn't a bad chap," sighed Rodas, dropping his voice as he let fall these last few words to his friend's memory; he had taken in the news between two heart-beats and already he felt it in his blood. "Well, it can't be helped now! We used to call him Velvet, because he never missed a chance and knew how to cadge special favours."

"According to the verdict he was sentenced as perpetrator of the crime, and you as his accomplice."

"But I had a defence."

"It was the advocate for your defence, in point of fact, who, knowing the President's views, asked for a death sentence for Vasquez and the maximum penalty for you."

"Poor chap. At least I'm alive to tell the tale."

"And you can go free at once if you want to; because the President needs someone like you, someone who has been inside for a bit for political reasons. It's a question of keeping an eye on one of his friends, whom he has reason to suspect of betraying him . . ."

"You mean . . ."

"Do you know Don Miguel Angel Face?"

"Only by name; he was the one who went off with General Canales' daughter, wasn't he?"

"That's the man. You'll recognise him easily because he's very handsome: a tall man, well built, with black eyes, a pale face, and silky hair, and moves gracefully. A dangerous customer. The Government wants to know everything he does, the people he goes to see, or talks to in the street, the places he frequents in the morning, afternoon and night, and the same for his wife; I'll give you full instructions and money for this."

The prisoner followed the Judge Advocate's movements stupidly, as with these words he took a pen from the table, dipped it in a large inkpot with a figure of the goddess Themis standing between two wells of black ink, and handed it to Rodas, saying:

"Sign here; tomorrow I'll give orders for you to be set free. Get your things ready to leave tomorrow."

Rodas signed. Joy was dancing through his body like a playful little bull.

"I'm very grateful, you know," he said as he went out; he almost embraced the soldier who was waiting for him, and went off to the prison like a man going to heaven.

But the Judge Advocate General was even more delighted with the paper Rodas had just signed, and which read as follows:

"I have received from Doña Concepcion Gamucino, known as 'Gold-Tooth', proprietress of the brothel known as The Sweet Enchantment, the sum of ten thousand pesos in the national currency, a sum which she gave me as partial compensation for the damage she had done me in corrupting my wife, Señora Fedina de Rodas, by taking advantage of her good faith and that of the authorities to offer her employment as a servant, and then enrolling her, without any authorisation, among the girls of her establishment.

                                        Genaro Rodás."

He heard the servant's voice calling through the door:

"Can I come in?"

"Yes, come in."

"I came to see if there was anything you wanted. I'm going to the shop to buy candles and I must tell you there were two

233

women from one of the brothels here, who told me to tell you that if you don't pay back the ten thousand pesos you robbed them of they'll go and complain to the President."

"And what else?" grumbled the Judge Advocate, looking annoyed and stooping to pick up a postage stamp from the floor.

"And a lady dressed in mourning came to see you; I think she's the wife of the man who was shot . . ."

"Which one of them?"

"Señor Carvajal."

"Well, what did she want?"

"The poor thing gave me this letter. I think she wants to know where her husband is buried."

While the Judge Advocate was reluctantly glancing over the black-edged pages the servant went on:

"I must tell you I promised to do what I could for her, because I felt sorry for her, and the poor thing went away full of hope."

"I've told you often enough that I don't like your sympathising with people. You mustn't encourage them to hope. When will you understand that you mustn't encourage people to hope? In my house the first thing everyone, down to the cat, has to learn is that there are never grounds for hope of any description for anyone. It's only possible to go on holding a position like mine if you obey orders; the President's rule of conduct is never to give grounds for hope, and everyone must be kicked and beaten until they realise the fact. When this lady comes back you must return her her letter, neatly folded, and tell her there is no way of finding out where her husband is buried."

"Don't be so angry, you'll make yourself ill; I'll tell her. God will take care of you and your affairs."

And she went out carrying the letter and dragging her feet, one after the other, one after the other, under her rustling skirts.

When she got to the kitchen she crumpled up the letter and threw it among the coals. The paper curled up in the flames like a living thing, and then suddenly turned into a mass of tiny worms made of gold wire. Along the shelves where pots of spices were arranged, like boats against a bridge, came a black cat; it jumped on to the stone seat beside the old woman, rubbed itself against her barren belly, purring like a four-legged embodiment of sound, and fixed its golden eyes with satanic curiosity on the heart of the fire where the letter was now burnt to ashes.

CHAPTER XXXIV

Light for the Blind

CAMILA was standing in the middle of the room, supported on her husband's arm and a walking-stick. The main door gave on to a patio smelling of cats and poppies. The window looked on to the town where she had been brought as a convalescent in a wheel-chair, and a small door led into another room. In spite of the sun setting alight the green fires of her eyes, and the air filling her lungs like a heavy chain, Camila wondered if it could really be she who was walking. Her feet felt too large, her legs like stilts. She seemed to be walking in another world, with her eyes wide open; she was new-born, disembodied. She was surrounded by phantoms, walking among a foam of cobwebs. It was as if she had died in a dream, without ceasing to exist, and had come back to life to find she could not distinguish dreams from reality. Her father, her home, her old nurse Chabela, all belonged to her previous existence. Her husband, the house where they were temporarily living, the servants, all belonged to her new existence. It was she, yet it was not she, who was walking about in this room. She felt as if she had returned to life in a new world. When she spoke of herself, it was of someone leaning on the walking-stick of her past life; she had an understanding with things that were invisible, and if she was left alone she got lost in this other world, sitting with her mind far away, with frozen hair, her hands lying in the lap of her long skirt and noises echoing in her ears.

She soon began to move about, but she remained an invalid none-the-less, or rather she remained absorbed in the evaluation of all the overwhelming things that had happened to her since her husband first pressed his lips to her cheek. It was all too much for her to take in, but she clung to it as the only thing that was really hers in an alien world. She looked with pleasure at the moonlight shining on the earth, at the moon itself opposite the cloud-capped volcanoes, and at the stars like golden lice in an empty pigeon-loft.

Angel Face was aware that his wife was shivering inside her white flannel garments, not from cold, not as people normally shiver, but as angels shiver—and he led her step by step back to her bedroom. The grotesque head over the fountain . . . the motionless hammock; the water as motionless as the hammock . . . damp flower-pots . . . wax flowers . . . passages patched with moonlight . . .

They went to bed, talking to each other through the wall. There was a communicating door between their bedrooms. Buttons came sleepily out of buttonholes with a gentle sound like that of cutting a flower-stalk; shoes fell to the ground with the noise of dropping anchors, and stockings were peeled from skin as smoke is peeled from a chimney.

Angel Face talked to her about the objects of his personal toilet ranged on a table beside his towel-rail, so as to create a foolish but intimate family atmosphere in this huge, apparently uninhabited house, and to remove his thoughts from that narrow little door, like the gateway to heaven, which led from one bedroom to the other.

Then he fell on to his bed with all his weight and lay there for a long time without moving, lapped around by the mysterious tide of the relationship that was continuously being created and destroyed between the two of them. He kidnaps her with the intention of making her his own by force; then out of blind instinct love develops. Abandoning his plan, he tries to take her to her uncle's house; the door is shut against them. So she is in his power again, and surely there is now no risk in making her his, since this is what the world believes. But knowing this, she tries to shun him. Her illness stands in the way. In a very few hours she gets much worse. She is dying. Death will come and cut the knot. He knows this, and at times he is resigned, although more often he is in revolt against these blind forces. Death's summons frustrates his dearest hope, and fate is waiting till the last moment to unite them.

Childlike before she could walk, she becomes an adolescent when she gets up and takes her first steps. In the space of a single night the blood has returned to her lips, her bodice has filled out with its fruit, and she is troubled and damp with sweat at the approach of the man she has never really thought of as her husband.

236

Angel Face jumped up from the bed. He felt that he was separated from Camila by something that was neither his fault nor hers; by a marriage to which neither of them had given their consent. Camila closed her eyes. His footsteps moved away towards the window.

The moon went in and out of floating niches in the clouds. The road flowed like a river of white bones under bridges of shadow. Now and again everything grew indistinct, with the patina of some old religious relic, only to reappear brightened with gold thread. A vast black eyelid intervened, and cut off this vision seen through flickering eyelids. Its enormous lashes seemed to come from the highest of the volcanoes and spread like a huge spider over the skeleton of the town, plunging it in mourning shadow. The dogs shook their ears like door-knockers, night birds flew through the sky, a moan passed from cypress to cypress and there was a sound of clocks being wound and set. The moon disappeared completely behind the tall summit of a crater and a mist like a bride's veil came to rest among the houses. Angel Face shut the window. In her bedroom Camila was drawing slow, difficult breaths, as if she had fallen asleep with her head under the clothes, or a phantom presence were sitting on her breast.

Sometimes they went bathing. The shadows of the trees dappled the white shirts of the travelling vendors of earthenware jars, brooms, mocking-birds in wicker cages, pine-cones, wood and maize. They had covered long distances walking on tip-toe without ever resting their heels on the ground. The sun was sweating with them. They panted and waved their arms about and then vanished like a flock of birds.

Camila stopped in the shadow of a hut to watch the coffee being picked. The pickers' hands moved among the metallic foliage like hungry animals; up and down they went, joining together as if crazily tickling the tree, then separating again as if unbuttoning its shirt.

Angel Face put his arm around her waist and led her along a path lying stricken under the slumberous heat of the trees. They were conscious of their heads and their torsos; the rest of their bodies, legs and hands floated along among orchids and bright-coloured lizards in a half-light which gradually changed to a honeyed darkness as they penetrated further into the wood. He could feel Camila's body through her thin blouse as one feels the smooth, silky, moist grains of maize through the young leaf. The wind ruffled their hair. As they went down to the bathing-place the sun was asleep in the water. Invisible presences were floating among shady tufts of ferns. The keeper of the baths came out of a zinc-roofed house, munching beans; he greeted them with a nod, swallowed the mouthful with which his cheeks were bulging, and looked them up and down with a self-important air. They asked for two bathing-boxes. He went to fetch the keys, and opened two little cabins separated by a partition. They kissed each other quickly before parting to go into their cabins. The bathing-box proprietor had a bad eye and he covered his face to protect it.

They felt strange, separated from each other, and with the forest noises all round them. A broken looking-glass saw Angel Face strip with youthful haste. Why must he be a man—when it would be so much better to be a tree, a cloud, a dragon-fly, a bubble or a humming-bird? Standing on the highest step of the swimming-bath, Camila shrieked to feel the cold water on her feet; she screamed again on the second step, more piercingly on the third, and more piercingly still on the fourth then—splosh! Her Indian chemise swelled out like a crinoline, like a balloon, but almost at the same moment the water saturated it, moulding her body in the garish blues, yellows and greens of the material: firm breasts and stomach, the gentle curve of the hips, smooth back, and rather thin shoulders. Her plunge over, Camila came out again, somewhat agitated by the watery silence of the reeds. But she heard her husband's voice at her door, asking if he could come in, and she felt safe.

The water frisked around them like a happy animal. Amongst the shining cobwebs of its reflection on the walls of the baths, they saw the reflections of their own bodies like monstrous spiders. The air was pervaded by a smell of water plants, by the presence of the distant volcanoes, the dampness of frogs' bellies, the breath of calves as they sucked in the white liquid into which the pasture had been transformed, the coolness of the waterfalls laughing as they fell, the restless flight of green flies. An impalpable veil of silent aitches enveloped them, together with the sound of someone singing in the ravine and the fluttering of a shara-bird.

The bathing-box keeper looked in to ask if the horses from La

Quebraditas were for them. It was time to dress and leave the baths. Camila felt a worm wriggling in the towel she had thrown over her shoulders to protect her clothes from her wet hair. For her to feel it, to scream, for Angel Face to come and deal with the worm was a matter of only a few seconds. But she was not enjoying herself any more; the forest had begun to frighten her; it seemed to be sunk in a damp, sleepless torpor, exuding worms.

The horses were flicking away flies with their tails under a fig-tree. The groom who had brought them came up to Angel Face, hat in hand.

"Oh, so it's you! Good morning! And what are you doing here?"

"Working! I've been coming here ever since you did me the service of getting me out of the barracks, nearly a year ago."

"How fast time goes!"

"It seems like it. The sun'll be gone soon now, boss, and we've some way to go."

Angel Face asked Camila if they should leave; he had stopped to pay the attendant.

"Whenever you like."

"But aren't you hungry? Don't you want to eat something? Perhaps we can buy something from the attendant."

"Some eggs?" suggested the groom, and from the pocket of his jacket (which had more buttons than buttonholes) he extracted a handkerchief with three eggs wrapped in it.

"Thank you very much," said Camila, "they look very fresh."

"Don't thank me, young lady, and as for the eggs they're goodness itself. The hens laid them this very morning and I said to my wife: 'Put them aside for me. I think I'll take them to Don Angel!'"

They took leave of the attendant, who was still wiping his bad eye and eating beans.

"And I've been thinking," the groom went on, "that it would be a good thing for the Señora to swallow those eggs raw, because it's quite a stretch from here and she might get hungry."

"No, I don't like raw eggs and they might make me ill," replied Camila.

"I thought the Señora looked as if she needed taking care of!"

"That's because I've only just got out of bed."

"Yes," said Angel Face, "she's been very ill."

239

"But now you're going to get better," said the man while he tightened the girths of the saddles. "Women are like flowers, they need watering; marriage'll soon put you to rights!"

Camila lowered her eyelids, blushing and confused, like a plant that finds eyes growing everywhere instead of leaves; she exchanged a glance with her husband—a glance full of mutual desire, silently sealing a compact that had been lacking between them hitherto.

CHAPTER XXXV

The Song of Songs

"SUPPOSE fate had not brought us together!" they used to say. And the thought of the risk they had run filled them with such terror that if they happened to be apart they would seek each other out, if they were together they embraced, if they were in each other's arms they held each other tighter, and not content with holding each other tighter they kissed each other and gazed into each other's eyes, and found them so alight with happiness that they passed into a transparent state of amnesia, in blissful accord with the trees, newly swollen with sap, and with the little morsels of flesh covered in bright-coloured feathers that flew about more swiftly than the echo.

But the serpents considered the question. If fate had not brought them together, would they have been happy? The right to destroy this useless and charming Paradise was put to auction among the infernal shadows; the evil spirits began to keep watch, and the uncertain voice of doubt sprouted from the damp vaccine of guilt, while the calendar spun cobwebs in the corners of time.

Neither he nor she could afford to stay away from the party the President of the Republic was giving in his country residence that night.

Their house suddenly seemed alien to them; they were at a loss what to do, and sat sadly surrounded by a sofa, a looking-glass and other furniture, instead of by the marvellous world of the first months of their marriage. They felt sorry for each other, and ashamed of being themselves.

The dining-room clock struck the hours, but it seemed such a long way away that they had the feeling that they would need either a boat or a balloon to reach it. And there they sat . . .

They ate in silence with their eyes on the pendulum which was bringing them closer to the party with each oscillation. Angel Face got up to put on his dress-coat, and felt cold as he thrust his arms into the sleeves, like someone wrapping himself in banana leaves. Camila tried to fold up her napkin, but it was the napkin which folded up her hands, and she sat between the table and her chair without the strength to take the first step. She drew back her foot. Now she had taken the first step. Angel Face returned to see what the time was and then went back to his room for his gloves. She heard his footsteps far away, as if in a tunnel. He said something. Something. His voice sounded indistinct. A moment later he reappeared in the dining-room carrying his wife's fan. He could not remember what he had gone to fetch from his room and had been hunting about vaguely everywhere. At last he remembered, but his gloves were already on his hands.

"Be sure and see that the lights aren't left on; put them out and shut the doors carefully; then go to bed," Camila told the servants who were watching their departure from the door into the passage.

They set off in a carriage drawn by well-fed horses, trotting in the river of clinking coins made by the harness. Camila buried herself in her corner; she could not shake off the torpor oppressing her, and the dead light from the street lamps shone in her eyes. Every now and then a sudden movement of the carriage jolted her off her seat, interrupting her smooth progress in rhythm with the vehicle. Angel Face's enemies had been saying he was no longer in favour, and it was hinted in the Club of the Friends of the President that he ought now to be called Miguel Canales instead of his own name. Rocked by the bounding wheels, he was savouring in advance the surprise that would be caused by his appearance at the party.

The carriage left the paved streets and glided down a sandy hill, the wheels making a hollow sound. Camila was afraid; she could see nothing at all in the darkness of the surrounding countryside, only the stars; nor could she hear anything from the dew-soaked fields except the song of the crickets; she was afraid, and she shrank back as if she were being dragged to her death along a path (or semblance of a path) with a yawning abyss on one side and, on the other, Lucifer's wing stretched out like a rock in the darkness.

"What's the matter?" said Angel Face, gently taking her by the shoulders and moving her away from the door.

"I'm scared!"

"Sh! Be quiet!"

"This man's going to turn us over at this rate. Tell him not to go so fast. Do tell him! Oh dear, didn't you hear what I said? Tell him! You're so silent!"

"These carriages . . ." Angel Face began, but stopped short because his wife clutched him and there was an unexpected bump on the springs. They felt as if they were rolling down the slope.

"It's all right," he said, pulling himself together, "it's all right—the wheels must have caught in a rut."

The wind was blowing over the rocks with a screech like tearing linen. Angel Face put his head out of the window and shouted to the driver to be more careful. The man turned his dark pock-marked face to look at him and slowed the horses to a funereal pace.

The carriage stopped at the far end of a little village. An officer in a cloak advanced towards them clicking his spurs, recognised them and told the driver to go on. The wind sighed through the dry and broken corn-stalks. The silhouette of a cow was barely visible in a yard. The trees were asleep. Two hundred yards further on two officers approached to see who they were, but the carriage hardly paused. And now that they were about to alight in front of the Presidential Residence, three colonels came forward to search the carriage.

Angel Face greeted the staff officers. (He was as beautiful and wicked as Satan.) A nostalgia for the warmth of home was floating in the inexplicable vastness of night. A light on the horizon marked the site of an artillery fort guarding the safety of the President of the Republic.

Camila lowered her eyes when confronted by a man with a Mephistophelian scowl, stooping shoulders, slit-like eyes, and long thin legs. As they came in, this man slowly stretched out his arm and opened his hand as if he were going to set free a dove instead of speak to them.

"Parthenius of Bethany," he began, "was taken prisoner in Mithridates' wars and carried off to Rome, where he taught the Alexandrian language. Propertius, Ovid, Virgil, Horace and I got it from him . . ."

Two elderly ladies were talking together at the door of the room where the President was receiving his guests.

"Yes, yes," one was saying, patting her hair. "I've told him they must re-elect him."

"And what did he say? I'm really interested . . ."

"He only smiled, but I know he will be re-elected. He's the best President we've ever had, Candidita. Do you know that ever since he was in office, Moncho, my husband, has always had a good job?"

Behind these ladies the Teacher was pontificating to a group of friends.

"The President wants to see you," the Judge Advocate was saying, turning to right and left, as he walked through the crowd. "The President wants to see you, the President wants to see you . . ."

"Thank you!" replied the Teacher.

"Thank you!" said a negro jockey with bow legs and gold teeth, assuming the remark was meant for him.

Camila would have liked to have passed unnoticed. But that was impossible. Her exotic beauty, her clear impassive green eyes, her exquisite figure sheathed in her white silk dress, her small breasts, her graceful movements, and above all the fact that she was General Canales' daughter, singled her out.

One of a group of ladies remarked:

"I don't think much of her. A woman who doesn't wear stays— anyone can see how common she is!"

"And she's had her wedding-gown altered into an evening dress," whispered another.

"People who don't know how to behave always make themselves conspicuous, you know," a lady with thin hair took the opportunity of adding.

"Oh, how unkind we're being! I said that about the dress because obviously they're hard up!"

"Of course they're hard up, and we all know why!" remarked the thin-haired one, adding in a low voice: "They say the President hasn't given him a thing since his marriage to that girl!"

"But Angel Face is completely loyal . . ."

"He was, rather. Because you know people are saying—for what it's worth—that Angel Face only ran off with his present wife so as to throw dust in the eyes of the police while his father-in-law, the general, escaped; and that he wouldn't have got away otherwise!"

Camila and Angel Face advanced among the guests towards

the far end of the room where the President was. His Excellency was talking to Canon Irrefragable, among a group of ladies who had forgotten what they meant to say as soon as they found themselves in the Leader's proximity, and looked as though they had swallowed lighted candles and did not dare to breathe or open their lips. There were bankers out on bail, with law-suits pending against them; secretaries with revolutionary sympathies, who never took their eyes from the President, but dared not greet him when he looked at them nor absent themselves when he turned away; village notables, whose political enthusiasms had lost their fire, but who showed a trace of outraged human dignity at being treated as mice when they were really lions.

Camila and Angel Face went up to shake hands with the President. Angel Face introduced his wife. The President gave Camila his cold little right hand and let his eyes rest on her as he uttered her name, as if to say: "You see what sort of a man I am!" Meanwhile the Canon was paying homage to a beauty with the same name and unique character as Albanio's beloved, by quoting some lines by Garcilaso:

> Nature desired but once to make
> A face so fair as this—
> And then the mould did break!

The servants were handing round champagne, little cakes, salted almonds, sweets and cigarettes. The champagne set a match to the as yet unlit fire of this official entertainment, gradually spreading an animation which looked more genuine when reflected in the quiet mirrors than in the drawing-rooms themselves.

"General," the President's voice was heard to say, "take the gentlemen away; I wish to have supper alone with the ladies."

The men hurried towards the doors opening on to the brilliant night in a compact group, without a word, some eager to carry out their master's orders, others trying to conceal their anger by their haste. The women looked at each other, not daring even to hide their feet under their chairs.

"The poet can stay," suggested the President.

The officers shut all the doors. The poet was embarrassed to find himself among so many ladies.

"Recite something, poet," ordered the President; "something good—the Song of Songs":

> The song of songs which is Solomon's,
> Let him kiss me with the kiss of his mouth!
> I am black but beautiful, oh ye daughters of Jerusalem,
> As the curtains of Solomon.
> Do not consider me that I am brown
> Because the sun hath altered my colour . . .
>
> A bundle of myrrh is my beloved to me:
> He shall abide between my two breasts . . .
>
> I sat down under his shadow whom I desired
> And his fruit was sweet to my palate,
> He brought me into the cellar of wine,
> He set in order charity in me.
>
> I adjure you oh daughters of Jerusalem
> That you stir not up, nor make the beloved awake
> Till she please
> Till she please . . .
>
> How beautiful art thou, my love;
> Thy eyes are dove's eyes;
> Thy hair is as flocks of goats
> Thy teeth as flocks of sheep,
> Which come up from the washing,
> All with twins;
> And there is none barren among them.
>
> There are threescore queens and fourscore concubines.

The President stood up with a baleful expression on his face. His footsteps echoed like those of a jaguar in flight on the stones of a dry river-bed; and he vanished through a door, pulling aside the curtains and brushing between them.

The poet and his audience were left astounded, shrunk to

insignificance and empty, in an atmosphere of uneasiness such as is felt after the sun has set. An usher announced that supper was ready. The doors were opened and, while the men who had been waiting in the passage came shivering back into the drawing-room, the poet came up to Camila and asked her to have supper with him. She stood up and was just going to take his arm when a hand from behind stopped her. She almost cried out. Angel Face had been hidden all the time behind a curtain close to his wife; everyone saw him come out of his hiding-place.

The wooden bars of the marimba had begun to vibrate and so had the resonators hanging like little coffins beneath them.

CHAPTER XXXVI

The Revolution

NOTHING was visible ahead. Behind them crept the track like a long silent snake unrolling its fluid, smooth, frozen coils. The ribs of the earth could be counted in the meagre dried-up marshlands, untouched by winter. The trees raised themselves to the full height of their thick, sappy branches in order to breathe. The bonfires dazzled the eyes of the tired horses. A man turned his back to urinate. His legs were invisible. The time had come for his companions to take stock of their situation, but they were too busy cleaning their rifles with grease and bits of cotton which still smelt of woman. Death had been carrying them off one by one, withering them as they lay in their beds, with no advantage to their children or anyone else. It was better to risk their lives and see what would come of that. Bullets feel nothing when they pierce a man's body; to them flesh is like sweet warm air—air with a certain substance. And they whistle like birds. The time had come to take stock, but they were too busy sharpening the machetes the leaders of the revolution had bought from an iron-monger whose shop had been burned down. The sharpened edge was like the smile on a negro's face.

"Sing, comrade," said a voice. "I heard you singing a little while ago!"

> "Why did you court me, hard-hearted
> With a mistress of your own?
> Better if you had left me
> Like a dead tree alone."

"Go on, comrade, sing!"

> "We went to the lagoon
> We hurried to the fair;
> This year there shone no moon

And there was no one there."

"Sing, comrade, sing!"
The quinine light of the moon was spreading over the country-side and the leaves were shivering on the trees. They waited in vain for the order to advance. A distant sound of barking showed where a village must be hidden. The sun was rising. The troops, waiting in motionless readiness to attack the first garrison that same night, felt as if some strange subterranean force was robbing them of their mobility and turning them to stone. The rain turned the sunless morning to soup; it ran down the faces and backs of the soldiers. Sounds echoed more loudly through God's falling tears. The first news they got was brief and contradictory, as if spoken by small voices, afraid to tell all they knew. Deep in the soldiers' hearts something like an iron ball or a splinter of bone was consolidating. The whole camp was bleeding as from a single wound. General Canales was dead. The news took shape in syllables and sentences, syllables out of a spelling-book. Sentences from the funeral service. The taste of cigarettes and brandy was tainted with anger and exclamations of grief. It was impossible to believe what was being said—yet it must be true. The older men were silent, waiting impatiently to hear the bare truth, some standing, others stretched or squatting on the ground; they took off their straw hats, threw them down beside them and scratched their heads furiously. The young men had hurried down into the ravine in search of more news. They were stupefied by the re-verberating heat of the sun. A flock of birds was circling in the distance. From time to time there was the sound of a shot. Evening began to close in. A raw sky beneath a torn cloak of clouds. The camp fires were put out and there was nothing but a grey shape-less darkness, a black solitude composed of sky, earth, animals and men. Then a galloping horse broke the silence with the rataplan! rataplan! of its hoofs, repeated by the echoes all through the multiplication table. It came closer and closer, from sentinel to sentinel, and soon it was here in their midst, and they thought they must be dreaming when they heard what the rider had to tell. General Canales had died suddenly, just after eating a meal, when he was about to lead his troops into action. And now their orders were to wait.

"They must have given him something, some chiltepe root

perhaps—it's a deadly poison which leaves no trace—for him to die just now," said a voice.

"He ought to have been more on his guard!" murmured another.

"Ahhhh!" They were all silent, all deeply stirred, down to their bare heels, buried in the ground. "His daughter?"

After a long and unpleasant pause, another voice added: "If you like I'll call down a curse on her; I was taught one by a witch-doctor down on the coast; he told it me when maize was short in the mountains and I went down there to buy some. What do you say?"

"Well," came the other voice out of the shadows, "I'm for it myself, because she killed her father."

Once more a horse was heard galloping along the track—rataplan, rataplan, rataplan; once more the sentinels' shouts were heard and once more silence reigned. The howl of coyotes rose like a double staircase towards the newly risen moon with its broad halo. The echo repeated it.

And each time anyone described what had happened, General Canales came out of his grave and died all over again: he sat down to eat by lamplight at a table without a cloth, they heard the rattle of cutlery and plates, the footsteps of the orderly, a glass of water being poured out and a newspaper unfolded, and then—nothing more, not even a groan. They found him lying across the table dead, his cheek resting on *El Nacional*, his eyes half closed, glassy, staring at something that was not there.

The men went back reluctantly to their daily tasks; they were tired of living like domestic animals, and they had joined Chamarrita's revolution—this was their affectionate nickname for General Canales—to make a change in their way of life, and because Chamarrita had promised to give them back the vineyards that had been taken away from them on the pretext of abolishing communities; to make fair distribution of water supplies; to suppress the pillory; to form agricultural co-operatives to import machinery, the best seed, pure-bred stock, fertilisers and technicians; to make transport easier and cheaper and so facilitate export and sale of products; to confine power to those elected by the people and responsible to the people themselves; to abolish private schools, institute proportional taxation, make medicine cheaper and doctors and lawyers available to all; to grant freedom in religion, so that the Indians should be able to worship their gods and rebuild their temples, safe from persecution.

Camila heard of her father's death many days later. An unknown voice told her the news over the telephone.

"Your father died of reading in the newspaper that the President of the Republic was a witness at your wedding."

"It's not true!" she cried.

"What isn't true?" said the voice, laughing disagreeably.

"It isn't true; he wasn't a witness! Hullo! Hullo!" But the unknown person had already put the receiver down very slowly like someone slipping away by stealth. "Hullo! Hullo!"

She sank into a wicker chair. She felt stunned. After a little while it seemed to her that the room had lost its old appearance and become different, with a different colour, a different atmosphere. Dead! Dead! Dead! Camila twisted her hands as though to break something, and broke into a laugh with set jaws and her eyes full of unshed tears.

A water-cart was going along the street; its taps were weeping and its metal tanks laughing.

CHAPTER XXXVII

Tohil's Dance

"WHAT would you like, gentlemen?"

"A beer."

"Not for me; I'll have a whisky."

"And a brandy for me."

"Then that's . . .?"

"One beer, one whisky, one brandy."

"And some cocktail snacks!"

"Then that's one beer, one whisky, one brandy and some cocktail snacks."

"Hullo there!" Angel Face's voice was heard saying as he came back, buttoning his fly-buttons rather hastily.

"What'll you have?"

"Anything. Bring me some mineral water."

"Ah! then it's one beer, one whisky, one brandy and one mineral water."

Angel Face pulled up his chair and sat down beside a man six feet tall, who had the appearance and gestures of a negro although he was white-skinned, a back as straight as a poker, a pair of anvils for hands and a scar between his blond brows.

"Make room for me, Mr Gengis," he said, "I want to sit beside you."

"With pleasure, Señor."

"I'll have my drink and then go, because the boss is expecting me."

"Oh," said Mr Gengis, "if you're going to see the President, you must stop being a damn fool and tell him the things they say about you aren't true—not true at all."

"That goes without saying," said another of the four, the one who had asked for brandy.

"I should know that," put in Angel Face to Mr Gengis.

"So does everyone," exclaimed the American, hitting the

* The God of rain in Maya-Guatemalan mythology.

marble-topped table with the flat of his hands. "Of course! But I was there that night and heard with my own ears the Judge Advocate say you were against the re-election, and friendly to the revolution like the late General Canales."

Angel Face made a poor show of concealing his anxiety. Under the circumstances it was foolhardy to go and see the President.

The waiter came up with their drinks. He was wearing a white jacket with the word "Gambrinus" embroidered on it in red chain-stitch.

"That's one whisky—one beer . . ."

Mr Gengis swallowed the whisky at a gulp without blinking, like someone taking a purge; then he took out his pipe and filled it with tobacco.

"Yes, my friend, these things have a way of getting to the President's ears just when one least expects it, and it's not very amusing for you, I'm afraid. Now's your moment to tell him straight out what's what. It's a tricky situation."

"Thanks for the advice, Mr Gengis. I'll see you later. I'm going to try and get a cab now, so as to get there quicker. Thanks again, eh? And I'll be seeing you all later."

Mr Gengis lit his pipe.

"How many whiskies have you drunk, Mr Gengis?" asked one of the men at the table.

"Eighteen!" replied the American, his pipe in his mouth, one eye half shut and the other—very blue—staring at the little yellow match-flame.

"And you're quite right! Whisky's splendid stuff, isn't it?"

"God knows. I couldn't say. You must ask people who don't drink it out of sheer desperation, like me."

"You mustn't say that, Mr Gengis!"

"Why not say it if it's what I think? In my country everyone says exactly what he thinks. Exactly."

"That's an admirable quality."

"Oh no—I like it better as you do here: you say what you don't think, so long as it's pleasant!"

"So in your country, you don't tell stories?"

"Oh no, absolutely not; except what are in the Bible!"

"Another whisky, Mr Gengis?"

"Yes I think I'll have another whisky!"

"Bravo, I like that, you're a man who's ready to die for his beliefs!"

"*Comment?*"

"My friend said you were a man who would die . . ."

"Yes, I understood about dying for one's beliefs. No, I'm a man who lives for his beliefs. I'm very much alive. Dying is not important; I shall die when God wills."

"Mr Gengis would like it to rain whisky!"

"No, no, why? Then they wouldn't sell umbrellas as umbrellas but for funnels," and he added, after a pause filled with pipe-smoke and a soft sound of breathing, while the others laughed: "Angel Face is a good chap; but if he doesn't do what I say he'll never be forgiven, but be sent packing instead!"

A party of silent men suddenly came into the bar; there were a lot of them—too many to come through the door at the same time. Most of them remained standing by the door, between the tables, or close to the bar-counter. They would not be there long, it wasn't worth sitting down. "Silence!" called a rather short, rather old, rather bald, rather healthy, rather mad, rather harsh-voiced, rather dirty man; he spread out a large printed notice, and two other men helped him fix it to one of the looking-glasses with black wax.

"CITIZENS:

"Merely by uttering the name of the President of the Republic we shed light from the torch of Peace upon those sacred interests of a Nation which, under his wise rule, has conquered and will go on conquering the inestimable benefits of Progress in every sphere, and of Order in every form of Progress!!!! As free citizens, conscious of our obligation to watch over our own destiny (which is also that of the Nation) and as men of goodwill and enemies of Anarchy, we hereby proclaim!!! That the welfare of the Republic depends upon the RE-ELECTION OF OUR ILLUSTRIOUS MANDATORY AND ON NOTHING ELSE BUT HIS RE-ELECTION! Why hazard the ship of State in unknown waters, when we have at its head at present the most accomplished Statesman of our day, whom History will salute as a Great Man among Great men, a Wise Man among the Wise, a Liberal, a Thinker and a Democrat??? Even to imagine any other than Him in this high office amounts to an attempt upon the Destiny of the Nation (which is our own destiny); and whoever dares to do so—if any such there be—deserves to be shut up as a dangerous lunatic, or if he is not mad, tried as a traitor to his Country according to the law!!! FELLOW CITIZENS, THE BALLOT-BOXES ARE WAITING!!! VOTE!!! FOR!!! OUR!!! CANDIDATE!!! WHO!!! WILL!!! BE!!! RE-ELECTED!!! BY!!! THE!!! PEOPLE!!!"

The reading aloud of this notice aroused universal enthusiasm in the bar; there were shouts and applause; and in answer to a general demand, a carelessly dressed man with long black hair and steely eyes got up to speak:

"Patriots, I think as a Poet, but I speak as a patriotic citizen! A Poet means a man who invented the sky; you must listen therefore to a disorganized harangue from the inventor of this useless, beautiful thing we call the sky. When that German whom the Germans did not understand—no, I do not mean Goethe, Kant or Schopenhauer—wrote of a Superman, he was undoubtedly foretelling the birth in America, to Father Cosmos and Mother Nature, of the first truly superior man who has ever existed. I am speaking, gentlemen, of him who excels the dawn in brightness, whom his country has called 'the Well-deserving', of the Chief of the Party and Protector of Studious Youth. It is the Constitutional President of the Republic, gentlemen—as no doubt you have all realised—whom I refer to as Nietzsche's Superman, the Super-unique . . . I say it and I repeat it from this platform." As he said this he banged on the bar-counter with his hand. "And so, compatriots, although I am not one of those who has made politics his livelihood, it is my disinterested, wholehearted and honest belief that since there does not exist among us another hyper-superman and super-citizen, we should be mad or blind, criminally blind or mad, if we allowed the reins of government to pass from the hands of this super-unique charioteer who now and for ever guides our beloved country, to those of another citizen, some ordinary citizen—a citizen, fellow citizens, who even if he possessed all the good qualities on earth must still remain a mere man. In the old, exhausted continent of Europe, Democracy has done away with Emperors and Kings; but we must realise—and we *do* realise—that now that it has been transplanted to

255

America, it has been injected with the almost divine graft of the Super-man, and is building a new form of government: Super-democracy. And now, gentlemen, I shall have much pleasure in reciting . . ."

"Recite, poet," cried a voice, "but not the ode."

". . . my Nocturne in C Major to the Super-Unique!"

The poet's magnificent oration was succeeded by others even more impassioned, aimed at the "infamous" party supporting the San Juan alphabet, the abracadabra system and other theological suppositories. The nose of one of those taking part began to bleed, and he shouted loudly between speeches, for someone to bring him a new brick soaked in water, so that he could stop the haemorrhage by sniffing it.

"By now," said Mr Gengis, "Angel Face is between the wall and the President. I like the way this poet speaks, but I think it must be very sad to be a poet; and to be a lawyer must be the saddest thing in the world. And now I'm going to have another whisky! Another whisky," he shouted, "for this super-hyper-ferro-quasi-carrilero!"

As Angel Face was leaving "Gambrinus", he met the Secretary of State for War.

"Where are you off to, General?"

"To see the boss . . ."

"Then let's go together."

"Are you going there too? Let's wait for my carriage, it won't be long. Between ourselves, I've just been visiting a widow."

"I know you're fond of merry widows, General."

"Now then, none of your musical talk!"

"I wasn't talking music, but Clicquot!"

"Clicquot nothing! A dish fit for a king!"

"Really?"

The carriage rolled silently along as if its wheels were made of blotting-paper. Gendarmes were posted at the corners of the roads and they heard them passing the signal along: "The Secretary of State for War. The Secretary of State for War."

The President was pacing his study with short steps; he was wearing a hat pulled down over his forehead, his coat collar turned up over a scarf, and his waistcoat buttons undone. Black suit, black hat, black boots.

"What's the weather like, General?"

"Cold, Mr President."

"And here's Miguel without an overcoat!"

"Mr President . . ."

"Rubbish. You're trembling, and you're going to tell me you're not cold. You're very unwise. General, send someone to Miguel's house for his overcoat at once."

The Secretary of State went out saluting—he nearly tripped over his sword—while the President sat down on a wicker sofa and offered Angel Face the chair next to it.

"You see, Miguel, I have to do everything myself and supervise everything, because I rule over a nation of 'intenders'," he said as he sat down. "And when I can't see to things myself I have to rely on my friends." He paused for a moment. "I mean by 'intenders' people with every intention of doing or undoing, but who from lack of will power do neither. They are neither fish, fowl nor good red herring. For instance, our industrialists spend their lives repeating over and over again: I intend to build a factory, I intend to set up new machinery, I intend this, I intend that, and so on *ad infinitum*. The agriculturalist says: I intend to try out new methods, I intend to export my products; the writer: I intend to write a book; the professor: I intend to found a school; the businessman: I intend to carry out such and such transactions, and the journalists—those swine with lumps of lard where their souls ought to be—I intend to improve the country. But, as I told you, nobody ever does a thing, and so naturally it is I, the President of the Republic, who has to do everything, and take all the blame as well. You might almost say that if it weren't for me Fortune wouldn't exist, as I have even to take the part of the blind goddess in the lottery . . ."

He stroked his moustache with his transparent, delicate reed-brown finger-tips, and went on in a different tone:

"This is all leading up to the fact that circumstances oblige me to make use of the services of men like you, who are useful to have close at hand but even more useful outside the Republic, where my enemies' scheme, intrigues and malicious writings are endangering my re-election . . ."

He let his eyes drop, like two mosquitoes gorged with blood, and went on:

"I'm not talking about Canales and his followers: death has always been my most trusty ally, Miguel! I'm talking of the people who are trying to influence North American opinion, in the hope of discrediting me in Washington. When a caged wild animal begins to moult, it doesn't mean that it wants to have the rest of its hair pulled out by force, does it? Very well, then. Am I an old man with a pickled brain and a heart as hard as ebony, as they say? Let the blackguards say what they like! But that the people themselves should, for political reasons, take advantage of what I've done to save my country from the onslaughts of these sons of bitches—that is a bit too much! My re-election hangs in the balance, and that is why I've sent for you. You must go to Washington and bring me back a detailed report on those dark clouds of hate, and those funeral ceremonies where the only respectable rôle—as in all funerals—is that of the corpse."

"Mr President," stammered Angel Face, divided between his desire to follow Mr Gengis' advice to put his cards on the table and the fear of losing, by some indiscretion, the chance of making a journey which he had realised from the first might be his salvation. "The President knows that I am unconditionally at his service for any purpose whatever; however, if I may say two words, since I have always wanted to be the last, but also the most loyal and devoted of his servants, before undertaking such a delicate mission I would like to ask the President to be so kind, if he sees no objection, as to give orders for an investigation into the truth of the unfounded charges of my being an enemy of the President's, made against me, by the Judge Advocate General for one . . ."

"But who is paying any attention to such tarradiddles?"

"The President cannot doubt my unconditional loyalty to his person and his Government; but I do not want him to give me his complete confidence before discovering whether the Judge Advocate's accusations are true or false."

"I am not asking your advice as to what I should do, Miguel! That's enough! I know all about it, and I'll go further and tell you that this desk contains the charge that the Judge Advocate General drew up against you at the time of General Canales' flight; and more still: I can tell you that the Judge Advocate's hatred of you derives from a circumstance of which you are perhaps ignorant. The Judge Advocate, in agreement with the police, had formed a plan of kidnapping the lady who is now your wife and selling her to the proprietress of a brothel, from whom, as you know, he had received ten thousand pesos in advance. The woman who had to suffer in her stead was a poor creature who has gone half mad as a result."

Angel Face sat quite still, careful not to show his master the slightest change of expression, and burying his feelings deep in his heart behind the guard of his black velvet eyes. He was pale and cold as his wicker chair.

"If the President will allow me, I would rather stay beside him, and defend him with my own blood."

"Do you mean you won't accept?"

"Absolutely not, Mr President."

"Very well then. All this is quite superfluous—mere words; tomorrow's newspapers will publish the news of your impending departure, and you cannot let me down; the War Office has orders to let you have the money you'll need for the journey today; I will send it to the station with my instructions."

Angel Face began to be aware of the pulsation of an underground clock marking the fatal passage of time. Through a wide-open window, his eyes looked out under their black brows and saw a bonfire burning beside a greenish-black cypress grove and walls of white smoke, in the middle of a patio half-effaced by the darkness. Groups of sentinels were standing about under the seedling stars. Four priestly figures stood at the corners of the patio, all four dressed in moss as water-diviners; all four with their hands covered in yellowish-green frog-skin; all four with the eye on the bright side of their faces shut, and the eye on the dark side open. All at once there was a sound of native drums: tom-tom, tom-tom, tom-tom, and a great many men disguised as animals came leaping in, in Indian file. Down the blood-stained, vibrant drum-sticks came crabs of falling air and worms of fire. The men danced rather than be rooted to the ground or to the wind by the sound of the tom-tom; they fed the bonfire with turpentine from their foreheads. From the dung-coloured semi-darkness emerged a little man with a face like a dried fruit; his tongue protruded between his cheeks, there were thorns on his forehead, he had no ears, and wore round his navel a woollen cord from which hung warriors' heads and calabash leaves. He went up to blow on the clustered flames, and to the blind delight of the men-animals he took some of the fire in his mouth and chewed it as if it was copal without burning himself. A cry came from the darkness enveloping the trees, and from near and far came the mournful voices of the tribes who had been fighting blindly since birth: with their entrails—for they were animals of hunger, with their throats—for they were birds of thirst, and with their fear, their nausea and their physical needs, crying upon Tohil, the Giver of Fire, to give them back the lighted torch of fire. Tohil arrived riding on a river of pigeons' breasts which flowed like milk. The deer came running so that the water should not stop flowing; their horns were as slender as rain, and their little hoofs fell on the cheerful sand as light as air. The birds came hurrying so that their reflections should swim on the water—birds with bones more delicate than their feathers. Rataplan! Rataplan! echoed from under the earth.

Tohil demanded human sacrifices. The tribes led their best hunters before him—with their blow-pipes held ready and their slings charged.

"And do these men hunt other men?" asked Tohil.

Rataplan! Rataplan! echoed from under the earth.

"We'll do as you ask," replied the tribes, "on condition that you, the Giver of Fire, will return fire to us, so that neither our flesh, nor the air, nor our nails, nor our tongues, nor our hair shall freeze any more! On condition that you do not go on destroying our lives, and subjecting us to a living death!" "I am content," said Tohil. Rataplan! Rataplan! echoed from under the earth. "I am content! I can prevail over men who are hunters of men. Henceforth there will be neither true death nor true life. Now dance the jicara in my honour!"

And each hunter-warrior blew on their gourds without pausing for breath, to the rhythm of the tom-tom, and the echo and the drumming which set Tohil's eyes dancing.

After this inexplicable vision, Angel Face said goodbye to the President. As he was leaving, the Secretary of State for War called him and gave him a wad of notes and his overcoat.

"Are you coming, General?" He could scarcely find words.

"I wish I could. But perhaps I shall join you there, or else we shall meet again some time; I have to stay here for the present, you see," and he twisted his head over his right shoulder, "listening to my master's voice."

CHAPTER XXXVIII

The Journey

THE river that was flowing over the roof while she packed the trunks did not debouch inside the house, but very far away, in the wide expanse leading to the open country or perhaps to the sea. A strong gust of wind forced open the window; the rain came pouring in as if the glass had been broken to smithereens, the curtains and papers blew about, doors banged, but Camila went on with her task, isolated among the trunks she was filling; and although she felt the lightning right to the roots of her hair, nothing seemed to her either complete or different—everything was alike empty, disconnected, weightless, without body, without soul, as she was herself.

"Is it better to live here, or where one is out of range of that monster—what do you think?" said Angel Face, shutting the window. "It was just what I wanted. Perhaps I'm running away though!"

"But after what you told me about those wild witch-doctors dancing in his house . . ."

"That's not worth worrying about!" His voice was drowned by a thunderclap. "And anyway what could they possibly find out by their divinations? After all, he's the one who is sending me to Washington; he is the one who's paying for my journey. And, good lord! everything may well look quite different when I'm far away. Anything's possible. You'll join me, with the excuse that you're ill, or else that I am, and after that he can look for us as hard as he likes!"

"But supposing he won't let me go?"

"Well then I shall come back and keep my mouth shut, and we shall be no worse off than before, shall we? Nothing venture . . ."

"You always think everything's so easy!"

"We've got enough to live on anywhere; and I mean live, really live, not just go on repeating all day long: 'I think with the President's mind therefore I exist, I think with the President's mind therefore I exist.' "

Camila gazed at him with eyes full of tears; her mouth seemed to be full of hair and her ears of rain.

"What are you crying about? Don't cry."

"Well what else can I do?"

"Women are all the same."

"Leave me alone!"

"You'll make yourself ill if you go on crying like that—for heaven's sake!"

"No, leave me alone!"

"Anyone would think I was dying or else about to be buried alive!"

"Leave me alone!"

Angel Face held her close. His hard, masculine cheeks were unused to tears, but two burning drops twisted their way down them, like reluctantly extracted nails.

"But you will write to me?" murmured Camila.

"Of course I will."

"Very often, please! You see we've never been separated before. Don't leave me without letters; it'll be agony for me if days go by without news of you. And take care of yourself! Don't trust anyone, d'you hear? Don't pay attention to what anyone says, least of all your compatriots—they're a bad lot. But above all, I beg you," her husband's kisses interrupted her, "I—beg—you—to—I beg you—to write—to me!"

Angel Face shut the trunks without removing his gaze from his wife's adoring eyes. It was raining in torrents. The water poured through the gutters like heavy chains. They were both choking with misery at the thought of the following day—now so close—and when everything was ready, they undressed in silence and got into bed, where they were kept awake by the sound of the clock clipping pieces off their last hours together—clippety-clack, clippety-clack—and the droning of mosquitoes.

"It's just flashed through my mind that I forgot to tell them to shut up the rooms to keep out the mosquitoes. Good heavens, what a fool!"

Angel Face's only reply was to hold her more tightly to him; she was like a little sheep, too weak to bleat.

He did not dare put out the light, nor shut his eyes, nor utter a word. They were so much closer in the light; the human voice creates such a distance between speakers, the closed eyelids are so great a barrier. And to be in darkness is a form of separation; and there was so much they wanted to say to each other this last night, that the longest of conversations would have seemed like a telegram.

The noise of the servants chasing a hen among the seedbeds filled the patio. The rain had stopped and the water was dripping into the gutters like a clepsydra. The hen ran, crouched and fluttered, trying to escape from death.

"My little mill-stone," whispered Angel Face in her ear, smoothing her rounded stomach with his hand.

"My love!" she said, pressing her body against his. Her legs moved under the sheet like oars resting on the rippling water of a bottomless river.

The servants were still running about and shouting. Palpitating and terrified, the hen escaped from their hands, its eyes starting from its head, its beak wide open, its wings spread out like a cross, its breathing reduced to a thread.

Tightly enlaced, they caressed each other with trembling fingers—fingers that were half-dead and half-asleep, insubstantial. "My love!" she said to him. "My heaven," he said to her. "My heaven!" she said to him.

The hen ran against a wall, or the wall fell on top of it. It felt the two things happen simultaneously. They twisted its neck. It flapped its wings as if it could fly even now it was dead. "The wretched bird has gone and made a mess!" cried the cook, shaking the feathers which had soiled her apron, and went off to wash her hands in the rain-water in the fountain.

Camila shut her eyes . . . Her husband's weight . . . A flapping of wings . . . A stain . . .

And, more slowly now, the clock went clippety clack! clippety clack! clippety clack! clippety clack!

Angel Face hastily looked through the papers that had been handed him at the station by an officer. As he left the town behind him, it seemed to claw at the sky with the grimy nails of its roofs. The documents had a calming effect on him. What luck to be travelling away from that man in a first-class carriage, sur-rounded with attentions, with no spy at his heels and his pocket full of cheques! He half shut his eyes, the better to preserve his thoughts. The fields came alive as the train passed through them, and began running after each other like children, one behind the other, one behind the other, one behind the other: trees, houses, bridges.

"What luck to be sitting in a first-class carriage, travelling away from that man!"

One behind the other, one behind the other, one behind the other. The house chased the tree, the tree chased the fence, the fence the bridge, the bridge the road, the road the river, the river the mountain, the mountain the cloud, the cloud the cornfield, the cornfield the labourer, the labourer the animal . . .

Surrounded with attentions and with no spy at his heels . . .

The animal chased the house, the house the tree, the tree the fence, the fence the bridge, the bridge the road, the road the river, the river the mountain, the mountain the cloud . . .

The reflection of a village ran along the transparent surface of a stream as dark as the depths of a pitcher.

The cloud chased the cornfield, the cornfield the labourer, the labourer the animal . . .

With no spy at his heels and cheques in his pocket.

The animal chased the house, the house the tree, the tree the fence, the fence . . .

With a lot of cheques in his pocket!

A bridge like a billiard-rest flashed past the window . . . Light and shade, ladders, steel fringe, swallows' wings . . .

The fence chased the bridge, the bridge the road, the road the river, the river the mountain, the mountain . . .

Angel Face let his head fall against the back of his seat. His sleepy eyes followed the low, flat, hot, monotonous coast-line, with a confused feeling of being in the train, of not being in the train, of lagging behind the train, further behind the train, further behind, still further behind, still further behind, further, further, further, further . . .

Suddenly he opened his eyes. He had been asleep with the unrelaxed sleep of a fugitive, the restlessness of someone who knows that danger may be filtering through the very air he breathes; and it seemed to him that he had just jumped into his seat in the train through an invisible hole. His neck hurt him, his face was sweating and there was a cloud of flies on his forehead.

Above the passing greenery, motionless clouds were gathering, swollen from the water they had sucked up from the sea, and with beams of light emerging like claws from behind their grey plush centres.

A village came and went—an apparently uninhabited village, a collection of toffee houses and dried maize leaves, grouped between the church and the cemetery. "How I wish I had the faith which built that church," thought Angel Face. "The church and the cemetery! Nothing is left alive now but faith and the dead!" His eyes were misted with the pleasure of escape. Yet this country with its slow-moving springtime was his country, his tenderness, his mother; and however much it might put new life into him to leave these villages behind, when he was among men of other countries he would always be a dead man among the living, eclipsed by the invisible presence of these trees and tombstones.

Station followed station. The train ran on without stopping, rattling over the badly laid rails. Here a whistle, there a grinding of brakes, further on still a hill crowned with a ring of dirty smoke. The passengers fanned themselves with hats, newspapers and handkerchiefs; they were suspended in hot air watered by a thousand drops of their own sweat; they were exasperated by the discomfort of their seats, by the noise, by the way their clothes pricked them as if insects' feet were hopping all over their skin, and their heads itched as if their hair was alive; they were as thirsty as if they had taken a purge, and as sad as death.

Dusk followed the harsh daylight, a shower of rain was wrung from the clouds, and now the horizon began to disintegrate, and far, very far away in the distance there shone a tin of sardines surrounded by blue oil.

One of the railway officials came along to light the lamps in the compartments. Angel Face straightened his collar and tie and looked at his watch. They were due at the port in twenty minutes —it seemed a century to him in his impatience to be safe and sound on the boat. He put his face close to the window trying to distinguish something in the darkness. There was a vegetable smell. He heard a river running by. And again further on, perhaps the same river.

The train slowed down among the streets of a small village, slung like hammocks in the darkness; it stopped very gradually, and after the second-class passengers had got out carrying bundles, it went on at a still slower rate towards the quays. Now he could hear the breaking of the waves and make out the indistinct pale shape of the Customs office with its smell of tar; he could hear the somnolent breathing of millions of gentle, salt-soaked creatures.

Angel Face waved a greeting from a distance to the man waiting in the station—it was Major Farfan. He was delighted to find a friend whose life he had saved at this crucial moment in his own. "Major Farfan!"

Farfan saluted him from a distance, and coming up to the window told him not to worry about his luggage—some soldiers were coming to take it to the boat. When the train stopped he got in and shook hands warmly with Angel Face. The other passengers got out in a great hurry.

"Well and how have things been going with you?"

"And you, my dear Major? But there's no need to ask—one can see from your face . . ."

"The President wired to me to look after you and see you had everything you want."

"Most kind of you, Major!"

It had taken only a few minutes for the compartment to empty itself. Farfan put his head out of one of the windows and shouted:

"Are they coming for the luggage, Lieutenant? What's the meaning of this delay?"

At his words a group of armed soldiers appeared at the door. Angel Face saw the trap too late.

"I arrest you by order of the President," said Farfan, revolver in hand.

"But, Major . . . if the President . . . it's impossible! Come with me, please come with me, and let me send a wire!"

"My orders are explicit, Don Miguel, and you'd better come quietly!"

"As you like; but I mustn't miss my ship. I'm on a mission, I can't . . ."

"Silence, please, and hand over everything you have on you immediately!"

"Farfan!"

"Hand it over, I tell you!"

"No. Listen to me, Major!"

"Come along, do what you're told, do what you're told!"

"It would be better if you'd listen to me, Major!"

"Let's have no more threats!"

"I have confidential instructions from the President in my possession—and you'll be responsible!"

"Search him, sergeant! We'll soon see who's master!"

An individual with a handkerchief tied over his face appeared out of the darkness. He was as tall as Angel Face, as pale as Angel Face and with hair of the same light brown as Angel Face; he took possession of everything the sergeant was abstracting from the real Angel Face (passport, cheques, wedding-ring engraved with his wife's name—this he slipped off his finger with the aid of a large dollop of spit—cuff-links, handkerchiefs) and disappeared immediately.

Much later the ship's siren sounded. The prisoner put his hands over his ears. His eyes were blinded with tears. He would have liked to break down the door, escape, run, fly, cross the sea, cease to be the man he was—what a restless river ran beneath his skin, what a scar had burnt into his flesh!—and become that other man, who was travelling to New York with his luggage and his name in cabin no. 17.

CHAPTER XXXIX

The Port

EVERYTHING was quiet in the hush that precedes a change of tide, except the crickets (damp with sea-spray and with stars glowing in their wing-cases), the reflection of the lighthouse, like a safety-pin in the darkness, and the prisoner, pacing up and down with his hair over his forehead and his clothes in disorder, as if he had just taken part in a riot. He was incapable of sitting down, and kept making the tentative gestures of a sleeper who defends himself with groans and muttered words from being dragged by God's hand towards his inevitable doom—wounds, disembowelment or sudden death.

"Farfan is my only hope!" he kept repeating. "Lucky it wasn't the Colonel! For all my wife knows, I may have been shot and buried already. Nothing to report."

There was a pounding noise on the floor as if two feet were thudding along the railway carriage, which stood motionless on the rails, guarded by pickets of sentinels; but Angel Face was far away among the little villages he had just passed through, sunk in the slime of darkness or the blinding dust of sunny days, eaten up with fear of the church and the cemetery, the church and the cemetery, the church and the cemetery. Nothing was left alive but faith and the dead!

The clock at Garrison Headquarters struck one. The chandelier shook. The large hand had rounded the cape of midnight.

Major Farfan lazily thrust first his right arm, and then the left, into his tunic, and with equal slowness began to fasten it, starting with the button over his navel; he saw none of the things that lay in front of him: a map of the Republic shaped like a yawn, a towel covered in dried mucus and sleepy flies, a saddle, a rifle, knapsacks. Button by button, he reached the collar. When he got to the collar he threw back his head, so that his eyes fell on something that he could not look at without saluting: the President's portrait.

He finished fastening his buttons, broke wind, lit a cigarette from the lamp, took up his riding-whip and went out. The soldiers did not hear him go; they were asleep on the floor, wrapped in their ponchos like mummies; the sentinels presented arms and the officer on duty got up with the object of spitting out a worm of ash, all that was left of the cigarette between his sleeping lips, and only just had time to wipe it away with the back of his hand as he saluted: "Nothing to report, sir."

The rivers were flowing into the sea like cats' whiskers in a saucer of milk. The liquid shadow of the trees, the heavy shapes of rutting crocodiles, the water in the malaria-haunted marshes, weary tears—all were moving towards the sea.

A man with a lantern joined Farfan as he entered the railway-coach. They were followed by two smiling soldiers who were busily undoing the knots in the rope with which the prisoner was to be bound. Farfan ordered them to tie him up, and they went off with him towards the village, followed by the sentinels who had been guarding the coach. Angel Face made no attempt to resist. In the major's manner and voice and the rigorousness he exacted from the soldiers, who would have treated him brutally enough without any incitement, he thought he divined a stratagem by which his friend could help him later on when they got to Headquarters without compromising himself beforehand. But he was not taken to Headquarters. When they left the station they turned off towards the farthest stretch of the railway line, where they forced him with blows to get into a goods-wagon with its floor covered in manure. They hit him without provocation, as if they had been given orders to do so.

"But why are they hitting me, Farfan?" Angel Face demanded of the major, who was following behind, in conversation with the man with a lantern.

The only reply he got was a blow with the stock of a rifle; but instead of striking him on the back they hit him on the head, making one of his ears bleed and sending him face downwards in the manure.

He took a breath, and spat out the dung; blood was dripping on to his clothes and he tried to protest.

"Will you shut up! Will you shut up!" cried Farfan, raising his riding-whip.

"Major Farfan!" cried Angel Face, holding his ground but almost frantic; there was a smell of blood in the air.

269

Farfan was afraid of what Angel Face might say, and struck him with the whip. It left its mark on the unfortunate man's cheek; with one knee on the ground he struggled to free his hands from their bonds.

"I understand," he said in a voice trembling with uncontrollable bitterness; "I understand. This exploit may earn you another star . . ."

"Shut up, unless you want . . ." interrupted Farfan, raising the whip again.

The man with the lantern held him back by the arm.

"Go on, hit me, don't stop, don't be afraid; I'm a man, and only eunuchs use whips!"

Two, three, four, five times the lash fell on the victim's face in less than a minute.

"Easy now, Major, easy now!" interposed the man with the lantern.

"No, no! I'm going to make this son of a bitch bite the dust. He can't get away with insulting the army like that. The swine! The shit!" He had broken his whip, but he was belabouring the prisoner violently with his pistol barrel, tearing off chunks of hair and leaving his face and head in ribbons, and with every blow he dealt he repeated in a stifled voice: "the army . . . orders . . . filthy swine . . . take that!"

They dragged their victim's almost inanimate body from the manure in which he had fallen, and carried him from one end to the other of the railway line, where the goods-train was making ready to return to the capital.

The man with the lantern got into one of the trucks, accompanied by Farfan. They had been talking and drinking at Headquarters until it was time to start.

"The first time I tried to join the Secret Police," the man with the lantern was saying, "a great pal of mine called Lucio Vasquez—known as Velvet—was one of them . . ."

"I think I've heard of him," said the major.

"They didn't get me that time. He was a pretty tough chap—that's why they called him Velvet—and instead I got a stretch in clink and lost what my wife and I—I was married then—had put into a little business as well. And they even took my wife to The Sweet Enchantment, poor thing . . ."

Farfan woke up at the mention of The Sweet Enchantment, but

the recollection of the Sow, that putrescent specimen of her sex, stinking of the latrine, who had once aroused his enthusiasm, now left him cold. He was like a man swimming under water, battling all the time with an imaginary Angel Face, who kept on saying over and over again: "another star! another star!"

"And what was your wife's name? I knew almost all the girls at The Sweet Enchantment."

"You'd be none the wiser if I told you, for she left as soon as she got there. We had a little nipper and he died there and it nearly sent her off her rocker. It was no place for her, you know! Now she's in the hospital laundry with the nuns. She'd never have made a whore!"

"But I think I did know her. Because I was the one who got permission from the police for the wake Doña Chon held for the baby; but I had no idea it was your little boy!"

"And as for me, I was fed up in clink, without a *real*. No thanks! If you start looking back at what you've been through, you feel like taking to your heels and running for your life!"

"And as for me, I didn't know a thing until a tart tried to get me into trouble with the President."

"This chap Angel Face was mixed up with General Canales; he was fast and loose with the daughter—he married her later on —and didn't carry out the President's orders, so they say. I know all this because Vasquez—Velvet—met him in a tavern called the Two-Step, a few hours before the general escaped."

"The Two-Step?" repeated the Major, searching his memory.

"It was an inn right on the corner. And, believe it or not, there were a man and a woman painted on the wall, one on each side of the door; the woman was saying—I remember the words still: 'Come and dance the two-step!' And the chap had a bottle in his hand and was saying: 'No thanks! I prefer the bottle dance!' "

The train slowly got under way. A small patch of dawn light was floating in the blue sea. Gradually, out of the shadows, came the straw huts of the village, the distant mountains, the wretched little cargo-boats and Garrison Headquarters—like a box of matches full of crickets in uniform.

CHAPTER XL

Blind Man's Buff

"He went away so many hours ago!"

On the day of departure, the person left behind starts counting each hour until there are enough to say: "He went away so many days ago!" But after two weeks the days are lost count of, and then it is: "He went away so many weeks ago!" A whole month. Then the months are lost count of. A whole year. Then the years are lost count of . . .

Camila was watching for the postman at one of the drawing-room windows, hidden behind the curtain so as not to be seen from the street; she was pregnant and was sewing baby-clothes.

The postman heralded his arrival by knocking like a lunatic on all the front doors. Knock by knock, he came level with the window. Camila left her sewing to listen and look, her heart leaping in her breast with agitation and pleasure. "At last I shall get the letter I long for! 'My beloved Camila,' in large letters . . ."

But the postman did not knock. Perhaps it was because . . . Perhaps later . . . And she took up her sewing again, humming a song to drive away her sad thoughts.

The postman came by again in the afternoon. It would have been impossible to sew a single stitch in the space of time it took her to get from the window to the door. Cold, breathless, all ears, she stood waiting for his knock; and, realising at last that the silence of the house was unbroken, she shut her eyes in terror, and was shaken by sobs, sudden retching and sighs. Why not go out on the doorstep? Perhaps . . . the postman may have forgotten— he's a fine postman!—and he'll bring it tomorrow as if nothing had happened.

Next day she almost wrenched the door off its hinges, she opened it so wide. She ran to wait for the postman, partly so that he shouldn't forget her, but also just for luck. But he was already going by as usual, evading her questions, dressed in pea-green (the colour of hope), with his little frog's eyes and his teeth bared like those of a skeleton in the anatomy-school.

A month, two months, three, four . . .

She no longer frequented the rooms looking onto the street; the weight of her grief drew her to the back of the house. She thought of herself as a kitchen utensil, a piece of coal or wood, an earthenware jar, mere rubbish.

"They're not just whims, but pregnant cravings," explained a neighbour with some knowledge of midwifery when the servants consulted her, more for the pleasure of talking than in search of a cure; as for remedies they had plenty of their own: they put candles in front of the saints, or relieved their own poverty and the burden on the house by removing small objects of value.

But one fine day the invalid went out of doors. Corpses float. Sitting huddled in a cab, avoiding the eyes of anyone she knew— nearly all of them turned away rather than greet her—she set off, determined to see the President at all costs. She breakfasted, lunched and dined off a tear-soaked handkerchief. She was still biting it as she sat in the waiting-room. What a lot of misery there was, to judge by the waiting crowd! Peasants sitting on the edges of their gold chairs; townspeople sitting in the middle and leaning against the backs. Ladies were directed to armchairs in low voices. Someone was talking in a door-way. The President! The mere thought made all her muscles stiffen. Her child kicked her in the stomach as if to say: "Let's get out of here!" There was the noise of people changing their positions. Yawns. Muttered remarks. The footsteps of staff officers. The movements of a soldier as he cleaned one of the windows. Flies. The little kicks of the child in her womb. "Don't be so rough! Why are you so cross? We're going to see the President to ask him what has happened to someone who doesn't know you exist, but will love you very much when he comes home! Oh, so you're impatient to come out and take part in what people call life! It's not that I'm against it, but you're better off and safer where you are!"

The President would not see her. Someone told her she had better apply for an audience. Telegrams, letters, official forms— everything was useless. He did not answer.

Night fell and dawn came, and her eyelids were hollowed by

lack of sleep or floated in lakes of tears. A large patio. She was lying in a hammock, playing with a caramel out of the Thousand and One Nights and a little black rubber ball. The caramel was in her mouth, the ball in her hands. Moving the caramel from one cheek to another, she dropped the little ball, which bounced on the floor of the passage under the hammock and rolled away into the patio a long way off, getting smaller and smaller until it vanished altogether, while the caramel in her mouth grew larger. She was not fully asleep. Her body trembled at the touch of the sheets. It was a dream lit both by dream lights and electric-light. The soap slipped out of her hands several times like the rubber ball, and her breakfast roll—she was eating it out of pure hunger —seemed to swell in her mouth like the caramel.

Everyone was at Mass and the streets were deserted when she went to several Government offices by turns, to watch for the Ministers to arrive; she did not know how to win over the grumpy little old porters—bundles of deformed flesh, who refused to answer her questions and threw her out when she became insistent.

But her husband had run to pick up the little ball. Now she remembered the rest of her dream. The big patio. The little black ball. Her husband getting smaller all the time, further away all the time as if seen through the wrong end of a telescope, till he disappeared out of the patio after the ball, while the caramel swelled inside her mouth—and she was not thinking about her child.

She wrote to the Consul at New York, to the Minister at Washington, to a friend of a woman friend and to the brother-in-law of a man friend, asking for news of her husband, and she might as well have thrown her letters in the dustbin. She heard through a Jewish grocer that the distinguished secretary of the American Legation, who was a detective as well as a diplomat, had definite news of Angel Face's arrival in New York. Not only were there official records of his disembarkation to be found in the port and hotel registers and the police files, but his arrival had also been reported by the newspapers and by people who had recently returned from the city.

"And now they're looking for him," the Jew told her, "and they must find him, dead or alive, although it seems as if he'd taken another boat from New York to Singapore."

"And where's that?" she asked.

"Where do you suppose? Why in Indochina," replied the Jew, with a click of his false teeth.

"And how long would it take a letter to get here from there?" she persisted.

"I don't know exactly, but not more than three months." She counted on her fingers. Angel Face had been gone for four.

In New York or Singapore. What a weight was lifted from her mind! What an immense comfort to think of him far away, to know that he hadn't been murdered at the port as some people said, that he was far away from her in New York or Singapore but thinking of her all the time!

She held on to the counter in the Jew's shop to prevent herself from fainting. Her joy made her feel ill. She walked away as if on air, as if on her husband's arm in a new country, leaving behind the hams wrapped in silver paper, the bottles in Italian straw, the tinned jams, chocolates, apples, herrings, olives, dried cod and muscat grapes. "What a fool, I was, tormenting myself like that! Now I understand why he hasn't written; but I must go on playing the part of a deserted woman, blind with jealousy, trying to find the man who has left her—or else of a wife who wants her husband beside her during the difficult ordeal of child-birth."

She reserved a cabin and packed her bags; everything was ready for her departure when she was refused a passport. A hole full of nicotine-stained teeth surrounded by a rim of swollen flesh moved up and down, down and up, to tell her that orders had been issued that she should not be given a passport. She moved her own lips up and down, down and up, in an attempt to repeat the words as if she must have heard them wrong.

And she spent a fortune on telegrams to the President. No answer came. She got no help from Government officials. The Under-secretary for War, a man who was naturally indulgent to women, advised her not to go on insisting, for no amount of effort would get her a passport; her husband had tried to trifle with the President and the position was hopeless.

They advised her to go and see a certain influential little priest, or else one of the mistresses of the man who provided the President with horses; and as a rumour that Angel Face had died of yellow fever in Panama was running round at the time, there were plenty who were ready to take her to the spiritualists to settle her doubts.

They did not wait for her to ask them twice. But the medium seemed a little reluctant. "I don't like the idea of the spirit of someone who was the President's enemy materialising in me," she said, her withered shanks shaking under her frozen clothes. But prayers and money together will move mountains, and by much greasing of her palm they induced her to agree. The lights were put out. Camila was terrified when she heard them summon Angel Face's spirit, and they had to drag her out practically unconscious; she was told that she had heard the voice of her husband, who had died on the high seas and was now in an inaccessible sphere of universal Being, lying in the most comfortable bed, on a mattress of water, with fishes for springs and the most delicious of pillows—non-existence.

Thin and wrinkled as an old cat, and with nothing left of her face but eyes—green eyes with dark rings round them as big as her transparent ears—she was barely twenty years old when she gave birth to a little boy. On the advice of her doctor she went to stay in the country for a while as soon as she got out of bed. Threatened by progressive anaemia, tuberculosis and madness, she held on to life by a fine thread, feeling her way with her baby in her arms, without news of her husband, searching for him in mirrors (the only place of return for drowned men) in her son's eyes and in her own as she slept and dreamed of him in New York or Singapore.

At last a day came which shed light on the dark night of her grief, as she wandered like a shadow between the pines, the orchard fruit-trees and the tall trees in the fields: it was Whit Sunday, when her son was anointed with salt, oil, water and the priest's saliva, and given the name of Miguel. The mocking-birds were caressing each other with their beaks—two ounces of feathers and endless trills. The sheep were busy licking their lambs. What a perfect sensation of Sunday well-being the movements of its mother's tongue over its body produced in the suckling lamb, flickering its long-lashed eyes under her caress! Foals raced after moist-eyed mares. Calves mooed with delight, their jaws slavering, as they nuzzled the swollen udders. Without knowing why, she pressed her baby to her heart when the christening chimes had ended, as if life had been renewed in her.

Little Miguel grew up in the country and became a country-man. Camila never again set foot in the city.

CHAPTER XLI

Nothing to Report

ONCE in every twenty-two hours the light penetrated between the cobwebs and stone mullions into the underground vaults; and once in every twenty-two hours a rusty old petrol tin was let down on a rotten, knotted cord with food for the prisoners in the underground cells. At the sight of the can full of greasy broth with scraps of fat meat and pieces of pancake in it, the prisoner in No. 17 turned away his head. He would rather die than eat even a mouthful, and day after day the tin descended and went up again untouched. But he was driven by sheer need, hunger had him with his back to the wall, his eyes had become enormous with glassy pupils, he talked aloud and ramblingly as he paced up and down his tiny cell, he rubbed his teeth with his fingers, tugged at his cold ears, and the day came at last when he rushed at the descending tin as if it might be withdrawn any moment and plunged his mouth, nose, face and hair into it, nearly drowning himself in his efforts to swallow and chew at the same time. He finished the lot, and when the rope was pulled up he watched the empty tin ascending with the pleasure of a satisfied animal. He could not stop sucking his fingers and licking his lips. But his gratification was short-lived, for he soon vomited up his meal amid curses and groans. The meat and the pancake glued themselves to his stomach and refused to budge, but each spasm left him leaning against the wall open-mouthed like someone leaning over the edge of a cliff. At last he got his breath again, but his head was spinning; he combed his damp hair with his hand, slipping it down behind his ears to clean the vomit from his beard. There was a ringing in his ears. His face was bathed in cold, sticky, sour sweat, like the water in an electric battery. And the light was already going—the light always began to go as soon as it came. By clutching on to his wasted body, as if struggling with himself, he succeeded in half sitting down, stretching his legs, resting his head against the wall and succumbing to the weight of his eyelids as to some powerful narcotic. But there was no comfort in sleep for him; his struggles to breathe in spite of the lack of air were followed by restless movements of his hands over his body, a compulsive drawing up and stretching out of each leg in turn, and feverish efforts to tear out the live coal which seemed to be burning his throat, with the little helmets of his finger-nails. As soon as he was half awake he began to open and shut his mouth like a fish out of water, to taste the icy air with his dry tongue; and, once fully awake, he began to shout in a feverish delirium, standing on tiptoe and stretching to his full height so that everyone should hear him. His cries grew fainter and fainter as they echoed through the vaults. He beat on the walls, stamped on the floor with his feet and shouted again and again, until soon his shouts had become yells . . . "Water, soup, salt, fat, anything; water, soup . . ."

A trickle of blood fell on his hand—the blood of a crushed scorpion . . . of many scorpions, for it was still flowing . . . of all the crushed scorpions in heaven turning to rain . . . He quenched his thirst without knowing whence came this gift of liquid, which was afterwards to be his chief torment. For he spent hours and hours crouching on the stone he used as a pillow, to keep his feet out of the puddle of water which collected in his cell in winter; hours and hours, wet to the very hair, distilling water, wet to the very bones, yawning and shivering, suffering torments of hunger whenever the tin of greasy broth was late in arriving. He ate as thin people do, to nourish his dreams, and he fell asleep standing up after the last mouthful. Afterwards another tin was lowered in which prisoners in solitary confinement satisfied their physical needs. The first time the prisoner in No. 17 heard it come down he thought it was a second meal, and as this was during the time he was refusing to eat he let it go up again without dreaming that it contained excrement; its stench was much the same as that of the soup. This tin used to pass from cell to cell and when it reached No. 17 it was half full. How terrible to hear it come down when he had no need of it, or to need it when he had perhaps deafened himself with beating on the wall like the clapper of a useless bell! Sometimes, as a further refinement of torture, his desire left him when he even thought of the tin, wondering if it would arrive or not arrive, or be late or even forgotten (this was not uncommon) or break its cord (this happened nearly every day) and give one of the prisoners a shower-bath. The thought of the fumes that came from it, the human warmth, the sharp edges of the square receptacle, the necessary effort, was enough to inhibit his desire and then he had to wait for the next time, to live through twenty-two hours of colic, strangury, tears, contortions, and obscenities, with the taste of copper in his saliva, and in the last extremity to relieve himself on the floor, emptying the stinking contents of his bowel like a dog or a child, alone with death.

Two hours of light, twenty-two hours of utter darkness, one tin of soup and one of excrement, thirst in summer, flood in winter; that was life in the underground cells.

"You weigh less every day," said the prisoner in No. 17 to himself in a voice he hardly recognised; "and soon the wind will be able to blow you to where Camila is waiting for you to come home! She must be tired out with waiting, she must have shrunk into something almost invisible! What will it matter if your hands are thin? She will warm them in her bosom! Dirty? She'll wash them with her tears! Her green eyes? Yes, like those pictures of fields in the Austrian Tyrol in *La Ilustracion,* or the green of sugar-cane, flecked with bright yellow and indigo. And the taste of her words, and the taste of her lips, and the taste of her teeth, and the taste of her taste . . . And her body, like a figure of eight with her slender waist, or the guitar-shaped cloud of smoke left by fireworks as they go out and lose their impetus. There were fireworks the night I stole her from death . . . The angels were walking, the clouds were walking, the roofs were walking with little steps like a night-watchman, the houses, the trees, everything was walking on air with her and with me."

And he used to feel Camila close beside him, like silken powder to his touch, in each breath he drew, in his ears, between his fingers, against his ribs as they were shaken like eyelashes by the blind eyes of his viscera.

And he possessed her . . .

The spasm would come about gently, without the slightest contortion; a slight shiver would pass along the twisted thorns of his spine, there would be rapid contraction of the glottis, and his arms would drop to the ground as though amputated . . .

The disgust it caused him to satisfy his needs in the tin, multiplied by the guilt that devoured him for satisfying his physical needs in so barren a manner with the memory of his wife, left him without the strength to move.

With the only metal utensil at his disposal, a little piece of brass torn from one of his shoe-laces, he engraved Camila's name and his own intertwined on the wall, and making use of the light which came every twenty-two hours, he added a heart, a dagger, a crown of thorns, an anchor, a cross, a little sailing-boat, a star, two swallows like the tilde on an ñ, and a railway-train with a spiral of smoke.

Fortunately his weakness spared him the torments of the flesh. Physically destroyed as he was, he thought of Camila as one smells a flower or hears a poem. He thought of her as the rose which used to flower every April and May in the window of the dining-room where he breakfasted with his mother as a child—an inquisitive little rose-tree branch. A series of childish mornings left him bewildered. The light was going . . . it was going . . . the light always began to go as soon as it came. The darkness swallowed up the thick walls as if they were wafers and soon afterwards the bucket of excrement would arrive. Oh for his rose! The harsh sound of the rope and the tin hanging crazily between the intestinal walls of the vaults. He shivered at the thought of the stench which would accompany this important visitor. Oh for his rose, as white as the milk in his breakfast jug!

In the course of years the prisoner in No. 17 had aged considerably, though more from suffering than from the passage of time. Countless deep wrinkles grooved his face and he sprouted white hairs as ants sprout wings in winter. Nothing left of his body . . . Nothing left of his corpse . . . without air, without sun, without movement, suffering from dysentery, rheumatism and neuralgia, practically blind, the last and only thing that remained alive in him was the hope of seeing his wife again, that love which sustains the heart against the emery-powder of suffering.

The Chief of the Secret Police pushed back his chair, tucked his feet under it, leant his elbows on the black-topped table, brought his pen closer to the light and with bared teeth and a sudden pinching movement of two fingers, succeeded in extracting the hair which had been giving his letters prawns' whiskers. Then he went on writing:

". . . and according to instructions received," the pen scratched its way over the paper from stroke to stroke, "the forenamed Vich made friends with the prisoner in cell No. 17, after he had been shut up with him for two months and made a pretence of weeping at all hours, shouting all day long and wanting to commit suicide every few moments. From friendship to words; the prisoner in No. 17 asked him what crime against the President he had committed to be sent to this place where all hope was at an end. The aforenamed Vich did not answer, but merely beat his head on the ground and broke into obscenities. But he insisted, until in the end Vich's tongue was loosened: A polyglot born in a land of polyglots, he heard of the existence of a country where there were no polyglots. Journey. Arrival. An ideal country for foreigners. Jobs here, friends there, money, everything. Then suddenly a woman in the street; the first hesitating steps in pursuit, almost against his will. Married? Single? Widow? The only thing he knows is that he has to follow her! What beautiful green eyes! A mouth like a rose! How gracefully she walks! He determines to get in touch with her, he walks past her house, manages to get inside, but from the moment he tries to speak to her he never sees her again, and an unknown man begins following him everywhere like his shadow. What does it mean, my friends? His friends turn away. Paving-stones, what does it mean? The walls tremble to hear him speak. The only thing that becomes clear is that he has been so rash as to want to make love to the President's mistr—a lady who was the daughter of a general and had done this out of revenge because her husband had deserted her, so they told him, before he was put in prison as an anarchist.

"The aforementioned Vich states that at this point he heard a noise like a snake rustling through the darkness, that the prisoner came up to him and begged him in a voice as weak as a fish's fin to tell him the lady's name, and the aforementioned Vich repeated it twice . . .

"From this moment the prisoner began to scratch himself as if his whole body itched, although he had no more sensation in it; he tore at his face to wipe away tears where there was nothing but dry skin, and raised his hand to his breast but could not find it: a spiders-web of damp dust had fallen to the ground . . .

"According to instruction received I handed personally to the aforementioned Vich, whose statement I have tried to set down exactly, eighty-seven dollars for the time he was imprisoned, a second-hand cashmere suit and his passage to Vladivostok. The death certificate of the prisoner in No. 17 has been filled in as follows: Died of infectious dysentery.

"This is all I have the honour to impart to the President . . ."

Epilogue

The student was standing rooted to the edge of the pavement as if he had never seen a man in a cassock before. It was not the cassock that astonished him, however, so much as what the sacristan whispered in his ear, as they embraced with delight at meeting one another at liberty:

"I've received orders to dress like this."

And he would have stopped there had it not been that a string of prisoners just then went by between two files of soldiers, in the middle of the street.

"Poor wretches," murmured the sacristan, while the student stepped on to the pavement, "this is the price they have to pay for pulling down the Cathedral Porch! Some things must be seen to be believed!"

"One sees them," the student exclaimed, "touches them, and still doesn't believe them! I'm talking about the Municipality."

"I thought you meant my cassock."

"They weren't content with forcing the Turks to pay for painting the Porch; they must needs carry their protest against the assassination of the 'man with a little mule' to the lengths of destroying the structure itself."

"Take care no one hears you, you chatterbox. Be quiet for God's sake! It's not certain."

The sacristan had more to say, but a little man who was running about the Plaza without a hat on came up, planted himself in front of them and sang at the top of his voice:

> "Figurine, what figure-maker,
> figured you?
> who gave you the face
> of a figure of fun?"

"Benjamin! Benjamin!" called a woman running after him, who looked as though she would burst into tears any minute.

"Not Benjamin the puppet-master?
no not he;
who made you a policeman
and a figure of fun?"

"Benjamin! Benjamin!" cried the woman, almost in tears now. "Don't take any notice, please, don't pay any attention to him; he's quite mad; he can't get it into his head that there's no Cathedral Porch any longer!" And while the puppet-master's wife made excuses for him to the sacristan and the student, Don Benjamin hurried off to sing his song to an ill-tempered gendarme:

"Figurine, what figure-maker
figured you?
who gave you the face
of a figure of fun?
Not Benjamin the puppet-master,
no not he,
who made you a policeman
and a figure of fun?"

"Please don't take him away, he doesn't mean any harm; don't you see he's mad?" begged Don Benjamin's wife, getting between the puppet-master and the policeman. "He is mad, I tell you, don't take him away—no, don't hit him please! He's so mad that he says he can see the whole town laid flat like the Porch!"

The prisoners were still going past. What must it be like to be them instead of the lookers-on who were so deeply thankful not to be them? Behind the procession of men pushing hand-carts came some who carried heavy tools over their shoulders like a cross, and behind them again were second rows of men dragging their chains like noisy rattlesnakes.

Don Benjamin tore himself away from the gendarme, who was arguing with ever-increasing violence with his wife, and ran to greet the prisoners with the first words that came into his head: "Just look at you now, Pancho Tonancho, and that knife of yours which eats into leather and likes making holes in a cork bedroom! Just look at you now, Lolo Cusholo, with your fantailed machete! Just look at you walking now, Mixto Melindres, when you used to ride on horseback; fresh water for your dagger, you sodomite and traitor! Who saw you with your pistol when your name was Domingo and who sees you now, as sad as a week-day, without it! She gave them nits, let her delouse them! Guts dressed in rags make no stew for soldiers! Anyone who's got no padlock to fasten his mouth had better put on handcuffs!"

The shop assistants were beginning to go home; the trams were full to bursting-point. An occasional cab, car, or bicycle . . . A little surge of life, which lasted as long as it took the sacristan and the student to cross the Cathedral square—the beggars' refuge and the rubbish-dump of the irreligious—and say goodbye outside the door of the Archbishop's Palace.

The student looked scornfully down at the debris of the Porch from a bridge of planks laid over it. A gust of icy wind had just raised a thick cloud of dust, like smoke without fire, or the remains of a distant eruption. Another gust brought a shower of pieces of useless official paper raining down on what had once been the assembly-room of the Town Hall. The remains of the tapestries on the fallen walls waved like flags in the current of air. Suddenly the shadow of the puppet-master appeared riding on a broom against a blue background covered with stars, with five little volcanoes of gravel and stone at his feet.

Splash! The chimes announcing that it was eight o'clock in the evening plunged into the silence—Splash! Splash!

The student arrived at his house at the end of a blind alley, and as he opened the door he heard (interspersed with the servants' coughs as they prepared to make the responses to the Litany) his mother's voice telling her rosary:

"For the dying and for travellers. So that Peace shall reign among Christian rulers. For those who suffer persecution by the law. For the enemies of the Catholic faith. For the desperate needs of Holy Church and for our own needs . . . For the blessed souls of Holy Purgatory . . . Kyrie eleison."

GUATEMALA, December 1922
PARIS, November 1925-September 1932

Miguel Angel Asturias, 1899–1974

A Guatemalan by birth, Miguel Asturias studied the myth and religion of Central America at the Sorbonne. While living in Paris (1923–1933), Mr. Asturias was a correspondent for several Central American newspapers. Mr. Asturias then pursued a diplomatic career, representing the Guatemalan government in Argentina, El Salvador, and Mexico. He was the Guatemalan ambassador to France from 1966 to 1970.

Miguel Asturias was awarded the Nobel Prize for Literature in 1967. His other works include: *El Papa Verde, Mulatta de Tal, Hombres de Maiz,* and *El Week-End en Guatemala.* In 1962, *El Señor Presidente* received an Ibero-American Novel Award from The William Faulkner Foundation.